Potent Male Flesh

She needed to make it clear that this wasn't how Marietta Dalrymple dealt with adversity. She was strong and self-sufficient. She didn't need a man to get her through anything. She didn't need a man. Period.

She turned around and nearly came up against his chest. Jax seemed even taller and broader in the close confines of the toilet stall. She held herself still, not wanting to come into contact with all that potent male flesh, but she couldn't stop her eyes from rising so she could look at him. When she did, he smoothed her hair back from her hot forehead, his expression almost tender. He no longer seemed angry.

"You shouldn't be in the ladies' room," she said, wondering why she was whispering.

"Who's going to throw me out?" The corners of his mouth curved upward. "Listen, arguing about this isn't getting us anywhere. I care about what's best for the baby. I assume you do, too."

"Of course I do," she answered weakly. He stroked her cheek as he talked, and he was so close that she could barely think, remembering all the things they'd done to each other in that Washington, D.C. hotel. As biological advantages went, his was definitely unfair.

"Good. It's settled then."

She was watching his mouth, which could be the most appealing part of him. She remembered his lips were softer than any man's had a right to be. "What's settled?"

He gave a short, decisive nod. "We're getting married."

Darlene Gardner

The Misconception

LOVE SPELL BOOKS ◆ NEW YORK CITY

*To my sister Adrienne and the rest of the Fritzes,
who should figure out why about halfway through this book.*

A LOVE SPELL® BOOK

May 2002

Published by

Dorchester Publishing Co., Inc.
276 Fifth Avenue
New York, NY 10001

ISBN 0-505-52481-3

The name "Love Spell" and its logo are trademarks of Dorchester Publishing Co., Inc.

Printed in the United States of America.

Visit us on the web at www.dorchesterpub.com.

The
Misconception

Chapter One

The newspaper in Harold McGinty's hands shook so hard the words on the page swam in front of his dull-brown eyes like shivering sperm.

So much for taking his mind off the promise he'd made to lend his less-than-studly body out as a breeding machine.

"Attention ladies and gentleman . . ."

The crinkling of the newspaper pages all but drowned out the tinny voice being broadcast into the airline waiting area. An elderly woman, her hair arranged in tight, white curls around her small head, glared at Harold over an open book while pressing a gnarled finger to her lips.

"Shhhh," she hissed.

Just my luck, Harold thought. A retired librarian who can't let go of the job.

With difficulty, he folded the paper into fours, ripping it right across the science page's feature story about the sexual reproduction habits of orangutans.

From what little Harold had been able to decipher of the dancing print, the males of the species skipped from female to female, haphazardly implanting their seeds before going on their merry way.

1

Darlene Gardner

Which was sort of like what Harold had been contracted to do, except his mission involved a singular, human female.

". . . begin boarding for Flight 707 to Washington D.C. in ten minutes."

Flight 707. Oh, gosh. That was his flight. The one that would fly him straight into the womb of the unknown.

He smoothed back the few hairs on his head, belatedly realizing his sweaty palms were dark with newsprint. But maybe that wasn't a bad thing. His remaining hairs were as black as ink. If some of the dark print transferred to his shining scalp, maybe that would make him look less bald. More virile.

The white-haired librarian pointed to his head, *tsk tsk*ing in her whispery voice.

Harold looked quickly away. Her disapproval was already hard to stomach. What if she guessed that he was at Chicago's O'Hare Airport because he was being flown nearly seven hundred miles to be paid to have sex with a woman he'd never met.

Oh, gosh. What had he been thinking when he'd agreed to the scheme? Sure, he could use the money to pay for the premium telescope with the wide-angle eyepieces he visited weekly in the electronics superstore. But the contract clearly stated she wouldn't pay him the bulk of the money unless his sperm hit the jackpot.

Who did he think he was anyhow? Super Stud? Able to impregnate willing women with a single spurt?

An overabundance of brain cells, unfortunately, didn't translate to an instructional experience in bed. His performance had been so miserable the last time he'd engaged in horizontal activity that the woman involved had never deigned to speak to him again.

"Mac? Mac McGinty?"

The deep voice cut into his thoughts, and he raised his still-quivering chin to a chiseled Adonis of a man with thick dark hair and friendly brown eyes. Something about the

2

The Misconception

slash of his high cheekbones and the long slope of his nose was vaguely familiar, but Harold couldn't place him.

"That is you, isn't it, Mac?" The man was as imposing as a 747, but he was dressed in a well-cut, double-breasted gray suit that screamed success. He had a black garment bag slung over one arm and a matching leather briefcase in his hand. "I never forget a face, and I swear we were on the football team together at Ridgeland High."

Harold squinted, trying to see past the muscles to the man underneath. He'd been the brains of his graduating class at Ridgeland, but he was sorely lacking in brawn. The only way he'd gotten close to the crushing excitement on the football field was by talking the coach into letting him act as manager.

Most of the players either teased him for failing to grow past five feet four or they ignored him. Only one had treated him like a teammate.

"Cash? Cash Jackson?" Overwhelmed by surprise, Harold stood up. His eyes were at the level of the middle button on the big man's suit. He looked up. And up. And even farther up. Finally, he focused on a row of straight, white teeth, which were bared in a grin.

"Yeah, buddy, it's me. But everybody still calls me Jax." The man mountain clapped Harold on the back with one of his big hands, which caused Harold to pitch forward and almost fall. "It's been too long. How many years has it been since high school? Ten years? Twelve?"

"Fourteen," Harold answered while he tottered.

Oblivious to Harold's balancing act, Jax laid his garment bag and briefcase down and lowered his big body into a seat. Once Harold regained his equilibrium, he figured he might as well do the same.

Leveling the playing field, they used to call it in high school. Except, when Harold sat down, Jax, who was a foot taller than him when they were standing, still topped him by nearly a head.

Darlene Gardner

"I didn't recognize you at first. You're bigger." That, Harold thought, was an understatement. Jax had never been a small guy, but Harold didn't remember his muscles being so developed. Even the cloth of his expensive suit didn't hide them. All the female eyes that hadn't been turned in Harold's direction before Jax sat down, and quite a few envious male ones, were riveted on them. "Much bigger."

"I work out with weights," Jax said, as though that explained everything. It didn't. If Harold took up weight training, all it would get him was tired.

"So, Mac," Jax continued, using the nickname Harold had so revered in high school. It had made him feel like one of the guys, as though he, a bookish academic, really fit in with a bunch of jocks. The problem was that Jax was one of the precious few people who'd ever called him Mac. "What have you been doing with yourself?"

"I'm a biochemist at a research testing facility for a pharmaceutical company in the greater Chicago area," Harold answered, waiting for Jax's eyes to glaze over the way most people's did when he told them what he did for a living. Instead, Jax let out a low whistle.

"Wow! I'm impressed, Mac. I always knew that brain of yours would take you to high places."

Harold's chest puffed out. Jax, one-time star of the Ridgeland Lantern football team, was impressed. Not for anything would he reveal that the job wasn't quite what he'd dreamed of, especially the salary part.

"How about you, Jax? What have *you* been doing with *yourself?* The last I heard you were at the University of Michigan on a football scholarship. Then I lost track of you."

"Yeah, well, football didn't work out the way I thought it would." Jax's smile was firmly in place, as though that hadn't bothered him at all. "I found out fairly early in the game I didn't have quite what it takes to make the pros."

4

The Misconception

Harold's eyes widened. After his high school experience, he'd lost interest in the game. He seldom read the sports pages and never watched football on television, but he'd been sure Jax had hooked on with an NFL team somewhere. With his imposing musculature and grace, he certainly looked like an athlete.

"So what did you do?"

"Improvised. I'm sort of a, well, an entrepreneur." Jax paused. "A businessman."

"Is that why you're going to D.C.? Because you have business there?"

"Exactly," Jax said, sitting back in his seat. "Why are you headed there, Mac?"

The question brought vividly to mind Harold's shivering sperm. The anxiety that had temporarily receded when Jax showed up came back like a charging linebacker. Harold couldn't possibly confide his reason for going to the nation's capital to Jax, a man whose sperm would no doubt rather fight than quit.

Quit.

As soon as Harold thought the word, he knew that's what he was going to do. He was five feet four, for Pete's sake, with muscles that had the consistency of corned-beef hash. He could live without the deluxe telescope that provided glimpses of the heavens if it didn't mean putting himself through hell to get it.

Not that having a strange woman waiting in D.C. for him to make love to her was hellish.

But Harold had to face facts. He could barely perform with a woman he knew. How was he going to fare with a stranger who wanted his deposit far more than she'd ever want him? How would he feel if she took one look at him and went sprinting in the opposite direction, offering an on-the-run explanation that she'd changed her mind?

"I'm not going." Harold was so relieved, he nearly shouted the words.

Jax's brows drew together. "But you have a boarding pass."

Harold glanced down at the stiff piece of cardboard he was tip-tapping against the side of a hand. His boarding pass. He'd completely forgotten he was holding his boarding pass.

"We will now begin boarding for Flight 707 to Washington D.C.," the loudspeaker voice rang out. "Anybody traveling with small children or needing assistance can now board."

"That is a boarding pass, isn't it?" Jax asked again.

"Yes." Harold nodded. He couldn't very well deny it when he held the truth in his hands. "Yes, it is. But I've decided not to go."

"You decided not to go? But there must have been some reason you were going."

"There is. I mean, there was."

The loudspeaker once again cut into the general airport terminal noise. "We're continuing boarding Flight 707 to Washington D.C. Passengers holding seats in the rear of the airplane from rows 12 to 19 may now board."

Jax didn't bother to rise, telling Harold he was probably holding a first-class seat. A privilege that meant his old friend could board whenever he wanted. Harold briefly wondered exactly what kind of entrepreneur Jax was before more pressing matters thrust the thought from his mind.

"I tell you, Mac, you're not making much sense. But it's your life, buddy. Can I let someone know you're not coming? I mean, there's not going to be anyone waiting for you at the airport, is there?"

Harold thought of the woman who would surely be standing in the designated waiting area when the passengers from Flight 707 deboarded. He winced. She'd stated in her correspondence that she'd chosen Harold after a rigorous examination of all the candidates who had applied. It didn't seem quite right to leave her standing there, holding a sign bearing the name of a man who was never going to show.

"Yes," Harold said, grabbing Jax's arm. Since the only address he had for the woman was a post office box, he doubted he could track down her phone number. Besides, it would be easier to pass on a message to Jax, who could then deliver it to the woman. "A woman will be waiting for me. Can you tell her I'm not coming?"

Jax's handsome face fell. "You're standing up a woman? Geez, Mac. Are you sure you want to do that?"

Harold thought of his sperm. Considering how he was feeling, they'd probably refuse to make an appearance if he followed through on his agreement with the woman. "I couldn't be more sure."

"Okay. I don't like it, but I'll break the news to her," Jax said, sounding resigned. Then something seemed to occur to him. "She's not going to get upset, right? I mean, this meeting wasn't for pleasure, was it?"

"Weeeellll," Harold drew out the word, biting his lip. It would be easiest to let Jax think the woman was strictly a business contact, but Harold had initially thought no-strings sex would be pleasurable. He didn't want to lie. Not to Jax, who'd always been so nice to him. "Sort of."

"Geez, Mac," Jax said again, looking decidedly unhappy. "Just tell me what she looks like before I change my mind about helping you."

Harold bit his lip. "I don't know what she looks like."

Jax let out a short, incredulous bark. "What do you mean, you don't know what she looks like? You just said you were meeting her for pleasure. How can you not know what she looks like?"

"We've kind of, uh, never met."

"Never met?" Jax shook his head. "I don't understand. You were flying to D.C. to visit a woman you've never met? What was this going to be? Some sort of blind date?"

"Yes, exactly. A blind date." Harold fastened on the term like a scientist on a microscopic irregularity. Let Jax believe

7

he and the woman were planning an innocent date. Going into specifics would be too embarrassing. "I need you to tell her I'm sorry. That circumstances prevent me from meeting her." He paused. "Now or at any time in the future."

Jax narrowed his eyes. "That's kind of harsh, Mac."

"Would you tell her? Her name's Rhea, and she'll be holding up a sign with my name on it. The sign is how I was supposed to find her."

"I don't like it." Jax rubbed a hand over his smoothly shaven jaw. "But, yeah, sure, I'll tell her. It'll be better than having her standing there waiting for you."

"Thanks," Harold said at the same time the loudspeaker announced it was time for all other passengers taking Flight 707 to board the aircraft.

Harold watched only long enough for Jax Jackson to disappear into the portable tunnel leading to the plane. Then he turned and walked quickly out of the airport.

His hands had stopped shaking, and his sperm, he imagined, were no longer shivering.

Chapter Two

Rhea, better known as biology professor Dr. Marietta Dalrymple, was not prone to bouts of anxiety. Nevertheless, she took her damp palms and accelerated heartbeat as good signs. She was much too educated about the A-word to let it get the better of her.

The trick was turning the anxiety to her benefit. If she let herself get too anxious, the task at hand would seem overwhelming, maybe even impossible. The proper degree of anxiety, however, would help her focus on what she wanted to accomplish.

She needed to remember, first and foremost, that it was perfectly normal to feel a tad anxious when a new situation loomed.

Considering she was heading to the airport to pick up the stranger she hoped would impregnate her, she figured she had a doozy of a new situation looming.

She inhaled deeply, drawing in an additional five hundred or so cubic centimeters of much-needed supplemental air, and pulled on her long, dark coat before heading for the front door of her townhouse. She opened it to a blast of chilly February air and a more vibrant version of herself on the doorstep.

"Hey, Marietta." Her younger sister Tracy looked up from her open purse and displayed a smile made more charming by the slight gap between her front teeth. "Boy, am I glad you're home. I think I forgot my key again."

The low-cut blouse Tracy wore with a short, denim skirt was firecracker red. So were her low boots and faux leather jacket. Her long, ruler-straight hair was tinted red, and she was wearing more makeup than Tammy Faye Baker. She dressed as outrageously as any other hairdresser Marietta had ever come across, which was only one of the reasons Marietta was urging her to pursue a college degree.

Tracy pointed to the silver-blue Lincoln Continental parked curbside on the narrow street in front of the townhouse. "Did you buy a new car without telling me?"

"I *rented* a new car," Marietta corrected, walking through the door. She gave her sister a quick hug, because Tracy was the person in the world she cared most about. "I didn't think you were going to be home for another few hours. Don't you have anthropology class Friday mornings?"

"The professor cut it short today," Tracy said, but her attention was on the shiny car that looked incongruous in front of the brick-front townhouses that reflected the historic ambiance of Old Town Alexandria. "Is there something wrong with your Volvo?"

"No. It's parked at the rental car agency."

"I don't get it. If your car's not in the shop, why do you need a rental car?"

Marietta let out a sigh, which hit the cold air and turned into a misty cloud. She'd wanted to avoid this conversation, but that was going to be impossible. "I'm on my way to the airport to pick up somebody, and I thought it would be better not to do it in my car."

"Oh, no!" Tracy held her hand over her heart in the same dramatic fashion she'd perfected in high school when cast as Macbeth due to a shortage of male thespians. "Please tell me today isn't the day you're meeting that . . . that *sperm whore.*"

"Today is the day," Marietta said, "but I prefer to call him a sperm supplier."

"But it can't be!"

"According to my basal body temperature, which I've been taking religiously every morning for months, it's the perfect day. I'm ovulating, Tracy. That means I'm fertile."

"I know what it means." Obvious frustration punctuated Tracy's syllables. "But I thought you weren't going through with this crazy Conception Connection until next week."

Marietta patted Tracy on her rouged cheek and smiled. "That's what I wanted you to think. No offense, Tracy, but are you familiar with the Shakespeare play *The Taming of the Shrew*?"

"Of course I am. You're talking to Macbeth, here." Tracy looked suspicious. "Why?"

"Lately, Kate the shrew doesn't have anything on you."

"Very funny."

"No. Very true. I calculated that the intensity of your arguments would increase in direct proportion to the proximity of the meeting. That's why I didn't tell you when I rescheduled the date."

She took advantage of Tracy's momentary speechlessness to slip past her. Grabbing the wrought-iron railing, she hurried down a half-dozen steps onto the redbrick sidewalk leading to her rental car. She tried telling herself she shouldn't feel guilty for not sharing her plans with Tracy. It didn't work. Her anxiety hiked up a notch, and she wiped her damp palms on the nubby fabric of her coat.

Focus, she told herself, which was difficult with her sister's boot heels *click-clack*ing behind her. Resigned to apologizing, Marietta turned at the same time the pointed toe of Tracy's boot caught in a crack. She pitched forward, arms akimbo, and Marietta was just quick enough to catch her as she fell.

"You can't do this, Mari." Tracy clawed her way up her sister's body until she was standing upright again. "You just can't."

Marietta paused, affected by the dismay on her sister's expressive face. "I'm sorry I didn't tell you I was meeting Harold today, honey, but my clock is tick-tick-ticking. It's so loud that most of the time it sounds like a boom-boom-boom."

"Then get a silencer!"

Marietta pursed her lips. "The next time I decide to do something like this, remind me not to confide in you."

"The next time! I don't think I can survive a next time. Once is bad enough."

"It was a figure of speech. I just told you. I'm primed for pregnancy. I know there's no guarantee that I'll achieve my objective on the first attempt, but hopefully I won't have to set up another meeting."

"Another meeting? You mean, another sexual encounter." Tracy fanned herself with one of her hands. "I think I'm going to faint."

"We've been over this before, Tracy." Marietta supported her sister's limp body, wishing she could make her understand. "Without sex, there can't be reproduction. And reproduction is essential for the preservation of the species. For a woman, the desire to become a mother is the strongest of all the biological urges. I have no intention of denying mine."

"I'm not proposing you deny it." Tracy still clung to her. Her green eyes were pleading. "I'm suggesting that placing an ad in a magazine for eggheads might not have been the best way to go about getting a baby."

"The magazine is for people of superior intelligence," Marietta corrected, peeling her sister's clutching fingers off her clothes as she talked. "The male's genetic material accounts for half the baby's makeup. By choosing someone with desirable qualities, I'm merely looking out for my baby's welfare. Surely you've heard of the terms natural selection and survival of the fittest."

"Natural selection! There's nothing natural about what you're doing. The natural process would be to fall in love with a man and have his baby."

Marietta sniffed, moved to her car and yanked open the door. "You know how I feel about love. Besides, you thought you were in love, and look what good it did you. What happened with Ryan merely proves my theory about the myth of the monogamous man."

The wounded look that was never far away appeared in Tracy's eyes, and Marietta wished she could take her words back. Her sister had been separated from her cheating husband for seven months, and she still wasn't over the snake.

"This isn't a lecture hall, and I'm not one of your college students. Besides, we're talking about you, not about me and Ryan," Tracy said, recovering admirably. "If you have to have a baby, why don't you try artificial insemination?"

"Now, there's an unnatural solution. Did you know that freshly collected semen have a much higher success rate than the frozen spermatozoa used in the artificial insemination process? That alone proves the natural way is better." Marietta forced herself to shrug. What good would it do to confide in Tracy that she was tempted, even at this late date, to take the easier route. "Besides, why do I need artificial insemination when I already have everything I want in a sperm supplier?"

Marietta punctuated her statement by getting into the car. Before she could reach for the door handle, Tracy positioned her body inside the open door and leaned down, banging her forehead on the door frame in the process. She held her head with one hand and grabbed Marietta's wrist with the other.

"Wait. Think about this logically and consider what could go wrong. How can you be sure this Harold doesn't have a communicable disease?"

"I have copies of his medical records."

Tracy bit her lip, a long-held character trait that meant she was thinking. "Okay. Then here's another. What if you do get pregnant, and he wants to play a part in the baby's life?"

"He can't. You know that, Tracy. I neither want nor need a man to help me raise my child. He's already signed a contract relinquishing all rights to any baby we might conceive."

"What if he changes his mind?"

"It won't matter, because I've taken precautionary steps to assure he won't be able to locate me if he does."

"What kind of steps?"

"I told him I wanted to be known by the alias Rhea. In Greek mythology, she was the mother of the Olympian gods. Don't you think that's clever?"

Tracy didn't even crack a smile. "What else?"

"The only address he has for me is a post office box, I made the hotel reservation under my alias and I'm not sharing any personal information with him. Why do you think I'm driving a rental car?"

Tracy didn't answer. Instead she looked hard at her sister, and uncannily zeroed in on the aspect of the plan that disconcerted Marietta most. "You do realize you're going to have to have sex with him."

Marietta tried not to shudder. In her opinion, sex was a sweaty, undignified, *unpleasant* experience. Some women, Tracy for instance, claimed to enjoy it, but Marietta had found the deed was mainly about male gratification. In the animal kingdom, for example, the act often took less than ten seconds, and females seemed spectacularly unmoved by it.

The Misconception

The only real benefit Marietta detected for most females, whether human or animal, was procreation. Which was what she needed to remember. For most of her life, she'd wanted to be a mother. As a child, she'd dressed her stuffed animals in diapers and pushed a toy baby carriage around the neighborhood. As an adult, her arms ached every time she saw a mother cuddling a sweet-smelling, cooing baby. If sex was the price she had to pay to get a child of her own, so be it.

"Of course I know I have to have sex with him. I'm a biology professor, remember?" The wind blew through the open car door, and she shivered. "Would you let me go? It's too cold to stay out here arguing with you."

Tracy's head dropped. Reluctantly, she released Marietta's wrist and backed away from the car. "You're not going to let me talk you out of this, are you, Mari? You won't even seriously consider that something could go wrong."

"I've planned everything to the most minute detail." She slammed the door shut, turned on the ignition and listened to the rental car roar to life. She maneuvered out of the parking spot, rolling down the window to make her parting point. "The plane's en route. The man who agreed to give me a child and then disappear forever is on it. What could possibly go wrong?"

As the plane did a bumpy landing dance down the runway, Jax theorized he'd gotten the wrong stomach when God handed out body parts.

Anyone looking at him would see a very large, exceptionally strong man who appeared able to weather any hardship. Who could guess that on the inside his stomach soared and dropped with every air pocket the plane hit?

Sweat broke out on his forehead. Geez, he hated to fly. Takeoffs and landings were so torturous, he had to call on all his willpower not to squeeze the hell out of the armrests.

He'd done that once, and the plastic had cracked like an egg shell.

He much preferred driving, but, unfortunately, that wasn't an option. Not only would it take too long, but it would look bad. Very bad. And one thing Jax Jackson hated to look was bad.

The plane finally skidded to a stop, causing everything he had drunk that day to slosh against the wall of his stomach before settling into an uneasy peace.

When he was certain the nausea-inducing flying machine was motionless, he got unsteadily to his feet. He made sure nobody was watching before he surreptitiously pinched his cheeks to restore his color. Then he smoothed down his suit pants with hands he wouldn't allow to shake and got into the stream of passengers deboarding Flight 707.

"I hope your flight was enjoyable." A pretty, blond flight attendant caught and held his eyes when he reached the cockpit. He summoned a grin. She had legs like a Rockette, and she'd found reasons to bend over in front of him often enough during the flight to make sure he noticed.

"It about made me want to sprout wings and take off myself," Jax said, automatically reaching for her hand when she held it out. She pressed something into his palm.

"That's not necessary." Her eye contact never wavered. "We're the ones who can make you soar."

Somebody toting an overstuffed carry-on bag bumped into him, propelling Jax out the door and down the loading tunnel leading to the terminal. He breathed deeply, grateful he didn't have to take another lungful of the recirculated stuff that passed for oxygen on the plane. He felt immediately better, but still wished he could stick his head outside a window for some fresh air.

A girl in her late teens wearing a fur jacket and a tight skirt her mama should have outlawed turned and gave him a come-hither look over her shoulder. Not wanting to be rude, he inclined his head in a brief nod.

The Misconception

The piece of paper the blond flight attendant slipped him was still in his hand, and he unfolded it, revealing her name and telephone number. He stuffed it into his pocket along with the number the brunette working the flight had given him. Their names were Bunny and Loralei, which would work just fine had they been porno stars.

Considering the possibilities the names brought up, he figured he just might call one of them later. Then again, maybe he wouldn't. Jax tried to separate business from pleasure, and he was definitely in town on business.

He didn't have to work until much later tonight, but he hadn't gotten where he was by sloughing off. He'd check into his hotel, load up on carbohydrates during a quick lunch and hit the weight machines for a couple of hours.

By the time he had his itinerary planned, he was inside the terminal. He bypassed the airline employee giving passengers information on connecting flights and was heading for baggage claim when a name on a sign stopped him.

Harold McGinty.

Oh, Geez. He'd forgotten all about breaking the news to Mac's mystery woman that he was standing her up. Why had he said he'd do it anyway? It wasn't possible to be thought of as one of the good guys while delivering bad news.

He took a few steps toward the sign, figuring he might as well get it over with, when the woman holding it shifted positions and he got a clear view of her.

The first thing he noticed was her dress, if you could call it that. It hung off her like a muted-plaid sack, stretching nearly to the floor and covering all but her ankles. Her hair, which was some shade between blond and brown, was secured in a loose bun at the back of her head, as though she couldn't be bothered with it.

Her face was in profile, revealing a longish nose, a small chin and full, unpainted lips that told him she didn't have much use for makeup. She turned to look at him with eyes

17

of an indeterminate color—Were they hazel? Gray? Brown?—and her jaw dropped. Then those kaleidoscopic eyes rolled.

She wasn't what you'd call pretty. Despite that fabulous mouth, her face was too stern, and perhaps a little too narrow. She was also too pale, as though she didn't spend any time in the sun, and she was neither model tall nor pixie short. He couldn't really tell because of the dress, but her curves seemed neither particularly lacking nor especially rounded.

All told, she was one of the sexiest women he'd ever seen in his life, which surprised the hell out of him.

"You must be Rhea," he said, walking toward her and wondering what she looked like under that sack, what her hair looked like down around her shoulders, what color her eyes turned when she was turned on.

A long moment passed before she nodded, and it seemed as though she had to force her head into the motion. Surprise, tinged by dejection, gripped Jax. It had been a long time since a woman looked at him as though she didn't like what she saw. Which, judging by this woman's eye roll, she most definitely did not.

"Don't tell me *you're* Harold McGinty." Her voice wasn't throaty. She didn't purr or linger sexily over the words. If anything, she sounded disappointed. And more than a little nervous.

"Actually, people call me Jax," he said, not wanting to lie. He gave a half bow, hoping to put her at ease, hoping to make her like him. "At your service."

She muttered something that sounded like, "You got that part right," but he couldn't be sure because her heavy sigh distracted him. She crossed her arms over her chest and shook her head, making him think he'd misread her and she wasn't nervous at all. But he obviously hadn't misinterpreted her disappointment.

18

"Oh, well." She heaved another sigh. "I suppose you'll have to suffice, Harold."

"Jax," he corrected automatically. "And, what do you mean, I'll have to suffice? What's wrong with me?"

Her eyes dropped to his size-fourteen feet, lifted to somewhere in the vicinity of his trouser front and widened. She closed her eyes briefly before bringing them back to his face. "You're substantially, uh, *bigger* than I imagined you'd be, Harold."

"Jax," he corrected again. He had the fleeting impression she was sizing up his penis, but surely that wasn't right. She must be referring to his considerable height, making it clear that she preferred short men. Like the real Harold McGinty. "I've never found how big I am to be a problem."

"Here's hoping it's not this time, either," she said, and again he got the fleeting impression that she was nervous. Then she squared her shoulders, looking anything but nervous as she gave the sign an authoritative toss into a garbage can and picked up a long, dark coat from a nearby chair. She barely glanced in his direction. "Shall we go?"

He stared at her, puzzled by her attitude. She thought they were going on a blind date, for cripe's sake. She should at least want to impress him just a little. But, so far, all she'd done was make it clear that *he* didn't impress *her*.

It was downright insulting, is what it was.

"Harold? Are you coming?"

Harold. She thought she was going on a blind date with Harold McGinty, not with Jax Jackson. Would she have preferred it if Harold, he of the inconsiderable height, had showed up instead of him? Would her delectable mouth have curved into the smile of welcome she hadn't bothered to give him?

"Harold?"

He should tell her he wasn't Harold McGinty right now. He had a hotel to check into, weights to lift, a schedule to keep. He should forget the way his libido had hummed

19

when he'd seen her standing there in her sack cloth. It had probably been a fluke, anyway.

His gaze snagged on her pouty, unpainted mouth. She had the kind of full, wide lips that didn't need lipstick to look rosy. They got a man to thinking of running his tongue over them before kissing her senseless. Of pressing her down into a mattress and begging her to use that mouth to do erotic things to him.

"Well?" She tapped her foot, drawing his attention to her ankle. Her very nicely shaped ankle.

"I'm coming," he said, making the snap decision to stand in for Harold on the blind date. By the end of it, he bet he could have her looking at him with something more than disappointment. Guilt over his deception bloomed within him, but he squashed it. What possible harm could it do? He deliberately gave Rhea the slow smile he'd been told could charm the habit off a nun. The corners of her mouth didn't even lift. "But only if you promise to call me Jax."

"I'll call you whatever you want," she muttered, "as long as you deliver."

Before Jax could figure out what she meant by that, she strode away. His eyes dropped to her rear, but she didn't call attention to it with the exaggerated hip roll that he was so used to from women.

Wondering why he found that sexy, he picked up his bags and followed her.

Chapter Three

The man named Harold who wanted to be called Jax had been talking nonstop since they'd left the airport, gaining high marks for verbal acuity and making Marietta wonder when she'd ever met a more talkative man. He launched into a joke about a skeleton who came into a bar and asked for a beer and a mop, and she had her answer: Never.

"You didn't laugh," he said, making it sound like an accusation.

"Maybe I didn't think it was funny," she replied, which he took as an invitation to tell another joke, this time about a dyslexic devil worshiper who sold his soul to Santa.

"You're still not laughing," he said.

Marietta managed to make her lips curve marginally upward. She didn't dare confess that she'd only been half-listening, because then she'd have to admit to herself that she wasn't sure she had the nerve to go through with her plan. And she had to go through with it, because he was the perfect candidate.

He had an IQ of 145, which put him in the top one percent of the population. He came from such excellent stock that nobody on his family tree had ever been felled by cancer, heart disease, or high blood pressure. He had 20-15 vision in both eyes, not to mention a professional job as a biochemist.

Any mother-to-be would be lucky to have access to his genetic material.

But who would have thought Harold McGinty would be such a towering, handsome hunk? Especially since, in rebellion to a beauty-obsessed society, she'd stated in her ad that looks didn't matter? She'd been expecting somebody with a less-than-stellar appearance, not the living reproduction of the statue of *David*.

She thought about what Michelangelo's statue wasn't wearing, and what the handsome hunk wouldn't be wearing when she got him to the hotel room, and fought off an attack of anxiety. Not good anxiety, as in the kind that helps you excel. But bad anxiety. Very bad anxiety.

". . . and the bartender said," Jax continued, as though she'd been paying close attention to the first part of his joke, " 'We don't get many fire-breathing dragons around these parts.' 'At these prices,' the dragon replied, 'it's no wonder.' "

Jax laughed at the punchline, telling Marietta she'd missed something. Then again, as bad as his jokes were, maybe she hadn't. Shaking off visions of his naked form, she pulled her rental car under the impressive porticoed awning of what was arguably the fanciest hotel in Washington D.C.

"Geez, you're like a laugh miser," Jax said when he stopped chuckling. "Don't you ever just let loose?"

She turned off the engine and removed the valet key from the ring. "I'm not prone to laughter."

"This should be interesting," he said, raising his eyebrows, "because I'm not prone to seriousness."

She opened the door, and he seemed to notice where they were for the first time. "Nice place," he commented as his gaze took in the elaborate Tudor facade of the Hotel Grande. "I take it this hotel has a grand restaurant?"

She turned to look at him, and her heart gave an extra ba-boom, which dismayed even though it didn't surprise. From her position as a biology professor at prestigious Kennedy College in Washington D.C., she had carved out a reputation as a national authority on the evolution of sex. She knew, from her vast warehouse of biological facts, that the reason she found his face attractive was because of its outstanding symmetry.

His heavily lashed chocolate-colored eyes, shaded by matching brows that arched at just the right degree, were mirror images of each other. The halves of his strong nose and sensuously slanted mouth couldn't have been more alike. His right cheekbone was at the same, lofty height as his left. The tip of his nose was lined up in the dead center of his square jaw.

Her subconscious, Marietta realized, had concluded those perfectly matched features meant he was a man better able to weather environmental hazards than his unsymmetrical brothers. That kind of subliminal thinking was a relic from the days man had spent in a hunter/gatherer society, but still packed a powerful punch.

Jax's symmetrical brows rose. "Rhea?"

Rhea. Who was Rhea?

"Rhea," he repeated, and it belatedly occurred to Marietta that *she* was Rhea. "Does this hotel have a good restaurant?"

"I'm quite sure that it does." Marietta snapped out of the trance his symmetry had caused and got out of the car. A valet rushed to her side, and she handed him her key.

"If you need help with your baggage," he said in clipped, polite tones practiced by hotel staff the world over, "our staff will be happy to assist you."

Marietta cleared her throat. She was an able woman with vast reserves of strength and intelligence. She needed to stop dwelling on naked skin and symmetrical features and take control of the situation.

"I checked in earlier. Room 414. Please have the gentleman's bags delivered there," she told him before Jax unfolded his long length, his very long length, from the car. He didn't even turn his head as the valet walked over to the bell captain to deliver her message.

"So what are you in the mood for?" Jax asked as they entered the hotel through beveled glass doors so pristine Marietta couldn't even discern fingerprint smudges. "I could go for a big, juicy steak, but I better stick to pasta. Do you think they have pasta?"

She peered at him. "What are you talking about?"

"Lunch."

"Lunch?" she repeated, seriously miffed. Hadn't they fed the man some peanuts on his flight? It was barely past eleven, well before the time he should have been thinking about food. He was in town, at her expense, specifically to get her pregnant. Didn't he have any sense of duty? Any sense of honor?

She stopped walking, and so did he.

"It's a little early, but I could eat," he continued, and it was obvious from his smile that he was oblivious to her displeasure. He was so unrelentingly cheerful that, if she weren't so determined to have her way with him and get him out of her life, she might actually start to like him. "I think lunch is the perfect way for us to start out our day together."

She shook her head, thinking that for a man with an IQ of 145, he wasn't very smart. One day was all they had. To maximize her chances of getting pregnant, they'd obviously have to do the deed as many times as she could stand it. Obviously, they should get started immediately.

"I'll tell you what, if you'd like to have lunch in the restaurant, go right ahead," she said in a clipped tone, figuring she couldn't get a club, bop him on the head, and drag him to the room. "I'll be waiting in room 414 when you're through."

That said, she turned on one of her low heels and walked quickly away. The heart of the hotel was beautifully appointed, with marble flooring, stained glass windows, brilliant chandeliers and a gurgling fountain shooting water six feet into the air. Marietta barely noticed the surroundings as she determinedly made her way to the elevator.

Did this . . . bewilderment on his face mean that, now that he'd met her, he'd decided there was no rush to have sex with her?

"Rhea, wait."

He'd get around to it eventually, of course, because that's the way men were made. But it stung that his stomach commanded more attention than she did. Sure, her features weren't as symmetrical as his. But she had all the things men historically looked for in a sexual partner: shiny hair, firm muscle tone, supple skin.

"Rhea!"

Not that she wanted him to be *too* interested. Even if she hadn't decided long ago that she didn't want a man, she wouldn't want this man. Sure, he was handsome. Sure, he was charming. Sure, he was uncommonly personable. But what had her sister called him? A sperm whore, that was it.

"Rhea!"

The female of the species was perfectly capable of raising a child alone, but Marietta couldn't respect a man who'd take money for his sperm. This man had even gone a step further. He'd signed a legal document surrendering rights to his child before it had even been born.

"Rhea, didn't you hear me calling you?"

If a hand hadn't touched her shoulder, Marietta wouldn't have bothered to turn around, although she'd been vaguely irritated that Rhea hadn't answered the man's calls.

The man, it turned out, was Jax.

"Rhea?"

Rhea. She nearly thumped her forehead. She'd forgotten her alias again. He peered at her through eyes that had gone soft with concern, which was another reason to like him when she shouldn't. She most definitely shouldn't.

"Are you hard of hearing?"

"Of course I'm not hard of hearing," she denied, then realized that would have conveniently explained her faux pas. She searched for another explanation. "It's just that Rhea's such a common name. I thought you were calling someone else."

Jax cocked his head, and a bemused smile touched his lips. Her assertion that a bunch of Rheas could be wandering around the lobby of the Hotel Grande was so idiotic that it was completely unbelievable. There had to be another reason she hadn't answered his call.

A ping sounded as the elevator doors opened. Instead of commenting on the Rheas, he followed her inside the elegantly padded box.

"It's okay with me if we have lunch in your hotel room," he said as she punched the button to the fourth floor.

She shook her head, looking decidedly unhappy, meaning he'd misread the situation. When she told him to have lunch in the restaurant, she'd sounded upset. He figured she'd been insulted at the thought that he didn't want to dine with her on room service. But maybe she hadn't been inviting him to her room. Maybe she was one of those people who felt uncomfortable eating in front of others. If that were true, she wouldn't want to eat in front of him. She certainly didn't seem to like him very much.

The elevator doors slid open at the fourth floor, and he followed her through them and down lush green carpeting slashing a long creamy hallway cleverly lit with recessed lighting. Soft music filled the space, and he recognized an old Beatles tune set to Muzak. Preprinted plastic cards hung from several doorknobs, reminding him of another joke.

The Misconception

"What did the maid do when she saw a 'Please make up' card hanging from the hotel door?" Rhea didn't attempt a guess, but that didn't stop Jax from plowing ahead. "She got out her mascara and lipstick."

Again, there was silence.

"You're determined not to laugh at my jokes, aren't you?" he asked. She didn't bother to answer, and he couldn't blame her for that. One of the big unsolved mysteries of his life was that few people laughed at his jokes. Granted, he wasn't fall-down funny like Nancy and Sluggo, but he was at least worth a couple giggles.

"All I want to do," she said as she put the key card in the door and the button flashed green, "is get this over with."

He followed her into the room, beginning to think they were speaking a different language. Get what over with? If his suspicion that she didn't like to eat in front of others was correct, maybe she intended to gobble her food.

He pulled the door closed while he tried to think of something to say that would put her mind at ease. All he could come up with was a banality about the perceived quality of the hotel food. "I'm sure it will be good."

Her eyebrows furrowed, and the corners of her sexy mouth turned down. She still hadn't smiled at him, he noted. "I'm sure *you* think so."

She disappeared into the bathroom, and he sank onto the mattress of a mahogany four-poster bed, a little surprised she'd reserved a room with a king-sized bed. She seemed very controlled, not at all the sort of woman who'd spread out in bed. He'd have thought she'd occupy one very small corner of it.

The room itself was surprising, because it qualified as a suite. The heavy reproduction furniture was fashioned of the same mahogany found on the bed and complemented by a brass chandelier and decorative fireplace.

Rhea couldn't be hurting financially if she could afford to stay in a joint like this.

27

A sharp rap on the door drew him to his feet, and he crossed the expensively decorated room, expecting a maid who'd forgotten to put fluffy, oversized towels in the bathroom.

Instead, a muscular young man stood in the hallway carrying his luggage. "I'll just put these bags inside for you, sir," he said, shouldering past Jax into the room. He had no choice but to move aside.

The young man deposited the bags and then looked at Jax expectantly, no doubt waiting to be tipped. But why should he tip him for making a mistake?

"I didn't tell you to bring those bags up here," Jax said.

The young man shifted uncomfortably. "No, sir, you didn't. I believe I saw the lady tell the valet to have the bags brought to your room, sir."

"It's not my—"

The bathroom door banged open to reveal Rhea, interrupting what Jax had been about to say. She obviously hadn't been inside the bathroom primping for their date. Her blond-brown hair was still in the loose bun, and she'd washed off what little makeup she'd been wearing. Her dress was wrinkled, and her skin even paler than before.

She looked so enticing that Jax's mouth watered.

"Oh, good," she said when she saw the bellboy. "Your bags are here."

She crossed the room, picked up her purse, withdrew a bill and handed it to the bellboy, who beat a hasty retreat out the door. He shut it, leaving them alone in the room.

Jax thought for a minute, but nothing he came up with made sense. She was standing six feet from him, as though carefully trying to keep her distance, which further confused the matter.

"Let me see if I've got this straight," he said slowly. "You told the bell staff to have my bags brought up to your room?"

"That's correct." Her words were bold, but she twisted one hand with the other, a sure sign that she was nervous. "Why?"

"For heaven's sake." The tempo of her hand twist reached double time. A muscle in her jaw twitched. "How do you expect to do it if we're in separate rooms?"

Jax stared at her, completely at a loss, but she wouldn't meet his eyes. "Do what?"

She put her hands on her hips, and the sack cloth bunched up against her body in a way that gave him his first glimpse of the shape underneath. Not that she was ever going to let him see that shape.

"Do what?" he repeated when she didn't answer.

"Have sex," she hissed under her breath.

Everything in his body went still, even the blood running through his veins. He banged one ear, then the other, because suddenly they weren't working correctly. "Excuse me? I don't think I heard what you said."

"Sex," she shouted, as though he should have comprehended the incomprehensible. Seeming to remember propriety, she lowered her voice. "We can't very well have sex if we're in separate rooms."

"You want to have sex with me?" His voice cracked, parts of his body leaped to attention, his mind whirled.

"Why on earth," she began, staring at the ceiling instead of him, "did you think I was taking you up to a hotel room?"

He'd thought they were going to have lunch. Jax had met his share of women on the make, and this wasn't the way the drill went. They smiled at him. They made eye contact. They found excuses to touch him. They moved in ways to get him to notice them. True, Rhea hadn't called off the blind date when she'd seen him, but she hadn't done any of those things.

"Why would you want to have sex with me when you don't even seem to like me?"

"Oh, for heaven's sake." She threw up her hands. "What's liking you got to do with it?"

Jax swallowed. Never, starting with the night Loretta Hood had invited him into the backseat of her daddy's Chevy convertible when he was fifteen, had he made love to a woman who didn't like him.

He was likable. Everybody said so. Just as everybody knew that liking the person they jumped into bed with enhanced the experience. That's why Jax wasn't inclined to one-night stands. He liked to build up to the lovemaking, possibly with dinner and a few drinks. Definitely with conversation. He and Rhea hadn't even talked. Well, that wasn't quite true. He'd talked. He wasn't sure she'd listened.

"Don't you want to know more about me first?"

"I know everything I need to know about you," she said, moving to the bed and sitting down. She patted the mattress, and he was pretty sure he saw her hand tremble, which didn't make any more sense than the rest of this. Women who boldly announced they wanted sex from a virtual stranger didn't suffer the trembles.

"But . . ." The reasons he shouldn't get on that bed with her were plentiful, but they died on his lips when she crossed her leg. Her dress had ridden up when she sat down, and the leg-cross offered him a view of shapely bare calf that exceeded his expectations. His gaze traveled upward, but the rest of her body was still covered by the sack. It got him to thinking that, if her leg looked that good, the other parts of her would match. His body hardened while he valiantly tried to remember what he'd been going to say. ". . . but I don't know anything about you."

"If you're worried about that," she said, sweeping her hand in his general direction, "take a look at those papers on the dresser."

Wondering what she could be talking about now, he turned, although it took a monumental effort to look away

The Misconception

from the inviting picture she made. A sheet of paper lay on the dresser, and he picked it up and scanned it.

"What is this?" he asked, puzzled. "Your health history?"

"It's a doctor's statement asserting that I'm free of communicable diseases."

She delivered the statement as though it made perfect sense that she would be in possession of such a document. He put the paper back down, wondering what possible zinger she'd surprise him with next. He caught sight of a stack of dog-eared books on the opposite side of the dresser. The top one was entitled *The Sure-fire Method of Natural Family Planning*.

She'd thought of everything, it seemed, even the birth control.

"Well?" His back was to the bed, but he knew what she was asking. "Are you coming?"

Jax liked sex as much as the next guy—okay, he liked sex more than the next guy—but it would be lunacy to make love in a hotel room before noon to a woman who didn't like him. Never mind about respecting her when they were through. Jax wasn't sure he'd respect himself.

He turned to tell her that, but she spoke first.

"If you don't mind," she said in that clipped, prissy way she had of speaking. "I'd like to get it over with."

"Get it over with?"

"Yes." She abruptly got up from the bed and moved to the window in that no-nonsense, no-swaying way she had of walking. The blinds were the room-darkening variety favored by hotels that catered to travelers who liked to sleep late, and she pulled them shut. The only light in the room came from a bedside lamp. She turned that off, too, plunging the room into darkness.

"What are you doing?" Jax asked.

"I'd rather you didn't see me when we, you know, do it."

Jax rubbed his forehead while his eyes adjusted to the darkness. "I have to tell you, Rhea, this has to be the strangest come-on in history."

"Oh, for goodness sake, someone had to make the first move," she said, but again he heard that strange little quiver in her voice, as though she wasn't as self-assured as she wanted him to believe.

Jax stood rooted to the spot, wondering if he'd have the strength of mind to walk away from this, when he noticed movement coming from the other side of the room. He could make out the shape of her arms stretching overhead, of her waist bending, of the sheets of the bed being turned back.

"What are you doing now?" he asked, although he was pretty sure he already knew.

"What do you think I'm doing? I'm taking off my clothes and getting under the covers."

She was taking off her clothes. The part of Jax that had relaxed at the bizarreness of the situation came back to life with a vengeance. His mouth went Sahara-desert dry.

From the instant he'd seen her, standing at the airport holding her sign, he'd fantasized about how she looked under that ridiculous sack dress. Now, here she was, alone in a hotel room with him. Naked.

His fantasy was very close to becoming reality.

His conscience screamed at him, but he shut it out. He was only a flesh-and-blood man, after all. There was only so much he could resist. And he couldn't resist Rhea.

He kicked off his shoes, shrugged out of his suit jacket and pulled off his tie as he walked slowly to the bed.

Then he turned on the bedside light and flung back the covers.

Chapter Four

A rush of cool air hit Marietta's naked skin, but it was offset by the hot wave of humiliation caused by having this man's brown eyes on her.

"Hey!" she said indignantly, trying to cover herself with her hands. Two of them weren't enough. She tried to get hold of the bed covers, but he was quicker than she was, yanking them off the bed with a supreme tug.

Tears sprang to her eyes, and she tried valiantly to blink them away, but it was to no avail. She'd used up all her bravado in the bathroom, when she'd given herself a pep talk about how she could—how she had to—bring herself to have sex with a handsome stranger. Her stomach had been churning with harmful anxiety, but she'd marched out of the bathroom, tipped the bellboy, and put the plan into action.

She'd only lost her nerve when it came to the lights. She thought turning them off was a reasonable request. Except he hadn't honored it. She was naked and exposed, and he was staring at her as though he'd never seen a woman without her clothes on. The embarrassment was almost too much to bear.

"Are you crying?" His voice was incredibly gentle, and the mattress sagged under his weight when he sat down on the bed. He reached out a hand, and she braced herself to withstand his intimate touch, knowing it was no more than she had invited. Instead of stroking her breasts or her thighs, however, his fingers came in contact with her forehead. He smoothed back the hair from her face. "Why are you crying?"

"I told you, but you didn't listen," she said on a sob, painfully aware that most of her was displayed before him. "I'd rather you didn't see me."

"Why not? You're incredibly beautiful." His eyes had darkened so they seemed more black than chocolate, and tiny goose bumps formed on her skin.

"I am not."

"Sure you are." His hand dropped, and he wiped away the tears under her eyes. Even though they were the only people in the room, he spoke in a whisper. A husky, sensual whisper. "You have one of the sexiest bodies I've ever seen."

"No, I don't." Marietta shook her head vigorously at his ludicrous statement. "I'm five, maybe ten, pounds overweight."

"You're the perfect weight." His eyes roamed over her as though to prove he meant what he said. "Neither too fat nor too thin."

"Look at my legs, then," she said, her voice shaky. "They're way too long in proportion to the rest of me."

He ran his fingertips from her ankle to her hipbone, sending delicious shivers over her. "I am looking at them. In my opinion, a woman's legs can never be too long, which makes yours extensively beautiful."

Marietta tried to dismiss the ludicrous compliment, tried again to make him see reason. "My stomach isn't flat. That's why I never wear a bikini. No matter how thin I get, it poufs out."

"Flat stomachs aren't sexy. Yours is."

The Misconception

His big hand covered her stomach, his dark skin providing a stunning contrast to her paleness as he lightly rubbed her soft skin. The fluttering feeling his touch induced caused Marietta to put her hands to her hot cheeks. The way things were going, she wasn't making much headway in convincing him she'd be more comfortable with the lights out.

"My breasts," she choked out. "They're too small. I barely fit into a B cup."

"Too small for what?" he asked and smiled. The hand covering her stomach skimmed over her ribcage and cupped one of her breasts. She gasped at the heated rush of feeling his warm hand elicited. "It fits perfectly, don't you think?"

Marietta tried to swallow, but she couldn't. She couldn't seem to do anything but feel. Jax's left hand joined his right until both of them were lightly kneading her breasts, his fingertips circling her nipples until they pebbled.

"They're getting bigger," she informed him.

"What's getting bigger?" he asked as he moved closer to her on the bed, skimming his lips across her cheek.

"My . . ." Sensation pooled low in her belly. ". . . breasts."

"Your breasts?" His mouth moved down to the body parts in question, and he kissed them, one after the other. She felt her back arch as she tried to get closer to his mouth. He laughed. "What do you mean your breasts are getting bigger? I thought, when a woman reached adulthood, they stopped growing."

Her brain was so muddled that it was difficult to think, but she managed to dredge up material from one of her more popular biology lectures.

"Female breasts enlarge up to twenty-five percent," she began, gasping as his tongue circled them, "and nipples swell by as much as one centimeter during, uh, you know."

"Sex?" He raised his head and smiled, looking straight into her eyes. "That is what you're trying to say, isn't it?"

Marietta was known around campus as one of the more erudite instructors. She was seldom at a loss for words. Now, she said, "Uh huh."

His lips moved to her right earlobe. His teeth tugged on it, then his tongue laved it.

"Did you know," she asked, more than slightly breathless, "that the earlobe is an erogenous zone?"

He chuckled softly near her ear. His warm breath sent shivers through her, making the tiny hairs all over her body stand on end.

"I love it when you talk brainy like that," he whispered, drawing back to look at her face. "Tell me more."

"Nostrils flare, and pupils dilate," she said, noticing that, despite the light, his pupils were so large she could barely make out the brown rim of color surrounding the black. She inhaled deeply, trying to draw in enough air. The scent of his cologne mixed with an intoxicating something else teased her senses. "Sweat glands open, releasing a signature scent. Some people call it a pheromone. In the insect kingdom, the female gypsy moth emits a specific kind of pheromone to attract a male."

He put his nose to her neck and breathed deeply. "You smell better than any moth I've run across." He put his lips where his nose had been and nuzzled the sensitive skin of her throat before trailing kisses over her jaw and across her cheek. He stopped when he reached the side of her mouth. "What happens to the lips?"

"They get redder." She licked them, already feeling the physiological changes. "They swell and become sensitive."

"I've got an idea," he said, moving his mouth so it covered hers. He whispered the rest of the words against her lips. "Let's try out your sensitive-lip theory and see if it pans out."

His mouth, which looked so hard, was incredibly soft. He seemed in no hurry to gain entrance to the inside of her mouth, instead running his tongue over her lips and kissing her over and over, on the corners of her mouth, at the center, as though he couldn't get enough.

The Misconception

A rush of heat enveloped her, and Marietta recognized what was happening. Her body was readying itself for sex. It wasn't something that hadn't happened before. Marietta was familiar with the tingling that preceded the actual act, although she couldn't quite remember the tingling being this intense.

She remembered the disappointment, though. After her partner had his fun, the disappointment was always the same.

She pulled back slightly from his ministrations, suddenly wanting to get the disappointment over with. "We can skip the preliminaries, you know."

He ignored her, as though he hadn't heard, and plunged his tongue into her mouth. She moaned as his tongue traced the roof of her mouth and then transferred its attention to the cellar. The tip of it ran over hers, coaxing her into a sensual session of give and take.

For a moment, she forgot about the impending disappointment and kissed him back.

He gathered her into his arms, and there was something amazingly erotic about having her bare skin against his clothing. One of his hands tangled in her hair, loosening the knot of her bun so her hair fell long and free, and his other hand cupped her bottom, kneading. She felt herself grow wet, her body readying itself for him.

He drew back slightly and smiled at her. "Unbutton my shirt," he invited.

A smidgen of sense came back to Marietta. She couldn't unbutton his shirt. That was an action that reeked of intimacy, and this was a business deal. It wasn't supposed to be sensual, wasn't supposed to be enjoyable.

"I . . . I couldn't," she began, but he silenced her by capturing her hands and bringing them to his shirt front.

"Go ahead," he urged. "I know you've probably seen the movie *Alien,* but I promise there's nothing under there but a chest. No monster's going to jump out at you."

A smile creased her mouth. This was bad, very bad. Above all, she wasn't supposed to let herself like him.

"Do you know," he said, tipping up her chin, "that's the first time I've seen you smile." He traced her curving lips with his finger. He made his eyebrows dance. "The second time is going to be when you get up the courage to unbutton my shirt. I have an amazing, alien-free chest."

She'd been clenching her fingers in an effort not to take him up on his invitation, but she couldn't resist his teasing. Couldn't resist teasing him back, especially when all she wanted to do was touch him.

"Oh, you do, do you?" she heard herself say as she reached for his shirt. "Let's just see about that."

When she'd finished with the buttons, he freed the tail of his shirt from his trousers and shrugged out of it. She stared at him. His chest was amazing, bronzed skin and golden-brown chest hair stretched over some of the most impressive pectoral muscles she'd ever seen.

"I look even better without my trousers," he prompted, but she was too stunned at the glorious sight of his chest to take him up on the hint. He laughed, lifted her easily off his lap and made short work of the rest of his clothes.

She watched him as he undressed, growing even more amazed. His body was the kind a sculptor would appreciate. Every muscle was defined, every sinew beautifully realized. It looked more like a work of art than a body. Michelangelo's David wasn't far off the mark. In fact, Marietta thought Jax had a better body than David. It was certainly larger than the statue man's.

The only marks marring his perfection were a large purplish bruise beside his hip and three slashes—from a cat's claws?—across the middle of his stomach. She started to ask how he'd gotten the injuries, but she forgot the question when he turned and she saw that he was fully aroused. She'd been right. He was big. Big and spectacular. His gaze followed hers, and she knew he could hear her breathing become ragged.

"Did you know," Marietta rasped, trying to camouflage her nervousness, "that respiration increases to four times its normal level during, uh, you know . . ."

"Sex?" he supplied again.

Now that he was naked, she expected him to be concerned with fulfilling his own needs. Instead, when he rejoined her on the bed, he caressed the arch of her foot and planted a soft kiss on her ankle.

"What . . . what are you doing?"

"What does it feel like I'm doing," he said, a chuckle in his voice. He kissed her calf, the underside of her knee, her thigh. "I'm kissing you all over."

"But . . . but . . . that wasn't part . . . oooohh." He'd reached the juncture of her thighs, and she felt the warm wetness of his tongue invade her. Nobody had ever done that before, and it felt wickedly good. "No . . . ooooohh."

Calling on her willpower, she pulled his head up. His fingers immediately replaced his tongue, taking over where it had left off, and he kissed the soft skin of her stomach. By the time he kissed his way up to her mouth, she was trembling.

"Touch me," he commanded, and she was powerless to do anything but obey him. First she smoothed her hands over his glorious chest, reveling in the hard ridges and soft chest hair. Then she moved her attention to his flat, rippled stomach, being careful not to aggravate the scratch marks. Finally, she found the most impressive part of him and encircled him with her fingers.

"Baby," he breathed into her mouth, "oh, baby, that feels good."

Her vocal cords could only seem to produce moans and murmurs or she might have told him not to call her baby. Then again, maybe she wouldn't have. As long as he kept doing what he was doing, whatever he called her was just fine.

He moved his body slightly and she moved with him. It was the most natural thing in the world when he slid into her. And it was like nothing Marietta had ever felt before. Instead of experiencing a vaguely pleasant fullness, multiple sensations crackled in the place they were joined and radiated outward. She wrapped her legs around his buttocks as he buried himself deeply inside of her and slowly withdrew.

"I don't think I can go this slow," he said when he'd finished the stroke.

"I don't think I want you to."

He moved, faster and faster, and she moved with him until she didn't think she could stand the sensual assault anymore. This is why some women enjoy having sex, she thought incredulously. This was bliss.

The scientist in Marietta knew there was some reason sex with this man was immeasurably better than she'd ever imagined sex could be. She didn't have time to analyze why as the hot gush signaling his release flowed into her, and she experienced a soaring storm of unfamiliar, exhilarating tremors that turned her body into a human earthquake. Then he collapsed on top of her.

Neither of them spoke for a few saturated minutes. Marietta couldn't even think coherently. Finally, he rolled over on the bed so that she was on top of him. He smiled up at her. "Wow."

Feeling suddenly shy, she tried to avert her face. He didn't let her. He put a hand on the side of her cheek so she had to look at him. His hair was tousled, his eyes were crinkling and he had the most endearing smile lines radiating outward from his mouth.

"Did you ever hear the one," he began, "about the little girl who came back from playing with some older neighbor kids and asked her mother what an orgasm was?"

The Misconception

Marietta shook her head, amazed that she still had the strength to complete the motion, amazed that Jax was telling her a joke while he was still inside her.

" 'I don't know,' the mother answered. 'Go ask your father.' "

Marietta smiled, although it really wasn't funny. Up until a few moments ago, when she'd had her very first orgasm, the joke would have rung more true. If Jax ever had a daughter, she'd never get that answer from her mother.

At the thought of Jax with a child, Marietta sobered. Even now, Jax's baby could be growing inside her. No, she mentally corrected herself. It wouldn't be his baby. It would be *her* baby. The baby who was the reason she was here, in this bed, with this man. The baby she'd forgotten all about until this moment.

"You've gone away from me. What are you thinking?"

"I was thinking," she said truthfully, "that the woman in your life would never give that answer."

"Not if I can help it," he said, and she felt his body come to life inside hers again. "I've got an idea. Why don't we try to give you another one?"

Before she could answer, his mouth covered hers in a searing, bone-melting kiss. Since she still didn't have the answer to why sex with Jax had been so transcendent, she owed it to herself as a scientist to repeat the experience. But, as his body moved inside hers, she forgot all about collecting data. She even forgot about the baby. All over again.

Sometime after making love to Rhea, summoning room service and eating lunch as quickly as he could so he could make love to Rhea again and yet again, Jax must have dozed.

When his eyes opened, the oversized red numbers on the bedside alarm clock were the first things he saw. When the numbers registered, he squeezed his eyes shut, not wanting them to be true. Slowly, apprehensively, he opened his eyes

41

again and groaned when the numbers still said the same thing.

Six o'clock. It was six o'clock, an hour past the time he was to have reported for work, and just an hour before things really got started. It would be the height of irresponsibility, and possibly the funereal march of his career, if he wasn't there when things got started.

Rhea was snuggled sweetly against his back, her soft curves reminding him of how they'd spent most of the past seven hours and tempting him to relive some of them. She was an incredible lover. Jax was usually nearly as talkative in bed as he was out of it, upfront about where he wanted to be touched and when. With Rhea, words hadn't been necessary. She'd seemed to know what he wanted, sometimes even before he knew himself. His body reacted to his erotic thoughts, and he had to fight himself so he wouldn't turn to take her into his arms.

He had to leave her bed. *Right now.*

Heaving a frustrated sigh, Jax pushed himself away from her and sat up. He caught a glimpse of his navy Jockey shorts, pulled them on, got up and began the hunt for the rest of his clothes.

He'd just shrugged into his shirt when he realized that she was watching him. The bedside light he'd turned on hours ago was still burning. She made such an appealing picture, even with a thin sheet covering her delectable body, that he wanted to crawl back into bed with her.

He smiled. She didn't.

"Are you going somewhere?" She anchored herself on an elbow and raised slightly from the bed. He noticed she was careful to keep the sheet covering her nakedness in place, and that made him sad.

"I have a business commitment," he said while he buttoned his shirt. "Believe me, if I could break it, I would. But I can't. It's completely unbreakable."

The Misconception

"But I thought . . ." Her voice cracked, and she started again. "I thought you were in town because of me."

Jax closed his eyes briefly, because he'd almost forgotten. She still thought he was Harold McGinty, who'd flown to D.C. specifically to see her. For the first time, he wondered why Rhea and Harold had arranged to meet. Had they been set up by mutual friends? Or, perhaps, were they Internet e-mail pals?

He should tell her about the mix-up right now. Maybe they'd even have a laugh about how anybody who knew both of them would never mistake five-foot-four Harold for six-foot-four Jax.

The trouble was that he didn't have time to explain. His career was on the line, and he needed to leave. He'd be back later. Nothing could keep him away. Then he'd explain. But right now, he needed to leave.

"It's something that can't be helped." He picked his suit jacket up from the floor and tried to shake the wrinkles out of it. "But I'll be back. You can count on that."

"Actually," Rhea said, sitting up straighter in bed, still clutching the covers to her chest, "that won't be necessary."

For the first time since he'd awakened, Jax went still. "What do you mean that won't be necessary?"

"We're done here," she said in the same clipped tones she'd used at the airport, before they'd spent hours tangled in each other's arms. "I'll have your bags delivered to another room. You can check which room at the front desk when you return."

"What?" Her nonsensical words drew him across the room to the bed. She backed up against the headboard, as though the intimacy they'd shared was a figment of his imagination. "What are you talking about?"

"You've served your purpose."

"My purpose? Am I missing something here? I just had the most incredible sensual experience of my life, and I

43

could have sworn it was you who spent all afternoon in bed with me."

"Sex is supposed to be sensual."

"What we had was more than sensual. It was special."

"What we had is a biological act millions of people engage in daily."

What had happened to the woman who'd moaned in his arms, who'd made him moan in hers? What had happened to that connection they'd shared that made words unnecessary? "You're deliberately misunderstanding what I'm saying," Jax said.

"No, you're misunderstanding me." She fixed him with a level stare. "I'll admit that the experience was extraordinary, but that's because you have a talent. Other men have a propensity for mathematics or music. You have a gift for sex."

Jax wasn't sure whether he'd just been complimented or insulted. Either way, he figured he should go with the flow. "Then let me keep on giving it to you."

"No." She shook her head decisively. "This is it. I don't need you anymore."

Time was ticking. His career was on the line. And she wasn't listening to him. In desperation, Jax dropped one knee to the bed and pulled her into his arms. She reacted instantly, as she had all afternoon. Her body went soft, her lips clung to his and she kissed him back as fervently as he was kissing her.

"You're attracted to me," he accused when he broke the kiss. He was slightly out of breath, and his heart hammered.

"Of course I am." She sounded breathless, too. "Your features are perfectly symmetrical."

"Huh?"

"Not to mention, you're well above average in height, you have clear skin, a square jaw, broad shoulders, a purposeful gait, good muscle tone. And high energy." She paused. "Let's not forget high energy. Of course I'm attracted to you. But it doesn't mean anything. I'd be attracted to anyone with those qualities. It's simple biology."

"There's nothing simple about it." He ran his hand through his hair. "Look, I've got to go. I'll be back as soon as I can, but it probably won't be before midnight. Then we can hash this out."

She didn't say a word, just peered at him through those hazel-gray-brown eyes. He reached across the bed, kissed her with everything he had in him and left the room.

Before he did, he glanced back at her. One of her hands was covering her eyes, as though she didn't want to look at him, as though she didn't want to face what had happened between them. But Jax would make her face it. When he got back from fulfilling his obligation and safeguarding his career, he would make her face it.

Five and a half hours later, Jax stood at the front desk of the Hotel Grande, rubbing his hand over the stubble that had formed on his lower face while he waited for the desk clerk to give him the extra key to Room 414.

Things had gone well tonight, but the usual high he got from a job well done was missing. Rhea hadn't answered the door when he knocked. He'd known she was disappointed when he left so abruptly, but, still, he expected her to answer his knock.

The clerk, a tall black man with a shaved head and a beautifully tailored white suit, moved to his computer terminal and punched a few keys. "I'm sorry, sir," he said with the kind of impersonal inflection that told Jax he wasn't sorry at all, "but the lady in that room has already checked out."

"She checked out?" Jax took a step back from the desk. He hadn't been expecting that. But that was okay. Even though she'd booked them into a hotel, he'd gotten the impression from the way she drove through Washington D.C. that she lived in the area. He'd simply go to her home to talk to her. "Could you give me her address?"

"Even if that information were listed here, which it isn't, I couldn't give it to you. The hotel has a strict confidentiality policy."

"But we were sharing a room!"

The clerk's eyebrows rose slightly, and Jax knew what he was thinking. If they were sharing a room, why didn't he know where Rhea lived.

"Look," Jax said. "It's not what you're thinking."

"I'm not thinking anything, sir."

"We were on this blind date," Jax began. "She wasn't saying much of anything, which is why I don't know much about her. But then the date, sort of, well, changed."

"Certainly, sir."

"And that's why I need her address," Jax finished.

"Very good try, sir, but the lady paid in cash and didn't leave an address. Which, even if she had, I couldn't give to you."

"Her last name? Did she leave a last name?"

The clerk's eyebrows rose again, and Jax launched into another explanation. "She's one of those people who prefers to use only one name in social situations. You know, like Cher. Or Madonna."

The clerk didn't comment, but lowered his eyes back to his computer screen. "It says here the lady's last name is Zeus."

"Zeus?"

"Yes, Zeus. Z-E-U-S. From Greek mythology. He was the god of the sky who ruled the Olympian gods." He squinted at the screen. "That's odd."

"What's odd?"

"Her first name is Rhea, who was the mother of the gods. If I'm not mistaken, she was Zeus's mother."

Unless her parents were rabid mythology buffs, Jax thought that probably meant Rhea Zeus was an alias. He remembered trailing after her in the hotel lobby, repeatedly calling out her name. She hadn't even turned, which lent credence to his theory that she'd used an alias. But why would she do that?

"There's a notation here on the computer that Miss Rhea Zeus did leave a message." He pulled open a drawer and withdrew a crisp white envelope with writing across it. "Are you Harold McGinty?"

The mention of Harold reminded Jax that Rhea didn't know his real name, either. "Sort of," he answered guiltily.

Looking suspicious, the desk clerk nevertheless handed over the envelope. Jax ripped it openly impatiently and withdrew the contents. Inside was the key to another hotel room and five crisp hundred-dollar bills with a note clipped to them.

For services rendered.

Jax hadn't kept track during their sexual marathon, but he suspected Rhea, or whoever the hell she was, had included a hundred dollars for every time they made love.

The desk clerk was looking at him with mild concern. "Are you all right, sir?"

He waved the bills in the clerk's face. "Apparently," he said, biting off the words, "I was more than all right."

Chapter Five

Two months later

Jax got out of his gleaming black Masserati in front of his mother's house and bit back a smile. Billy, the elder of his two younger brothers, was in the driveway rubbing at a spot on the hood of his old convertible with a worn rag.

Billy's lower lip was thrust forward, his concentration so intense he hadn't even heard Jax pull up. His hips swayed slightly to the beat of the rock music blaring from a too-loud boom box. Jax made a mental note to buy him headphones for his next birthday.

Billy straightened from the car and cocked his head as he regarded his handiwork. His golden hair was in wild disarray, dipping into his eyes and covering his neck, but it didn't disguise his good looks. His baggy shorts were slung low around his hips and his shirt was unbuttoned, revealing a sinewy body that belonged more to a man than a kid.

His little brother had grown up right under his nose. Billy not only had an old Ford Mustang he called his own, but had almost finished a year of college at Michigan State.

The Misconception

Jax was paying for the college, but his mother had forbidden him from buying Billy a car. That his little brother had done on his own.

Billy spit on an edge of his rag, leaned over and diligently rubbed at a spot on the windshield. Life in the Chicago suburbs, Jax thought, was far removed from the life he'd pulled his family from five years before.

It was a glorious day in April, and Billy was worried about spit-shining his car, no doubt to impress some girl, instead of helping his mother scrape enough money together to feed her family. He lived in a luxurious climate-controlled house in a neighborhood with yards resembling thick green blankets instead of a stifling two-room apartment surrounded by cement. Eviction wasn't a word that ever entered his mind.

Everything, in short, was exactly as it should be.

"Hey, Billy," Jax called as he crossed the lawn to the driveway. Billy turned, his face breaking into a grin. "What goes through an insect's mind last before it splatters against the windshield?"

Billy gritted his teeth, as though preparing for a particularly nasty blow. "Oh, no." He put his hands in front of his face. "Don't make me guess, Jax. Please don't make me."

Jax ignored him as he kept walking. He smiled, anticipating his brother's laughter. "His butt."

Billy groaned. "God, that was lame."

"It was not." Jax shook his index finger. "Admit it, Billy. That was one of my funnier jokes."

"Funnier? But doesn't that erroneously assume some of your other jokes are funny?"

Jax advanced toward his brother, surprised anew that Billy was only two or three inches shorter than he was. He remembered when his brother barely reached his waist. He ruffled his blond hair roughly.

"Erroneously? What's that? College-boy talk? If you're such a smart guy, how come you don't get a haircut? Your date's gonna bark when she sees you 'cause that mop on top of your head makes you look like Lassie."

"Lassie?" Billy's golden brows rose, and he moved swiftly away from the car, toward the hose. Jax recognized his intention, glanced down at his Italian loafers and tailor-made casual clothing, and hotfooted it toward the house. He wasn't fast enough. Spray cascaded over him, followed by Billy's teasing laughter. "Now who's the smart guy? You don't call a man with access to a hose Lassie."

Covering his head, laughing despite himself, Jax sprinted the rest of the way to the house and let himself in through the front door. He stood in the foyer, dripping on the wooden floor he'd insisted on paying extra for when he'd moved his mother from the inner city. She'd protested that the floor was a needless extravagance, but he thought extravagance was just what his mother needed after a lifetime of insufficiency.

His younger brother appeared in the entranceway to the kitchen, holding half a sandwich even though he'd probably eaten lunch just an hour ago. Drew was blond like Billy, a trait they'd inherited from the father who'd left them before either were out of diapers.

Eddie Bagwell hadn't been much of a father, but at least he'd been married to their mother for a brief while. That was more than Jax could say for his own father, whose name he bore but whose face he'd never seen. The result of Sheila Drayton Bagwell's romantic liaisons were identical, though. Both times, she'd ended up with sole responsibility for children who should have grown up with two parents. At the very least, his mother's men should have helped her support the children they'd helped create.

"What happened to you?" Drew asked before he finished chewing. Their mother liked to say her youngest son was a work in progress, but the world better watch out when he added the finishing touches.

The Misconception

Four inches shorter than Jax, Drew was an even six feet. His features were too large for his face, and he wore his hair preppy short, but the net effect was so compelling it was hard for strangers not to stare at him.

He struggled with his weight, but only because his high school wrestling coach had decided he should compete at 171 pounds. This past wrestling season, that decision had resulted in serious dieting plus a sectional championship. In the off-season, Drew made up for the dieting by eating everything in sight.

"What happened to me?" Jax repeated. "Billy happened to me. Let me give you some advice. Don't ever call him Lassie. Especially when your clothes are dry clean only. Throw me a towel, okay?"

"Sure thing, bro." Drew took another bite of his sandwich before he disappeared into the kitchen. By the time he reappeared and threw Drew a towel, the sandwich was gone.

"You call this a towel?" Jax held up a square of material roughly one foot by two. "Looks more like a handkerchief to me."

"It's all I could find," Drew said while Jax toweled himself off with the oversized hanky. He managed to dry his face and one muscular arm before the cloth was saturated. He hoped he wouldn't look too wilted when his clothes dried. He'd spent too many years wearing hand-me-downs and blue-light specials to not strive to look his best now.

"Hey, you know that wrestling camp I'm going to?" his brother asked, making no move to get him another towel. "We had a guest instructor this morning. Guy by the name of Manny Ramirez. Name ring a bell?"

Although it was as though the bells of St. Mary's were chiming in his head, Jax shrugged. "Should it?" he asked with all the nonchalance he could muster.

"Should it? Yeah, of course it should, man. Ramirez said he was the guy who pinned your ass in the state tournament when you two were high school seniors."

"Oh." Jax shrugged again, as though the name of the opponent who cost him a state championship wasn't burned in his mind. Football had been so popular at Ridgeland High that he'd been well known for his outstanding play at linebacker, but wrestling had always been his first love. "*That* Manny Ramirez."

"Yeah, *that* one." Drew affected a wrestler's stance, bouncing on the balls of his feet with his legs apart and his elbows close to his body. "He sure remembered you when I asked if he knew you. He even gave me some pointers on how to take you down. Let me try it, Jax."

Jax rolled his eyes. "We've already been over this, Drew. I was a heavyweight, remember, and I weigh even more now than I did then. I'm too big for you to take down. And I'm, what, fourteen years older than you."

"Manny says size and strength aren't nearly as important as speed and technique. Come to think of it, old man, youth is also an advantage."

"Thirty-two isn't old."

"Then prove it," Drew said, still bouncing. "Let me try."

"Cash? Is that you, Cash?"

The stairway leading to the second floor was off the foyer, and Jax turned at the sound of his mother's voice, smiling at the way she persisted on calling him by the name she'd given him at birth.

He temporarily forgot about his bouncing brother until Drew shot forward and down, hooking an arm under Jax's right knee. He pivoted, driving his shoulder into the back of Jax's leg.

"Hey, stop that," Jax protested, but it was too late. His leg buckled and, aided by the water his other brother had doused him with, slid out from under him. He fell to the floor in a landing so hard a crystal vase bounced off the foyer table and shattered, spraying water and flowers.

In defeat, Jax lay flat on the floor and closed his eyes. When he opened them, both his mother and Drew were staring down at him.

The Misconception

"I knew I could do it," Drew said. "I knew I could take you down!"

"Really, Cash. If you miss wrestling this much, why did you ever leave it?" His mother had her hands on her ample hips. She was shaking her head in a way that, for just a moment, reminded Jax of that bewildering woman in Washington D.C. who had paid him for sex. "Surely there's a high school somewhere that needs an experienced coach."

Jax anchored himself on an elbow and made a face at his brother. He rubbed his smarting hip. "What are a wrestler's favorite colors?"

"Oh, no," Drew moaned, putting a hand on their mother's arm. "I sense one of his jokes coming. Please, Mom, make him stop."

Jax ignored him. "Black and blue," he said, threw back his head and laughed. He was the only one of the three who did. His unsmiling mother patted the top of his head consolingly.

Drew extended a hand and helped him to his feet, and their mother came forward to enfold him in a soft embrace. The top of her head came to the middle of his chest, reminding Jax he must have inherited his size from the son of a bitch who'd fathered him and split as though nothing momentous had happened. In Jax's estimation, that was the lowest thing a man could do.

"I'm not even going to ask why you're wet," his mother said when she drew back from the embrace. She wasn't yet fifty, but her face was deeply lined, showing evidence of the hard life she'd led. "Come into the kitchen with me, and I'll get you a towel and something to eat. Drew, since you attacked your brother, you can clean up this mess."

Jax wasn't really hungry, but he knew better than to argue with his mother when the subject was food. She'd fed him a lot of hot dogs and macaroni and cheese while he was growing up, and she seemed intent on making up for it now that money was no longer scarce.

Darlene Gardner

The kitchen was a cook's dream with wall-to-wall maple cabinets, marble countertops, a floating island, and an attached sunroom that was the perfect setting for leisurely meals. Jax's mother had chosen wallpaper shot through with yellow and orange, a choice that shoved aside the memory of the dark little kitchen in the dingy apartment where they had lived for so many years.

Jax pulled up a stool to a counter where his mother was assembling sandwich fixings. Although he could handle himself in the kitchen, his mother wouldn't hear of him making his own sandwich. Years ago, he'd made plenty of meals for Billy and Drew while she'd labored to bring home a paycheck. She thought it was payback time now, and he couldn't convince her otherwise.

"I'll replace the vase, Mom," Jax said as he dried himself with the towel his mother gave him. "You were right. Drew and I shouldn't have been wrestling in the house."

"Pshew, you buy me too many things already," his mother said with a wave of her hand. Unfortunately, it was the hand that held a knife. Jax backed up his stool. "I can do without another vase."

"That's the point. I don't want you to do without anything."

She paused in making his sandwich, reached across the counter and patted his cheek. He kept an eye on her knife hand while she did so. "You're a good son, Cash, but I worry about how much you spend. That fancy place you have in town must have cost you a pretty quarter."

"A pretty penny," Jax corrected.

"Don't you give me that. The price of that place was a lot closer to a quarter than a penny."

Jax smiled. "Mom, stop. I can afford it."

"But are you happy with what you're doing? When you were teaching at the high school and coaching the wrestling team, you seemed so happy."

The Misconception

Drew came into the kitchen and pulled up a stool next to Jax. "Leave him alone, Mom. He's raking in the bucks, and that's what life's all about."

"Life's about being happy," she countered, slicing a tomato with a vicious chop, "and he was happy coaching wrestling."

"Everyone knows wrestling doesn't pay." Drew reached out and peeled a slice of cheese from a nearby stack. Their mother rapped his hand, but he smiled at her and popped it into his mouth.

"Actually, that's not true," Jax said. "Pro wrestling pays plenty."

Drew made a rude noise. "Pro wrestling? Now there's a joke. That's why serious wrestlers get so little respect. It's because of guys like the Undertaker who make up moves called stupid things like the Tombstone Piledriver—"

"Did you know that the Undertaker is six feet ten?" Jax interrupted.

"—and ridiculous duos who slam dance in the ring like those Headbanger guys—"

"Mosh and Thrasher," Jax supplied.

"—and other guys who have these elaborate entrance acts that are just laughable. The biggest joke of all is that so-called wrestler who calls himself something like the Secret Stallion."

"I think it's the Secret Stud."

"Yeah, something stupid like that. When he comes into the arena, he has these women who—"

"Do we have to talk about pro wrestling?" their mother interrupted. "Can't we have a normal conversation that doesn't have to do with thrashing and funeral directors?"

"Undertakers," Drew corrected.

"Whatever. It's too silly to talk about." She slapped the last piece of bread on the sandwich, sliced it in half with another tremendous chop and handed it to her eldest son. "I want to hear more about Cash's job."

"My job? No, you don't, Mom. It's awfully boring. Bore-you-to-tears boring, in fact."

"How can it be boring when you're so successful at it? You're always jetting here and there. I swear, you're away from home more than you're home. And I'm not even sure what company you work for."

Jax rearranged himself on the stool. "It's not a company, per se. I'm more of an independent contractor." He played his trump card, the one that always killed the conversation before it could go too much further. "We deal in stocks and bonds, securities, that kind of thing."

As Jax expected, their mother's eyes glazed over. Drew, however, looked thoughtful.

"If that's where the money is, that's where I want to be," Drew said. "Maybe I should look into majoring in finance if I get accepted to MIT. Why don't you tell me more about it, Jax?"

Jax hadn't anticipated the question. He figured Drew's interests would be more in line with Billy's when college rolled around, and Billy wanted to do something that enabled him to spend time outdoors. Who would have guessed Drew would opt to become a financial wizard?

"What do you want to know more about?" Jax wondered if he could bluff his way through this from what he'd gleaned from his accountant. "Equity funds? IRAs? Tax-free bonds? Overseas markets?"

"How about explaining how the stock market works."

"I'm sure that would be very interesting, but that's enough about Cash's job," their mother said, an almost desperate edge to her voice. Jax hid a grin. Despite what she'd said earlier, she clearly didn't want to engage in business talk. "Stocks and bonds are, um, interesting, but I'd rather hear about his love life. Have you met any nice girls lately, son?"

Jax's mind immediately drifted back two months to the brief, earth-shattering time he'd spent with the woman who called herself Rhea Zeus. Despite the fact that they'd spent most of their time in bed, he'd sensed a connection that went deeper than the physical. Between bouts of incredible sex, he'd thought, when he could think at all, that she was the kind of woman his mother would like.

"You have met somebody special, haven't you?" His mother stared at him through narrowed eyes. "When am I going to meet her?"

"There's nobody to meet." Jax emphasized his words by shaking his head. "I haven't met anybody special."

"Pshew. It's a sin to lie to your mother. I can tell from your face that you met somebody."

"Okay, you're right. But only partly. I thought I'd met somebody special, but I was wrong." Boy, was he ever. Jax remembered the sinking feeling that had assailed him as he'd stood in the lobby of the Hotel Grande holding five one-hundred-dollar bills. He'd decided on the spot not to waste any of his valuable time trying to discover Rhea Zeus's true identity. He didn't want any part of whatever game she'd been playing. "Whenever I do find a good woman, you'll be the first to know."

His mother seemed to accept the explanation. "Speaking of good women, Alexis Trumble is back in town."

Beside him, Drew sniggered. Jax had a vague memory of Alexis Trumble from high school as a sturdy, tuba-playing girl with a hint of a mustache. He sensed the conversation was heading into murky territory, where he'd be sucked into a date if he weren't careful.

"I ran into her mother the other day at the supermarket, and she said—"

Jax slapped the table theatrically, and his mother abruptly stopped talking. So far, so good. Now all he needed to do was employ what, in football, was called a misdirection play. If he could successfully change the subject, she might forget about the mustachioed woman.

"I hate to interrupt, Mom, but I just remembered that I need to call my machine and check messages. I'm expecting a really important phone call."

"It's so important you can't hear what I have to say about Alexis Trumble?"

"Yes, it's that important." Jax rose and moved to the telephone. He punched in the number for his home telephone and then provided the code for his answering machine. He slanted an apologetic look at his mother. "I'll just be a minute or two."

At least, he thought as he listened to the mechanical voice come over the line, he had messages. Four of them, to be precise. The first was from his travel agent, confirming the dates of his flights for later in the week. Star Bright, his business manager, had left the second, asking Jax to call him back. The third was from some woman named Bambi he didn't remember meeting. The fourth message was the strangest.

"Jax, this is Mac McGinty. Remember? From high school and the O'Hare Airport? The reason I'm calling is, uh, that I just, uh, got a really big check in the mail from Rhea. You remember Rhea, don't you? The thing is that I didn't earn this money. And I was just wondering if you, uh, delivered my message." His voice changed, went up a decibel. "You didn't deliver anything else, did you, Jax?"

That was it, aside from a number where Jax could reach him. Jax hung up, immediately punched in the number and had Harold McGinty on the line within seconds.

As he listened to the little man's bizarre story, his mouth opened in increments until a tennis ball could have fit into it. When he hung up the phone, he felt as though all his blood had drained to his feet and seeped onto the floor.

"Cash." His mother was instantly at his side. "Is everything all right?"

Jax shook his head mutely. After what he had just learned, he wasn't sure anything would ever be all right again.

"Cash, you're scaring me. Tell me what I can do to help you."

He cleared his throat, and looked down at his mother's concerned face. "You don't, by any chance, happen to know the name of a good private detective, do you?"

"A private detective. Why would you need a private detective?"

"You don't want to know. Let's just say there's somebody out there I need to find." He stopped, raised his eyes to the ceiling and blew out a breath. "Correction. Make that two somebodies."

Chapter Six

Marietta Dalrymple leaned weakly against the restroom stall while the lyrics of a golden oldie reverberated in her head. Except, instead of "turn, turn, turn," she bastardized the words to "churn, churn, churn." Which was precisely what her now-empty stomach was doing.

In the past few weeks, she'd become intimately acquainted with the inside of stall number one in the first-floor restroom of the Camelot Building. That's because it contained the toilet closest to her office.

If she continued this way much longer, she'd anoint herself Kennedy College's Porcelain Princess.

She walked to the nearest sink on unsteady legs, reached into her purse and extracted the toothbrush she kept precisely for incidents like this. The minty smell of toothpaste hit her nostrils, and she reeled. Her olfactory nerve must be way out of whack if even the scent of toothpaste made her nauseous.

She collected herself, held her breath, and brushed her teeth as quickly as possible. When she was through rinsing her mouth, she splashed water on her face and raised her eyes to the mirror. The sight that greeted her was enough to make her want to scream.

She looked like Casper the Friendly Ghost's scary older sister.

Her normally fair skin was milky-white except for the dark half-moons under eyes that looked even more washed out than usual. Even her lips, which she'd always thought were too large for her face, were colorless.

Pregnancy was definitely not agreeing with her.

She placed a hand over her still-queasy stomach, a gesture that never failed to get her through her bouts of morning sickness. She already loved the baby growing inside of her and thanked providence daily that she was one of the lucky women who had no trouble conceiving. The only hitch in her plan was that it had taken so long to find a suitable sperm supplier that she hadn't been able to time the birth for the summer months.

The baby was due in mid-October, which meant she'd have to take the fall semester off from teaching. But that was a minor inconvenience considering the tremendous payoff. No price on earth was too steep to pay for the wonder of motherhood. Not even the thousands she'd mailed to the baby's sexy sperm supplier.

At the thought of Jax, warmth spread through her stomach, directly over the place her baby nestled. Memories of Jax in her bed, making procreation seem much more like recreation, assaulted her with hot fingers. She could probably come to orgasm just thinking about him.

Which was why she had to banish the warm thoughts and think about him as a stud-for-hire with a talent for making whoopee. He wasn't her baby's father any more than a donor who leaves a deposit at a sperm bank.

Her baby didn't need a father, anyway. She, or he, only needed Marietta.

She rummaged through her purse for the little-used lipstick and blush her sister Tracy had thrust at her during her latest unsuccessful let's-make-over-Marietta kick. After painting on the color, she surveyed the result and suppressed another scream.

Great. Now she looked like a ghostly apparition with Adobe-Sands cheeks and Very-Berry lips.

The restroom door swung open. Through it walked a college coed no more than five feet tall and so brimming with health and vitality that Marietta felt like ducking under the sink. The coed smiled, all white teeth, dark hair, and olive skin. Then she clapped her face with both hands.

"Oh, my God. You're Dr. Dalrymple, aren't you?" Marietta nodded, taking a step backward to protect her ears from the squealing. "Oh, my God. I can't believe it. This is so radical."

"What's radical?" Marietta asked suspiciously.

"Running into you in the restroom, that's what. This is so great. The rest of the FOCs are going to be so jealous they'll have a cow. Nobody else had to go."

Marietta was at a loss as to why the girl was acting like she was a rock star instead of a Ph.D. specializing in evolutionary biology. True, up to this point, her career had been remarkable. She'd finished her dissertation at the shockingly young age of twenty-seven. After teaching at Kennedy for three years, she was putting together a tenure package that would come up for review next year. Her class was popular, in large part because her specialty was biological matters relating to sex, but that hardly qualified her as a celebrity.

"I don't understand," Marietta said. "Although, as a biology professor, I need to inform you that foxes can't have cows. Animals mate within their own species."

The girl laughed. "That was a good one," she said, clapping her dainty hands. "I didn't say foxes. I said FOCs. We're people, not animals. FOC is an acronym for Feminists On Campus. I'm Vicky Valenzuela, the president. I'm the one who organized the group to come sit in on your class."

"You're going to listen to my lecture?" Marietta was proficient enough at lecturing that she didn't harbor any false modesty, but her audience typically consisted of students taking the class for college credit. "Why?"

"Why?" Vicky's mouth dropped open. "You're kidding, right? You've been like a role model for our group since that feature story in the *Washington Post* last week. I picked up the academic journal that published your article and photocopied it for all the other FOCs. I even thumbtacked it to the bulletin board in my dorm."

"You thumbtacked 'Motherhood Without Males' to your dorm bulletin board?"

"Yes," Vicky answered enthusiastically. "That was absolutely brilliant. We FOCs wholly embrace the notion that females, who have wrongly been thought of as the weaker sex, can do anything they choose whether a man is involved or not. It's the ultimate feminist viewpoint."

Marietta's stomach did a roll not quite as acrobatic as the one that had led her to the restroom. She pulled some crackers out of her purse, tore open the package, chewed and swallowed.

"Actually," she said, "I believe you missed my point. I wasn't stating a feminist viewpoint. I was giving my opinion as a biologist who has studied animal behavior related to sex.

"When was the last time, for example, you saw Mallard ducklings following their father? The mother's the one they need. It's the same thing with baby alligators. The mother stays near them for a year or more. The father, whom I prefer to call the sperm supplier, splits before the mother even lays her eggs. She does just fine without him."

"Cool," Vicky said, leaning back against an adjacent sink. The mirror reflected the scene: The tiny ardent feminist and the much-larger nauseous biologist. "Just like I said: A woman doesn't need a man to succeed. I can hardly wait to hear today's lecture. What are you going to talk about?"

"We're studying mating behavior so I'm going to talk about the reasons women and men are attracted to one another. Then I'm going to present my theory on why love is a four-letter word for sex."

"What does that have to do with feminism?"

"I told you I'm a biologist, not a—"

"Oh, now I get it," Vicky interrupted. "You're going to instruct college-age feminists like the FOCs about the manipulative ways of men so we can better compete in today's sexist climate."

Marietta rubbed at one of her eyes, intending to tell Vicky that wasn't her intention at all, when her vision went blurry. "Oh, no," she wailed. "I've just lost one of my contacts."

"Hold still. Hold perfectly still," Vicky ordered, stepping forward. "Now lean down so I can search your face." Marietta bent over until her face was inches from Vicky's, who looked like one of those larger-than-life images on roadside billboards. "I'll help you find it. Look up. Now look down. Oh, drat. It's not in your eye." She ran her fingers over Marietta's cheeks as though reading Braille. "It's not on your face either. Maybe it's on the floor."

She took a step back and bent down to survey the area. "Oops," she said after a minute. "You don't wear hard contacts, do you? Most people wear soft, you know."

"Hard contacts are the only kind that work with my eyes. Why?"

"Because I think I see half of it."

"Half of it?" Marietta's stomach did some more tumbling maneuvers that had nothing to do with morning sickness and everything to do with dread.

"The other half's on my shoe. I can't believe this. I just crunched my idol's contact lens. I'm super sorry, Dr. Dalrymple. I'll do anything to make up for it. Please let me."

The Misconception

Marietta tried to focus on the girl, but her near-sighted eye couldn't synchronize with the eye with the corrected vision, resurrecting her nausea. She saw two mouths, both of them frowning in misery. She wondered how Vicky would atone for her mistake, and had a vivid picture of the girl lobbying to get her elected as president of NOW.

"That won't be necessary, Vicky. Mistakes happen. Don't worry about it." Marietta went to the sink, popped out her other contact and reached into her purse for the pair of eyeglasses she always kept there. She tossed two tissues, a pillbox, and three packages of crackers onto the counter before she remembered switching from her large brown purse to her small black one that morning.

Accessorize, Tracy was always telling her. Never, ever carry a brown purse when your dress was predominantly black. Foolishly, Marietta had listened to her, even though her black purse didn't have nearly enough room for all her things. Come to think of it, Tracy was the one who'd persuaded Marietta to get the contacts. And look what had happened.

She was a professor known for her vision who couldn't see a foot in front of her face unless someone stuck one there.

"Can I help you with anything?" Vicky asked, her voice contrite.

"Oh, no. You've done quite enough already." Somehow Marietta managed to smile, just like she'd manage to get through the class that should be starting right about now. If she held her notes close enough to her eyes, she'd be able to read them. It didn't really matter how well she could see her students.

"It was such an honor to meet you, Dr. Dalrymple," Vicky called after her as she exited the restroom. Marietta spun to acknowledge her with a wave, turned back around and promptly collided with the door frame. Dazed, as well as nauseous and near-blind, she headed into the hall.

"Marietta, do you have a moment?"

The hall was blurry, like the reception on a cheap television that wasn't hooked up to cable, but she could identify the man who'd asked the question.

None of her other colleagues had quite the same shape as Professor Robert Cormicle, who sort of resembled a fuzzy lamp post. His body was tall and lean, which, unfortunately, made his rather large head look out of proportion. If Marietta hadn't been so versed in biology, she might have thought his head needed to be large to house his brain, which was enormously impressive.

"Robert! I'm so glad I ran into you. I need you to do me a really big favor. I'm late for class or I'd do it myself. Could you call my sister Tracy and ask her to bring me my brown purse?" Before he could respond, Marietta rattled off her home phone number.

"Of course I will, but—"

"Do you need me to repeat that?"

"No, of course not. I have an excellent memory. That's not what I was going to say."

"What were you going to say?"

"I just . . . I wanted to . . . I thought you and I might . . ." Robert, who could spout chemical equations as easily as elementary students reciting the alphabet, couldn't complete a sentence. Marietta wished she could see his face to get a clue to what he was thinking, but all she saw was a blur.

"I don't mean to be rude," she told the blur, "but could you please just say whatever it is you want to say. I'm already late as it is."

"Will you go out with me?" Robert's words came out in a rush, surprising Marietta with their intensity. She'd known Robert for six months, ever since he'd joined the biology department, and didn't have a clue that he considered her as anything other than a colleague. "To dinner, I mean. Or a movie. Or, well, anywhere."

The Misconception

"Robert, I—" Marietta began.

"I know you're off to class, Marietta. Don't say anything now. Just think about it. Please?"

She didn't want to hurt his feelings, but she didn't need to think about it. She wasn't in the market for a man. If she were, he'd be six feet four and so sexy he made her heart threaten to beat down the walls of her chest cavity. While Marietta tried to reject that ridiculous thought, Robert walked away so quickly she didn't have a chance to say anything at all.

Resigning herself to turning him down later, Marietta squinted. She walked the rest of the way to class, feeling as though somebody had opened the doors and let in fog.

Reaching the podium in front of the class in the giant lecture hall seemed like a miraculous feat. She shuffled her notes until she had them in a vague order and then peered at the class. From what she could make out, the lecture hall was remarkably full.

She wondered if more people were here today because of the article that had appeared in the *Washington Post*'s Style section, airing her unorthodox views on love, sex, and man-free motherhood.

A flash of red crossed her eyes, and she realized it was Vicky Valenzuela, the tiny contact-crunching feminist from the restroom. The FOC took a seat in the front row beside a string of females. The rest of the foxes, no doubt.

Marietta adjusted the microphone and cleared her throat. "I take it advance word must've gone out that today's lecture is about sex."

Standing in front of a crowd always gave Marietta a case of the jitters, which she could quickly dispel by getting the students on her side. Laughter filled the room. The FOCs, who apparently hadn't been versed in classroom decorum, clapped.

"Notice that I said sex, not love," Marietta continued. "Sex is absolutely essential for our survival as a species.

Darlene Gardner

Love isn't. But I'll get to that later in the lecture."

Now that her jitters had subsided and she had the attention of her students, Marietta launched into a well-researched lecture that included traditionally accepted dogma about mating behavior. Whenever she said anything that could be vaguely construed as pro-female, the FOCs, who she'd come to regard as her own personal cheering section, applauded.

"As you can see, men and women choose their sexual partners because of deep-seeded evolutionary tendencies that began to develop in hunter-gatherer societies," she said deep into her talk.

"Men subconsciously seek out women who have youth and good health, positive signs of fertility. They're looking for a vessel in which to spread their seed, because this response is deeply ingrained within them.

"Women subconsciously want men who transmit signals of strength and power. In the societies of old, when food was scarce and predators plentiful, it was extremely important for females to have males who would help provide for them."

She took a breath, because she was about to get into the part of the lecture that had, at its heart, no heart.

"Love simply didn't play into it. It doesn't play into it. In short, love doesn't matter."

One of the FOCs whistled her approval as the others clapped, and murmurs spread through the classroom like wind chimes carried on a breeze.

"That's the most ridiculous thing I've ever heard."

A male voice from the back of the lecture hall exploded into Marietta's consciousness. She was so surprised to be interrupted that she could barely believe it had happened.

"Excuse me?"

"That's the most ridiculous thing I've ever heard."

A heckler. Here she was, at the front of a college biology class giving a lecture, and she had a heckler. Never, in all her years of teaching, had it happened before. Sure, she'd had students stop her and ask her to clarify a point. If she had time at the end of the lecture, she made a habit of opening the subject up for debate. But never had a student baldly dismissed what she'd said.

Never had a student heckled her. This wasn't the Improv. This was Kennedy College. And this was unthinkable.

"I heard you the first time, but this is a college class," Marietta said firmly. "We'll have a question-and-answer period at the end of the lecture. But my lecture itself is not open to debate."

"It should be. You just presented an opinion as though it was fact."

The voice was angry, ridiculously so, as though something in her lecture had touched him on a personal level. It was also familiar. It sounded, in fact, just like her sperm supplier's voice. Marietta squinted to get a look at the speaker, but he was sitting at the back of the class, too far away to see—with or without her contacts. Besides, it couldn't be Jax. He didn't know where she was or even who she was. It couldn't be him.

"You're wrong. I've formed educated convictions based on facts. There's a difference."

"But you're talking as though love doesn't exist!"

Marietta's stomach rumbled. The baby, she thought, responding to its sperm supplier's voice. Which was as ridiculous a thought as her suspicion that Jax was in her classroom. But, for somebody who wasn't Jax and couldn't possibly be Jax, he sure sounded like Jax.

"On the contrary, I'm not saying that love doesn't exist. A mother loves her child, certainly, and siblings can develop love for each other. I'd even venture to say that some couples eventually come to love one another. But that blush of attraction between males and females has nothing to do with love and everything to do with sex. There are numerous examples I can cite that back me up on this fact.

Darlene Gardner

"The male praying mantis, for example, has such a strong urge to mate that he risks cannibalization every time he does. At any time during copulation, the female may twist around and tear off his head. I assure you she's not doing this out of love."

"Oh, come on." This was one student, it seemed, who wouldn't be placated. "You're comparing humans to insects. You're talking about instincts and completely ruling out the power of emotions."

"Some humans let their perfectly good instincts be overruled by messy emotions better left out of the equation," Marietta said, getting into the debate despite herself. "Sex, which leads to the survival of our race, is what matters in the long run. Not this thing we call romantic love."

Her heckler laughed. He actually laughed.

"That reminds me of a joke," he said, and Marietta told herself not to panic. Just because her heckler was telling a joke didn't mean she was right. It didn't mean he was Jax. Especially if the joke was funny. Please, God, let his joke be funny.

"What's the best way to a scientist's heart?" He paused before answering. "By sawing open her breast plate."

Nobody laughed. There must have been two hundred people in the room, and nobody laughed. Not one of them.

Marietta, however, swooned.

The combination of her morning sickness and her growing suspicion of who was in her classroom was too much. She clasped the edge of the dais and willed herself not to faint. A woman ran up on stage, and when she got close enough Marietta saw it was Vicky Valenzuela.

"Pull yourself together, Dr. Dalrymple," she whispered urgently. "Pull yourself together right now. The future of feminism on campus is at stake."

"What are you talking about?"

"We must not show weakness in the face of male oppression. You have a right to be heard, and you must stand

70

fast against masculine opposition so you can be a leader in the feminist movement."

Marietta knew it was useless to try to tell her, once again, that she was a biologist, not a feminist. Vicky was right about one thing, though. The end of the hour was near, and she needed to pull herself together long enough to dismiss the class.

After all, just because nobody laughed at her heckler's jokes didn't mean he was Jax. The world was full of the humor-impaired. A mere glance at the sitcoms on television proved that much.

"Thank you for that humorless joke," she said into the microphone, pleased that her voice sounded strong. "I'm sure the class, however, will back me up when I ask that you refrain from entertaining us in the future."

Vicky returned to her seat. The rest of the FOCs, bless their loyal little feminist hearts, applauded.

"In closing, I'd like to leave you all with this thought. Remember, this is a conclusion I've reached from all my years of study. You are free to reach your own conclusions.

"Our mothers have always told us not to use four-letter words, especially in regard to sex. Count the letters while I spell the following word: L-O-V-E.

"Love: It's the ultimate four-letter word for sex."

Before the heckler could interject his unwanted opinion, Marietta gathered her papers and moved away from the dais. She was grateful that the FOCs in the first row had once again burst into applause, drowning out the other classroom noises.

She walked gingerly toward the short flight of stairs that led to the floor, but unfortunately three steps had blurred into one. She thought briefly of asking somebody to help her negotiate them, but rejected the idea.

Most of what Vicky Valenzuela said was off base, but she wasn't entirely wrong. Marietta couldn't afford to show weakness, not when she was entrusted to educate and command the respect of hundreds of students.

She stepped forward, missed the first step completely and pitched down the stairs straight into the arms of a mountain of a man who caught her as easily as if she were a rag doll.

His clean scent overwhelmed her, but it was intoxicating instead of nausea-inducing. Even before she looked up into his grim, handsome face, she knew who she would see.

Still, she couldn't stop her eyes from climbing upward and confirming the impossible: Her baby's sperm supplier was pressed up against the stomach that held the child.

"Hello, Rhea," he drawled, putting emphasis on the alias Marietta just now realized also had four letters. "Remember me?"

Chapter Seven

Marietta felt her already ghostly face go whiter and would have sunk to the floor in a horrified heap if he hadn't been holding her up.

The eyes she remembered looking at her with melting warmth were as cold as a chocolate popsicle. He was gazing at her as though he had something to be upset about. As though he were perfectly within his rights, with thousands of her dollars stuffing his pockets, to bulldoze his way into her world and disrupt her life.

Those thoughts gave her the courage to pull herself up to her full height, which was about the level of his chin, and glare right back at him.

"What are you doing here, Harold?" She deliberately used his formal name instead of the nickname she knew he preferred, making her voice as chilly as a blast from an open freezer. He still held her by the upper arms, and her frostiness contrasted vividly with the warmth that had gathered under his hands. Irritated at her epidermal sensitivity, she shrugged away from him.

"You have to ask that question?" He let out a short bark of what sounded like disbelief, and Marietta had a premonition of doom. His eyes were narrowed, his mouth unsmiling, his jaw hard. He didn't look like a man who took the money and ran. He didn't look like he intended to go anywhere. "And the name, as I told you before, isn't Harold. It's Jax."

"I don't care if you want to be called Ishtar. You and I have nothing to discuss."

"I wouldn't have hired a private investigator to find you if I didn't think we had plenty to discuss." He looked deliberately at her abdomen before raising his eyes to hers. "I believe you have something that belongs to me."

"Belongs to you?" She affected the bravado that had always carried her through the sticky situations in life, but she felt faint, which simply wouldn't do. She needed to heed the words of the FOC heading her fan club. *Stand fast against male oppression.* She couldn't let herself be bullied by a man who had signed a contract relinquishing the very thing he was trying to claim. "Nothing of mine belongs to you. You have absolutely no right to come here and harass me like this."

He laughed, but the sound held a bitter undertone. "You don't want to get into an argument with me about rights, Marietta," he said, emphasizing her name, "because you'll lose."

"Dr. Dalrymple? Is this man bothering you?" The voice of salvation came out of Vicky Valenzuela's mouth. The FOC president, with panache befitting her position, walked straight up to Jax. She came so close that Marietta's near-blind eyes could make out the girl's features as she leaned back her head and looked way, way up at Jax. Her lips parted, and her eyes widened. Her brain, unfortunately, seemed to go stone-dead.

"As a matter of fact, he *is* bothering me," Marietta answered, but Vicky wasn't listening. She wasn't doing anything but staring spellbound at Jax, who was dressed in another of those beautifully tailored suits that were no doubt made for him. This one was chocolate brown, like his eyes.

"Of course I'm not bothering her." Jax switched on the charm, smiling down at Vicky. "Marietta and I are old friends. In fact, you could strip her bare and there's not a man alive who knows more about her than I do."

"Really?" Vicky said breathlessly, telling Marietta she hadn't processed a word he said. Her lips formed a silent word that even Marietta could make out. It was "Wow."

"Oh, for heaven's sake. What kind of feminist are you?" Marietta exclaimed in disgust, even though she understood the effect Jax was having on the young woman. It was no more intense than the effect Jax had on Marietta. Vicky was not only reacting to his symmetrical features, but the evolutionary truth that conditioned women to seek out men emitting signs of power and strength. With his great height and incredible physique, Jax had an unfair advantage.

Still, she'd expected more of the head of the FOCs. Vicky must know that men had a strong biological urge to spread their genetic material around. Jax, and every other man Marietta had ever come across, merely had to look at an attractive young woman to want to make love to her. Which is why you couldn't trust any of them.

"Snap out of it, Vicky," Marietta said harshly. "Remember what you said in the restroom? That I was your role model. Well, you're ogling the man who was heckling your role model."

"Heckling," Vicky repeated, but she still wasn't operating on all cylinders. Whatever bolts kept her brain in place had seriously loosened.

"Heckling?" Jax looked taken aback. He transferred his attention from Vicky's starry eyes to Marietta's hardly seeing ones. "I wasn't heckling you. I was disagreeing with you, which I wouldn't have done in the first place if you hadn't said such ridiculous things."

Darlene Gardner

"Ridiculous things?" The insult cut into Marietta, taking precedence, for the moment, over her questions as to why he was here at Kennedy College making ridiculous insinuations about rights he should well know were legally non-existent. This was her profession he was insulting, her passion. She put a hand on her hip. "I suppose this means you think you're in love with someone?"

Confusion crossed his good-looking face, and Marietta knew in that instant that she had him. A corner of his mouth twitched, as though he didn't want to admit the inevitable.

"Well, no, actually I'm not in love." A smile of triumph lit Marietta's face at the admission, and he quickly added a qualifier. "But I could be." The ray of hope that crossed Vicky's face was so dazzling even Marietta couldn't miss it. "I mean, I will be. One day."

"I assume," Marietta continued in her most scholarly tone, "that means you've never been in love?"

Jax hesitated, as though sensing she was laying a trap for him but not sure which way to step. "If you're talking about romantic love," Jax said finally, "I'd have to say that's true."

"The sexual encounters you have had, then, weren't motivated by love. In fact, I maintain they had nothing to do with love."

"You're twisting—"

"So that proves my point," Marietta finished triumphantly. "Sex is what makes the world go round. Not love."

"Professor Dalrymple." Vicky, it seemed, had at long last found her voice. "Don't you think you're being too hard on him?"

"Too hard on him?" The idea was so laughable that Marietta actually laughed, right in Jax's handsome face. "Hah! How could I possibly be too hard on someone so mercenary he'd sell his soul if he could find a way to extract it from his body."

"Now, wait just a minute. You don't know anything about me." A red flush peeked through Jax's olive complexion, and Marietta was perversely glad. After what he'd done, he ought to be ashamed of himself. He certainly didn't have the right to take the moral high ground, and she wasn't going to let him.

"I know that you took thousands of dollars of my money for something priceless. That's all I need to know, buster."

"Oh, come on." The words were laced with disgust. "I'll say this in professor lingo, so you'll understand. You've reached a faulty conclusion. I don't want your money. I never did."

Reaching into his suit jacket, Jax withdrew two envelopes from an inner pocket. He tried to hand them to her, but she backed up, rendering him so blurry that she could no longer make out his expression.

"What's going on?" Vicky asked, but Marietta ignored her. As did Jax.

"Oh, no," she said. "I am not taking that money back. I am not going to let you renege on our deal."

"If you'd listen to me for one minute, you'd realize we don't have a deal."

Marietta shook her head so vigorously some of her hair loosened from her bun and swung into her face. She swiped it back. Great. She was having a bad-hair day in the midst of a crisis of staggering proportions.

"A deal's a deal, and I've got the documentation in my office to prove it." She turned on the low heel of her sensible shoe and walked away from him, squinting to give herself a better view of the surroundings. It didn't help. She misjudged the aisle and bumped into the edge of the first row of seats. Then she forgot about the descending single step that led to the door connecting the lecture hall to the outside hallway. She tripped, righting herself inelegantly on the door frame before she could fall.

"What's wrong with that woman?" Jax asked under his breath. The anger he was trying hard to hold back simmered just beneath the surface of his skin, making his blood bubble.

"She can't see," Vicky answered.

"You're right about that. I've never met anyone so stubborn about seeing another person's point of view."

"That's not what I meant. She can't see, literally. I stepped on her contact lens in the ladies' room, and she didn't have her glasses with her."

That was just great, Jax thought. The woman carrying his baby was navigating Kennedy College as though she were a bumper car come to life. Hell, yes, he had rights. And the most pressing one involved the right to assure that she didn't smash his baby before it was born. He took off in the direction Marietta had gone.

"Wait," Vicky called after him. He didn't stop moving, but glanced backward over his shoulder. "I find you very attractive."

"Uh, that's nice." Jax noticed her appearance for the first time. She was petite with classic features and dramatic coloring, the kind of woman who probably attracted a lot of male attention. He wasn't interested, but that didn't mean he had to hurt her feelings. "You're very attractive yourself."

"Wait," she called again. He was already at the door, but he paused once again when all he wanted to do was talk sense into Marietta. Darn his mother for drilling good manners into him. "Are you in favor of the equal-rights amendment?"

"Uh, yeah."

"Good. It's been a wonderful boon for us dating feminists who like to do the asking out. Dinner and dancing would be fine with me. So would sex. Sex would be very fine."

Jax's eyes widened. He felt as though he were lost in the Land of the Romantically Impaired. Wasn't there anybody at Kennedy College who believed that taking the time to develop a certain affection for each other, even if it didn't amount to love, should be a prerequisite for sex?

"Sorry," he said, although he wasn't sorry at all, "but I can't go out with you, or do any of the other things you mentioned. I'm involved with your professor."

"You're involved with Dr. Dalrymple?" The tiny feminist's brows rose. "Does *she* know this?"

"She will soon," Jax said under his breath and gave chase. She had thirty yards on him, and she was walking in the dead center of the hall. The better, he thought, not to crash into anything. Her hair was mussed, and she was wearing another one of those amorphous tent dresses, this one in dreary shades of black and gray. On top of it, she'd thrown on an unstructured black jacket. From behind, she looked like a walking sack.

Jax still thought she was the sexiest woman he'd ever seen.

"Hey, wait a minute," he yelled, running to catch up with her. The bottoms of his fine leather shoes echoed in the hallway, and she walked even faster. He'd almost caught her when she took an abrupt turn and rammed into the side of an office door.

"Oof."

"Careful," Jax said, noting that the name on the door was her own. Ignoring him, she threw open the door and bumped into the edge of a shining mahogany desk on the way to her file cabinet. Rubbing her leg with one hand, she rummaged through some file folders with the other. After a few moments, she drew out one and handed it to him.

"There," she said, sounding as though she'd just won a battle. "You can't argue with that."

Jax read the heading of the file folder in his hands: Coolidge Effect on male sexual behavior. Because he couldn't help himself, he flipped open the folder.

The first page contained an anecdote about President Calvin Coolidge and his wife being given separate tours of a government chicken farm. When Mrs. Coolidge witnessed

Darlene Gardner

a rooster copulating with a hen, she asked the attendant how often the rooster engaged in such behavior. "Dozens of times each day," the attendant answered. She requested that he please tell that to the president. The president, after hearing about the randy rooster, asked the attendant if the rooster always copulated with the same hen. "Oh, no," replied the attendant, "always a different one." The president reportedly quipped, "Please mention that fact to Mrs. Coolidge."

Jax laughed.

"I don't see what's so funny," Marietta said.

"Do you think President Coolidge actually said that or is it an apocryphal tale?"

"What?" Marietta came across the room, uneventfully this time, and snatched the folder from his hands. She took out the top paper and held it inches from her eyes. "I obviously gave you the wrong folder."

"You didn't answer my question. Do you think he said that?"

"Of course he said it." She moved back to the file cabinet. "The Coolidge Effect is an accepted scientific term."

"Meaning?"

"It means that males have a tendency to lose interest in their current sexual partners whereas they can be stimulated indefinitely by a variety of partners."

Jax could just make out the shape of her delectable rear as she bent over the cabinet. If they hadn't had more important matters to discuss, he would have disputed the Coolidge Effect. Having sex with her hadn't diminished his interest in the slightest. Despite what she'd done.

"There," she said, extracting another folder and handing it to him.

This one was entitled: Conception Connection: Contracts, Medical clearance forms, etc. He flipped through it with growing amazement, because it documented Marietta

Dalrymple's deliberate search for what she called a "sperm supplier."

The wording of an advertisement she'd evidently placed in a national publication had the emotional intensity of lint. "Well-adjusted, financially independent professional female will pay cash for sperm. Qualified sperm supplier must submit proof of superior intelligence, excellent health lineage and professional credentials. Intercourse required."

The ad was followed by a handful of completed application forms from what Jax figured were Marietta's sperm-supplier finalists. Judging by the red pen circling the remark, one man had apparently doomed himself by noting in the "fetishes and other foibles" section that he was an armpit smeller. Harold McGinty, Jax noted, had wisely left that section blank.

The last ten or so pages were comprehensive legal documents signed by Harold relinquishing his rights to any child he and Marietta might conceive. Considering she'd gone to the additional trouble of concealing her identity, Marietta obviously hadn't wanted to take any chances on paternal involvement.

"There's your proof," she said when he closed the folder. She crossed her arms over her chest. "You signed away any rights you might have had, especially when you accepted the payment. So you can just keep the money and forget you ever met me, Harold."

"I keep telling you my name isn't Harold. It's Jax."

"Listen, I don't have the patience to stand here and listen to your nickname preferences. You got your money, and I expect you to uphold your part of the deal."

"You're not listening to me. You have a deal with Harold McGinty. He's the one who signed the papers, not me."

"Are you trying to tell me you're one of those people with a split personality? That you were Harold McGinty then, but now you're somebody else." She tapped her forehead with a finger. "Don't tell me, because I can figure it out. Jax must be short for Jackson, so you're either the reincarnation of Andrew Jackson or you're—I've got it," she snapped her fingers, "Michael Jackson."

"My name's Cash Jackson," he said, unamused. Humor was necessary for a happy life, but nothing about this was funny. This covertly sexy biologist, who had accused him of disrupting her life, had completely altered his existence two months ago by luring him into her hotel-room bed. How was he supposed to know she had babies on her mind when he hadn't been able to think straight?

"I don't believe you," Marietta said, giving a superior little shake to her head.

He was too miffed to speak, so he reached into the back pocket of his trousers, pulled out a wallet, extracted his driver's license, and held it out.

"You can't prove what isn't true," Marietta said, staring at the small, square piece of plastic in his hands as though it were poisonous. She knew what it was, but she didn't want to look at it. The risk, it seemed, was too high.

"Look at it." Jax said, his voice firm.

"I don't need to—"

"Just look at it." She met his eyes, saw the challenge there and snatched it away from him in irritation. She'd been careful. She knew who she was dealing with, and it was a money-grubbing sperm supplier named Harold McGinty.

At first, the image on the driver's license was blurry, but it slowly came into focus as she brought it closer to her eyes. It was Jax, all right, in all his glorious symmetry. With growing dread, she swung her eyes to the name alongside his outrageously good-looking face. *Cash Jackson.*

She ran her finger over the print, checking for anything that felt phony, such as stick-on letters over his real name. She scratched, but nothing came off.

As the news sunk in that the man before her really was Cash Jackson and not Harold McGinty, her legs buckled. She braced herself against her desk.

The Misconception

"Oh, no. Oh, no. Oh, no," she repeated while she took shallow breaths. Jax was instantly at her side. He lifted her onto the desk as though she weighed little more than a paper weight and peered at her with concern.

"Lower your head between your legs and take deep breaths." She was about to protest, but then she thought of the baby. The baby needed air as badly as she did. She lowered her head and breathed. "That's right. In and out. In and out."

After a few miserable minutes, she raised her head. Jax was leaning over her, looking every bit as solicitous as an expectant father. Suddenly enraged, she put both hands on his boulderlike shoulders and shoved as hard as she could.

Caught by surprise, he staggered backward, but righted himself with the grace of an athlete. "Hey." His voice was injured. "What was that for?"

"For telling me you were Harold McGinty, that's what!"

"I didn't say I was him. I told you right off the bat to call me Jax."

"But you didn't tell me who you were. You didn't tell me you weren't Harold McGinty."

"That's because I didn't want to hurt your feelings. Harold is an old high school classmate of mine. When I ran into him at the airport, he was planning to stand you up. I told him I'd let you know he wasn't coming."

"So instead you decided to see if I could make you come, is that it?"

Jax rubbed his chin. Despite his dark looks, he didn't have a heavy growth of beard, and she remembered how good his skin felt. Smooth, warm, electrifying. Remembering made her angrier, because she should never have touched him in the first place.

"Of course that isn't it. I thought you and Harold were meeting for a blind date, for Christ's sake. How was I supposed to know you had some crazy conception scheme?"

"Crazy?" He was making her crazy. Her heart rate was up, her body temperature rising at an alarming rate. "It was a perfectly logical plan until you showed up and ruined it."

"Logical? Are you nuts? There's nothing logical about advertising for a candidate to father your child."

"That's not what I did. I advertised for a sperm supplier. That's an entirely different thing."

"Oh, excuse me. That makes it entirely logical."

"You don't need to be sarcastic."

"What do you expect? I think I'm going on a perfectly innocent blind date, and two months later I end up an expectant father."

"You are *not* an expectant father."

"I didn't sign those contracts, Marietta," he said ominously. He took the envelopes of cash and threw them on her desk. "And I never said I'd accept money from you. One of those envelopes is from Harold, returning the money you sent him for a, how did you put it, 'mission accomplished.' But the other contains the five hundred dollars you left for me at the front desk of the Hotel Grande.

"So, you see, sweetheart, we didn't have a deal. That means I have as much right to that baby growing in your belly as you do."

"No, you don't," Marietta exclaimed desperately. She had to do something, so she tried throwing him off track. "You can't even be sure that I'm pregnant!"

The second the statement left her lips, her stomach did a roll worthy of one of the logs that fancy-stepping contestants tried to keep afloat and revolving during those crazy he-man competitions.

"Marietta." Jax's voice seemed to come from far away. "Are you okay? You look really pale. I mean, ghostly pale."

Marietta didn't answer. She couldn't, because the contents of her stomach were rising. She hopped off the desk and dashed for the restroom, dimly aware that her actions confirmed that she was pregnant.

The Misconception

When she got to her knees in front of the toilet in stall number one, however, all she had was a case of the dry heaves. Someone lifted the fallen mass of hair off her hot neck, and she closed her eyes as a wave of shame washed over her. Jax had followed her.

"False alarm?" he asked softly.

"Only because there's nothing in my stomach besides salted crackers," Marietta said as he helped her to her feet. His touch was ridiculously comforting . . . and nice. But the calming effect of skin-to-skin contact was a noted biological response. New mothers soon discovered it was the best way to soothe cranky babies. Anybody could have elicited the same response in her. That it was Jax meant nothing, except that she had let him see her in a moment of weakness.

She needed to make it clear that this wasn't how Marietta Dalrymple dealt with adversity. She was strong, self-sufficient. She didn't need a man to get her through anything. She didn't need a man. Period.

She turned around and nearly came up against his chest. He seemed even taller and broader in the close confines of the toilet stall. She held herself still, not wanting to come into contact with all that potent male flesh, but she couldn't stop her eyes from rising so she could look at him. When she did, he smoothed her hair back from her hot forehead, his expression almost tender. His beautiful dark eyes ran over her face, as though assuring himself that she was all right. He no longer seemed angry.

"You shouldn't be in the ladies' room," she said, wondering why she was whispering.

"Who's going to throw me out?" The corners of his mouth curved upward. The overhead fluorescent lights shone on his face, making it even more appealing. "Listen, arguing about this isn't getting us anywhere. We both made mistakes, but the fact of the matter is that we have to deal with this situation. Agreed?"

Marietta didn't nod, not wanting to get caught in a trap. Just because she yearned to lean her body against his didn't mean she could trust him.

"The way I see it is this," he continued. "I care about what's best for the baby. I assume you do, too."

"Of course I do," she answered weakly. He stroked her cheek as he talked, and he was so close that she could barely think, remembering all the things they'd done to each other in that Washington D.C. hotel. As biological advantages went, his was definitely unfair.

"Good. It's settled then."

She was watching his mouth, which could be the most appealing part of him. She remembered his lips were softer than any man's had a right to be. "What's settled?"

He gave a short, decisive nod. "We're getting married."

Chapter Eight

"Married?" The notion was so shocking that Marietta fairly shouted the word. After an hour lecturing her biology students about the intricacies of mating behavior, she'd been caught off guard because she'd nearly succumbed to lust. "Did you just ask me to marry you?"

"Marietta?" A third voice rang out in a restroom Marietta already thought too crowded. Worse, she recognized the voice. "Mari, it's Tracy. Is that you in the stall? Are you talking to yourself?"

"Who's Tracy?" Jax whispered.

"My sister," she hissed back, mortified. Tracy had been against her conception scheme from the beginning. What would she say if she found Marietta cavorting in a restroom stall with the sperm supplier who had not only hunted her down, but was trying to stake a claim on her baby?

"Marietta? That is you in there, isn't it? Robert Cormicle called and asked me to bring your glasses."

Jax opened his mouth, so Marietta clamped a hand over it. "It is me, Tracy," she answered, warning him with her eyes to keep quiet.

The stall doors were high, but not high enough that part of Jax's head didn't peek over the top. Marietta prayed that Tracy wouldn't look up.

"Were you just talking to yourself about marriage?" Tracy asked, her voice even closer to the stall.

Marietta closed her eyes. It was useless to deny it, so she had to come up with an explanation. "I'm practicing for a lecture."

"You're giving a lecture about marriage?" Tracy sounded dubious.

"Yes, I am." Marietta looked straight at Jax while she elaborated on her answer. "I'm going to air my opinions on the instability of the institution and the extreme likelihood of any union ending in divorce."

"You've got to be kidding," Jax exclaimed so loudly that his voice carried through her hand. She removed the useless barrier and glared at him.

"There's a man in there with you!" Tracy said. "What is a man doing in there with you?"

"Now you've gone and done it," Marietta whispered angrily. Jax shrugged and opened the stall door. Tracy gaped at him with the awed expression Marietta imagined every female wore when she got her first look at Jax.

"It's a pleasure to meet you." He gallantly held out his hand as though he were greeting her sister at a cocktail reception instead of inside a ladies' room. Tracy, of course, took it. "I'm Cash Jackson, but you can call me Jax. I take it you're going to be my new sister-in-law."

"Omigod." Tracy broke the shake and gestured wildly with her hands. "Were you proposing to her in there? In the toilet stall?"

"He wasn't proposing—" Marietta began, but Tracy kept right on talking.

"I can't say that's the most romantic proposal I've ever heard of, but I can go with it if you can." She stepped forward and embraced Jax as she talked. "This is wild. I never

88

thought this would happen for Marietta." She let Jax go and moved to Marietta, flinging her arms around her and hugging tight. "Oh, Mari. I'm so happy for you. I'm so glad you didn't mean it when you said you were never getting married."

Tracy was squeezing so hard that Marietta couldn't speak until she let go. The grin on her sister's face was rivaled only by the one on Jax's. Marietta wasn't smiling.

"I am not getting married, Tracy," she said firmly. "He didn't mean it anyway."

"I did so mean it," Jax refuted.

Marietta turned on him, fuming. Now that he was no longer so close to her, imposing his biologically unfair advantage, she could think more clearly. Especially since she was far enough away that he looked like a very large blur. "You did not! You just want to get your hands on my baby."

"It's my baby, too."

Tracy gasped. "*You're* the sperm whore."

"Sperm supplier," Marietta corrected.

"I'm neither of those things." Jax turned to Tracy, and Marietta could imagine the plea for understanding he was putting into his expressive eyes. "It was all a colossal mix-up, Tracy. I never contracted with your sister to supply sperm. That was somebody else."

"But you did have sex with her?"

"The last I checked, that's how babies were made," he said with a smile in his voice.

"I told you, Marietta." Tracy, always one to say I told you so, did just that. "I told you not to do this."

Marietta took the glasses Tracy was still holding and perched them on her nose. She could immediately see better, but nothing was clear. Least of all what she was going to do about the six feet plus of delicious man in the ladies' restroom, especially since her improved vision crystallized his biological perfection.

"I can't take this anymore," she muttered.

Darlene Gardner

"Then I'll drive you home," Jax offered. "Just tell me the way."

"Didn't your private investigator do that already?"

"You hired a private investigator?" Tracy interjected, looking at Jax. If she were like Vicky, the traitorous feminist, she wouldn't be able to stop looking at him.

"What can I say? Your sister didn't leave a number where she could be reached, and I'm a resourceful man." He returned his attention to Marietta. "My PI did give me an address, but not directions on how to get to it."

"I'll tell you," Tracy offered.

"Don't you dare." Marietta shook her finger. "Not that it matters anyway. I wouldn't go anywhere with him even if I didn't have classes for the rest of the afternoon."

"You can't teach class. You're not feeling well," Jax protested.

"I'm pregnant. Not sick. There's a difference."

He looked thoughtful. "Okay. I'll accept that. It's probably better for the baby if you're active during the pregnancy anyway. How about this? I'll meet you when you get off work, and we can hash out the details of the wedding then."

"Weren't you listening? There's not going to be a wedding."

"There's not?" Tracy, blast her, sounded disappointed. "I think you should consider it, Mari. Jax is the father or your child, after all. It says something about a man's character when he's willing to own up to his responsibilities. I kind of like him."

"Thank you," Jax said.

"You're welcome." Tracy smiled at him.

Marietta pinned her with a stare. Was her sister, too, becoming a victim of impeccable symmetry? "Whose side are you on, Tracy?"

"This isn't a war, Marietta," Jax said. "We're discussing the future of our child."

The Misconception

"I'm not discussing anything with you," Marietta said, knowing she was being unreasonable. The ability to think logically and analytically was what separated man from animal, but right now she preferred to act like a rabbit and make a run for it. Everyone expected pregnant women to act irrationally anyway. She pushed through the door, intent on escape.

Jax started after her, but Tracy laid a hand on his arm and took a step sideways until she blocked his path. His muscles were tense and his jaw clenched, as though nothing were more important than chasing down the mother of his unborn child and making her see reason. Tracy nearly sighed at the romanticism of it all.

Unfortunately for Jax, he didn't know Marietta very well. Her sister was so opinionated that what she considered to be perfectly reasonable was often what others thought was just plain wacko.

"I think it would be best," she said as gently as she could, "if you gave her some time to cool off."

"But she's pregnant, and she's upset. I don't want her to be upset."

Tracy reached up and patted his cheek. He seemed genuinely concerned about Marietta, and that made her like him even more. From the look of him and the tension that had sizzled between them, she'd bet he'd changed Marietta's low opinion of sex, too. "I'll go after her. It's a pretty safe bet that having you chase her isn't going to calm her down."

He ran a hand through his thick brown hair, obviously considering her advice. He was outrageously good looking, this man of Marietta's, with his high cheekbones, broad shoulders, and doe-brown eyes. He was well-coifed, too. Tracy knew clothes, and the suit, she'd venture, was Armani. The shoes were made of expensive leather, Italian, she'd bet. But his looks weren't all he had going for him. Tracy saw intelligence in his eyes, goodness in his soul.

"Okay," he said finally. "You're right. I don't want to upset her any more than she already is. I'll give her time to cool off and then talk to her."

"She usually gets home around six. You might pick up a couple of points if you brought dinner. Her townhouse is in Old Town Alexandria just a few blocks from the Potomac. If you have a street address, it shouldn't be hard to find."

"I'll find it. You can count on that."

She smiled at him then, because she didn't doubt it was true. Jax had the air of a man who could be counted on. Giving a little wave, Tracy exited the restroom and immediately spotted Marietta disappearing around a corner at the end of the hallway. Only one classroom was in that direction, so Tracy didn't hurry.

As she walked, she thought about her sister's predicament. Sure, it must have been a shock to discover that your sperm supplier wanted to be a family man, but Marietta would be a fool to refuse a man that fine. Why, he was nearly as appealing as Ryan.

Tracy frowned, as she reluctantly admitted that wasn't quite true. Even an unquestionable hunk like Jax couldn't compete with Ryan. Since leaving her soon-to-be-ex-husband nine months ago, Tracy had compared every man she met to him, hoping one would measure up.

Not one of them had.

It was starting to seem as though nobody on God's green earth was as appealing as Ryan Caminetti.

Tracy put her feet down harder as she walked, trying to stamp out thoughts of Ryan. It didn't do any good. Since this morning, when she'd called the salon to check on her appointments, she'd been thinking of him even more than usual. Every slot but one was filled by regulars. The exception had been claimed by a man named Ryan who wanted a cut and blow dry.

The Misconception

It could have been a coincidence. Lots of men went by the name Ryan, after all, but her assistant said the man requested her by name. Tracy pressed, and the girl remembered his voice was deep and sexy.

Ryan Caminetti's voice was deep and sexy, though not as sexy as the rest of him. His hair was silky and black, his body lean and muscular, his eyes so dark she felt like she was falling into them whenever they made love.

Marietta had pointed out that everything about him made Tracy go as weak in the brain as she did in the knees. Which was why Tracy had immediately packed up and left him when she discovered how he'd wronged her.

He'd wanted to explain, but she wouldn't let him. She'd hung up on him when he called, slammed the door in his face when he'd showed up at Marietta's looking for her and insisted they communicate only through divorce lawyers.

Eventually, he'd given up trying. He hadn't attempted to get in touch with her for a good eight months. Until yesterday. When she'd seen that name scribbled in her appointment book.

She reached the door to Marietta's classroom and peeked inside. Her sister was sitting behind the desk, her head in her hands. The irony of the situation struck her. Tracy would have come to Kennedy College seeking out Marietta's opinion even if she hadn't been asked to deliver the glasses. But now it was Marietta who was more in need of counsel.

Since all the desks were empty, it was obviously too early for class to begin. Tracy dragged a chair across the room and sat down catty-corner from her sister.

"Want to talk about it?"

Marietta raised her head and shook it. "I don't even want to think about it." She pasted on a smile Tracy knew was fake. "I'd much rather talk about you."

"Me? But, Mari, it's not every day the father of your unborn child proposes in a toilet stall. Don't you think that's a more interesting topic than little old me?"

"You haven't even given me an update lately on your anthropology classes," Marietta said, ignoring her question. "Has Professor Bingham given his lecture on biological-physical anthropology yet? He has the most fascinating theories about Java Man."

"Java Man?"

"Aren't you paying attention in class, Tracy? Java Man is an early form of human whose fossils were found in the 1980s. Anthropologists believe he lived between 800,000 and 2 million years ago. What's fascinating is—"

"Actually," Tracy interrupted, "I've been doing a lot more thinking about a real, live man instead of a fossilized one."

Marietta's regard sharpened. "Did you meet somebody new? You didn't tell me you met somebody new."

"I didn't meet anybody new."

"Is it somebody you already know? Take a piece of advice from me, Tracy, you better go into it with your eyes wide open this time. As long as you keep in mind that you can't trust anybody with a Y chromosome, you'll be in a position of strength. You can't be naive the way you were with Ryan. Now who is this man?"

"Actually," Tracy said, taking a breath. "I was talking about Ryan."

"Ryan?" Her sister said the name as though it were a dirty word. "I thought you were all through with Ryan. Your divorce will be final in another three months."

"Actually," Tracy said, clearing her throat. "It's another seventy-one days."

"So? What's the problem?" Marietta's face fell. "Oh, no. Don't tell me he's tried to contact you."

"Well, actually, no, but . . ."

"Because if he does, you just tell him you aren't going to talk to him. Do you hear me, Tracy? This is serious. You got everything you wanted in the divorce settlement, and you can't put that in jeopardy. You absolutely cannot talk to him."

The Misconception

"But what if he wants to explain what he was doing in a hotel with that woman?" Even referring to the incident that had wrecked her marriage sent a shard of pain through Tracy. "I was so angry at him, Mari, that I never let him explain."

"There's nothing to explain. I was there that day, remember? You should thank Providence I invited you to lunch or you never would have seen him with that blonde at the elevator. They were all over each other."

"But maybe . . ." Tracy's voice got small, because she knew how ridiculous this was going to sound, even though more and more she wanted to believe it. ". . . maybe it was her who was all over him."

"And that's your explanation as to why Ryan registered for a room? Remember, Tracy, I got the desk clerk to show us the registration records. Ryan's name was listed, even though you two only lived a few miles from that hotel."

"I know, but—"

"There are no buts in this. I know it hurts, but you have to face facts. Ryan Caminetti is just as predisposed to mate switching as every other man on this planet. Sure, you could have stayed in the marriage, knowing he'd keep on cheating, but then you'd be just as miserable as our father made our mother."

Their parents. Even though Dad had died four years ago and Mother a short time afterward, Marietta regularly resurrected them in conversations about the interplay between the sexes. She seemed to regard their father as a template for members of the male sex. "Just because Dad cheated," Tracy said, uttering an oft-repeated refrain, "doesn't mean every man cheats."

"Ryan cheated. And remember the way I found Bobby Lancer with Betty Jo Kowalski?"

"Bobby Lancer? But that was in high school."

"Let's skip ahead to college then. Jeff Granger cheated on me, too. Hours after he told me he loved me. To think how stupid I was back then."

"You know, Marietta," Tracy said softly, "none of that means this new man in your life would do the same thing."

"Not only isn't he the new man in my life, but you're completely wrong. Men are predestined to stray. It's a biological fact. If I gave Jax the chance, he would do exactly the same thing as all the others. But we're not talking about me. We're talking about you and Ryan. Stay away from him, Tracy."

Tracy nodded. She doubted she'd get a chance to heed the warning anyway. She'd overreacted when her assistant told her a man named Ryan with a very sexy voice had specifically made an appointment to have her cut his hair.

This Ryan was probably seventeen with pimples or seventy with sagging skin.

He probably wasn't anything like the man she had once loved with every particle of her heart.

Chapter Nine

Ryan Caminetti stopped at the door of The Cutting Edge and looked through the glass window. A half-dozen beauticians cut, combed, and styled the hair of the clients sitting in front of them. But only one of them interested Ryan.

Tracy Dalrymple Caminetti. His wife.

He still thought of her that way even though she'd been his wife in name only for almost as long as they'd had a real marriage. Fourteen months. He'd had just fourteen months with her before she walked out. For all he knew, she didn't even use his surname any more.

She was wearing one of those cute little getups she always dressed in for work. A lime-green T-shirt hugged the breasts that could drive him wild and bared a sliver of the satiny-smooth skin at her midriff. Royal-blue bicycle shorts hugged the long, lean legs that used to wrap around him when they made love. Lime-green high-tops completed the picture. He used to tease her about having a Hairstyle of the Month, and this month's flavor was long, tight curls that made her look like a sexy Shirley Temple doll.

She laughed at something somebody in the shop said, throwing her head back so her curls bounced. He couldn't hear her through the door, but knew her laugh sounded like the tinkling of the crystals on a wind chime. He used to try to think up funny things to say just so he could hear that laugh.

God, he loved her. He always had, and he'd recently accepted that he always would. Nine months of separation hadn't dimmed that feeling. All it had done was make him want her more.

He had to stop himself from throwing open the door, striding across the shop, and hauling her into his arms so he could kiss her senseless until she no longer cared whether or not she trusted him.

But he couldn't do that. If he did, his victory would be built on rocky ground that wouldn't allow anything, least of all trust, to take root. If the past nine months had taught him anything, it was that a marriage without trust could never survive.

It wasn't her forgiveness he wanted. Until she trusted him again, trusted him completely, he couldn't ask her to give their marriage another go. He couldn't kiss her. He probably shouldn't even touch her.

He could, however, make damn sure he didn't give her up without a fight. Even if it were a sneak attack, sort of like the soldier who infiltrated the enemy camp in the dead of night. Only Tracy wasn't the enemy: Her lack of faith in him was.

He forcefully wiped out the desire he knew was on his face. If he let Tracy see the desire, he'd lose the battle before it was fought. Taking a deep breath, he pushed open the door.

Incessant chatter, the whir of hair dryers, and the smell of chemicals assaulted him, freezing his feet in place just inside the salon. Mirrors lined the establishment, making it seem as though there were twice as many rows of chairs as there actually were. Making it seem as though there were two delectable Tracys instead of one.

The Misconception

Her expression was animated as she talked to the teenage boy in the chair, her quick fingers teasing a line of dyed-purple hair skyward into a mohawk. If it hadn't been spring, Ryan would have figured the boy for a color-blind Geronimo headed for a Halloween party.

He saw a flash of something shiny on her left hand as she worked and realized, with a jolt of pleasure, that it was her wedding ring. If she hadn't taken off the ring he'd put on her finger, he refused to believe that all hope was lost.

Something, a sixth sense perhaps, made Tracy pause. Then both her faces, the one belonging to the living, breathing woman and that of her mirrored image, turned toward him. Ryan focused on just one of them. The real thing, he thought as his heart stampeded in his chest.

Her green eyes went saucer-wide. Her sensuous little mouth hung open, revealing the adorable little gap between her front teeth. The comb dropped from her fingers, wedging in the teenager's mohawk.

"Ryan." She croaked out his name, telling him she hadn't been expecting him. His spirits fell. He'd made an appointment in the hopes that she'd see his name and start thinking about him, start remembering how very much she'd once loved him.

"Hi, Trace." He greeted her as though it were a few hours instead of endless months since he'd last seen her. Smiling wasn't a problem, because it was so damn good to be in the same room with her again.

She leaned down and said something to the boy in the chair, who was trying to extract the comb from his mohawk, and made her way over to where he was standing. She was tall for a woman, just a few inches shorter than he was, another thing he'd always liked about her. She stopped well shy of him, being careful, he supposed with a hurtful pang, not to touch him.

"What are you doing here, Ryan? You and I have nothing to talk about." She was trying to sound stern, but she was

99

Darlene Gardner

nervously biting her lip while her voice shook, giving Ryan more hope.

"I didn't come here to talk." If he told her why he was really here, she'd give him no more chance to explain than she'd given him when she'd seen him at the hotel with that woman. "I came here to get my hair cut."

"There are a lot of hairdressers in Northern Virginia."

"And only one of them cuts my hair the way I like it." Ryan forced himself to sound nonchalant. "I haven't had a decent haircut since you left me."

"Since you drove me away, you mean."

It took willpower not to respond to that, but Ryan managed it. Just barely. "Come on, Trace. I need a haircut. You're a hairdresser. I even made an appointment. Surely you're not afraid to cut my hair."

She rose to the bait, just as he knew she would. His Tracy was nothing if not courageous. "Of course I'm not afraid."

"Then I'll take a seat and wait until you're done with the purple Geronimo." He flashed a smile and sat down before she could reply, picking up a magazine and pretending to leaf through it.

Tracy glanced back at him when she returned to her station, noting that this Ryan was even more gorgeous than the one in her daydreams. He was wearing a long-sleeved denim shirt that made him look virile and, combined with the five o'clock shadow on his jaw, a little dangerous. She dragged her eyes from him, then immediately let them drift back again. Because it just registered that he was holding a copy of *Cosmopolitan.* Cosmo? For a man who worked as a housing contractor and subscribed to *Field and Stream*?

"Who does he think he's fooling?" she muttered in a low voice. She picked up a comb from her work area and vigorously dragged it through the boy's grape mohawk.

"Ow!" he yelped. His pain-filled eyes met hers in the mirror. "You really think I look foolish?"

The Misconception

"Sorry." Tracy gave him an apologetic pat on the side of his shaved head. It was time to improvise. She couldn't tell him what she really thought, which was that he looked like a little boy playing a really weird game of dressup. "I didn't say you looked foolish. I said that purple hair won't be fooling anyone."

"No joke. Anybody who thinks purple hair grows out of my scalp would be pretty lame, huh?"

"Yeah," Tracy said, because it was expected. She spent an inordinate amount of time putting the finishing touches on the mohawk, more to avoid dealing with Ryan than because she thought she could make the grape concoction look any better.

She simply didn't believe that he'd turned up mere months before their divorce was to become final just to get his hair cut. The more logical assumption would be that he was here because he wanted her back. Maybe that was it. Maybe he was going to beg for her forgiveness and ask if she'd forget about the divorce and move back home with him.

Maybe he was going to turn on the lights and banish the nightmare the past nine months had been.

By the time she'd finished with her customer and asked Luanne, the shampoo girl, to wash Ryan's hair, Tracy's hands were trembling. She'd been so angry and hurt when she saw him cheating on her that she hadn't thought she could ever forgive him.

But now, after so many months of missing him, of craving him, she wasn't sure what she would do if he wanted her back. She knew the precise moment Luanne finished washing his hair, but she didn't trust herself to watch him walk across the room toward her. She knew, even without looking, he'd be the first customer she thought looked sexy in wet hair and a maroon cape. Then he sat down, and she couldn't avoid looking at him any longer.

"What do you want done today?" She tried the breezy tone she used with all her customers, but her voice cracked, ruining the effect.

His dark, dark eyes met hers in the mirror, and she remembered the first time she'd seen him. She'd been sitting alone at a table in a sundae shop, reveling in the taste of chocolate fudge, when she spotted him staring at her from across the room. He hadn't released her gaze, just picked up his own sundae, walked deliberately to her booth and sat down across from her.

"You know what I want," he said now, and her breath hitched. She was right. He wanted her back. Because it had been easier that way, she'd tried to convince herself that the long months of silence meant he no longer loved her. But he'd simply been giving her time to forgive him. Could she? Would she? "You've cut my hair enough times."

"What?"

"Don't tell me you forgot. Short on the sides, longer in the back. I'm not like you, Trace. I don't change hairstyles month to month." He paused, pinned her with those eyes. "Is something wrong?"

"Wrong? No, of course not. Nothing's wrong. What could be wrong?" Mortification spread through Tracy as she picked up a pair of scissors. He wanted a haircut. Just a haircut. He didn't want her, after all. She forced herself to be professional, but touching the wet warmth of his scalp was sweet torture. His hair was so silky that running her fingers through it had been another one of the sensual pleasures of living with him. She snipped, because it was expected of her, but wasn't sure whether she'd made the cut in the right place.

"So, how've you been?"

How had she been? Desperately trying to convince herself she wasn't miserable without him. "Great," she said brightly, snipping again and again. "Just great. And yourself?"

"A little lonely, but getting by."

"Lonely? You?" Snip, snip. "I find that hard to believe."

"You always did have trouble believing in me." Before she could argue, pointing out it was difficult to believe in your husband when he was making out with a stacked blonde who looked like a Barbie doll, he continued. "But you made it clear you don't want to talk about that. So let's talk about you instead. There must be something new in your life in the past eight months."

"Nine." She lifted a hank of his hair and snipped it off. "It's been nine months."

He smiled, and his eyes crinkled at the corners in that way that never failed to charm her. "Okay. Anything new in the past *nine* months?"

Was he asking if she had a new boyfriend? Is that what he wanted to know? "Like what?"

"Like your acting. Are you doing any community theater?"

Theater. He wanted to know about her theater. She could answer that. "There's a new company in Arlington called the Put Up With Us Players. We're doing an experimental play that opens in a couple of months."

He nodded, as though filing away the information. "You'll have to let me know when. I might want to check it out."

"You might not want to," she said, panicked at the thought of him in the audience watching her, the way he was watching her in the mirror. "It might be a little weird."

"I can handle weird." A corner of his mouth lifted. "Anything else new?"

"I'm taking some college courses at Kennedy toward a degree in anthropology," she said, trying to keep the conversation on safe topics.

"You are? Why?"

"Why? Do you think I want to be a hairdresser all my life?" she asked, repeating the question Marietta often asked her.

"Yes," he said, nodding. She cut off a piece too close to his scalp. "Don't move your head," she warned.

"Yes," he repeated. "You love being a hairdresser. There's nothing wrong with being a hairdresser."

"There's nothing wrong with having goals in life, either." That was another thing Marietta often told her.

"Then open your own shop. Forgive me for being blunt, Trace, but this anthropology thing sounds more like Marietta than you. You shouldn't let her talk you into something you don't want to do."

"I don't let her talk me into things," she snapped, snipping.

"Yeah, you do. I know you love her, but she has a weird way of looking at the world. You should take that into account when she's giving you advice. Especially when she's giving you advice about relationships."

"What's that supposed to mean?"

"It means men aren't animals. Just because monkeys are indiscriminate about who they mate with doesn't mean men are. If your sister would give some man a chance, she might find that out."

Even though his observations about Marietta had a grain of truth, Tracy sprang to her sister's defense. "You're wrong about Mari. For your information, she's pregnant."

His jaw dropped. "By a man?"

"Of course, by a man." She paused. Marietta wouldn't want her to repeat this, but she had a point to make. "He's asked her to marry him."

"Wow! You're kidding? Who would have called it? I'm surprised she even gave the guy a chance. Let me guess. He's a professor, right? Somebody with ideas as wacky as hers."

Tracy shook her head. "He's definitely not a professor."

"So what's he do for a living? Is he a chemist? A mathematician? What?"

The Misconception

Tracy frowned, because she hadn't thought to ask, but Jax had been beautifully dressed in clothes only a prosperous man could afford. "I'm not sure, but I think he's some kind of businessman. Whatever he does, I'm sure it's respectable."

"It better be," Ryan said, smiling at her and making her heart swoon, "or Marietta isn't going to give him the time of day."

He didn't say anything for a while, and Tracy tried to concentrate on his haircut. Instead, she reveled in the sensations of touching him again. Even in the midst of winter, she'd always gotten a warm sensation when she stood next to him, and she had it now. But, when she brushed the satin skin at his nape with the backs of her fingers, she was the one who shivered.

"You still like R.E.M., don't you?"

She nodded, wondering what he was getting at. He kept watching her in the mirror, which made Tracy nervous but which was preferable to Ryan watching himself. Without a doubt, she was giving him the worst haircut of all time. "They're playing at RFK next weekend."

"I know." Disappointment shot through Tracy, and she realized it was because he was making small talk. Now that she was ready to hear him apologize for being with that woman, he didn't seem inclined to discuss the incident. "I tried to get tickets, but they've been sold out for months."

"I mentioned it, because I have an extra ticket. I thought you might want it."

She was dragging a comb through his hair, intending to trim his ends. Instead, her scissors closed near his scalp. "Are you asking me out?"

He laughed. "Of course not. You've made it clear you want this divorce, so I'm not going to stand in your way. I just don't see any reason we still can't be friends. Remember, Tracy, we were always friends, too."

105

"I remember," she said softly as her mind dwelled on what he hadn't said. They'd been lovers, too. Insatiable lovers.

"Remember Steve and Sue? They're going. So are George, Jenny, and Anna. I bought the last ticket for another friend, but she can't go. It's yours if you want it. No strings attached. You don't even have to sit beside me."

No, she thought darkly. Anna, who'd always had her eye on him, would probably do that. She should refuse. If she didn't, she wouldn't hear the end of it from Marietta. Then again, she didn't have to tell Marietta. And what would it hurt to be at the same concert with him, especially when it featured music from her favorite band?

Plenty, she thought.

He reached into his back pocket, withdrew a wallet, extracted a ticket, and held it up. "You don't even have to drive there with me, if that's what you're worried about. Just meet us."

She hesitated a moment, gazing at the ticket of temptation. Too weak to resist, she took it from his fingers and laid it on her counter.

"I'll think about it," she said, but she'd already made her decision. She was going.

Chapter Ten

Old Town Alexandria was just five miles from the urban bustle of Washington D.C., but it had the feel of a quaint eighteenth-century village plunked down in the middle of suburbia.

Gas-powered streetlights illuminated the main streets of town, which were lined with antique stores, specialty shops, and restaurants. Bradford pears, resplendent in their shiny white blooms, sprang from tree boxes cut into the herringbone sidewalks.

As Jax turned away from the commercial area and navigated a cobblestone street that was easy on the eyes but hell on his rental car's shock absorbers, he almost expected George Washington to step out of one of the well-preserved residences.

Jax figured the nation's first president had popped into his mind for a reason. Good, old George wouldn't have let a simple "no" stop him from getting what he wanted. If Martha had refused to marry him, he probably would have called in the Continental Army to persuade her to change her mind.

Jax would take his inspiration from George. He was going to stick by the vow he'd made even before he'd gotten over the shock of Harold McGinty's telephone call informing him that the steamiest sex of his life had produced a baby. Marietta *would* marry him before he became a father.

A father! He could barely believe it was going to happen. Not that he didn't want a baby. Hell, he'd always wanted that.

It just hadn't been on his agenda this soon. He'd kept his eyes and his heart open, waiting for that bowl-you-over kind of love that would deliver him a mother for his unborn children, but so far he was still standing.

In all the years he'd been ogling women, only once had the sight of one nearly toppled him. That had been when he'd spotted Marietta, with her snowy complexion and frightfully bad fashion sense, in the airport holding aloft her sign.

He'd wanted to make love to her on the spot, but he certainly wasn't *in love* with her.

What man could love a woman who schemed to gain access to grade-A sperm but didn't have enough sense to realize her baby deserved access to both a mother and father?

Jax had that truth drilled into him every time he saw a father playing catch with his son or lifting his daughter onto a swing. His child wasn't going to look into a mirror, as Jax had, and wonder if he resembled a father he'd never seen. Jax was going to be there from his child's first step and beyond, from infancy to adulthood.

Marietta would just have to get used to that. She'd invited him into her bed, and now they both were going to have to lie in it. Which, come to think of their combustible sexual attraction, might be a perk to the whole impossible situation.

Armed with the street address the private investigator had provided, Jax found her townhouse with little trouble.

The Misconception

Located down a narrow side street within walking distance of the heart of town, it oozed charm. The snowy blooms of dogwood trees fluttered in the breeze, adding to the picturesque quality of the string of single-row houses that graced the block.

Designed in the colonial style with brick facades and elegantly designed wrought-iron railings, the two-story townhouses were no wider than a single room. Marietta's boasted a sextet of street-view windows lined by dark-green shutters and a triangular pediment positioned above a door of the same color. Yew bushes and ivy provided a rich green blanket for the azaleas that splashed the front of the residence with color.

A FOR SALE sign on the townhouse next to Marietta's drew his attention. Jax thought of his antiseptic apartment in downtown Chicago, which had as its main feature a dearth of charm, and let himself covet the place for a moment. Then he took the brick stairs two at a time, lifted the brass door knocker and let it fall. It was nearly half-past six and the porch light was on, so it was a safe bet that Marietta was home.

Whether or not she'd let him in was another matter. But he hadn't come this far to be turned away. He jammed his thumb over the peephole and waited for the door to open. When it did, it was only a crack.

"Who is it?" Marietta asked in her unmistakable highbrow way.

He stuck the bag of food in her face, obstructing her view of him. "Delivery."

"But I didn't order anything." The door opened wider, and he got a good look at her. She'd changed from the unattractive sack cloth she'd worn to work to equally unattractive comfort clothes. She'd topped a pair of baggy sweat pants with a Kennedy College Biology sweatshirt, and her hair was pulled back in a sloppy ponytail from a face scrubbed clean of makeup. Her glasses were brown and oversized, the kind that had gone out of fashion years ago.

She looked ravishing, even with the sour expression that surfaced on her face.

"Oh," she said, a frown on her luscious mouth, "it's you."

"I brought dinner." He held up the bag of food. "If you invite me in, I'll share. Then we can talk."

"I've already told you we have nothing to talk about," she said, then sniffed. Her nose wrinkled, and her lips curled. "What do you have in that bag? Isn't dinner supposed to smell good? Is that . . ." She sniffed again. ". . . soy sauce?"

Actually, it was bean curds, soy pasta, and wheat germ. It had taken all his willpower to bypass the amazing array of restaurants the city offered in favor of a health-food store whose owner had insisted that pregnant women needed to eat protein-rich foods, but Jax had done it.

He'd even ordered double portions, figuring it was only fair if he choked down some of the food with her.

"Dinner's a surprise." He refrained from adding it wasn't a particularly good surprise. "You only get to look in the bag after you let me in."

"Go away."

She tried to shut the door in his face, but he put out a hand and forcibly kept it open. "Not until we talk."

"We have nothing to talk about."

"C'mon, Marietta. How are we going to make our marriage work if we don't talk to each other? Haven't you ever heard how important communication is in a marriage?"

Her jaw hardened, and her eyes narrowed. "I am not going to marry you."

Oh, yes, Jax thought, you are. Saying so aloud, however, didn't seem like a good idea at the moment. Not with her peering at him through her ugly glasses and compelling, multicolored eyes as though she wanted to rake her nails down his face.

"If you didn't want to marry me," he said, "you shouldn't have lured me into your bed and gotten pregnant."

The Misconception

"Lured you into my bed?" She swung the door all the way open and put her hands on her hips. Color crept up her neck and onto her cheeks. "I did not lure you into my bed. And even if I did, I don't remember you protesting. Besides, I had a perfectly legitimate reason for doing what I did. What's yours?"

"Lust."

His eyes never left hers as he uttered the admission, and the word did a sultry dance over Marietta's skin, raising the tiny hairs on her arms and legs. Biology, which by all rights should have been her ally, kept acting against her. Apparently, it had also acted against him. She waved a hand in the air.

"Fortunately, that shouldn't be a problem much longer."

"What shouldn't be a problem much longer?"

"Your lust. It's going to fade. That is, if you still feel it."

"Oh, I still feel it." His throaty admission triggered reciprocal lust in Marietta, which flowed through her like a warm river. Damn the man for being such a specimen of evolutionary perfection. He smiled a lady-killer smile and leaned one broad shoulder against the side of the door, his eyes full of skepticism. "Mind telling me what's going to make it fade?"

"Pregnancy." She cleared her throat. "It's thickening my waist. Studies have shown men are most attracted to females with waists two-thirds the size of their hips. Soon, my numbers will be way out of whack."

His eyebrows rose, and his smile got deeper. "You're serious, aren't you?"

"Of course I'm serious. Biology is a science, and you can't argue scientific fact."

"I hate to burst your bubble, honey, but I must be the exception to the rule." His eyes deliberately ran down her body, making the river of lust flow faster. "I lusted after you even before I saw your waist and hips. Those sacks you wear aren't exactly form-fitting."

111

She crossed her hands over her chest, miffed at the crack he'd made about her clothing. Not all females catered to the notoriously roving eyes of the male species by putting their bodies on display. She was about to tell him so when he slipped past her into the house, looking around with obvious interest.

"I don't remember inviting you in."

"I don't remember you inviting me in, either." He pulled the door closed, shutting her inside with him, making her even more aware of his masculinity.

His shirt was charcoal-colored, his suit a lighter shade of gray that complemented his tawny skin tones and hung on him like it was custom-made. Of course, it must have been. Nobody made off-the-rack clothes for men built like Greek gods.

He was so tall and powerful that her knees went a little weak. Fighting the evolutionary instinct to feel protected when in the presence of a man of such great height wasn't easy when you were shoeless. To counteract his biologically unfair advantage, she yanked open the closet door where she and Tracy kept their shoes. Over her floppy white socks, she slipped into a trendy black pair of chunky clogs that belonged to Tracy.

Jax still towered over her, although by about four fewer inches, which wasn't ideal, but better than before. He cut his eyes at Tracy's shoes, shrugged, and continued surveying her home. She followed his gaze as it ran over her gleaming hardwood floors, decorative fireplace, and Federal Period reproduction furniture.

"This is a lot bigger than it looks from outside," he said.

"That's the way it's designed," she said, frustrated that he hadn't offered an opinion on the home she so loved. "The rooms are situated north-south instead of east-west. It's a form of architecture that was used in the British colonies."

He nodded, annoying her.

"Well?" she asked.

"Well what?"

He was going to make her ask, darn it. "Well, do you like it?"

That grin appeared again, the one that crinkled the corners of his eyes and made him look even sexier. "Does it matter if I do?"

"Of course it doesn't matter," Marietta snapped. "I was just curious."

"Do you know why a woman is so much more curious than a man?"

Marietta's annoyance fled, replaced by quick dread. "This isn't a joke, is it?"

"Shh," he warned. "You'll ruin the punchline."

"I thought you were going to do that."

"Come on, be a sport and answer the question. Do you know why a woman is so much more curious than a man?"

"No," she said, figuring that arguing with him would just prolong the agony.

"Neither do I. I've never been curious enough to ask." He grinned. "Get it? I'm a man, so of course I wouldn't have asked."

The joke was so mind-bogglingly bad and his expression so amused that she felt as though she'd been transported into another universe where the bizarre was commonplace. Come to think of it, she had been. Jax was trying to change his status from sperm supplier to husband and father, wasn't he?

"For the record, I do like your place." He moved past her with a bravado and confidence her evolutionary foremothers had once found hard to resist in their male counterparts. Marietta, however, was determined to resist. For her good and that of her baby. "Some clutter here and there would make it more homey, but other than that, it's very charming. Is the kitchen this way?"

He didn't wait for an answer, so she didn't have any choice but to try to walk in Tracy's clogs. Feeling as though

113

she were wearing cement overshoes, she clomped after him through the narrow house to her kitchen, where her microwave was thawing a frozen meal. He peered inside the appliance and turned it off.

Marietta could only gape at him. "What do you think you're doing?"

"I told you. I brought dinner." He put his bag down on the counter and extracted the containers, holding each one up as though it were a carnival prize. "The lady at the health store said you can't beat soy pasta for protein enrichment. Or bean curds. Or wheat germ."

Marietta made a face as her appetite fled, and the contents of her stomach boiled. She didn't know which was worse. Having him striding about her house as if he owned it or having him bring her a gift of bean curds.

"You know what? Why don't we hold off on dinner and talk?" Marietta pulled out a kitchen chair and gratefully sat down on it. Her feet were killing her. Feet weren't designed to lift ten-pound weights, which is what hers had been doing repetitions of since she put on the clogs. "That's what you wanted, isn't it?"

He nodded, looking surprised that she had capitulated so easily, and sat down catty-corner from her. She immediately edged her chair farther away from his, but he closed the distance by putting his elbows on the table. She leaned back in her chair. "Yeah, actually, it is. I wanted to talk about—"

"Me first," she interrupted, determined to ask the questions that had haunted her all afternoon. If she didn't suspect she wasn't going to like his answers, she would have viewed his appearance at her door as a golden opportunity. "What's your IQ?"

"My IQ?" He shrugged. "I don't know, but I'm sure it falls into the average range."

Average? She closed her eyes. It was just as she feared. She'd gone to great lengths to enlist a sperm supplier of superior intelligence, and instead she'd gotten one who proclaimed himself average.

"Don't worry," Jax continued, "compared to the rest of my family, I'm actually pretty bright. My sister's so dumb she thinks blood vessels are some kind of ship. She can't even count to twenty without taking off her shoes first."

Marietta's head pounded, but she forced herself to ask the next question for the good of her baby. "Do any diseases or health problems run in your family?"

"We're a pretty healthy bunch," he said slowly, regarding her through narrowed eyes. "Physically, that is. Mentally, all bets are off. My Aunt Martha thinks the reason she's always bumping into things is because her children's toys come to life when she's asleep and rearrange the furniture. And Great Uncle Wilbur collects his nail clippings and tries to sell them at the corner store as slivers of ivory."

"Really?" Marietta asked as horror dawned.

"Oh, yeah. So many Jacksons have been committed to insane asylums that, in some parts of Chicago, they no longer refer to them as mental patients. They just call them Jackson patients."

"You can't be serious," Marietta wailed.

"Of course I'm not serious," Jax retorted, emitting a short, unamused laugh. He removed his elbows from the table and sat back in the kitchen chair. "Not only don't I have a sister, but I don't have an Aunt Martha or Uncle Wilbur either."

Marietta thumped the table with the palm of her hand. "How could you tease me like that?"

"What do you expect when you ask those kinds of questions?"

"I was merely trying to get a handle on my unborn child's genetic makeup."

"*Our* unborn child, Marietta. *Our child.* For Pete's sake, conception isn't like custom building a home. You can't custom build a child. All of it's chance. You take what you get."

Marietta already loved the baby growing inside her and knew she'd love him or her no matter what, but she didn't feel like sharing that information with Jax. They had more important things to discuss, such as her determination to go through with single motherhood.

"I am going to take what I get," she said firmly. "I'm taking the baby. It's you I don't want any part of."

"Tough," he said, sitting up straighter, "because I'm part of the package."

"You can't still be under the delusion that I'm going to marry you." Marietta would have laughed if her throat weren't so tight. "I'm not going to marry anybody. Ever. Least of all you."

He straightened from the table in a ploy she recognized. He was using his height to speak to her from a position of strength. If her feet hadn't protested at the thought of standing in the four-inch heels again, she would have gotten up, too.

"Why's that exactly?" he asked, crossing his arms over his chest, calling attention to how broad it was, to what a fine physical specimen he was. If Marietta had been born a couple of millennia ago, she would have snapped him up, spurred by the knowledge that he would protect her from enemies. But she hadn't been born in the Stone Age, and in this time period *he* was the enemy.

"Why? You have to ask why? For starters, you're a stranger. I don't even know where you're from or what you do for a living."

His body twitched slightly in what Marietta thought was a wince, but she must have imagined it because he answered easily enough. "I'm a businessman from Chicago. But I wasn't asking why you're opposed to marrying me. I'm asking why you're opposed to marriage."

"Because it's an unworkable institution."

The Misconception

"Lots of people make it work."

"Wrong." She raised her finger in a professorial gesture. "Nearly half of all marriages in this country end in divorce. Of the couples who stay married, are you really so naive to think that most of them are in good marriages? Haven't you read the statistics on how many men cheat on their wives?"

"How about wives cheating on their husbands?"

"That happens too, but not nearly as often. A man is predisposed to stick around only until his drive for variety and sexual excitement gets the better of him. Then, driven by his urge to spread his genetic material as widely as possible, off he goes, his penis leading the way."

Jax's face reddened, and, if Marietta hadn't known better, she would have thought he was embarrassed. But this was a man so expert at lovemaking that he'd caused her, who was privy to the biological undercurrents of it all, to never want to leave his bed.

"You don't mince words, do you?" he asked. "But none of those words matter. You're pregnant with my child so you're marrying me."

"But that's ridiculous! Even from you. You're the one who claims to believe in love. You can't possibly think you're in love with me."

"Of course I'm not in love with you." He didn't even hesitate before he answered, which was nothing less than Marietta expected but as piercing as a lance. If he had to be in love with somebody, what was wrong with her?

"Then what is it?" she forced herself to ask. "Do you want to do right by me because I'm pregnant?"

"It has nothing to do with you," Jax said, and it was like he'd just thrown a handful of salt in her lance wound. Nothing to do with her? She was the one who was pregnant. "This is all about our child. Our baby has a right to be born into a house with married parents. He, or she, isn't going to start life at a disadvantage if I can help it."

Darlene Gardner

She rapped the table in frustration. "Being raised by a single parent doesn't make a baby disadvantaged!"

The phone rang, but Marietta was so agitated she let her answering machine pick up. She heard the machine click on, her voice instructing the caller to leave a message.

"It damn well does." He brought his face, with all its maddening symmetry, down close to hers. "You're marrying me, Marietta, so you just better get used to the idea."

"Of all the arrogant, overbearing, egotistical—"

"I'm calling for Dr. Marietta Dalrymple on behalf of the television show *Meet the Scientists*." The professional voice on the answering machine stopped Marietta's tirade. "A guest we had scheduled for Thursday's program on evolutionary biology just canceled. Because of your views on sex and evolution, you've been recommended as a replacement. Since it's already Tuesday, the catch is you'd have to fly into New York tomorrow so we can prep you on what'll happen on Thursday's program. Please call me as—"

Marietta got out of her chair, hitting the top of her head on the bottom of Jax's chin in the process. She rubbed it, bumped her leg on the kitchen table, and hurried to the phone.

She snatched it up before the representative of the most well-regarded talk show—okay, the only talk show—about science in America, could hang up. Breathlessly, she listened as he outlined a plan that involved her flying to New York the next day, spending the night in a hotel, and taking a limo to the studio for the taping of Thursday morning's show.

"Does that sound workable?"

"Yes." Marietta barely refrained from shouting the word. She'd have to get permission from Kennedy College's dean of biology first, but the plan was eminently workable. She'd gladly crawl to New York for the opportunity to air her views nationally even if the viewing audience on public television was small. "Yes, it sounds very workable."

118

The Misconception

When she hung up the phone, she was giddy with excitement.

"I take it that was good news," Jax said, grinning at her.

"Stupendous news. Marvelous news." In her excitement, she forgot she was angry at him and hurried across the room to where he stood. She looked up at him, beaming, her enthusiasm unspoiled by the realization that he towered over her because she'd left the clunky clogs under the table. "Douglas Donaldson saw the article about me in the *Washington Post* and had his assistant phone to invite me to be on Thursday's show of *Meet the Scientists.*"

"Forgive me for asking, but what exactly is that?"

"It's a public-television show. It's sort of like *Meet the Press,* only with scientists. Guest scientists discuss a different topic each week. They want me to talk about sex." She clapped her hands. "Isn't it wonderful?"

"It is wonderful." He opened his arms, and she went into them. Picking her up, he whirled her around until she, Marietta Dalrymple, actually giggled. "It's incredibly wonderful," he added.

"It is, isn't it?" she asked when she stopped revolving. At least, she was pretty sure she wasn't spinning anymore. Since he was holding her so her mouth was level with his, she couldn't tell much except that he was smiling. The thought that he would take joy in her pleasure warmed her almost as much as the contact of his body against hers. She moved her lips forward just a fraction, but it was far enough to make contact with his mouth.

His lips were as soft as she remembered, and they tasted as richly sinful as the chocolate cheesecake she had stashed at the back of the freezer. She leaned into the kiss, playing with his lips, smiling against them at the pleasure of it all.

She started to slide down his body so she wrapped her arms around his neck to prolong the contact, tangling her fingers in his thick, dark hair. He was hard and warm, like living, breathing, pliable rock. Her toes touched the floor just as his tongue slipped into her mouth, caressing her with slow erotic strokes.

Shivers did a jig over her skin, invaded her pores, radiated inside of her. The river of lust that had begun to flow when she'd seen him at her door was raging now, like whitewater rapids. She tilted her head back to give him better access to her mouth, and she kissed him back, matching his thrusts with her own tongue.

One of his hands cupped her bottom while the other traveled up her side, tracing slow, dizzying circles near her breasts. She felt herself grow damp and rubbed against him, feeling the hard outline of his sex against her body. He groaned, kissing and stroking for moments that were all too brief. Then he lifted his head. Still clinging to him, she opened her eyes, so blind with lust she couldn't see anything for long moments. Until her vision cleared enough to notice that her glasses had fogged up and his eyes were twinkling.

"If I didn't have business," he said, tracing the lips he'd just kissed with gentle fingers, "I'd talk you into taking me to New York and booking a room with a king-sized bed."

A king-sized bed. Like the one in the Hotel Grande where they'd had sex until her muscles were weak from pleasure overload. Where she'd made the biggest mistake of her life. She made herself disentangle her fingers from his hair, but her body still sizzled where it touched his.

"That would never happen," she said, her voice shaking with the aftereffects of his sensual pull.

"That's okay," he said, stroking her face. "We don't need to go all the way to New York to indulge ourselves. We could do it right here."

"You deliberately misunderstood me." Because her body seemed to have developed an insatiable craving for his, stepping back from him was one of the hardest things Marietta had ever done. "I meant it's not going to happen at all."

"Don't lie to me, Marietta." He tipped up her chin so she had to look at him, and she saw his eyes were still burning.

The Misconception

"You can't deny that you're attracted to me. Not after that kiss. Not after that afternoon we spent in bed. Weren't you the one who said I had a talent for sex?"

"I wouldn't think of denying it." Marietta stepped back so his finger fell from her face. "Of course I'm attracted to you. I'm as attracted to you as I would be to any man with your outstanding muscle tone and superior facial symmetry. But that doesn't mean I'm going to succumb to instincts shaped millions of years ago and mate with you."

"In case you hadn't noticed," he said, stepping forward to pat her belly, "you've already mated with me."

Her expression was so confused and miserable that he took pity on her and backed off. He didn't doubt that he could press his advantage and kiss away any doubts she had of going to bed with him again. After all, he was still so turned on that he hurt. He only resisted because sex wouldn't get him any nearer to his goal of marrying her. Especially when she stubbornly insisted that making love to him had more to do with million-year-old instincts than present-day chemistry.

"I have no intention of having a platonic marriage," he said softly.

When she made her reply, she still wouldn't look at him. "I have no intention of having a marriage of any kind."

If she hadn't been pregnant and showing the effects of her condition, he would have argued with her. But the dark half-moons under her eyes and her snowy pallor told him she was tired. And probably hungry, too. Maybe he was pressing for too much too soon. She was a thinking woman, and she needed time to get used to the prospect of marriage with him.

He frowned, remembering her dry heaves earlier that day and the bland frozen meal she'd had thawing in the microwave. She needed somebody to take care of her, too. Since he was the man for the job, he might as well get started on it.

Darlene Gardner

"Sit down," he ordered, more than a little surprised when she obeyed. She must be more tired than he thought.

He opened one of the kitchen cupboards in search of dinner plates, and hit pay dirt the first time. He took one out and dumped some of the food from the containers on it. Then he went to the refrigerator, extracted a jug of milk, and poured some into a glass he found in another cupboard.

"What are you doing now?"

"Getting your dinner ready." He walked to the kitchen table and set the plate of food in front of her. "Now that you're eating for two, you need to keep up your strength."

They both looked down at the food on the plate. It not only smelled unappetizing, it looked the part, too. Everything was either brown or beige, except the bean curds, which were a rather sickly green. Jax didn't blame her when she made a face. "Do you really expect me to eat this?"

"Are you going to argue with me about everything?"

She looked up at him and gave him a hint of a smile. "Well, now that you ask, yes."

He laughed. "Listen, I'll make you a deal. You promise to eat this, and I'll get out of here. You need time to get used to the idea of marrying me anyway."

She waved a fork at him. "I'll never get used to the idea."

"I couldn't stay more than another hour anyway," he continued, "or I'd miss my flight."

The fork froze in midair, and the corners of her mouth drooped. "Your flight? Do you mean you're leaving?"

"You sound almost disappointed," Jax said, and she immediately shook her head, disappointing him.

"Not disappointed. Surprised. I thought you were going to stick around here and make my life miserable."

"I'd love to stay, but I can't. I told you. I have business."

She dropped her fork, and wrinkled her brow. "What kind of business? You never told me what kind of business you're in. You are a professional, aren't you?"

The Misconception

"Of course, I'm a professional," Jax said, thinking that, at least, was true. Now, however, was not the time for confessions, especially when his wouldn't win any points with her. "I'm a professional with important business. Now, is it a deal? Will you eat your dinner if I leave?"

She seemed to think about it long and hard before she answered. "Yes," she said finally. Before she could object, he bent down and planted a swift kiss on her lips. Even that brief contact made something *ping* inside of him.

"Don't look so smug," she groused. "Agreeing to eat bean curds is a far sight from agreeing to marry you."

She took a bite of the curds, swallowed, and made a face. He figured that was his signal to leave. He was halfway to her front door when he muttered with a small, optimistic smile. "If I can talk you into eating bean curds, I can talk you into anything."

"I heard that," she shouted. "You're dreaming, pal. I'm not going to marry you."

His only reply was to shut the door, but he could still hear her through it. "Do you hear me? I'm not going to marry you."

"Oh, yes," Jax said to himself so softly that his words were swallowed in the night breeze, "you are."

He knifed his fingers through his hair. That is, if he could manage to get a ring on her finger before she figured out what sort of ring he worked in for a living.

Chapter Eleven

Every one of the twenty thousand people crammed inside Pittsburgh's Mellon Arena seemed to be either talking, cheering, or just plain shouting. Some of them waved homemade signs with messages like Destroy Demolition Dan, and Crack Some Bones, CrackerJack. Excitement buzzed through the crowd like giant, mutant bees.

The Ultimate Wrestling Alliance was in town.

"Uwa, Uwa, Uwa," somebody in the crowd shouted, making a word with a catchy, junglelike beat from the UWA acronym.

"Uwa, Uwa, Uwa." A few hundred other professional wrestling fans joined in the chant, which spread through the arena until the crowd was reciting it as one. "Uwa, Uwa, Uwa."

An emcee crawled into the ring and stood at its center as the rafters of the domed stadium fairly shook with the chant. In his black suit, crisp white shirt, and black bow tie, he looked ready for a cocktail party instead of a night of ferocious brawling. Strobe lights in hues of orange, green, and yellow danced over the crowd like fireflies gone mad.

The Misconception

Jax stood in the wings, watching the excitement build, feeling it spread through him. His body tensed when the emcee began to talk, because it meant that the start of the show was just moments away.

"Ladies and gentleman," the emcee began in a booming voice and waited for the chorus of "uwa's" to subside. When the din was more manageable, he continued. "Tonight we are proud to bring you the thrill-a-minute ultimate in bone-crushing, mind-numbing enjoyment: The unparalleled Ultimate Wrestling Alliance! Are you ready? Are you rrrrready? Are you ready to rock 'n' roll?"

The crowd erupted into cheers, resuming their "uwa" chant and sending Jax's pulse pounding even faster. He waited, along with the emcee, for the cries to once again die down.

"We begin the festivities with an unbeatable opening act. Tonight we have another matchup that is the ultimate in UWA entertainment. Tonight, in one corner, we have the dastardly demon, the one, the only Smashingggg Headhunterrrr."

The spotlight swung away from the emcee and toward the top of the pathway leading to the ring. A bare-chested Goliath of a man, weighing at least three hundred pounds and wearing long tattered trousers with combat boots, appeared. He waved a stick from which dangled three shrunken heads he insisted were authentic. The crowd booed lustily.

"Smash your own head, Headhunter," someone yelled from the cover of darkness.

Smashing Headhunter brayed long and loud, pounded on his own shaggy-haired head with his free hand and sprinted for the ring with loping strides. A child of seven or eight stepped in front of him, holding out a piece of paper for the Headhunter to autograph. The wrestler snatched it from the kid's hands, crumbled it into a ball, popped it into his mouth, and swallowed.

125

Fresh outrage spread through the audience, but it only seemed to fuel the Headhunter. He sprinted past the sobbing kid and vaulted over the ropes. He paced like a big cat, waving the miniature heads, looking like he was ready to smash anything in sight.

Adrenaline shot through Jax like a river of blood.

"In the other corner," the emcee announced, sending fearful glances at the pacing Headhunter, "is a man who makes Don Juan look like Don Knotts. Yes. It's the ultimate loverboy, and one of your favorites: the Secret Stuuuuud."

The spotlight swung again, and this time it hit Jax full in the face. Music with an energetic beat blared from loudspeakers positioned in various spots throughout the arena. The lyrics were so familiar Jax knew them by heart, but the fans cheered so loudly all he could make out was the chorus: *He's a studmuffin, he's a studmuffin, he's a studmuffin.*

Jax took in a deep, bracing breath, because this was the part of the act he could do without. He focused on the ring through the slits in his black mask and affected the walk his manager, the self-named Star Bright, called the studly boy strut.

"You go, Stud," a female voice shouted before screaming in what sounded like ecstasy.

The Studettes—a brunette, a blonde, and a redhead dressed in shimmering gold halters and matching microshorts—accompanied him to the ring, swaying to the music. The brunette hung on his arm, staring at him with goo-goo eyes. The blonde stroked his chest, squeaking with pleasure as she did so. The redhead put her palm to her forehead, as though the very sight of him made her swoon.

Jax could relate. Every time he caught a glimpse of himself in the mirror wearing the sleeveless ruby-red singlet that clung to him like skin, he felt like passing out himself. He looked like one of those preening, muscular contestants in a Mr. America contest.

He's a studmuffin, he's a studmuffin, he's a studmuffin.

The Misconception

The fervent voices over the loudspeaker sang on as his quartet reached the ring. The three women, who had even more skin showing than Jax, stood in line. They fanned their hands back and forth across their faces, as though he really were a studmuffin.

Not for the first time, Jax thanked God for the mask that hid his identity. He already knew how the people in his life would react to his secret. His mother would be embarrassed; his brothers, especially Drew, appalled. The male-bashing professor pregnant with his child would stand firm on her ridiculous assertion that she wasn't going to marry him.

He's a studmuffin, he's a studmuffin, he's a studmuffin.

The lyrics reverberated in his head, and Jax climbed into the ring. A referee, who in reality was nothing more than ornamentation, was already present. The emcee was gone.

Smashing Headhunter, his UWA "archenemy," threw down his trio of shrunken heads and let out a tremendous roar, even louder than the one he'd practiced yesterday. The noise never ceased to amaze Jax. Outside the ring, the Headhunter spouted lyrical poetry and talked in a voice so low you could hardly hear him. But the roar was part of the act, just like the child who'd been planted in the audience with the autograph sheet Headhunter wasn't supposed to sign.

Jax grinned and postured, because that was part of the Secret Stud's shtick. Feminine screams erupted from the vast legions of fans in the arena.

"Nobody messes with the stud except those little ladies alongside the ring," Jax said, uttering his signature line.

Then, the silliness dispensed with, he circled Smashing Headhunter with steps made light by his adrenaline rush. The crowd gave off a manic energy that transferred itself to Jax. He soared to a natural high he got from nothing else, if he didn't count making it with Marietta Dalrymple.

As he dodged one of Smashing Headhunter's furious charges, the irony of the situation hit Jax. Even though he was ashamed for it to be known that Cash "Jax" Jackson was the Secret Stud, he loved the grandeur and sheer excitement of pro wrestling.

He loved the storyline casting the villainous Smashing Headhunter as a descendent of the Jivaro people of eastern Ecuador. The Jivaro were actual headhunters who'd once shrunk and preserved the heads of enemies slain in battle, believing it would prevent the return of their vengeful spirits. As the UWA story went, Smashing Headhunter's forefathers had massacred all but one of the Secret Stud's forefathers. His vindictive spirit lived inside the Stud. Never mind that neither wrestler had any ties to Ecuador.

Jax launched into his signature move, a flying one-hundred-eighty-degree kick off the ropes called the Stud's Super Special. His foot connected with Smashing Headhunter's chest, and the other wrestler went down hard, the sound of him hitting the mat amplified by the piece of plywood underneath it.

Yeah, he thought as the audience cheered. He loved pro wrestling.

The roar of the raucous crowd sounded to Jax more like a dim buzzing once he was inside the locker room. If it hadn't been for Star Bright's effervescent chatter, he would have thought it almost funereally quiet.

"Brilliant show tonight, Jax. Just a brilliant show. Loved it when that doll jumped into the ring and tried to stop Smashing Headhunter from smashing you." Star threw back his head and laughed. "Talk about master touches. It was like the finishing stroke from Van Gogh's paintbrush."

"Did you set that up, Star?" Jax asked as he removed his black mask and sat down on the bench. The excitement of the wrestling portion of the match was fading, replaced by the reality of being the Secret Stud. His eyes narrowed. "Because, if you did, you should have told me. I wasn't expecting her, which means she could have been hurt."

The Misconception

Star managed to look injured, an expression that didn't fit with the rest of him. He was a tall, broad man in his early sixties who teased his excess of white hair until it resembled an albino fright wig. He favored colorful suits decorated with sparkles and spangles. Tonight, he wore canary yellow.

"You know I wouldn't do that to you," Star said, then laughed his rolling belly laugh. "Then again, maybe I would've. That doll had more moxie than half the wrestlers that get into the ring with you. Maybe I should hire her for your next match. The Studettes are too smart to get into the ring until the match is over."

"Don't, Star." Jax shook a finger in warning. "It was damn embarrassing when she jumped into my arms and plastered me with kisses."

"Really great theater, is what it was. Really great theater."

"Come to think of it," Jax continued, staring down at the muscles rippling through his red singlet, "wearing this costume is damn embarrassing."

"I know you'd rather wear black, Jax, but the dolls like red. It reminds them of Valentine's Day. I suppose we could switch it, though. How does fuchsia sound? Or chartreuse?"

"It's not the color. It's the act. I think it's time we came up with another one."

Star threw up his hands. "Another act! What blasphemy! Secret Stud has never been more popular. We've been over this before. Pro wrestling is a popularity contest, and right now you're Mr. Congeniality. In this business, popularity is green."

Jax closed his eyes, because he'd initially gotten into the business because of the very reason to which Star was alluding: Money. He'd enjoyed working as a teacher and coaching high school wrestling, but the pay was so low he hadn't been able to support his mother and brothers the way he wanted to.

Darlene Gardner

Then the misfortune of one of his former college football teammates became Jax's gain.

The teammate had just begun competing on some of the smaller pro-wrestling circuits when he was felled by a bum knee that needed reconstructive surgery. His fledgling act was uncommonly popular, so much so that the promoters didn't want to lose it.

In a fit of largesse, the teammate, who had a similar body type as Jax, phoned and asked if Jax wanted to assume his role as the Secret Stud. The only catch was that he'd have to assume the wrestler's business manager, too, who back then had been known as Harvey Smith.

Jax said yes, never dreaming that three years down the road he'd still be arguing with Star Bright while he enacted a role that was at worst sexist and at best silly. Not to mention very lucrative, which was why his mother could live in an upscale neighborhood and Billy and Drew didn't have to worry about college costs.

"I know the Secret Stud is popular. But that doesn't mean another act wouldn't be just as successful," Jax argued. "Who's to say the audience wouldn't like me just as well if I wrestled as myself? I could even use a different last name. How about Jax Rules?"

"Cute. Very cute. But that's a no go. Secret Stud is tried and true, and the UWA loves him. They wouldn't just let you change your act. It's too risky. You know that, Jax. When the tide turns against you in this business, it's hard to swim back to shore. And we're already on shore, baby. We're already there."

Jax's heart sank, because Star was right. The last thing he could afford, with one brother in college and another just months away, was to jeopardize his paycheck. Especially because, the way things were going, he'd make enough money in the next twelve months to pay off the entire higher-education bill.

Still, the knowledge that he had to play the Secret Stud for another year stung. Sometimes, he'd awaken in the middle of the night and play around with the idea of telling his family and friends what he did for a living. But he would never confess while he was still the Secret Stud.

"All this talk of changing your act brings up something I need to talk to you about." Star affected a smile as fake as the oversized diamond ring on his finger. Jax mentally termed it his cubic zirconium smile. "You know that the UWA's fifth anniversary is approaching?"

"Yeah?"

"The promoters want to do something really special, something cementing UWA's status as a league that can compete with the WWF and the WCW. I've been talking to them about this very subject, and the talks involve you." Star pointed to him with a flourish.

"Yeah?" Jax asked again, disliking the direction the conversation was taking. The UWA would go to almost any lengths to capture the audience of the World Wrestling Federation and the World Championship Wrestling leagues.

"The Secret Stud is one of UWA's most popular acts, so it only makes sense that you would be prominently featured at the wrestling extravaganza marking the fifth-anniversary celebration."

"Get to the point, Star," Jax said, uncommonly irritated. He didn't even feel like telling a joke.

Star cleared his throat. "They want you to take off your mask, Jax. Then you could drop the Secret and wrestle as The Stud."

"No way!" The words erupted from Jax as he got up from the bench. He took a few steps forward until he was face-to-face with his fright-haired manager. "There's absolutely no way I'm doing that, so you can just forget it."

"Aw, come on, Jax. You're a good-looking guy. You're already popular, but this unmasking could make your popularity skyrocket into the stratosphere."

"No!"

"At least think about it." Star's voice trailed after him as Jax headed for the trainer the league kept on call during matches. "Remember the color of popularity is green."

"I've thought about it all I need to," Jax shouted back, "and the answer's no."

He had tag team coming up, Jax thought as he approached the trainer, and he could use some heat on his sore left shoulder.

What he couldn't use was a public unmasking that would forever alter the way people thought about him and wreck his chances straight to hell of convincing Marietta Dalrymple to marry him.

Chapter Twelve

A persistent, clamorous ringing pulled Jax out of an apocalyptic dream in which Marietta Dalrymple, her legs crossed and her expression suspicious, watched him as he applied a flying body block to an opponent.

As he flew out of the wrestling ring, landing atop Sumo Man, she rose from her front-row seat and strode right up to the spot where the carnage was taking place. She pointed at him in triumphant recognition, ignoring two pairs of flailing arms and legs and the banshee-like keening of the Secret Stud's beaten opponent.

"I don't care if you are a studmuffin, Jax," she was yelling when the phone rang. "You stay away from me and my baby."

Struggling to come fully awake, the ringing filling his ears, Jax groped for the receiver. He knocked over a lamp and banged his forearm on the nightstand before he succeeded in picking it up. " 'lo."

"Good morning. This is your wake-up call," a cheery, mechanical voice came over the phone line. "It is eight-forty-five."

Darlene Gardner

He banged the receiver back down on its cradle and lay back in bed, thankful that the phone had roused him from the terror of the dream. With the Secret Stud's mask back in place, he could rest as easily as he ever did a night after an UWA match when his body felt like one big bruise.

But what had possessed him to request a wake-up call at eight-forty-five when he usually didn't wake up until ten? After last night's performance, he'd had an earlier night than usual. He'd excused himself from the hotel bar after a single drink with The Bug-Eyed Alien, an innately shy man named John Smith with a passion for etymology's creepiest critters in his nonwrestling life.

It wasn't that Jax didn't find The Bug-Eyed Alien's discourse on cannibalistic praying mantises and swarming, stinging killer bees oddly fascinating. He did. He just needed to get some sleep since he had, for some reason, requested a wake-up call for eight forty-five.

Which isn't why he'd turned down the invitation of a nightcap the leggy redhead had issued in the elevator. By the way she'd looked at him through half-closed eyes, he could tell she was more in the market for a sexual romp than an alcoholic beverage.

Jax was no saint, but he wasn't about to have carnal relations with one woman while another was pregnant with his child. Besides, the leggy redhead hadn't interested him in the slightest. Even if it flew in the biological face of Marietta's ludicrous assertion that all men were on the prowl for variety and sexual excitement.

Marietta. Something having to do with Marietta had caused him to request that wake-up call, but why at eight forty-five?

His eyes popped open as the answer came to him. He hadn't asked to be awakened at eight forty-five, but at seven forty-five. Because the television program, *Meet the Scientists,* started at eight o'clock with Marietta as one of its guests.

The Misconception

He scrambled out of bed, squinting to locate the television in a room kept night-dark by the heavy blinds covering the window. Hurrying to turn it on, he bumped hard into an armchair. He automatically placed both his hands on the cushion, leap-frogging the chair as though it were another wrestler in the ring.

Bringing his face close to the controls on the television, he pushed buttons until a picture appeared. He moved swiftly through the channels, afraid he'd blown his chance to watch her. As he clicked the controls, the images on the screen passed so quickly that he moved right past Marietta on the first go round. He backtracked and smiled.

Marietta sat stiffly on an uncomfortable-looking leather chair, wearing an unbecoming tweed suit that had orange as a base color. The camera panned in on her, and lettering at the bottom of the screen proclaimed her an evolutionary biologist from Kennedy College in Washington D.C. Considering they were just introducing her, apparently he hadn't missed much at all.

Jax thought it was all quite impressive until he got a good look at her face. It was light green, sort of like the effect St. Patrick's Day revelers got when they spray-painted their faces in an effort to capture the holiday spirit.

He moved closer to the television, trying to find the controls for tint so he could fix the facial tones. Then the camera switched to the host of the show, who wasn't green. Douglas Donaldson's telegenic face glowed with health and the usual warm tones that made up skin. Donaldson said something Jax couldn't quite hear, and the camera panned back to Marietta.

Yep, she was still green. To make matters worse, the chair she sat on was a rich burgundy. Jax winced. The orange of Marietta's suit wouldn't have been such a bad contrast to burgundy if it hadn't been mixed with green.

A sick feeling crept into his stomach, but he bet it was nothing like the one churning inside Marietta's. He'd seen firsthand evidence of her morning sickness.

Darlene Gardner

Marietta said something, and he turned up the volume just as the camera returned to Douglas Donaldson.

"We're very happy to have you here today, Dr. Dalrymple," Donaldson said. Jax backed up until he was sitting on the bed, never taking his eyes off the screen. "We heard from other scientists earlier in the show who talked about evolution's effect on physiology, social structure, and survival skills. I understand you're going to talk about sex."

Marietta nodded. "Specifically, sex and motherhood."

"Yes. You have a somewhat unorthodox take on the subject, as evidenced by your recent scientific paper, 'Motherhood Without Males.' "

Motherhood Without Males?

Jax tried to catch the breath that had suddenly whooshed from his lungs. He'd thought she was going to talk about Sex Without Love or Quantity Versus Quality or any of a hundred other topics on which he was sure she had drastic views.

But Motherhood Without Males? When the seed he, a male, had planted was growing in her belly?

"Yes, that's correct, Mr. Donaldson."

"But isn't motherhood without males a classic oxymoron?"

"It isn't an oxymoron at all. Considering the options women have today with artificial insemination, at least some part of a man has to be present at conception. That's an inarguable truth." Despite her greenness, Marietta's voice was strong. Jax would have been proud of her for fighting through the nausea if she'd been discussing anything else. "My point is that, for some women, men become superfluous after conception. They simply aren't needed."

"Like hell they're not." Jax shouted at the screen at the same time Donaldson cleared his throat.

"That's certainly an interesting viewpoint," he said, "but I'm not sure I understand the scientific basis for your argument. Throughout time, women have needed men to play integral roles in familial structures."

"Way to go, Douglas, my man," Jax told the host, even though he suspected Donaldson wasn't his type of man at all. It looked as though not a hair on the man's very erect head would move if he slapped him on the back.

"With all due respect, that's simply not true," Marietta replied. She swayed a little, but righted herself admirably. Sweat broke out on her lime-colored brow. "Some women, without a doubt, desperately need the resources men can provide to help them raise their children. But that is not true of *all* women."

"So what's your point?" Jax asked the screen.

"It would help if I gave you a little history on the subject," Marietta continued as though she hadn't heard him, which of course she hadn't even though he was talking in a voice several decibels too loud. "In societies of old, women were poor and essentially powerless compared to men. So it made evolutionary sense for women to seek out men with resources.

"Going back even further in time to the Ice Age and the dawn of humans, life was so rigorous for prehistoric women that they needed men to help them and their children survive. They never knew when a mastodon or a saber-toothed tiger would appear on the scene."

Jax relaxed a little. He didn't see where Marietta was going with her argument, but now she was making as much sense as she ever made. Despite it all, he couldn't help being impressed by how brainy she sounded.

"That's all well and good, but I'm afraid I don't see how you made the leap that mothers don't need men," Donaldson said, echoing Jax's thoughts.

"Simple." Marietta closed her eyes briefly before continuing. "We live in a brand new world. Females have made tremendous strides in the workplace, and an entire class of economically independent women has sprung forth. It's women like us—I'm including myself in the equation—who don't need men."

"Bullshit," Jax shouted.

Two heavy raps sounded on the connecting wall between Jax's room and the next one down the hall. "Hey, keep it down. I'm trying to sleep in here," a gruff voice that sounded familiar shouted back, proving conclusively that even the best hotels could use thicker walls.

Donaldson screwed up his perfect brow. "I'd respectfully have to disagree with you on that point, Dr. Dalrymple. I'm a married man myself. Because my wife is a lawyer who works long hours, we split child-rearing duties. I maintain that our three children need me as much as they need her."

"You're damn right they do," Jax said, making an effort not to shout.

"That may be true in your case, but I maintain that it isn't true in all cases." Marietta, true to character, wouldn't listen to reason. "We can look at the animal kingdom for examples. It's the norm, rather than the exception, for male animals to take no part in rearing their young.

"The female elephant, for example, uses the male for copulation but has decided he's more trouble than he's worth. The mother and her calf live in a herd of females with no paternal involvement, thus proving the utter uselessness of the male."

Donaldson, to his credit, kept a better grasp of his cool than Jax did. "But how pertinent is it, Dr. Dalrymple, to apply animal behavior to human behavior?"

"Yeah. How can you do that?" Jax's voice rose to crescendo proportions, but he couldn't help it.

Two more raps sounded on the wall. "I said keep it down," the voice screamed in now-recognizable fury. It belonged to Savage Knight, whose name fit him just as well outside the ring as it did in.

"Guess the Knight's not much of a morning person," Jax muttered.

The Misconception

"There's a direct correlation." Jax forgot about Savage Knight as Marietta pursed her lips and, if possible, got a darker shade of green. She didn't say anything for long moments, and Jax hoped Donaldson kept empty receptacles on hand. But Marietta managed to hold onto her stomach and started to talk again. "Which woman do you think is most likely to divorce? The one who can support her children on her own? Or the one who is financially disadvantaged? Women today are constantly deciding in favor of motherhood without males, just like the elephants."

"I'd like to ask you a question, Doctor."

Marietta nodded but didn't answer. Instead, she not-so-surreptitiously took out a small plastic packet from her suit-jacket pocket and opened it. Jax recognized her bounty as a salted cracker just before she popped it into her mouth.

"You're an attractive woman." When she wasn't the color of an avocado and munching on crackers, Jax amended. "If you were expecting, and the man who got you pregnant offered to help out, wouldn't you take him up on the offer?"

"She is pregnant," Jax yelled at the screen. "And I have offered."

The pounding from the adjacent room got more savage, which made sense considering the other wrestler's act consisted of using the ropes like giant rubber bands to bodily fling himself at opponents while emitting savage screams. "Hey, I'm a reasonable man. But I asked you to KEEP IT DOWN IN THERE!"

Jax turned up the volume on the television as high as it would go to drown out the ruckus next door and waited for Marietta's answer. She was so unpredictable he had no idea what she was going to say. Maybe she'd confess she was pregnant and advocate that like-minded women try a more secure version of her Conception Connection scheme. Or maybe she'd announce her plans to build a space station that allowed mothers and children but no men.

Darlene Gardner

Either way, it was adamantly clear to Jax that she hadn't listened to a word he'd said. She had no intention of marrying him and letting him play an integral role in their child's life. He might as well been talking to air for all the attention she'd paid him.

"Well?" Donaldson prodded when Marietta didn't answer.

Marietta put up a hand while her face went into contortions that were painful to watch. They were the same facial contortions Jax had witnessed in her office just before she'd sprinted for the bathroom. To the eye untrained in Marietta's morning sickness, it probably seemed like she was considering a particularly difficult question. Marietta swallowed and stared into the camera.

"You know as well as I do, Mr. Donaldson, that scientists strive not to let personal experience color their pursuit of scientific truths. But my answer is that women have to learn to rely on themselves instead of on the unreliable promises of men."

The credits began running across the bottom of the television screen, and Donaldson announced that was all the time they had. Jax's hand accidentally hit the remote. The channel changed, and Marietta's green and determined face was replaced by that of a young, long-haired beauty shot in soft focus and holding up a beautifully designed box that contained a diaphragm.

"The next time he reaches for you," she said in a breathless voice, "reach for Sperm Shun, birth control you can rely on."

Jax picked up the remote and switched off the television. He'd been willing to give Marietta time to come to her senses about marrying him and giving their child a two-parent home, but the little stunt she'd just pulled on national television convinced him he needed to take drastic measures.

The Misconception

The task at hand was Herculean, but he wasn't daunted by it. He meant to infiltrate her world, and he knew exactly how to do it.

But first, he was going to have to deal with the savage who was now trying to knock down his hotel-room door.

Chapter Thirteen

Business. Jax had said he had business he couldn't get out of, which was exactly what he'd claimed in the hotel room when she'd believed him to be Harold McGinty.

Not for the first time, Marietta wondered what kind of business was so important it drove a man to leave steamy sex in a hotel bed and then a nauseated woman he'd made pregnant.

Her concentration too shot to focus on her article for the *Journal of American Biology,* she pushed her wheeled chair back from her computer desk and rose. She'd been in the middle of a sentence describing the eight-second mating act of the baboon, but her baboon would just have to live with coitus interruptus.

A warm breeze blew through the open window in her den, bringing with it the scent of Spring. The white blooms of the dogwood trees visible through the window did a wind-aided dance, rivaled in beauty only by the shimmering pink of nearby cherry trees.

The Sunday-afternoon splendor was so mesmerizing that Marietta would have forgiven herself if it were the weather distracting her. But she wouldn't lie to herself. Thoughts of Jax had sidetracked her from the usually enthralling subject of primate mating habits, and that was unforgivable.

She hadn't had any choice but to think about him after he'd issued that ridiculous, eminently unworkable proposal in the toilet stall and bribed her into eating bean curds before rushing away on *business,* but that was two weeks ago.

Worrying about whether he really would claim his paternal rights had occupied the better part of a week, during which he'd bombarded her with telephone calls.

But, in the end, rebuffing him had been ridiculously easy. She'd turned off her home answering machine, told the biology department secretary she wasn't taking his calls, and hung up whenever he managed to get her on the phone.

After three days, he'd given up, proving he was just like every other irresponsible man she'd ever met. Sure, one of his sperm had managed to penetrate the membrane of her ovum, but he had millions more where that one came from.

Jax talked a good game, but he was a man, and men had inexhaustible, replenishable supplies of reproductive material. Because of that, his single-sperm investment in her unborn child was extremely low.

Which was precisely why she should concentrate on holding food down and getting enough rest rather than wasting any more time thinking about Jax. Especially because she was glad—very glad; no, make that intensely, exceedingly glad—that he'd reverted from expectant father back to sperm supplier.

As such, he didn't warrant another thought. No matter how deep-seated her evolutionary desire to hold onto a man who could protect and provide for her.

She'd been standing at the window for five minutes, but only now did her mind process what her eyes, with their newly fitted contact lenses, were seeing. Parked in front of her row of townhouses was a white moving truck with an open trailer hitch, from which spilled extremely large,

Darlene Gardner

broad-shouldered men toting heavy, predominantly wood furniture.

It could only mean one thing. A man was moving into the vacant townhouse next to hers. Because she was sure the for-sale sign had been up just last week, that was more than a little odd. Unless her previous neighbor had decided to rent instead of sell, there hadn't been time to finalize a deal.

The phone rang just as two movers hoisted an overstuffed cinnamon-colored sofa from the truck, and Marietta crossed the room to answer it. "Hello."

"Tracy?"

"No, it's Marietta."

"Of course. I'd forgotten how alike you two sound." The man's voice was familiar, but Marietta couldn't quite place it. "Is Tracy there?"

"No, she's not," Marietta said slowly, her stomach clenching as a suspicion of the caller's identity gripped her. But she had to be mistaken. It couldn't be who she thought it was. "Can I take a message?"

"Sure. Just tell her Ryan called and the gang from the R.E.M. concert is still meeting at Paddy's Pub tonight at nine."

"Ryan." Marietta ground out the name, hardly able to believe her suspicion had proved correct. "Ryan Caminetti."

"Last I checked, that was still my name." A click sounded on the other end of the line, signaling an incoming call. "Listen, Marietta, I've got to go. I'm expecting an important call. Nice talking to you."

The phone line went dead, and Marietta stared at the receiver in dismay before she put it back on the cradle. Her sister's no-good husband had some nerve calling here, acting as though he were still on good terms with Tracy. Remembering what he said, alarms chimed in her head. He hadn't issued an invitation, but confirmed one that had already been extended. And what did the reference to the concert mean? Did it mean Tracy had been meeting with Ryan?

She heard the rattle of a car's engine through the open window and hurried to look outside, watching as her sister's battered cherry-red Honda pulled up to the curb behind the moving truck and a low-slung black sports car she didn't recognize.

Tracy got out of the car, smiled widely, and dashed across the lawn to where one of the behemoth moving men stood with his back to Marietta's townhouse. Then she anchored a hand on his shoulder, stood on tiptoe to reach his cheek and kissed it.

Marietta staggered backward in shock. Cavorting with her no-good ex-husband. Kissing strange moving men. What had gotten into her sister?

She dashed down the stairs, wondering which subject to tackle first. Ryan. Definitely Ryan. Smooching a stranger wasn't her sister's brightest move, but it paled in comparison to reestablishing contact with Ryan of little faithfulness. Besides, she could understand the buss to the behemoth. From the back, the man had a magnificent build rivaled only by the physique of the man she swore she wasn't going to think about anymore.

She flung open the door before Tracy could open it herself. Her sister's smile seemed even sunnier than usual, probably because she was wearing canary-yellow leggings and a matching overshirt decorated with brightly colored geometrical shapes.

"Hey, Mari, you'll never guess who—"

"You just had a phone call," Marietta interrupted. "From Ryan. He said something about you meeting him tonight at Paddy's Pub."

Her sister's smile disappeared. "Don't look at me that way, Mari. I should have mentioned he might call, but it's no big deal."

"No big deal? We're talking about Ryan Caminetti here."

Darlene Gardner

"Who's Ryan Caminetti?"

The rich, sexy voice came from behind Tracy, shocking Marietta into silence. Her eyes slid past her sister and zinged upward to the man's symmetrically proportioned features before it came to rest on his incredibly soft lips. Jax. The behemoth Tracy had been kissing wasn't a moving man at all. It was her baby's sperm supplier.

How could she have missed him when she'd thrown open the door? How, for the second time in a matter of weeks, had she allowed herself to be stunned by his appearing act?

"Ryan Caminetti is my husband," Tracy answered, moving into the house. "We're separated."

"So what's shocking about him calling you?" Jax asked as he trailed after Tracy. "Hey, Marietta."

Not one of her muscles had moved since he'd invaded her sanctuary, not even the ones controlling her mouth, which she feared was still open in shock. She forced her jaw to close, but it just dropped open again when she took in his appearance.

Instead of the impeccably tailored suits in which he looked oh-so-fine, he was wearing well-fitting khaki pants and a chocolate-colored polo shirt that hugged his eye-popping pectoral muscles and the spectacular broadness of his shoulders. The color also brought out his chocolate-colored eyes and the wind-tousled disarray of his chocolate-colored hair.

The part of her still programmed to react like her evolutionary foremothers longed to take a chocolate-colored bite of him. Or, better still, to cover herself in chocolate.

Fortunately, the modern-day portion of her brain switched on before she could do something incredibly stupid, like lick him. Jax showing up unannounced at her townhouse was bad news. Very bad news.

"What are you doing here?"

"It's nice to see you, too. How's the nausea? Getting any better? I heard it helps to eat complex carbohydrates like buckwheat groats. You ever try buckwheat groats?" She didn't answer, because her stomach, which still wasn't over the horror of ingesting bean curds, was trembling. She was a biologist. Of course, she'd heard of a buckwheat groat. She would just never eat one. "No? I'll pick up some for you next time I go to the grocery store."

He gave her a good-natured grin before following her sister down a hallway leading to the kitchen. Marietta's taste buds immediately rebelled. Considering his dreadful culinary taste, she shouldn't let him anywhere near her kitchen. Who knew what ideas he'd get while he was in there.

"Just where do you think you're going?" She trailed after him, feeling the situation spiral out of control like a top teetering close to the edge of a table. What was he doing here in the first place?

"Tracy's getting me something cold to drink."

"Wait just a minute." With an act of supreme will, she pulled back from the edge and stopped the top from spinning. She lifted her chin and regained her poise. "You can't just come into my home and invade my kitchen."

Since they'd already entered the kitchen, his very presence mocked her words. He leaned back against the counter and crossed his arms over his chest, stretching the material even tighter across his well-developed pecs. She clenched her teeth against the oh-so-predictable surge of attraction he unleashed.

"Sure I can," he said. "Tracy invited me."

Marietta swung her gaze to her sister, thankful she had an excuse to look at something other than Jax's chest. "Tracy? Is that true? Did you invite him?"

Tracy took a glass out of the cupboard and placed it next to the pitcher she'd already removed from the refrigerator. "Of course I invited him. He's the father of your baby, remember?"

"There's more to being a father than supplying sperm," Marietta snapped.

"Which is why I'm here," Jax interjected, as though that explained anything. Before she could demand more answers, he turned to her sister. "So are you meeting your husband tonight, Tracy?"

Her sister's hand jerked, and the iced tea she was pouring missed the cup and spilled over the counter. Marietta's jaw clenched. If the mere mention of the man rattled her sister like that, what would being in his presence do to her? Break her heart again, perhaps?

"He's not her husband anymore," Marietta said as she retrieved a miniature sponge from behind the sink. Tracy took it from her and mopped up the spill.

"Actually, yes, he still is my husband." Tracy's head was down, as though she were concentrating hard on sopping up the iced tea from the counter, but her voice didn't have any *oomph* behind it. "Our divorce isn't final yet."

"But it will be soon if you stay away from him, Tracy," Marietta said. "You have to remember how he hurt you. You can't give him a chance to do it again."

She was tangentially aware of Jax coming deeper into the kitchen and filling his glass the rest of the way with iced tea. "Don't you think that's Tracy's decision to make?" he asked as he took a swallow of the cool liquid.

Marietta took a moment to glare at him, but it was Tracy's pinched, unhappy face that demanded her attention. Her sister could be on the verge of making a huge, hurtful mistake. She'd have to deal with Jax later.

"Ryan said something about an R.E.M. concert," Marietta said gently. The last thing she wanted was to put her sister on the defensive, but she needed the facts if she were going to help her. "Did you go to a concert with him?"

"Not exactly." Tracy hugged herself, looking miserable. "He gave me a ticket, and I went. We didn't even sit together."

Marietta let out a breath. This was worse than she first thought. Tracy wasn't on the verge of letting Ryan back into her life. She'd already done it. If only Tracy had been more practical from the start, instead of imagining that what she felt for Ryan was everlasting love. "I don't think—"

"I love R.E.M.," Jax interrupted, figuring it was time he changed the subject. Marietta clearly didn't understand that Tracy's feelings about Ryan Caminetti were something she needed to work out on her own. "In fact, I love music. But, wouldn't you know it, I can't sing at all. By the way, do you know how you can tell if someone's musical?"

Both women looked at him blankly, but he didn't let that bother him. This was a stressful time in both of their lives. They needed levity. Fortunately, he was excellent at providing that.

"By the chords in their neck." Neither of them smiled, but continued to stare at him with empty looks. "Get it? Musical chords? Cords of muscle? It's a play on words."

Under normal circumstances, the punchline was funny enough to crack up anybody within hearing range and make them forget what they'd been talking about. These apparently weren't normal circumstances. Marietta turned from him to Tracy, continuing where she'd left off.

"I don't think you should go anywhere near him, Tracy," she said. "You know what a slick talker he is. Why, he could talk a turtle into crawling out of its shell."

"Ryan's not trying to talk me into anything."

Marietta started to respond, but Jax interrupted. Tracy had been nothing but kind to him since they'd met, even recommending the name of a realtor after answering one of his repeated calls to Marietta. He owed her. "Sounds to me like this is between Tracy and her husband, Marietta. It really isn't any of your business."

"None of *my* business? I'm her sister. I love her. It's none of *your* business." Color flooded her face. "You shouldn't even be here. I made it perfectly clear I didn't want to see you again, so what are you doing here?"

Darlene Gardner

Her arrogant assumption that she could brush off the father of her child as though he were a piece of lint irked him. So much so that he was going to enjoy dropping the verbal bomb he held. "I'd call it getting to know my neighbors better."

"What neighbors? We're not your neighbors," Marietta said at the same time that a crash, followed by a muffled curse, sounded outside her front door.

Jax winced. "I sure hope that wasn't my stereo system. You know how much I like music. Of course, it'd be worse for the moving man if that was one of my barbells."

Horror bloomed in Marietta's eyes, but Jax hardened himself to it. Considering she was carrying his baby, she'd have to get over that. Babies, even unborn ones, thrived on tranquillity, not horror.

"What exactly are you trying to say?" she asked.

Although he wouldn't think of borrowing the incredibly unbecoming sweater he put on at the start of every show, he borrowed a line from Mr. Rogers. "Hi, neighbor."

She covered her face with hands that shook. "This can't be happening. Please somebody tell me this isn't happening. How can this be happening?"

"Simple. The last time I was in town, I noticed the place next door was for sale. Tracy recommended a realtor. He called the owner, told him my offer and, voila, I have a townhouse. We don't close for another couple of weeks, but he's letting me move in ahead of time."

"Tracy?" Marietta gazed at her sister with huge, betrayed eyes and sank into one of her kitchen chairs. "How could you have done that to me?"

"Maybe I did it *for* you, Mari," Tracy said, backing out of the kitchen. As she passed Jax, she patted his shoulder in what felt like a gesture of support. "I'm going to run some errands. What you have to talk about doesn't have anything to do with me."

The Misconception

"Don't be angry at Tracy, Marietta," Jax said the moment the younger woman was out of earshot. "I would have bought the townhouse even if she hadn't recommended a realtor. All she did was have the courtesy not to hang up when I called, which is more than I can say for you."

Marietta didn't reply for a long moment, giving Jax an opportunity to study her. Instead of one of her customary tent dresses, she wore an unstructured shirt and slacks every bit as ugly as the tents. They were also black, a color that bleached her already pale skin and highlighted the dark smudges under her eyes. She'd secured her hair so firmly to the back of her head it looked like you could bounce rubber balls off her taut temples.

Jax was suddenly, inexplicably so turned on that, if the timing had been different, he would have talked her into engaging in horizontal rapture. He might as well derive some pleasure from the predicament she'd thrust him in, even if, judging from the set of her jaw, the next few minutes weren't going to be particularly pleasant.

"Why are you doing this?"

"Why am I doing this?" He gave a short laugh. "What did you think I was going to do after that little stunt you pulled on *Meet the Scientists*?"

"You saw that?"

"Of course I saw it. You were so excited about going on the program that I wouldn't have missed it."

"Tell me something." She screwed up her forehead as though the answer really mattered. "Did you notice anything untoward about the way I looked, especially at the end of the show?"

An image of her avocadolike face came back to him, and he realized she was asking if her nausea was obvious. He nearly told her that only somebody with a black-and-white television could have missed the green hue of her skin, but he didn't see what purpose that would serve. Especially since she'd managed to convey her ridiculous beliefs quite succinctly.

"You looked fine."

"You didn't think I looked, well, sick?"

"If you're talking about morning sickness, it's a perfectly natural reaction. It's nothing to be embarrassed about. I've been reading up on pregnancy, and nearly half of all pregnant women have morning sickness." She didn't interrupt him, which encouraged him to go on. "Just hang in there. It's supposed to go away after the third month, which means you're about there."

"You've been reading up on pregnancy? Why?"

He shook his head at the question. "Why? Because you're pregnant, that's why."

"But my pregnancy has nothing to do with you."

"It has everything to do with me, which, in case you haven't been paying attention, is why I'm here. If you had listened to anything I said the last time I was here, you would have known that. You certainly wouldn't have gone on television spouting that 'Motherhood Without Males' mumbo-jumbo."

"It isn't mumbo-jumbo. It's a well thought out response to the realities of evolutionary biology and the strides today's professional women have made."

"It's mumbo-jumbo. What would you say if I got on television and jabbered on about fatherhood without females?"

"That's impossible. You can't have one without the other."

"Which is exactly my point about motherhood without males."

"Then you weren't listening very closely to what I said on the show." Her multicolored eyes narrowed. "A mother does not need a father in order to raise her child."

"When it's my child, she does. You should have thought about that before you picked me to father yours."

The Misconception

"I didn't pick you. You . . . you . . ." Her face grew red as she tried to come up with the right word. ". . . *infiltrated* my womb."

The assertion was so ridiculous that Jax couldn't help smiling. She acted as though she honestly believed he was at fault for the sticky situation she'd created with her insane scheme to get pregnant. She obviously hadn't considered the way she'd disrupted his life with a pregnancy that was, to him, completely unplanned.

Hell, she probably even thought he *wanted* to marry her when all he wanted was to provide his child with the best possible atmosphere in which to grow up. If she came as part of the package, so be it.

"If you think I've infiltrated your womb, wait'll you see what I do with your life."

"What do you mean by that?" she asked with a show of bravado, but the tremor in her voice betrayed her.

"You're the one with the high IQ. You figure it out."

He turned and walked out of her townhouse, but not before he caught a glimpse of her stricken face. Damn it all if he didn't feel sorry for making her look that way.

Chapter Fourteen

Her heart beating hard, Tracy Dalrymple Caminetti slipped out of the front door of the townhouse and pulled it shut very gently behind her.

Even though Marietta was still at Kennedy College and wouldn't be home until much later, Tracy felt more like a sneaky teenager trying to pull one over than a twenty-five-year-old woman heading out to meet friends at Paddy's Pub.

She smoothed down the skirt of her clingy red dress, the one that had never failed to make Ryan bug-eyed, and noticed that her hands were shaking as much as her heart.

A part of her very much feared that Marietta was right and having any contact with Ryan was like inviting him to unclasp the safety pins that barely held her together. But the alternative—to never see him again—was worse.

Marietta kept a wrought-iron chair on the townhouse's tiny porch, which Tracy had long thought looked about as comfortable as a porcupine's lap. Tonight, she sank into it, heedless of comfort, thinking only of whether she was doing the right thing by going to Paddy's.

The pub was in neighboring Arlington, just a few miles from the charming little house she'd once happily shared

Join the Love Spell Romance Book Club
and **GET 2 FREE* BOOKS NOW–**
An $11.98 value!
Mail the Free* Book Certificate
Today!

Yes! I want to subscribe to the
Love Spell Romance Book Club.

Please send me my **2 FREE* BOOKS**. I have
enclosed $2.00 for shipping/handling. Every other
month I'll receive the four newest Love Spell Romance
selections to preview for 10 days. If I decide to keep
them, I will pay the Special Members Only discounted
price of just $4.49 each, a total of $17.96, plus
$2.00 shipping/handling ($23.55 US in Canada).
This is a **SAVINGS OF $6.00** off the bookstore
price. There is no minimum number of books I must
buy and I may cancel the program at any time. In any
case, the **2 FREE* BOOKS** are mine to keep.

*In Canada, add $5.00 shipping and handling per order
for the first shipment. For all future shipments to Canada,
the cost of membership is $23.55 US, which
includes shipping and handling.
(All payments must be made in US dollars.)

NAME: _____
ADDRESS: _____
CITY: _____ **STATE:** _____
COUNTRY: _____ **ZIP:** _____
TELEPHONE: _____
E-MAIL: _____
SIGNATURE: _____

If under 18, Parent or Guardian must sign. Terms, prices, and conditions subject to change. Subscription subject
to acceptance. Dorchester Publishing reserves the right to reject any order or cancel any subscription.

with Ryan. He still lived there and still met with their friends at Paddy's while she'd left that world behind. Should she risk going back, even if only for a night?

At least, this way, on the fringes of Ryan's life, she'd be able to satisfy the constant thirst she had to drink in the sight of him. She bit her lip so hard she almost cried out. But that pain was nothing compared to the ache in her chest. The ache caused by the realization that the craving she had for Ryan no longer seemed reciprocal.

That day in the beauty salon, when she'd given him the world's worst haircut, she thought his passion for her might have survived their split. When their eyes met in the mirror, she felt as though she'd been zapped by lightning. She'd spent the week leading up to the R.E.M. concert trying to figure out what to say when he asked her to take him back.

Not only hadn't he asked, but he hadn't even taken the seat next to her at the concert. He'd treated her, in fact, no differently than he had the rest of his friends. She'd had to content herself with stealing glances at him while the band played on stage.

She glanced down at her red dress. It fairly screamed "Notice Me," which she supposed was the message she wanted to send. But did she really want Ryan Caminetti to notice her in the way that had once sent her knees trembling and her heart knocking? Did she really want to open herself to the possibility of all that pain again?

Was she really brave enough to put herself on the line— again? Was she even courageous enough to walk into Paddy's Pub without knowing for certain what she'd find? He said the gang from the concert would be there. That included Anna Morosco, who stole as many glances at Ryan as Tracy herself did. Maybe Anna would be there in a clingy red dress, trying to get Ryan to notice *her*.

Tracy put her hands to her face, which felt hot even though the temperature had dipped below sixty. Oh, God. She didn't know whether she could do this.

The faint sound of lively piano music seeped into her consciousness, surprising her enough that she dropped her hands. The tune was coming from the newly occupied townhouse next door. She cocked her head, trying to identify it, smiling when she did.

"Gray skies are gonna clear up," she sang with the music as she tried to follow the song's advice and put on a happy face.

She smiled as an idea struck her. Maybe she wouldn't have to go to Paddy's Pub alone. Maybe the show-tune-loving piano player, whom she'd already designated a surrogate big brother, would go with her.

Before she could change her mind, she skipped down the stairs leading from Marietta's door to the sidewalk and skipped up the ones leading to Jax's. Then she picked up the ornate brass door knocker and let it fall.

Jax pulled open the door a few minutes later, smiling with what seemed like genuine pleasure when he saw her. The music had stopped, which could mean only one thing.

"Was that you playing 'Put on a Happy Face' on the piano?" she asked, delighted at this new knowledge of her neighbor.

"You heard that?" He made a face. "Okay, I admit it. I needed a break from unpacking so I was practicing. But I wish you had heard 'Hello, Dolly' instead. I'm just learning 'Happy Face,' but I play a killer 'Dolly.'"

She giggled. Asking him to help her wasn't going to be as difficult as she imagined. "Jax? Remember when you said you owed me a favor for finding you that realtor?" He nodded, his smile still in place even though he was knee deep in half-empty boxes. "I was hoping I could take you up on that tonight."

What if Tracy didn't show up?

Ryan blew out a worried breath and looked at the clock that hung on the wall over the worn green felt of the pool table. Ten minutes to ten, two minutes later than the last time he'd checked it. He was sure he'd told Marietta to let Tracy know the gang was meeting at Paddy's Pub at nine.

Considering how Marietta felt about him, maybe he shouldn't have trusted her to pass the message along. The last time he saw Tracy's sister, she'd told him he was worse than a pied flycatcher. Her meaning was a mystery to him until he consulted an encyclopedia and found out the pied flycatcher was a polygamous bird.

Marietta could definitely have clipped the wings of his plan to win back Tracy's trust. But what if Tracy herself had decided not to come to Paddy's, because it reminded her of the good times in their marriage? What if she'd seen enough of him to last a lifetime? What if she didn't still love him with the same searing intensity that burned inside him every time he so much as thought of her?

What if their marriage really were over?

"Hey, Ryan. You gonna throw that dart any time soon, or is it permanently attached to your finger?"

Ryan forced himself to stop thinking about Tracy long enough to regard Anna Morosco, whom he'd known since she was a freckled-face, pigtailed second-grader. She raised a brow at him as she cocked a hip. Her hair was short and sassy now, but he still had the urge to tug on it, stick out his tongue, and sprint away before she could catch him.

"Didn't your mother ever teach you that patience was a virtue?" Ryan asked.

"Yeah," she shot back, sucking on the end of a finger and blinking her heavy lashes at him. Had she accidentally smashed her finger or was something in one of her eyes? "And procrastination a sin."

Not able to help himself, he did stick out his tongue. He risked another ultimately disappointing glance at the door before he eyed the center circle, drew back the red-tipped dart, and let it fly.

157

Darlene Gardner

It hit the wall surrounding the circle and fell to the floor with a clunk.

"No offense, pal, but you stink tonight." His best friend George, an ever-present Orioles hat pulled so low his eyes were barely visible, gave off a laugh as hearty as he was round. George owned the other half of Ryan's construction business, but the hard work they both insisted on sharing hadn't shaved any pounds off his large frame. "You sure don't look like the house champ. House chump is more like it."

Ryan grinned, and raised both arms overhead. "Mark my words. This chump will some day be a champ again."

He lowered his arms, turned around to check the door again and froze. Tracy stood just inside the entrance, her hair curled wildly about her head in a style as cute as she was. As he watched, she gracefully unwrapped from one of the funky shawl-like garments she wore when the weather was cool. The smile teasing the corners of his mouth faded.

She was wearing The Dress. The red one that dipped low in the front, clung to less skin than it revealed and ended well above her knees. The one she'd never worn for more than a few minutes, because he couldn't resist the urge to tear it off. By wearing The Dress tonight, was she sending him a signal? Did she want him to get her alone, tear off The Dress and do all the things to her he'd been dreaming about for the past nine months? The things that used to make her scream his name and beg for more?

Was The Dress the signal he'd been waiting for?

Slowly, feeling as though he were navigating a heavy fog, he walked toward the door and his knockout of a wife. He was halfway there when he spotted the hand of a very large, very good-looking man resting on the back of The Dress. Ryan's own hand immediately curled into a fist, getting ready to knock out the man who dared touch her.

Then Tracy, who had yet to glance in his direction, turned, looked up into the man's face and smiled. Ryan's fist stayed bunched as every bit of his blood dropped to his feet, but he didn't have the right to start swinging. He and Tracy were separated, and the model-handsome, Goliath-sized man was her date. Tracy would probably say he had more rights than Ryan did.

She turned back around, her green cat's eyes scanning the bar crowd until they fell on him. They looked wary and watchful, not at all like the eyes of a woman who'd worn a red dress to lure the husband she still loved into seducing her. The lips she'd painted with that sexy red lipstick she was never without curved slightly upward before she reached behind her, took Goliath's hand and headed toward him.

Maybe, Ryan thought darkly, she'd worn The Dress in the hopes that Goliath would tear it off. Ryan felt as though he'd been hit in the solar plexus with a stun gun, but he forced himself to smile.

"Ryan," she said when they were inches apart. Her cloud of perfume wafted into his nostrils, reminding him of the luscious way she smelled when they made love. "I want you to meet somebody. This is Jax Jackson. Jax, Ryan Caminetti."

He reluctantly pulled his gaze from his wife's lovely face and raised it to the man's smiling one. Goliath was even more imposing and better looking up close, the kind of man who could easily lift a woman if by some miracle he didn't sweep her off her feet. Goliath's big hand was outstretched. Ryan gripped it, barely conquering a childish urge to squeeze as hard as he could.

"Ryan, it's good to meet you," Goliath said, slapping their clenched hands with his free one. He looked around at their surroundings with appreciation once they were finished shaking hands, taking in the dart boards, pool table, wooden booths, and half-dozen televisions turned to various sporting events. "I was wondering why we were driving out of Old Town when there are so many bars right there.

Now I know. This is a great place. Nothing artificial about it."

"We like it enough that we've been coming here for years," Ryan said through clenched teeth before he remembered that he couldn't speak for Tracy anymore.

"Have you heard the one about the neighborhood bar and the pickle?"

"Jax, Ryan's not much for jokes." Tracy laid a hand on Goliath's arm with maddening familiarity. "I'm sure he's not in the mood to listen to one."

She'd got that one right, Ryan thought darkly. About now, all he was in the mood for was a barroom brawl even if the good-natured, good-looking Goliath was a good three inches taller and fifty pounds heavier than he was.

"Sure, he's in the mood. Everybody likes a good joke. Okay. A big, juicy pickle comes into a bar and asks for a beer." Goliath paused, as though trying hard not to laugh at the thought of a pickle walking into a bar. Ryan's lips twitched in response. He had to admit, the idea of a walking pickle was pretty funny. "The bartender says, 'Sorry. We don't serve food here.'"

Ryan tried to control the guffaw that escaped from his lips, but it was impossible. Damn. He might hate the big guy's guts, but he sure could tell a good joke.

He was vaguely aware that a number of people had been within hearing range of the joke, including Tracy, and not one of them laughed. Strange.

"You liked that one, huh? I got another."

"Jax," Tracy said, her face solemn, "maybe we've had enough hilarity for one day."

"No. No. I got to tell this one. It's a gut-buster. What do cannibals call kids on bicycles?" He paused a beat. "Meals on wheels!"

Ryan laughed again, although it was the last thing he should be doing with the man trying to steal Tracy. Unfortunately, he couldn't help it. Goliath was a regular comedian, much funnier than Robin Williams and Jerry Seinfeld, who hardly ever got Ryan to crack a smile.

Goliath slapped him on the back and gave his shoulder an affectionate, masculine squeeze. "I can't say I've heard real good things about you, but you're my kind of guy, Ryan."

His comment doused Ryan's laughter like a reservoir of water does a flame. So Tracy had been discussing him with the big, funny guy. The knowledge stuck in Ryan's craw and burned.

"That's strange," Ryan said, wiping away the tears of laughter from his now-serious eyes. "This is the first I've heard of you."

"That's not true, Ryan," Tracy cut in, even though Ryan knew it was very true. If she had told him she was dating Goliath, no way he'd have forgotten. "I told you about Jax when I cut your hair a few weeks ago."

"No," he said, shaking his head. "You didn't."

She raised her eyebrows. "Sure, I did. Jax is . . ." She stopped, looking decidedly uncomfortable. ". . . the man who . . ."

"Proposed to her sister," Jax finished with a smile.

The comment had the same effect as a light bulb in a dark room. It banished the blackness in Ryan's heart and replaced it with the brilliance of hope. Goliath was involved with Marietta, not Tracy, which was pretty shocking in itself.

"You're Marietta's *man?*"

Jax shrugged. He was pretty sure Marietta wouldn't put it that way, but it sounded good to him. "I guess you could say that."

"Wow. Somehow I, uh, expected you to be, uh, shorter." Ryan nodded once. "Definitely shorter. And, uh . . . not so, uh . . ." He stopped again, started. ". . . muscular or, uh . . ."

"Normal?" Jax supplied.

Darlene Gardner

"Yeah." Ryan nodded and gave Jax a sheepish grin, then hastened to add, "not that Marietta's *abnormal*."

Jax wrinkled his brow, pretty sure he didn't agree with that one. Marietta Dalrymple was a lot of things—smart, sexy, and incredibly obstinate among them—but normal was not a word he'd use to describe her. Normal women didn't advertise for sperm suppliers. Nor did they appear on national television advocating maleless motherhood.

"I hear you, pal," Jax said, his standard reply when he didn't have something nice to say. The jukebox was playing an old Willie Nelson tune about stardust and memories. He bent slightly at the waist to get closer to Tracy's ear. "Hey, Trace, you want me to get you something to drink?"

She didn't reply, although he'd practically blown the words into her ear. That's because she was staring at Ryan as though he were the only man in the room. Obviously she had it just as bad as Ryan did. It wasn't hard to see why, even though Ryan was sporting the worst haircut Jax had ever seen. Entire sections of his hair were longer than others, creating a sort of patchwork quilt effect that had no business on the human head.

Despite the haircut, Ryan possessed a magnetism that went far deeper than his skin. It didn't hurt that he was the first person—okay, the only person—in recent memory who laughed at Jax's jokes.

Jax wondered what happened between these two to threaten their marriage, especially since the torches they were carrying for each other were bright enough to blind a convention of ophthalmologists.

"Trace?" he asked again, louder, and she started. "How 'bout you go with Ryan, and I get you a drink."

She nodded, although he wasn't altogether convinced what he'd said had sunk in. No matter. He'd order a glass of one of those mild wines all women seemed to like. From the looks of her, Tracy wouldn't taste what she was drinking anyway.

162

The Misconception

Then he'd find out if any of the couple's friends had a sense of humor anywhere near as well developed as Ryan's and try to stop himself from wondering what Marietta was doing tonight.

The scent of smoke assailed Marietta the instant she walked into Paddy's Pub, and she braced herself for the wave of nausea that seemed to accompany every new smell. It didn't come.

She took a trial sniff. Nothing. No roiling belly. No urge to make a dash for the restroom. Great, she thought. The only substance that didn't make her squeamish was one that wasn't good for her baby.

If things went as planned, she wouldn't be inside Paddy's long enough to breathe in too many fumes. She figured she'd locate Tracy, talk her into leaving and then convince her she was making a mess of her life. That is, if Tracy were even here.

Right. Of course Tracy was here. Marietta had seen her face when she'd relayed the invitation from Ryan. Cinderella had worn the same look when she'd found out the prince had invited her to the ball.

Marietta took a few steps farther into the bar, aware that her tweed suit, altered slightly at the waist to make room for her expanding middle, labeled her an outsider.

Is this how the lone stranger felt when he walked into one of those wild west saloons where everybody knew each other? She half expected somebody to saunter up to her and ask, "What's your business here, partner?"

Shaking off the image, Tracy set off to take care of business. Her eyes swept the establishment, looking for her sister. Instead, they riveted on Jax.

He was standing with his back to her, but she knew instantly it was him. How many men, after all, had a waist that narrow, shoulders that broad, and hair that luscious shade of chocolate?

A delicious little thrill ran through her. Without pausing to wonder at its origins, she walked purposefully toward Jax, stopping a few feet from him when she realized he wasn't alone.

A beautiful redhead wearing tight jeans, a snug top that showcased her considerable bustline and a sultry smile walked red-tipped fingernails up Jax's chest. From her glassy eyes, Marietta figured she'd been drinking for hours. The jukebox stopped playing, and Marietta could clearly make out what she was saying.

"I only live a few blocks from here. Why don't you walk me home?" The woman's voice was low and sexy. "You could talk me into showing you my etchings."

The breath caught in Marietta's lungs as disillusionment filled her. She was at once angry at herself for being disillusioned and at Jax for being like every other man on the planet. Why had she expected, even for a moment, that he wouldn't seize every sexual opportunity that came his way?

"I'm not into etchings."

Not into etchings? Had Jax just said he wasn't into etchings? The beautiful redhead giggled, and plastered herself up against him. Since her breasts looked like they were filled with silicon, Marietta wondered why she didn't bounce off him.

"How about some Sex on the Beach then?" Jax must have looked puzzled, because the woman giggled again. "It's a drink. You mix something green with something pink and you get something brown that tastes really good."

"Don't you think you've had enough to drink?"

"Take me away from all this then," the woman purred. "And stop worrying about your girlfriend. I won't tell her if you won't."

Marietta crossed her arms over her chest, waiting for Jax to succumb the way men were programmed to, telling herself it wouldn't hurt when he did.

The Misconception

"I don't have a girlfriend." Typical, Marietta thought. Here she was pregnant with his child, and he was denying the existence of a girlfriend. "But I'm taken. Definitely taken. In fact, I have a fiancée."

A what? Did he just say he had a fiancée?

"Anything that's taken," the redhead cooed in a low, throaty voice, "can be taken away."

Jax spanned the woman's waist with his hands, lifted her off her feet and gently extracted himself from her clutches just as the music started up again. Marietta didn't hear his next words, but they seemed to mollify the drunken red-head, who patted his chest and turned away. Jax turned, too, and spotted her. A slow, sexy grin instantly enhanced a face that was already way too symmetrical.

He closed the distance between them until he was so close she could feel his warm breath on her face. "Hi," he said, smiling into her eyes.

"Hi," she answered, which seemed to be the extent of her vocabulary at the moment. She couldn't make sense of his interaction with the redhead. There had to be some explanation for it.

"Were you grading papers?"

She dredged up another word from her seriously depleted lexicon. "Huh?"

Slowly, gently, he reached out and touched the corner of her mouth. His forefinger rubbed lightly against her skin, proving that any part of the body could be an erogenous zone.

"You've got a smear right there. It looks like a pencil mark." Never taking his eyes from hers, he licked his finger, returned it to her face and rubbed. Electricity crackled, the world shifted, and Marietta jerked backward.

She forced herself to think, and came up with the only explanation that made sense. Jax had rebuffed the woman, because he'd seen Marietta walk into the bar. That had to be it.

165

Darlene Gardner

"I'm not your fiancée," she said, trying to sound firm. Instead, she sounded shaky.

"How long have you been here? I didn't see you come in."

"You didn't?"

"Nope. But you're right about not being my fiancée. We're practically engaged, but not actually engaged, so you're my fiancée-to-be." He tipped his head as though he found her fascinating. Unfortunately, no doubt due to his amazing physical presence, that's exactly how she found him. "What brings you here?"

"You know what brings me here," she said. "I was just wondering the same about you."

"I came with Tracy." He glanced over his shoulder. "She's in back with Ryan. Nice guy, that Ryan. Great sense of humor. They're playing darts, I think. I offered to get her a fresh glass of wine."

"How could you?"

His brow furrowed. "She was finished with her last one. I thought it would be a nice thing to do."

She made a face at him. "I'm not asking how you could get her more wine. I want to know how could you encourage her this way? You heard our conversation about Ryan. You know they're practically divorced."

His lips twitched. "The same way we're practically engaged?"

She jabbed her index finger into his chest, which felt just as hard as it looked. Who was he anyway? Superman? Able to wow unsuspecting women with a single touch? "I'm not going to let you twist my words around. Not this time. I will not have you aiding and abetting Ryan Caminetti's ploy to get Tracy back."

His eyebrows rose as though he didn't know what she was talking about. Yeah, right. "All I did was agree to come here with Tracy. I'm not butting into anybody's business, which is more than I can say for you."

166

"What?"

He tapped the side of his face with a forefinger. "Let me see if I've got this right. You worked late, even though you should be taking it easy considering your condition." She was about to object, but he talked faster so she didn't get the chance. "When you realized your sister might take Ryan up on his offer to meet him, you drove straight to Paddy's Pub. And now you plan to convince Tracy to go home with you."

"You're wrong. My car wouldn't start, so I took a taxi," she corrected, belatedly realizing she'd confirmed his account.

"Tracy is a grown woman who's old enough to make her own decisions. Her relationship with her husband is her business, not yours."

"You don't know what you're talking about." She rubbed her temples. "You don't know what he did to her."

"I take it you do?"

"Of course I do. I saw him at the hotel with another woman. I know he was cheating on her."

"The same way you saw me with a woman when you came into the bar? Tell me something, Marietta. If you'd walked away instead of overhearing our conversation, would you have thought I was cheating on you?"

Yes. The answer made her pause, made her wonder if what she and Tracy had seen that day had been what it appeared, or if Ryan, too, had been innocent. But Jax, she reminded herself, wasn't innocent. No matter what he claimed, he'd known she was behind him. He must have. Men didn't turn away beautiful women without a good reason.

"Stay out of this, Marietta." He took a step closer to her, reminding her of a dangerous, primal cat. She wouldn't have been surprised had he growled.

"What?"

"You heard me. Stay out of it. I know you love Tracy, but this isn't the way to help her. What do you think it's going to do to your relationship if you march back there and yank her out of here? I don't see any good coming of it."

As much as she didn't want to listen to him, what he said made sense. Tracy would be furious at her for interfering. Maybe, by trying to pull her sister away from Ryan, she'd be pushing them closer. She swallowed, feeling her pride sliding down her esophagus.

"What exactly do you propose I do?" she asked with as much dignity as she could muster.

"I propose that you get out of here before Tracy sees you. Give me a minute. I'll get her the drink and let her know I'm leaving. Then I'll drive you home."

"And why should I let you drive me home? Especially considering you've been drinking for the past hour?"

"All I've been drinking is ginger ale," he said. "I'm giving up alcohol for the next six months or so."

The time frame didn't make sense to Marietta. "The next six months? Why would you do that?"

"I figured you couldn't drink until after the baby was born, so why should I?" He touched her face. "A Maserati is a darn sight more comfortable to a pregnant woman than a taxi. What do you say to that ride?"

She stared at him, dazed by the realization that he'd given up alcohol when he needn't have. There had to be an explanation, maybe he was one of those rare men who didn't like alcohol. That had to be it.

"Well?" he prompted, arching an eyebrow and reaching out to tuck a strand of her hair behind one of her ears.

Since he was traveling in the same direction as she was, refusing him would be churlish. That, and not the little shivers that danced on her skin where his fingers brushed, was the reason she was going to accept his offer.

"I'll wait for you by the door," she said in a low voice.

The Misconception

His expression softened and a corner of his mouth lifted, throwing his symmetry off kilter but still making him look so darn tempting that she wondered if, by doing right by Tracy, she was doing wrong by herself.

Chapter Fifteen

As he'd proven many times in the wrestling ring, Jax was a cooperative kind of guy.

When he performed a leg drop, instead of crushing his prone opponent's windpipe, he landed on his butt so his leg didn't touch the other guy's neck.

When he walloped another wrestler with a folding chair, he made sure to hit him across the beefiest part of the back, where it hurt the least.

He never, ever drove his opponent's head into the mat when he had him in a bulldog headlock. He just made sure it looked that way.

His cooperative skills had never been put more to the test than after he discovered that, through no design of his own, Marietta was pregnant.

He could have kept on ranting and raving at her for duping him, but he hadn't. He'd tried instead to comprehend her incomprehensible conception scheme. When that failed, he put the past behind him and focused on the best interests of their unborn baby. The truce, the marriage proposal, the move next door: They'd all been in the interest of cooperation.

He'd gone so far above and beyond the call of cooperation, it was scary. And now he'd moved into the realm of involvement, clearly demonstrated when he'd sagely advised Marietta to leave Tracy alone. By doing so, he'd probably saved her relationship with her sister.

That's why it irked the hell out of him that Marietta didn't seem to know the meaning of the word cooperation. She'd fought him at every juncture and now . . . now she'd gone as silent as a convention of mimes.

Fourteen minutes into the fifteen-minute drive from Paddy's Pub to their side-by-side townhouses, anybody would have thought she'd lost the ability to speak.

He'd tried everything to get her to open up, including jokes about Captain Hook having trouble telling time because his second hand kept falling off and nobody being sure which position the Invisible Man played on the football team. In response, he'd got nothing. Not a laugh. Not a chuckle. Not even a request to shut up.

By the time he pulled his Maserati curbside behind Tracy's jalopy in front of their townhouses, he was considering getting his crowbar out of his toolbox to pry open her teeth. Then the Red Sea of her mouth parted, and she spoke.

"Why didn't you tell me at the bar that Tracy didn't drive to Paddy's Pub?"

Since Marietta's mind moved in strange ways, Jax was a little freaked out that he immediately grasped the implications of what she was asking. He got out of the car, came around to the passenger's side and opened the door while he considered how to answer. He could lie or play dumb, but that wasn't his style. So he told her the truth.

"Because I thought you might not leave with me if I told you Ryan was going to give her a ride home."

His hand was outstretched to help her get out of the low-slung automobile, but she ignored it and got out herself.

"Damn it, Jax. How could you do that?"

"Tracy didn't seem to mind."

"Of course she didn't! She still thinks she's in love with him."

Marietta slammed the car door. The harsh sound cut through the still night, echoing her fury. She walked quickly to her door, which was in darkness since she hadn't left on a porch light.

Jax stood on the sidewalk, his hands jammed in his pockets, watching Marietta rummage through her purse for her keys. Minutes ago, he'd been thinking about how uncooperative she was. Now he added unreasonable to the equation. All he'd done was try to keep the peace between the sisters by pointing out that Tracy needed to make her own decisions.

He shouldn't attempt to reason with Marietta any more tonight. He should disappear into his own townhouse and shut the door on Marietta's anger, which was exactly what she deserved.

He'd no sooner taken a step toward his place when he saw her swipe at something on her face. Oh, hell. It was a tear. He could walk away from anger, but he couldn't walk away from tears. His feet changed directions before his mind reconsidered the wisdom of reasoning with the unreasonable.

She was still riffling through her purse when he reached her, so he put two fingers under her chin and forced her to face him. As he suspected, her eyes glimmered with unshed tears. Something wasn't right here. Marietta's reaction was much too strong. He suspected whatever it was went deeper than her concern over Ryan and Tracy.

"I don't know what's come over me," she said, blinking rapidly to keep the tears at bay. "It must be true what they say about pregnant women being overly emotional."

"That's not all of it, Marietta. Something's wrong. It might help if you told me what it was."

"I'm worried about Tracy, that's what's wrong." Her voice had lost all its anger. "She fell for Ryan's lines once. Chances are she'll fall for them again."

The Misconception

Jax wasn't fooled into believing there wasn't more to Marietta's pain, but worry over her sister certainly seemed to be part of it. He smoothed the hair back from her face, which looked pinched and upset.

"What if they're not lines?" he asked softly. "If Ryan did cheat on her, what if he regrets it? What if he truly loves her and wants to make their marriage work?"

"Oh, please." She swiped at another escaped tear. "Men like Ryan don't love. They lust. He's only lusting after Tracy, because he's been without her for a while. If he gets her back, it won't be long before he's lusting after someone else. It's a never-ending pattern perpetuated by the male of the species."

He stared hard at her until the tough facade she wore like a mask slipped, revealing the vulnerable woman underneath. Her eyes were dewy with moisture, her chin quivering with emotion.

"Who did this to you?"

She lowered her head. "I don't know what you're talking about."

"Who hurt you so much that you can't trust any man?" he asked, willing her to tell him, to let him into her life.

"Nobody hurt me," Marietta said so harshly he knew it couldn't be true. Even if she believed it were. "I don't trust men, because evolutionary evidence supports the fact that they can't be trusted."

He shook his head, still studying her. He advanced a step, and she retreated, until her back was against the door and only the breeze was between them. "I don't buy that. Somebody did something to make you this way. Who was it? An ex-husband?"

"I've never been stupid enough to get married."

"A fiancé, then?"

"I've never been stupid enough to get engaged, either."

"Then a boyfriend. Was it a boyfriend?"

It was on the tip of her tongue to tell him about all the men in her life who had wronged her, starting with the father who wronged her entire family by cheating on her mother. But that would only lend credence to his ridiculous theory that her views had been shaped by personal events instead of biological evidence.

"Academia," she said through clenched teeth. "It was academia that caused me to think this way."

"Really?" Hardly any space separated them, but he moved forward anyway so that the length of his body was barely touching hers. The night was cool, but she was suddenly so overheated she had an almost irresistible urge to take off her jacket. "What does academia have to do with you and me? With the way we make each other feel?"

She couldn't pretend she didn't understand he was referring to the hot sizzle that connected them like pancakes to a griddle. "We're both young and healthy," she whispered. "It's perfectly natural for us to be sexually attracted to each other."

He tangled his hands in her hair, and she couldn't move, could barely breathe. His breath was hot on her face. "A few minutes ago, when you were giving me the silent treatment, I was so irritated I almost stopped the car and told you to get out and walk."

"So why didn't you?"

He cracked a smile. "Hell if I know."

"So what's your point?" she croaked.

"My point is that you're making me crazy. If this were only about sexual attraction, don't you think it would have burned out by now?"

"Not necessarily." She forced herself to ignore the delicious shivers dancing over her skin. "Research shows that—"

"To hell with research," he interrupted. "I'm not Calvin Coolidge's rooster."

"Excuse me?"

"The rooster," he answered as he removed the pins from her hair. She was so intent on making sense of his words that she didn't try to stop him. "The one that wants to copulate with every hen in the henhouse. That's not me. I only want to copulate with one hen."

She bit her lip to stop her mouth from dropping open. "Are you telling me you get turned on by animals?"

He let out a sigh. Of disbelief, she hoped. His eyes crinkled at the corners as he gazed down at her. "I'm telling you that you're the hen, Marietta. You're the one who turns me on. Do you honestly believe I want every woman I meet as much as I want you?"

"Don't you?"

He laughed, a low, seductive sound deep in his throat. "If every woman affected me the way you do, I couldn't get through the day. I doubt I could even walk."

Something shifted inside Marietta and softened. Despite all academic evidence to the contrary, she wanted to believe that only she, and not a hundred other nubile young women, could elicit this response from him. She wanted to believe, which made her traitorous psyche every bit as dangerous as his staggering appeal.

"Really?" she asked. He lowered his head and laughed again, his mouth so close to hers that she felt his breath on her lips, felt his laugh echoing inside her.

"Really," he answered and dipped his mouth farther.

Even though she'd kissed him before, she still wasn't prepared for the way he overwhelmed her senses. She saw his eyes darken, felt his mouth soften, tasted a hint of ginger ale on his lips, touched the pliant muscles of his spectacularly developed shoulders and inhaled the clean, male scent of him.

All the while, she felt as though she were falling, falling into a sensuous abyss from which there was no escape. The kiss went on and on, scrambling her mind, heightening her senses. His hungry hands roamed over her body, caressed her breasts, cupped her bottom. She gasped in protest when he drew back, but he only smiled.

"I want to come inside, Marietta." He met and held her eyes. "I want to spend the night in your bed making love to you."

Love.

The single word snapped her out of the trance his kisses had caused. The word was a lie. Jax didn't want to make love to her. He wanted to have sex with her, which was what Marietta wanted, too. But having sex with him, at this late date, wouldn't serve any useful purpose. She was already pregnant, so procreation was out. It would only complicate things.

Somewhere from deep inside herself, she dredged up the will to resist him. "No."

"No?" He laughed, a harsh sound of disbelief. "What do you mean no?"

"I'm not going to have sex with you."

"Why not?" His hands dropped from her shoulders, and he looked honestly puzzled. "It's not like we've never done it before."

"Just because we did it once—"

"Five times," he interrupted. "We did it five times."

She started over. "Just because we've done it five times doesn't mean we're going to do it a sixth."

"You can't tell me you don't want me." He put his hand over her heart, and she knew he could feel it beating a rapid tattoo against his palm. "I can feel how much you want me." His other hand cradled her head, tilting it up for his inspection. "I can even see it. Your pupils are dilated, and your skin is flushed. Didn't you tell me those were signs of arousal?"

Marietta licked her lips, which she was sure had reddened in sexual response to him. "I never said I didn't want you, but wanting you has nothing to do with it."

"Of course it does. That's the best reason to make love."

The Misconception

"No. The best reason is to perpetuate the species, and we've already done that. I'm already pregnant."

Jax cursed and let go of her. "You're unbelievable, is what you are. Do you mean to tell me you think we can live next door without sleeping together?"

Her chest felt suspiciously cold. She had the idiotic thought that rebuffing him had robbed her of warmth, until she looked down and saw that the buttons of her blouse were agape, letting in the cool breeze. She made a stab at rebuttoning, but her hands were trembling so much that she gave up. She squeezed a response through her dry throat. "That's exactly what I'm saying."

He narrowed his eyes. "This is because you don't trust me, isn't it?"

Marietta didn't need to consider that one. "Of course I don't. I'm not foolish enough to believe this moment means anything more to you than it would to an orangutan in heat."

He took a step backward, looking as though she'd slapped him. His eyes drew together, his mouth drooped, his face paled. "Is that what you think of me, that I have no more control than an orangutan?"

His stricken expression cut so deep that Marietta wished she could take the words back, but she didn't say anything. He stared at her for a moment before turning away. Within seconds, he'd opened the door of his townhouse and disappeared inside.

Marietta leaned against her door for a long time, staring out into the black night and wondering why the wounded look he'd given her weighed so heavily on her soul. But, no matter how hard she tried, she couldn't come up with an answer.

Tracy's fingers were so used to cutting hair that she didn't need to have her mind switched on to do it correctly. She simply let her scissors do the thinking, giving them free rein to fly over Ryan's head with expert snips.

The wall clock, which had a face that depicted a summer meadow, showed it was nearly one in the morning, but Tracy didn't feel tired. She and Ryan had walked the few blocks to the house they'd once shared after the gang had dispersed.

Ryan would have driven her straight home, but she'd insisted they go inside so she could fix the Dagwood Bumstead Special she'd given him at the beauty salon.

Here, in the country kitchen she'd decorated herself with calico curtains, homespun wallpaper, and hanging pots and pans in shiny copper, she felt comfortable enough to accomplish anything.

Nearly ten months after she'd left it, the house still felt like home. Her girlfriends used to tease her after visits, calling her decor Country Bumpkin Casual. They hadn't understood why somebody as thoroughly modern as Tracy filled her house with everything old-fashioned. Ryan had. He'd known, without her telling him, that the folksy furnishings, so unlike the modern decorations that had filled her parents' house, spoke to Tracy of comfort and security.

"There," she said when she'd taken a final snip. "I'm all through. Turn around so I can see how it looks."

Ryan turned. His silky black hair was more closely cropped than she'd ever seen it, so short on top that some of the pieces didn't lie flat. For a moment, she felt a pang of remorse, because she'd always thought his longish hair was unbearably sexy.

She angled her head to one side, then the other and it dawned on her that the hair didn't matter. It never had. Ryan Caminetti, with his flashing dark eyes and tawny skin, would be unbearably sexy even if he were as bald as a cue-ball.

"Well?" His grin, as drool-inducing as the rest of him, made an appearance. He brought a hand to his hair, touched the short strands. "Feels short. How does it look?"

"It looks great. I'll get you a mirror and you can see for yourself."

"I don't need a mirror," Ryan said before she could leave the room. "You've cut my hair a hundred times, Trace. I'm sure it's fine. It always is."

"That's not true. I made a mess of it the other day when you came into the shop. I still can't believe you waited this long to get it fixed."

"The only reason I got it cut again is because you insisted. Believe it or not, I usually don't end a night of hanging out with a haircut."

Tracy had to bite her tongue to keep from asking if his nights out usually ended with a female in his bed. Her gut twisted at the thought of Ryan making love to another woman in the bed they shared, in the house she decorated. Anna Morosco, who'd done everything to get Ryan to notice her tonight outside of stripping in front of him, would certainly be willing to fill the bill.

Despite what Tracy had seen at the hotel elevator, she had difficulty imagining Ryan with Anna or any other woman. Somehow she knew he wouldn't bring another woman here. Not to this house, where they'd been so happy.

"You needed a haircut. A good one, this time. Are you sure you don't want a mirror?"

"Tracy." His eyes pinned her to the spot. "I trust you."

For just a moment, Tracy thought he emphasized the last word in his declaration, but then he stood up and she figured she'd imagined it. Ryan wouldn't allude to trust, would he? Especially when he'd so cruelly shattered hers.

He took a broom and a dustpan out of the narrow supply closet, and she automatically crossed the room to his side, silently offering her help. He handed her the broom and crouched down, angling the dust pan to catch the hair.

His eyes swept the length of leg her dress left bare, and a warm shiver started at her toes and moved upward. It made her realize how much she had missed making love to him. Nobody else could turn her on with a glance.

Any second now, he was going to ask her to come upstairs with him. Considering their history, considering she was wearing the red dress, that would be the logical end to the evening. But would she go with him? Did she want to?

His gaze traveled the length of her body until his dark eyes met hers. Bedroom eyes. She'd always thought he had bedroom eyes, dusky and sleepy and sexy. Her stomach dropped. Yes. She definitely wanted to go upstairs with him.

"I never thought I'd say this . . ." He paused, and Tracy held her breath as she waited for him to ask her to make love with him. Yes. She was going to say yes. ". . . but I really like Marietta's fiancé."

The breath whooshed from Tracy, making her feel deflated. "What?"

"Jax, Marietta's fiancé." Ryan straightened and emptied the dustpan of hair in the trash. "I really like him. I never laughed so hard in my life as when he told that joke about Batman keeping his goldfish in the bat tub."

"I heard you," Tracy said, barely believing she was hearing him now. She'd thought he was going to ask her to make love, and he was talking about Batman. He couldn't be trying to get her in the mood. She'd never found Batman, who was six feet tall and dressed in tights, for God's sake, particularly sexy.

"How did you say they met?"

"Marietta advertised for a man to supply her with sperm so she could have a baby, and he showed up," Tracy deadpanned. Ryan stared at her for a moment with an incredulous expression, then he laughed.

"That's a good one, Tracy. Did Jax feed you that line?"

"Actually," Tracy said. "No."

"It's a good one anyway." He took the broom from her and put it back in the closet. "Are you ready to go?"

The Misconception

"Go?" Had she heard him correctly? Did he really intend to take her home tonight? When she was wearing the red dress?

"Yeah. It's past one o'clock. Don't you have work tomorrow morning?"

Did she? Tracy's mind had been so far away from the mundane details of everyday life that she had to search it for the answer. "I don't have to be in until one, but I do have an anthropology class at nine o'clock."

"Anthropology, huh?" He put his hand on her shoulder. The heat of it burned through her body, igniting her all over again, but he merely escorted her toward the door. "I still don't see you as an anthropologist. A beautician, yeah. An actress, sure. But if that's what you really want . . ."

What she *wanted?* She nearly shouted that what she wanted, what she'd always wanted, was what she'd had. An unassuming little house in a working-class neighborhood in Arlington. A job as a beautician. And him.

The hand of the man who was no longer hers was still on her shoulder as he guided her out the front door of the house in which she no longer lived.

The night closed in on her and gripped her heart with darkness. Two out of three. She'd lost two out of the three things most important to her, and she didn't have a clue as to how to get them back.

Chapter Sixteen

Marietta smoothed the material of her black crepe skirt over her not-so-flat stomach and frowned at her reflection. She wasn't one to preen in front of a mirror, but circumstances demanded it. After all, this would be her first date with Professor Robert Cormicle and she didn't want to open herself up to any embarrassing questions.

Such as, "You don't happen to be pregnant, do you?"

She turned sideways to the mirror. Over the skirt, she wore a lightweight kelly-green sweater that extended to midthigh. The ensemble should have hidden her condition, but a shrewd eye would be able to tell that her stomach was poking out. Since the rest of her body was as thin as ever, her stomach might give away her secret.

She couldn't hide her condition indefinitely, but she wasn't ready to broadcast it. With Jax living next door, she'd have just as hard a time convincing her followers she was practicing Motherhood Without Males as she did convincing Jax to leave her alone.

She moved to her closet, intending to get out one of her airy, comfortable dresses that provided the ultimate in poufy-stomach coverage. She was halfway there when the doorbell rang. Darn. Why hadn't she remembered that Robert was always a full fifteen minutes early? She'd attended enough staff meetings to know that.

Throwing open her closet door, she pulled out her roomiest suit jacket, which just happened to be red. She took one more look in the mirror and grimaced. The red jacket combined with the green sweater made her look like the Grinch Who Stole Christmas. If Tracy had been home instead of working an evening shift, Marietta's fashion-conscious sister would have been horrified.

The doorbell sounded again. Figuring Robert would have to live with the Grinch for an evening, she walked down the stairs. The additional weight she'd put on made her feel clumsy, and a pang of something that felt suspiciously like guilt hit her.

Would Robert have issued one of his repeated dinner invitations if he knew she were pregnant? Would she have accepted if she weren't?

She thrust the bothersome questions out of her mind, plastered on a smile and threw open the door. The man standing there wasn't what she expected. But then, Jax never had been, not from the first time she'd seen him in the airport.

She tried to stop her eyes from sweeping the length of him, but it was as impossible as looking away from a work of art. Since she'd seen him naked in the hotel room, he'd kept his magnificent body covered by well-fitting, expensive clothes. That wasn't the case tonight. He'd obviously been working out, because the long, ropy muscles of his legs were visible beneath his nylon athletic shorts and his impressive triceps exposed by a University of Michigan T-shirt. She swallowed so she wouldn't drool and strove to gain control of herself.

"I wasn't expecting you," she said as the specter of their recent argument rose between them.

"Yeah, well, I wasn't expecting to come over here." His ever-ready smile didn't appear, and she found that she missed it. With a nod, he indicated the large box he was holding. "The UPS man asked me to sign for this when neither you nor Tracy were home this afternoon. Where do you want me to put it?"

For the first time, Marietta looked at the box instead of at Jax. It was imprinted with the name of a trendy mail-order catalogue, which meant that Tracy had undoubtedly ordered another batch of funky clothes. That didn't bode well for her sister's shifting relationship with Ryan. Some women gorged on chocolate when things weren't going right. Tracy bought clothes. The more outrageous, the better.

"You can set it down here, inside the foyer." Marietta stepped backward to allow Jax entry to her home. He did as she asked, not even bothering to close the door. When he straightened, he turned his very broad back to her, obviously intending to leave. But she didn't want him to leave. Not yet.

"Jax," she said before he could take a step. He went still. Tension knotted his back and shoulders, made the muscles of his neck go rigid. He didn't turn around.

"Yes?"

She wet her lips. She hadn't slept well the night before, worrying about his reaction to what she'd said, but she wasn't certain how to put things right. As if they'd ever been right in the first place.

"About last night. About what I said in regard to the orangutan." She paused. She was still talking to his back, which meant he didn't intend to make this easy on her. "I didn't mean to insult you. Even if you are almost twice the size of most females, that's about all you and an orangutan have in common. For example, you don't have an air sac hanging down from your throat. And your technique with

184

the ladies is better. Okay, *much* better. An orangutan wouldn't have stopped last night. You did."

He turned around to face her, bewilderment imprinted on his perfect features. "Was there an apology in there somewhere?"

Marietta couldn't come straight out and say she was sorry without divorcing herself from her longheld belief that the sexual habits of man were analogous to the behavior of their animal brothers. So she did the next best thing. She prevaricated. "Sort of."

He shrugged his unparalleled shoulders, raised the corners of his flawless mouth. "Then I sort of accept your apology."

She met his eyes, which had warmed considerably since she'd opened the door, then glanced away when her nerves jumped.

"Does this mean we've sort of called a truce?" he asked.

"I think it's more like a cease-fire."

He laughed then, a rich, warm sound that made her smile, made her look at him again. Goodness gracious, he was magnificent. "Before you start firing again, have dinner with me." He reached out and brushed some errant strands of hair back from her forehead. "I was just going out for a bite."

Even though he'd probably take her somewhere that served vitamin-enriched gruel, Marietta was startled by how much she wanted to go with him. She bit her lip and cursed herself for giving in to Robert's persistent invitations. "I can't."

"You can't?" His eyebrows rose. "What if I let you choose the place and promise not to say anything about what you order? I can do that as long as you promise to ask for a glass of milk. You can't skimp on the calcium."

"You don't understand," Marietta said at the same time she heard a car door slam shut in front of her townhouse.

Jax was so focused on her that he didn't turn around. "I have a date."

"A date?" Jax screwed up his forehead. "With who?"

Marietta moved her head to the side so she could look past Jax and pointed. "With him."

Jax whipped around so fast he displaced some air, which whooshed over Marietta's head and rustled some of the strands of hair she hadn't managed to catch in her bun.

Robert walked gingerly toward them on his skinny legs. He lifted his too-large head, got a look at Jax, went as white as Ichabod Crane and dropped the bouquet of long-stemmed red roses he was carrying. Marietta didn't blame him. How often did a man show up for a date and find an oversized, scowling man on the doorstep?

Robert probably did feel like the fictional character Marietta had long imagined he resembled from the "Legend of Sleepy Hollow." Ichabod Crane, the lanky, pasty-faced schoolmaster, vying against local hero Brom Bones for the affection of a woman.

That meant Jax would be Bones.

She tried to shoulder past Jax so she could help Robert pick up the scattered flowers, but Jax took a side step, preventing her from passing. She could only wait while Robert picked up the flowers himself and continued his journey to her door.

"Nice evening tonight, isn't it?" Jax asked cheerfully. Marietta gave him a sharp sideways glance. The scowl was gone, replaced by a bright, suspicious-looking smile, which could only mean he was up to something.

Robert raised his eyes to the sky, which was so covered with clouds it made the night appear gray instead of black. The wind whipped his thin, fair hair around his face. He looked unsure whether to agree or disagree. "I suppose," he said finally, walking slower now. "Hello, Marietta."

"Hi, Robert. This is—"

The Misconception

"Cash Jackson, but my friends call me Jax." Jax thrust out a big hand. Robert hesitated a moment, then tentatively put his hand out. Marietta thought she saw him grimace when Jax squeezed. "Until we get to know one another better, you can call me Mr. J. And you are?"

"Robert Cormicle," he said, his tone a bit bewildered.

"How do you know Marietta?" Jax asked, slinging an arm around her shoulders. Marietta tried to shrug it off, but Jax was holding tight. Robert looked incapable of speech, so Marietta answered.

"Robert's a colleague at Kennedy College who specializes in microbiology. He's done some brilliant work in breaking down the biological composition of rare types of fungi." She paused. "He's taking me to dinner."

"Cool," Jax said, making Marietta suspicious all over again. Cool? What did he mean by cool? "I travel so much it's good to know Marietta has friends to keep her company when I'm not around."

Robert cleared his throat, clearly perplexed. "Excuse me?" he croaked.

"Friends? You and Marietta are *friends,* right?"

Robert looked toward Marietta, who was too speechless with shock to help him with this one. "Well, um, yes, uh, of course," he answered, then added. "Mr. J, sir."

"Good," Jax said heartily. "I'm glad we got that straight."

"What are you talking about?" Marietta asked, this time managing to get out from under the umbrella of Jax's arm. "What did we get straight?"

"That you and Robert are friends." Jax smiled at Robert, then at Marietta. "You wouldn't want him to get the wrong idea about this dinner considering your condition."

"Her condition?" Robert asked, his eyes wide. "What condition?"

Marietta thought about clamping a hand over Jax's mouth, but her reflexes weren't quick enough. She managed to jab him in the ribs with her elbow, but it didn't do any good. "We're expecting, Marietta and I," he said.

"Expecting?" Robert looked shocked, then downright confused. "Expecting what?"

Marietta glared at Jax, silently trying to get him to shut up. But he patted Marietta right on her poufed-out stomach. "A baby. What else would we be expecting?"

Marietta closed her eyes as horror washed over her. How could Jax have blurted out the news when it was her body, and she wasn't ready to tell?

"She's pregnant?" Robert asked.

"Yep. So do me a favor when you have her out tonight. She needs her rest, so I want her home early." He descended the steps, acting the part of the solicitous host. "Give me those flowers. I'll put them in water so you two can hurry and get back soon."

With the flowers in hand, he came back up the steps to where Marietta stood. She opened her eyes, narrowed them, stood on her tiptoes and hissed close to his ear. "The cease-fire is over, buddy."

"I'll miss you too, pumpkin. But don't worry. I'll wait up," Jax said loudly, leaning down to plant a quick kiss on her lips. "Robert, you make sure she orders milk and eats something healthy."

Before Marietta could comment on Jax's outrageous behavior, he turned and disappeared into her townhouse, presumably to find a vase for the flowers. Marietta composed herself, turned to Robert and tried a dignified smile, ignoring his stricken, frightened look.

"Are you ready?"

Marietta was going to kill him.

On second thought, death would be too good for Jax after the way he'd scared poor Robert half to death. Surely, Marietta thought as she pounded on the door to his townhouse, she could come up with something worse. Such as Chinese water torture, although she wasn't exactly sure what that entailed and didn't have time to look it up now.

Marietta had expected to enjoy a relaxing meal at a fine restaurant, but Jax's performance had ruined that. Robert had pulled up to the drive-through window at a fast-food restaurant, where he'd insisted on ordering skim milk and a flavorless salad for her while he'd gulped down a greasy cheeseburger that made her mouth water. Then he'd brought her home.

She hammered on the door again, bypassing both the doorbell and brass door knocker. She wanted to pound on something and Jax's head wasn't available. Why wasn't he answering? Barely a half-hour had passed since he'd scared away the first date she'd accepted in eons. She was pretty sure he was home, because his Masserati was parked curbside, lights shone through the windows and she could hear the television through the door.

Couldn't he hear her? Or was he trying to avoid her until she cooled down? As though she were going to cool down any time soon. In desperation, she tried the doorknob and found that it twisted freely in her hands. She shoved open the door, his privacy be damned.

The inside of his townhouse was the mirror image of hers, but a world apart. Whereas she delegated the room just off the entranceway as an elegant dining area, he'd made it into a weight room. Stainless steel machines filled the space, which explained a lot about his physique but was curious for a businessman who spent so much time on the road.

She walked deeper into the townhouse, past so much leather furniture a look at the place would give a cow incentive to learn how to sprint. She stopped dead when she spotted the Baby Grand piano, then approached the instrument with incredulity.

The sheet music on the stand was open to "The Pajama Game." She fingered through the sheets behind it—"Oklahoma," "West Side Story," "Hello Dolly"—as relief rushed through her. Music had been ringing in her ears for weeks, which she'd suspected was a malady similar to tinnitis, only slightly, very slightly, more melodic.

She never would have guessed, in a million moons, that the he-man next door had a weakness for show tunes.

Leaving the piano behind, she approached what she suspected was the family room. The closer she got, the louder the television became. She could make out people cheering over some atrocious pop music and wondered what on earth he was watching.

Jax sat on a leather chair with his back to her, his feet up on a coffee table, his big hand wrapped around a coffee mug. He hadn't changed from his shorts and T-shirt, so he resembled Adonis at rest. At the moment, Adonis's attention was focused on an oversized television screen.

She got ready to lambaste him, but what she saw on the screen struck her speechless. Three shapely woman in skimpy costumes danced around a muscular masked man who wasn't wearing much at all except a sleeveless, leg-baring piece of crimson spandex. The audience was going wild.

She couldn't hear much of the accompanying sound track over the screams, but she was positive she caught the word "Studmuffin."

The camera backed up for a panoramic shot. Thousands of people surrounded what looked like a postage-stamp sized ring. Marietta blanched, recognizing what she was seeing. Professional wrestling. The man who wanted to claim the child inside of her was watching professional wrestling.

One of the nearly naked bimbos on screen jumped into the big wrestler's arms and kissed him. She thought she heard Jax mutter, "Oh, brother," but couldn't be sure because the chorus of the song was coming through clearly now.

He's a studmuffin, he's a studmuffin, he's a studmuffin.

The Misconception

Not able to take any more of the sexist propaganda, Marietta propelled herself into the room, directly into Jax's line of vision and put up a hand, palm forward.

Jax gaped at the woman in front of his television screen and dropped his mug. Marietta! Coffee splashed onto the front of his T-shirt, but he barely noticed as he made a wild grab for the remote control on his coffee table and clicked it.

His VCR switched off, and The Secret Stud immediately disappeared from the screen, replaced by Arnold Schwarzenegger repelling a bullet with his bare hand. Since Marietta looked like she wanted to kill him, he hoped she didn't have a gun. Unlike Arnold, he wasn't bulletproof.

He pressed another button on the remote control, and the picture went black. But it was too late. He was sure Marietta had seen the Secret Stud swaggering up to the wrestling ring. The question was, had she recognized him?

"What was that?" she asked, her voice sharp with suspicion.

He cleared his throat. "Arnold the Invincible?"

"No, before that." She narrowed her variegated eyes, and he wondered again how much she had seen. Enough, it turned out. "Were you watching professional wrestling? On *videotape?*"

Jax squirmed uncomfortably, only now aware that the front of his shirt was soaked with coffee. The truth was that he'd been watching a taped broadcast of one of his matches so he could learn from it and improve his performance, but he couldn't very well tell her that.

"I *like* professional wrestling."

"It figures," she muttered.

He reached for his sweatshirt, which was draped over the back of a nearby sofa, and mopped up some of the coffee on his lap and the leather chair. "What do you mean, it figures?"

Darlene Gardner

Marietta shook her head in that maddening way of hers. "It figures you would be attracted to television programming that panders to one of man's basest urges."

He rolled his eyes. "Oh, no. Don't tell me you're going to make pro wrestling about sex, too?"

"I was going to say violence, which, by the way, begets more violence. There's a growing body of research that indicates watching violent entertainment is linked to subsequent aggression."

"If that's true, maybe I should get you to watch a sexy movie with me. Would that beget sex?"

She put her hands on her hips. "You're not taking me seriously."

"How can I take you seriously when you say things like that? Pro wrestling isn't popular because it's violent. It's popular because it fulfills society's needs for archetypes. You have your villains, and you have your heroes. And you have a stage where good triumphs over evil in the end."

"That wrestler you were just watching. That *studmuffin*." She said the word with heavy disdain. "I suppose you're going to tell me he's a hero."

"Of course, he's a hero." Jax looked down at the floor. "He's somebody men and women can look up to."

She let out a laugh. "You're kidding me, right? How could anybody look up to somebody who bills himself as a stud? You know where the name comes from, don't you?" Reluctantly, he shook his head. "A stud is a horse kept for breeding purposes."

She was getting in so many digs that he couldn't resist one of his own. "Kind of like what you advertised for, in human form, when you decided you wanted to get pregnant?"

She ignored him, which he'd noticed was her standard response when she didn't have a good comeback. "This wrestler who's billed as a studmuffin is an antihero," she continued. "He's an extreme example of a sexist he-man,

192

The Misconception

somebody who sets women's lib back fifty years. That portrayal was so distasteful it's no wonder the man wears a mask. He's probably ashamed to show his face in public."

Jax's stomach pitched, because it was exactly the view he feared she'd take. Exactly the view, in fact, that he took. But along with apprehension came aggravation. She was commenting on something about which she knew absolutely nothing. If she'd watch a pro wrestling match clear through, she'd understand it took tremendous athletic skill and strength to pull off the show.

"That man is a fine wrestler, not to mention an outstanding athlete."

"Yeah, right. It takes a lot of talent to display your body for the pleasure of female viewers before pretending to slam somebody else into the mat."

"You don't ever watch pro wrestling, do you?"

"Of course I don't."

"Because if you did, you'd appreciate the skill it takes to slam somebody into the mat."

She put her hands on her hips. "Don't tell me you're going to try to convince me pro wrestling is real?"

"Of course it's real, in the sense that any form of entertainment is real. The wrestlers are *supposed* to put on a show, but it's an extremely physical, demanding show. If they're not in excellent physical condition, they're going to leave the ring in a stretcher."

"Then the studmuffin you just had on screen better keep a robe handy or he's going to be awfully embarrassed when he gets to the emergency room. Either that, or awfully popular."

Jax took a breath, strangely hurt by her flippancy. "Did you barge in here to argue with me about pro wrestling?"

"I didn't barge in. You didn't answer the door, and it was unlocked. I came in here to talk about what you did to Robert."

Darlene Gardner

Jax leaned back in his chair, blew out a breath, mentally preparing himself for Round Two of their argument. "Ah, Robert. And what exactly did I do to Robert?"

"You scared him to death by implying that you were my . . . my . . . lover!"

"Correct me if I'm wrong, but I've been your lover."

She ignored that, of course. "Then you had the audacity to tell him I was pregnant."

"You mean the same way you had the audacity to accept a date with another man when my child is growing inside you?"

She stammered, but nothing came out of her mouth.

"Don't bother arguing with me, Marietta. What you did was plain wrong. I don't know what kind of moral system you subscribe to, but in my world pregnant women keep company with the men who got them pregnant. In case you've forgotten, that happens to be me and not Ichabod Crane."

Her eyes widened. "Did you say Ichabod Crane?"

He nodded, although he hadn't expected her to latch on to that part of his answer. "Nobody really knows what Ichabod looks like, of course, but that professor fits the description. Lanky, pasty-faced, a school teacher." He suddenly realized why she'd asked. "You think he looks like Old Ich, too, huh?"

"What I think is immaterial. And his name is not Ichabod. It's Robert Cormicle."

"Whatever. The point is that you had no business making a date with him." He got out of his sticky chair, picked up the empty mug off the floor and moved toward the kitchen. He put the cup in the sink, wet a wash rag, and wiped off his shirt, which only soaked the material more.

"You're serious, aren't you?" She'd followed him, as he'd known she would.

"Of course I'm serious. I don't know what you were trying to prove tonight, but it wasn't fair to either me or Ichabod."

194

"Robert," she corrected.

"Any fool who took a look at the guy clutching those roses could tell he's got a thing for you, the same way any fool could tell you're not romantically interested in him."

She pursed her lips, and he suspected she was trying to come up with a way to contradict him. But he already knew her well enough to realize she wouldn't consciously lie. Claiming she had the hots for Ichabod would be a whopper.

"That's because I'm not romantically interested in anybody."

He blew a breath out through his nostrils and took off his now-sopping shirt. "Oh, excuse me. Let me rephrase in words your biological mind will understand. Any fool could tell you're not *sexually* interested in Ichabod."

"You mean in the way I'm sexually interested in you?"

He leaned back against the kitchen counter, crossed his arms over his chest, and looked at the way she was openly gaping at his bare skin. She was not wearing the look of a woman who wanted to play tiddlywinks with him. "You said it."

"You're not helping matters any by parading around half-naked!"

"I'm only half-naked because you made me spill my coffee. Besides, if you weren't sexually interested in me, it wouldn't matter if I was buck naked."

She actually harrumphed. "What woman wouldn't be sexually interested in you? I mean, look at you. Symmetrical features. Broad shoulders. Long legs. Well-developed chest. My goodness, you even have a jumbo-sized penis. You're the epitome of the biological imperative."

"I'm not even going to ask you what that is, because I don't want to know." He cut his eyes at her, then looked down at the bulge in his shorts. From the inadvertent glances he'd gotten of the equipment of other men in various locker rooms, he knew he was big. But jumbo-sized? "I appreciate the compliment, though."

Darlene Gardner

The phone rang, saving him from having to listen to her explain the biological imperative. He snatched it after the first peal and almost groaned when Star Bright's nasal voice came over the line.

"Jax? Thank the stars in heaven that I've reached you. Did you know your phone was out of service?"

"The telephone company just hooked it up today, Star. I told you I was moving into a new place."

"Yeah, well, there's not time to talk about the mundane details of everyday life right now. We have important business to discuss. Vital business. I met with the UWA brass today about the anniversary show. The big brass. The really big brass."

"Yeah. So?" He took a look at Marietta, who was watching him carefully. Suspiciously, he thought.

"So they want the unmasking to be the climax of the show, Jax. They think Secret Stud Unmasked will send the ratings through the roof."

"No," he shouted, then instantly regretted the violence of his reaction. Marietta was already paying far too much attention to the conversation. He cradled the phone, turned away from her and lowered his voice. "No. I've already told you I'm not going to do that."

"But you have to think green, Jax. This is business. Think like a businessman. A green businessman."

"No," he repeated.

"That's your final word?"

"That's my final word."

"Well, then, I have a problem."

Jax closed his eyes as apprehension swamped him. He knew from experience that, if Star had a problem, he did, too. "What kind of problem?"

"I already told them the mask was as good as gone."

Jax held back the explosion of angry words behind his teeth and mentally counted to ten before he answered. "Listen, Star. I can't talk about this. Not now. I'll have to get

196

back to you, and you'll have to get back to them saying it's a no-go."

"But—"

He replaced the receiver on the phone before his manager could say another word. When he turned, Marietta was regarding him closely. "Who was that?"

"Nobody." He mentally slapped his forehead, trying to unscramble his panicked brain. What kind of answer was that? Of course, she knew it was somebody. He improvised. "I meant nobody important. It was just Star Bright." At her raised eyebrows, he added, "My business partner."

"You're in business with somebody named Star Bright?"

"It's a nickname." Think, Jax, think. "He doesn't use it professionally, just socially."

"What kind of business?" She tapped a finger against the side of her mouth. "I don't think you've ever told me what kind of business you're in."

"Stocks, bonds, that kind of thing."

"Really? I didn't know a job like that involved so much travel."

"Mine does." Gosh. What was she playing? Twenty Questions? Make Jax Squirm? "I'm like a traveling salesman."

"A traveling salesman of stocks and bonds? With a partner named Star Bright?" She sounded downright dubious now. She looked at his marble kitchen table, which was as expensive as the rest of the furnishings in his home. "You must be quite successful."

"I'm successful enough."

"Then maybe you could do some investing for me."

"Investing's not all it's cracked up to be," he said in what was surely the most inane comment he'd ever made. Desperately, he cast about for a way to change the subject. If this conversation went much further, she'd ask him the difference between an international stock fund and a municipal bond fund. He didn't think she'd accept "a whole lot of letters" as a knowledgeable answer. "But weren't we in the middle of a conversation when the phone rang? It seems to me we were talking about my jumbo-sized penis."

Just as he hoped, her face colored. For a biologist, she sure blushed a lot when the topic came around to sex. He walked toward her, deliberately puffing out his bare chest. He was pleased to see that her face got redder the closer he came.

She moved away, scurrying backward like a crab all the way down the hall and to the front door. She reached for the doorknob as though it were a lifeline.

"Any time you like, you can give it another try," he called when she wrenched open the door. "All you have to do is let me know. I'd be happy to oblige."

She didn't say anything, just whirled and fled. He closed the door behind her, wishing instead that he could call her back. He wanted Marietta in his life. It was the prospect of the Secret Stud Unmasked that he wanted to shut out.

Chapter Seventeen

Boom-boom-boom-boom-boom-boom-boom-boom-boom-boom-boom.

A half-hour after hearing her baby's rapid heartbeat on the fetal monitor at her monthly checkup, Marietta walked through the hallway at Kennedy College, the joyous booms resounding in her own heart.

Euphoria wiped out her nagging backache. A balloon of words waiting to explode rested on her tongue, tapping at her teeth. The fact that there was an entirely new human being inside of her, announcing its existence with a beating heart, was miraculous. Even for a biology professor.

She wanted to tell everyone she saw, maybe even ride the elevator upstairs and shout it from the rooftop.

My baby lives!

She giggled aloud, something she almost never did. Maybe Jax would like to accompany her to the next appointment so he, too, could experience the thrill. She should ask him tonight. No, better yet, she should call him right now and describe what she'd heard.

She quickened her pace, intent on reaching her office as quickly as possible. She should have brought a tape recorder to the appointment. Then she could play it for him. The Baby's Booms, she'd call it. She giggled again.

"Dr. Dalrymple. Can I have a moment?"

The unmistakable voice stopped her feet, because it belonged to the one man who had the power to make her life miserable. Dean Gerard Pringle, who would hold her life in his thin, vein-encrusted hands when she came up for tenure next year.

She composed her features, turned and felt the world tilt on its axis. Robert, his black clothing a prediction of doom, was walking alongside the dean. Under any other circumstances, Dean Pringle would have overshadowed him as completely as a bald eagle does a wren. The dean's clothing was more expensive, his carriage more erect, his dusky skin and closely shaved scalp more vivid, his presence more commanding.

But the dean didn't know that the professor drawing national attention to his biology department for her radical views on male-free motherhood was pregnant by the man living next door. Robert did.

She forced herself to remain calm. Because Robert knew her secret didn't necessarily mean he'd blabbed it. "Hello, Dean Pringle, Robert."

Robert nodded but didn't meet her eyes. Dean Pringle cleared his throat, as was his habit. The joke around campus was that a frog too afraid to come out lived inside.

"While you were out, you had a call from National Public Radio that was put through to me. It seems members of your fan club have been peppering them with calls advocating that you be a guest on one of their shows."

"My fan club?" Marietta screwed up her nose. "But I don't have a fan club."

"That's what I thought, but the lady from NPR was quite adamant that you did. She said all the calls were from females who said they were foxy. Either that or foxes, she couldn't be sure."

The Misconception

Marietta let out a short laugh as understanding dawned. She'd made the same mistake the first time she'd met Vicky Valenzuela. "She heard wrong. They're FOCs. It's an acronym for Feminists on Campus."

"Whatever." The dean waved off her explanation. "What's important is that their call-in campaign worked. One of the NPR reporters was interested enough to view your *Meet the Scientists* tape. She was so impressed they'd like you to do a segment later this week on *All Things Considered*."

"They want me to talk about Motherhood Without Males on *All Things Considered*?" Marietta asked in a voice that cracked. She deliberately avoided looking at Robert.

"I'm not certain of the topic, but that seems a likely bet." Dean Pringle's eyes dropped, and Marietta was positive they focused on her stomach. Had Robert told him she was pregnant? Would the dean suggest she tell the listening audience she was excluding her baby's father from their lives?

The frog in Dean Pringle's throat croaked again, and he swept his index finger toward her abdomen. Her blood rushed so quickly to her feet that she swayed. Oh, no. She was right. He knew.

She looked down in defeat—and spotted an ant's paradise of crumbs from the crackers she'd eaten in the car clinging to her nubby suit jacket. Crumbs. He'd been pointing at the crumbs.

"Check with my secretary for the contact person at *All Things Considered*," he said while she brushed off her clothes. He cleared his throat again, and Marietta felt sorry for the frog. "Keep up the good work, doctor."

Dean Pringle walked away, his heels clicking as sharply as if he were performing a goose step. Robert started to follow, but Marietta couldn't let him go, not until she knew his intentions.

"Robert, could I talk to you a minute?" she called after the departing duo. Robert hesitated, then cut his eyes right and left, as though searching the deserted hallway for Jax. The dean gave him a curt nod, granting his tacit permission, and continued on his way.

Robert turned, appearing decidedly unhappy, like Ichabod the first time he'd seen the headless horseman. He looked down at his feet, shuffled them. Marietta wet her lips. She couldn't seem to do anything but get straight to the point, which was her fear that Robert would gab about her baby the way Ichabod talked about what he'd seen.

"Are you going to tell him?"

"Tell who what?" Robert's eyes flashed up, then down again.

"Dean Pringle. Are you going to tell him I'm pregnant?"

He looked up again, his expression puzzled. "Why would I do that?"

"Because you're angry at me for what happened on our date the other night," Marietta supplied, then could have kicked herself for spoon-feeding him a reason.

A long silence greeted her statement. In the distance, Marietta could hear the hum of conversation as a class let out. "You should have told me you had a boyfriend," Robert said finally.

"He's not my . . ." Marietta started to deny it, but trailed off because she doubted Robert would believe her after the way Jax had acted. Besides, she'd been very wrong to accept a date with Robert when her ulterior motive had been to prove to Jax that he couldn't run her life. "You're right. I should have told you. I'm sorry I didn't. Can you forgive me?"

The Adam's apple in Robert's throat bobbed as he swallowed. Then he nodded. Marietta felt so badly for him that, if she had believed in love, she would have searched for a nice woman to fix him up with.

"Then you won't tell him?" Marietta prompted. "You won't tell anybody?"

The Misconception

"I was never going to tell anybody." Robert's eyes met hers in a look as direct as any he'd ever given her and branded him as one of the good guys she had such trouble believing in. "That's your job, don't you think, Marietta?"

He didn't wait for an answer, but turned and walked away. Marietta didn't move, thinking about his parting question. A few minutes before, she'd been so thrilled over hearing the baby's heartbeat, she'd been ready to shout the news to Jax and anyone else who would listen. But how could she, the nation's premier advocate of Motherhood Without Males, reveal she was pregnant without opening herself up to frightening questions?

She could hear them now: Who's your baby's father? What role will he play in your lives? How does he feel about you advocating that fathers have no part in raising their children?

She should be euphoric that a show as respected as *All Things Considered* wanted her as a guest. Instead, she felt as though a vacuum had sucked the happiness out of her.

Deep in thought, Marietta bit her lip as she slowly made her way down the hall to her office. Maybe, just maybe, she didn't have to talk about Motherhood Without Males on *All Things Considered*.

She had a half-dozen other provocative topics. Sex Without Love. Breaking Up Is Easy To Do. Animal Adultery. Surely, she could convince the programmers that a fresh topic was more interesting than a rehashed one.

In doing so, she'd buy herself more time to figure out what to do about Jax.

She glanced down at her stomach, which was getting rounder by the day. She was starting her fourth month, which meant she couldn't hide her pregnancy much longer. But even a little time was precious.

By the time Marietta returned home that night, flush with the success of getting *All Things Considered* to agree to a topic switch, she'd convinced herself it wouldn't hurt to tell

Jax about the baby's heartbeat boom-boom-booming inside her.

She wouldn't seek him out, of course. All she'd need do is wait until he decided to pester her. Two hours after walking through the door, Marietta was still waiting. She'd started toward his place a half-dozen times, but always stopped herself. No need to appear too eager, which she definitely was not. Jax would come to her. That was the pattern with them. He always came to her.

A rustling outside the door brought a smug smile to her lips. She put down the magazine on motherhood she hadn't been able to concentrate on and edged forward on the chair, prepared to answer the doorbell when he rang it.

Instead, the door opened and Tracy came through it, dressed from head to toe in a color Marietta hadn't known existed in her wardrobe. Black. She hadn't even brightened the outfit with one of her crazy scarves. Instead, her stylish jeans, low-heeled boots and short-sleeved shirt were unrelentingly black. She'd even had her curly auburn locks artificially darkened. She looked like she was advocating a new style—Grim Reaper Chic.

"Hey, Marietta," Tracy said. She sounded tired, another thing previously alien to her nature.

"Hi, Tracy. Long day?"

"Um, hmm." Tracy crossed the room and plopped down onto the sofa across from Marietta, letting her head fall back against the cushions. "I've been running since I took Jax to the airport this morning. He fixed your car, by the way. Just popped the hood, took a look inside, did a couple of things and, presto, it ran. Isn't it amazing how men can do that?"

Only the first part of Tracy's answer registered on Marietta. She felt her face sag. "You took Jax to the airport? You mean he's not home?"

"Nope. He won't be for two weeks. He has business, then he's going to Drew's high school graduation."

"Drew?"

"His brother."

"Jax has a brother?"

"He has two brothers." Tracy lifted her head and peered at her. "Geez, don't you guys ever talk?"

"Not about his family." Marietta was suddenly curious about the people related to him, but she couldn't ask Tracy to fill her in. If she did, Tracy would assume she was interested, which she was, but not for the reasons her sister would dream up.

"Drew, the one graduating from high school, just turned eighteen. His passion is wrestling, and he should be hearing any day now whether he got into MIT for the fall semester. Billy's a year older and just finished his freshman year at Michigan State. He's interested in a career having to do with the outdoors. They live outside Chicago with their mother, whose name is Sheila. She's fifty. The father isn't in the picture." Tracy lifted a brow. "Is that what you wanted to know?"

"I didn't ask you to tell me about them."

"Yeah, right." Tracy dropped her head back on the sofa and closed her eyes. "Your lips were pressed so tightly together you were injuring them."

"Don't make this into something it's not, Tracy. Curiosity is an evolutionary adaptation. Early primates dwelled in trees and resembled squirrels in their habits. Curiosity, like grasping hands, is an arboreal adaptation."

"Spare me the biology lesson, Marietta," Tracy said without opening her eyes. "I may only be a hairdresser, but I'm smart enough to know you wouldn't be curious about just anybody."

"That's not tr . . ." Marietta paused in the middle of her denial. "What did you mean by 'only a hairdresser'?"

"Just what I said." Tracy sat up straight and looked at her with sad eyes. "I know you don't have a very high opinion of hairdressing as a career."

"Whatever gave you that idea?"

"Oh, let's see." Tracy tapped her lip, pretending to think. The truth was that she didn't need to think about it anymore. That's all she'd been doing since Ryan pointed out there was nothing wrong with who she was: a hairdresser who loved her job. "The way you keep pushing me to become an anthropologist."

"I thought you wanted to become an anthropologist."

"No," Tracy said, surprised at the passion behind the denial. She wouldn't be saying any of this if she weren't in such a foul mood, but it was past time it came out. "I want to be exactly what I am: a hairdresser. I *like* cutting hair, Marietta. I like helping people feel better about themselves by making them look good. It makes me feel needed."

"Then why didn't you tell me?"

Tracy sighed, emotionally drained by her tirade. "I didn't tell you, because you're such an intellectual. I didn't tell you, because I thought you'd be disappointed in me."

"Disappointed?" Marietta's voice cracked on the word. Through the tears gathering in her eyes, Tracy could see her approaching the sofa. Then her sister's arms were around her, the way they hadn't been in too long. "I could never be disappointed in you, Tracy. I only want you to be happy."

The tears fell in thick rivulets down Tracy's cheeks as she clung to her sister. The closeness they'd always shared wrapped around her like a warm blanket, and in that instant she felt she could tell Marietta anything. "How can I be happy," she asked on a sob, "without Ryan?"

"Oh, honey. You still think you love him, don't you?"

"I do love him. I know you don't believe in love, Mari, but a part of me is missing without him. It's a constant physical ache. It's like half the cells in my body were cut away, but I'm still expected to function. I can still laugh and smile, but it takes so much more effort than it used to."

"If you're thinking about taking him back, you have to ask yourself some hard questions." Marietta's voice was gentle. "Could you ever trust him again?"

"I don't know. I just don't know." Confusion descended on Tracy like rain from a stormy sky. She no longer knew what she thought about the scene she'd witnessed in the hotel lobby. It seemed surreal. She knew the woman had been in Ryan's arms, but things had been so ideal between herself and Ryan, and Ryan so loving, that she could barely believe it had happened. "But I don't think I'll get to make that decision."

"What do you mean, honey?"

"I don't think he wants to get back together." Tracy choked out her fears. "I wore the red dress, and he didn't even notice. He doesn't touch me. He says . . . he says he wants us to be friends."

Tracy could no longer hold back the downpour of tears, so she wept in her sister's arms, grateful that Marietta didn't say anything, but just held her and stroked her hair.

Three hours prior to showtime and a full sixty minutes before the gates opened to the public, the arena was empty except for the two wrestlers in the ring and the crews of workers setting up the sound and light systems.

Jax was in sweats, but Drilling Drake was already decked out in his dentist finery. A white lab coat worn so it gaped open to reveal a massive chest shorn of hair topped skintight white shorts. Considering Drake was several inches shorter but at least seventy-five pounds heavier than Jax, the wrestler didn't resemble any dentist Jax had ever seen.

Drake clenched teeth that had been professionally whitened until they glistened, held up a household drill, and took a few tentative steps forward. "Okay, here goes." He sounded nervous, as though he were the patient instead of the dentist. "Open your mouth and hold still. Very, very still."

Feigning fear, Jax retreated until his back was against the ropes. Then he scowled and put out a hand, stopping the other wrestler's glacierlike progress. "Wait a minute. Why isn't the drill turned on?"

"Aww, Jax," Drake wailed. "I told you. We haven't practiced it enough yet. I don't want to turn on the drill until I'm sure I'm not gonna knock out your teeth."

Jax crossed his arms over his chest. "Stop worrying about my teeth and start thinking about the act. If we don't rehearse this, we're not going to get it right tonight."

Drake made a face and rubbed a hand over his lower jaw. "I don't know about this, pal. I appreciate you giving me the idea and all, but are you sure I need to add a drill to my act?"

"Are you kidding? You're a demented dentist. The audience is supposed to hate you. Can you think of a better way to get them going than taking a drill to their hero's mouth?"

"Considering you're their hero, I woulda thought you'd think of a better way. You're a sick man, Jax. Did you know that?"

Jax laughed, crossed to Drake and switched on the drill. The overhead lights shone on his perfectly bald, irregularly shaped head, making it gleam like a newly polished Easter egg. In that moment, he did look demented. Jax thought he looked perfect.

"Relax, Drake." Jax shouted to be heard above the drill. "If we do it right, the drill won't even touch me. Just get me into a headlock and I'll open up. Bring the drill close enough so it only looks like you're drilling. The audience will eat it up."

Drake shut off the drill. "You sure?"

"I'm sure."

"What are you going to do after I take it out?" Drake asked, and Jax understood he was stalling. Didn't he see the potential in the act? Didn't he realize this kind of theater was what made pro wrestling so perfect?

The Misconception

"I'm going to moan like a hero with aching teeth, of course." Jax said. "I might even juice myself."

In pro-wrestler speak, juicing meant causing yourself to bleed. The way it was usually done, the referee handed off a sliver of a razor blade to the "injured" wrestler. Being careful not to hurt himself, the wrestler made a small incision in the crease of his brow, causing blood to flow.

"Won't work," Drake said. "You should be bleeding from the mouth, not the brow. Besides, isn't the ref gonna be looking the other way when I bring out the drill?"

That was another standard of pro wrestling. Whenever the villain did something truly dastardly, the referee was never in position to see it. That way, the crowd had more reason to boo.

"I didn't think about that. I guess screaming in pain will have to be enough."

The demented dentist shuddered, as though imagining Jax would be screaming in real pain if he didn't keep the drill steady. Jax figured it was time to lighten him up. "Hey, Drake. Why did the wrestlers have to compete in the dark?"

Drake gave him the blank stare most wrestlers affected before the punchlines to his jokes. Jax figured they thought themselves too macho to react. "Because their match wouldn't light," he finished.

Jax laughed. Drake, predictably, fought off his hilarity.

"Don't tell me," Drake said. "If I don't turn on the drill, you're going to tell another joke, aren't you?"

"You need 'em, buddy. Why did the—"

Drake switched on the drill, which made a whirring sound that ran through Jax like the thrill kids got from the dips on a roller-coaster ride. This was going to be great. He smiled, then opened his mouth wide.

Ten minutes later, with Drake's face the color of Jax's still-intact teeth, Jax checked his watch. Thanks to Tracy, his pipeline to news of Marietta, he knew exactly what time she was scheduled to do her guest spot on National Public Radio.

"I hate to do this, but I need to take a break, Drake." Jax vaulted over the rope and landed softly on the floor of the arena. "You've got the act down anyway, don't you?"

"I'm not sure." Drake leaned against the ropes and peered down at him. "I was trying so hard not to pulverize your teeth that I forgot to practice looking crazed."

"You can always use a mirror for that. I've got something I need to do." Jax never broke stride as he headed for the locker room. Drake fell into step behind him.

"What do you have to do?"

"Nothing important," Jax said, but knew Drake wouldn't leave it alone. Pro wrestlers traveled so extensively they became a loose-knit family, spending as much time together out of the ring as in it. Jax knew a few of them, Drake included, as well as he did his own brothers. When Drake got hold of a subject, he didn't let go. Last year, he'd pestered Gargoyle Dan so relentlessly for the secret to his newly trim waist that the embarrassed wrestler finally admitted to liposuction.

"If it wasn't important, you would of stayed in the ring longer," Drake said, following Jax into the locker room. Jax resigned himself to the other man's company, because he didn't have time to get rid of him. Marietta was going to be on any minute. He reached into his locker and took out a portable radio, fiddling with the dials until he found the right station. The program's theme music blared out from it.

"Hey, that's NPR." Drake smiled like a kid who'd been given jelly beans and Coca-Cola for breakfast. "I love NPR. I didn't know you were a fan."

"Shhh," Jax said, sinking to the metal bench in front of his locker. "They're already introducing her."

"Introducing who?"

The Misconception

"Shhh," Jax repeated as a reporter with a voice so richly melodious it reminded him of one of his favorite show tunes recited Marietta's credentials. He steeled himself to hear the hated phrase—Motherhood Without Males—as the reporter welcomed Marietta to the show.

"Your controversial views of evolutionary biology and how they relate to human sexual behavior have been drawing attention throughout the country, Dr. Dalrymple. I understand that today you're going to tackle another contentious subject: Mate switching."

Drake's eyes got large in his bald head. "She's going to talk about *swingers?*"

"She said switching, not swinging," Jax said. "Now shut up."

"Don't misunderstand. I'm not referring to couples switching partners for a night. That's a different subject entirely." Marietta's voice, which Jax hadn't heard in nearly two weeks, washed over him like a soft, warm rainfall. With a start, he realized he'd missed her. "In this context, mate switching refers to our deep-seated desires to rebel against a society that pushes us to try to be faithful to one mate."

"To *try* to be faithful?" The reporter's voice cut in. "Are you saying fidelity is an impossibility?"

"Not at all. I'm aware that some people manage it, but infidelity is much more conducive to human nature, especially as it regards the male of the species."

Beside Jax, Drake let out a tremendous harrumph. "What is she? A female chauvinist pig?"

Irritation bubbled in Jax, and he was shocked that it was because of Drake instead of Marietta. Yes, she was a female chauvinist pig, but he didn't want to hear Drake call her one.

She went on to describe a university study in which researchers enlisted unusually beautiful women and stunningly handsome men to approach strangers of the opposite gender to ask for sex. All of the approached women refused,

211

but seventy-five percent of the men, many married or in serious relationships, accepted.

"Because they're biologically programmed to ensure the survival of our species, men are driven to spread their seed as widely as possible," she said, repeating something she'd told Jax before. "Females, too, have an irresistible need to procreate. But, since they must nurture the demanding new life well beyond the nine-month gestation period, they have more at stake when engaging in sex."

Jax held his breath while he waited for the motherhood-without-males illogic that would surely follow. Instead, Marietta paused and the interviewer asked a question. "So you're saying females are less prone to infidelity than men?"

"Not exactly," Marietta countered. "Neither sex is cut out for monogamy. If you want proof, look at our country's spiraling divorce rate. Then consider how many people would be better off divorced, but stay together because of societal pressure. Humans are genetically predisposed to separate. To mate-switch, if you will."

After Marietta answered a few more questions along the same vein, the segment ended and Jax switched off the radio. Drake looked as though someone had zapped him with a stun gun, paralyzing his vocal chords. All good things, however, came to an end. As did Drake's silence.

"That was the biggest bunch of shit I ever heard."

Jax bristled. "Hey, watch your mouth."

"You're not saying you agreed with her? How could you? Sure, some of that shit had a grain of truth. I mean, I tried to score with every woman I could until I met Ruthie. But, since I got married, I wouldn't cheat on Ruthie. I love her too much."

"Of course I didn't agree with her," Jax groused while he tried to sort out his jumbled feelings. On one hand, Marietta's opinions made him mad as hell. On the other, she stated them so eruditely that he was actually proud of her. "I don't have to agree with her to respect her opinion."

The Misconception

Drake narrowed his eyes and peered at him. "Just who is this woman to you?"

"A friend," he answered quickly. Too quickly.

"A friend you're sleeping with?"

"That's none of your business."

"Oh, it's that way, is it?" Drake tipped his bald head, looking infuriatingly wise. Like an inflated Yoda. "Does this *friend* know you're the Secret Stud?"

Jax looked down at the locker room floor. "You know better than to ask me that. Nobody in my private life knows I'm the Secret Stud."

Drake tapped his fat finger against his bristly chin. "You better not tell the professor that then. Especially if you're serious about her."

"Why not?" Jax asked, only now aware he'd been thinking about doing exactly that. He was tired of evading her questions about what he did for a living, tired of pretending he was something he was not. If he could get Marietta to accept she was pregnant by a pro wrestler, he could get her to accept anything. Even marriage.

"Why?" Drake laughed. "You're kidding, right? Think about it, Jax. That Secret Stud act of yours plays into every stereotype there is about a man not being able to stay faithful to one woman."

"It's just an act," Jax muttered, feeling it was more like an albatross around his neck pulling him deeper into a pit from which he couldn't escape.

Drake got up and slapped him on the shoulder. "You know that, and I know that, pal. But I don't think a professor who gets on NPR and talks about humans being genetically predisposed to mate-switch will see it that way."

He affected a sneer, lowering one corner of his mouth while his eyes nearly disappeared into his cheeks. "How's this for a demented look?"

"You look more like a bald, seriously upset Santa Claus than a demented dentist."

213

Drake's sneer disappeared, and his mouth drooped. "I do?"

"No, but it was fun telling you that," Jax said and suffered a serious attack of jealousy. He wished he could be the demented dentist brandishing the drill. Hell, at the moment, he'd leap at the chance to change places with one of UWA'S bottom-feeders, such as the wrestler who dressed in black, waved a pitchfork, and called himself the Dregs of the Underworld.

Anything would be better than being stuck acting like an immoral stud when he was trying to gain the trust of a woman who was going to have a devil of a time giving it.

Chapter Eighteen

Marietta's back didn't just hurt, it ached like a centipede with sore legs.

After work, she should have sat in a stiff-backed chair. Or done exercises to strengthen her abdominal muscles. Or, better yet, called Jax and griped. Expectant women complained to their men all the time, mostly because the men weren't the ones who got pregnant.

Except Marietta didn't have a telephone number for Jax, wouldn't ask Tracy for it, and had surrendered her inherent right to grumble when she'd discovered that Jax hadn't known she was angling to get pregnant.

So she'd stripped to her underwear, thrown on a nightgown, and crawled beneath the covers instead.

Now, an hour after she'd gotten into bed, not even the guilty prospect of the article on sexual cues and miscues she needed to finish for the *Biology Review* could drive her out of it. Especially since Tracy had indulged her with dinner in bed.

Now that the hubbub of finals week was over and her work schedule had slowed down considerably, she preferred to indulge herself by lying there in the semidarkness with the privacy of her thoughts. If nobody knew she was wondering when Jax would return from his endless business trip, nobody could attach any importance to her wondering.

A knock sounded at her half-open door. Tracy, no doubt.

"Come on in," she called and almost swallowed her tongue when the door swung the rest of the way open. Jax. Resplendent in chocolate-brown slacks and a cream dress shirt rolled up at the sleeves, baring his magnificent forearms. He'd loosened his tie and unfastened the first button of his shirt, which would have made him look like a sexy corporate rebel if it hadn't been for his extraordinary physique. Instead, he could have been a well-dressed poster boy for The Body Beautiful.

The distance from the bed to the door wasn't great enough to hide the way his symmetrical features warmed at the sight of her.

Her heart did a *boom-boom-boom* worthy of her unborn baby's quick metabolism, and the drabness of the last two weeks disappeared, replaced by vibrant color. He leaned against the door frame, hooked a thumb in the pocket of his slacks and grinned. "Hi."

She should ask what he was doing in her bedroom or at least tell him he needed to call before popping in. She should order him away with a finger as straight as a hunting dog's tail. She shouldn't, under any circumstances, smile at him.

"Hi," she said, feeling the corners of her mouth lift skyward. In response, his grin got bigger. Something was curiously off-kilter about it, but it was still so dazzling that she didn't bother to try to figure out what it was. "Tracy let me in on her way to the grocery store." He straightened, gestured with one of his big, well-shaped hands. "Mind if I come in?"

Her gaze snagged on his hand, which she imagined stroking her naked skin in that silky way she couldn't forget. Her

The Misconception

breath caught. "You want to get in bed with me?"

He laughed, showing his perfect teeth. "Actually, I do, but I was asking if I could come in your room."

Feeling foolish, Marietta scrambled to a sitting position, frantically finger-combing her hair. She should tell him that of course she minded, that they weren't on intimate enough terms that he'd be any more welcome in her bedroom than in her bed.

"No, I don't mind," she heard herself say.

Jax walked toward her in the easy way he had of moving, not quite a strut but not the walk of a mere mortal either. His steps were longer, his gait so smooth it seemed he moved to a rhythm playing in his head. If the rhythm were from a show tune, she'd guess one of the upbeat, sexy songs from *West Side Story*.

Her bedroom was decidedly feminine, with lace curtains, pine furniture, and an off-white color scheme softened by coral-hued accents. Jax looked large and potently male inside of it, but somehow he also managed to look as though he belonged. Inches from her bed, he stopped. Then she realized his mouth was no longer symmetrical. "Do you have a fat lip?"

He rubbed the puffy part of his lower lip, which had thrown his mouth slightly off balance. "It's not quite fat. Plump, maybe. But not fat."

"How'd you get it?"

"Don't know. Probably bumped into something," he said absently, which wasn't a satisfactory answer. She meant to question him further, but then he slowly lowered his head, and she went a little dizzy.

She shut her eyes and got ready for the onslaught of his lips, telling herself she should stop him but knowing she wouldn't. A sensation of brightness penetrated her closed eyelids, which didn't square with ordinary biological responses, meaning she'd need him to kiss her more often so she could research the phenomenon.

Except he didn't kiss her at all. She opened one eye, then the next, and her pupils constricted. The lamp. He'd switched on the bedside lamp, throwing the previously dark room into brilliance.

"What do lightning bugs yell before they take off?"

She squinted at him. "Excuse me?"

"Lightning bugs," he answered as though it were perfectly logical for him to walk into her bedroom after an absence of fifteen days and start talking about lightning bugs. "What do they yell before they take off?"

"I didn't know lightning bugs could talk."

Jax frowned. "Well, they can't. But, if they could, what would they yell before they took off?"

She didn't answer, so he did. "All systems glow!"

She waited until he stopped laughing, thinking about what had just happened. She'd thought he intended to kiss her and instead . . . "Was that a joke?"

"Of course it was a joke. It was funny, wasn't it?"

She didn't answer, not that he seemed to expect her to. He patted the bed beside her. "May I?"

Before she could ask may he what, he lowered himself onto the bed. The mattress compressed under his weight, throwing her thigh against his side. She inhaled sharply at the contact, and scooted away so they weren't touching. This close, she could smell him, an intoxicating blend of shampoo, soap, and man. Pheromones at work.

"What's wrong?" he asked.

"Wrong?" She considered the soft light of concern in his eyes. Since he'd come back into her life, she'd made a point of being honest with him. She didn't see any reason to stop now. "I wasn't comfortable with the rush of sexual arousal that occurred when my thigh touched your side, so I moved away."

His brown eyes brightened, the lines around his mouth deepened and he laughed. He tapped her on the nose. "Has anyone ever told you how cute you are?"

Marietta shook her head, eyeing him suspiciously. She was an expert in evolutionary biology who dressed in tweed suits, wore little makeup, and kept careful rein on her hair. Cute was not the image she was trying to cultivate. Her hand flew to her hair as she remembered taking out the pins before getting into bed. She found it long and loose, just the way it had been in that hotel room months ago when they'd indulged in mating bliss.

"It's the hair, isn't it?"

"What's the hair?"

"The reason you said I was cute. Nobody's ever said that to me."

He laughed again, captured a lock of her hair and twirled it around his finger, holding her to him in silken bondage. This time, he kissed her on the cheek before letting the hair unwind. "Then nobody's taken a good look at you. With your hair down like that and wearing that piece-of-nothing nightgown, you look like a cute sex goddess."

"Now you're teasing me."

"The way you blush is cute, too." He touched cheeks that she knew had gone hot, a reaction she wasn't sure whether to attribute to embarrassment or the sexual tumult brought about by his nearness. "Now are you going to tell me what's wrong?"

"I already told you. I wasn't comfortable with the rush of sexual—"

"I wasn't asking why you moved away from me, silly. I was asking why you're in bed at eight o'clock at night."

"Oh, that," she said, trying to sound offhand. Considering her face felt as red as a chameleon hitching a ride on a fire engine, she couldn't be fooling him.

Her response elicited another grin. "Yes, that."

"It's nothing. Just a backache."

No sooner had she said the words than the mattress sprang back into place. She gazed up in shock as Jax, who'd just returned, prepared to leave. Disappointment swirled through her like windblown snow in a blizzard. She tried to bank it, but couldn't. "Where are you going?"

He gave her a cheeky look over his shoulder. "Are you saying you want me to stay?"

"No," she said quickly, then realized he might misconstrue her answer as meaning she wanted him to leave. "It's only that you just arrived. You haven't told me anything about your trip."

"You want to know about my trip?"

"Well . . ." Marietta paused, considering his question. The answer she came up with almost knocked her back on the pillows. "I suppose I do."

"Hold that thought," he said and strode out of the room. Marietta watched him go, her hands on her hips. Of all the nerve! Striding into her bedroom; casually brushing her thigh with his big, sexy body; neglecting to do more than buss her on the cheek; and striding back out.

Ten minutes later, when he strode back into her bedroom, this time without knocking, she was still quietly fuming. Until she saw what he was carrying. "Is that a heating pad?"

"Uh, huh. I used the microwave, but it still took me a while to warm it up." He came closer to the bed. "Now lean forward."

She did, and he propped the heating pad behind her back. Soothing warmth immediately assailed her, chasing away the dull ache. She closed her eyes, savoring the feeling. When she opened them, he was studying her. She couldn't help but smile at him. She didn't even want to try not to. "Thank you."

"You're welcome." He sank back down on the bed. This time, when her thigh brushed his side, she didn't move. Instead, she luxuriated as the same delicious warmth that spread through her back moved from her leg to the rest of her body, although this time the cause of the warmth was strictly sexual. "I want to thank you, too," he said.

The Misconception

"For what?"

"I listened to you on *All Things Considered*." He paused. "I was prepared to hear you say that babies don't need their fathers, but you didn't. I wondered why."

She could tell him the omission was coincidental, but she wouldn't lie. She owed it to him to try to be honest, even though she was still sorting out her thoughts on the subject.

"I didn't think, under the circumstances, that it would have been the right thing to do." She paused, looked down at the bed, cleared her throat. "The males in some species of animals share the raising of their young with the females. After the female emperor penguin hatches her egg, for example, she goes in search of food and leaves the male holding the egg for nine weeks."

He grinned, brushed his knuckles against her cheek. "In our case, I think maybe you better send me off in search of the food. I wouldn't know what to do with your egg."

"Of course you wouldn't," she answered, refusing to be charmed. "The emperor penguin has a fur-lined pouch on his feet. You don't. My point is that Father Penguin helps with the feeding and care after the baby is born as well."

He tipped her chin up so she had to look at him. "Are you trying to say you think I'd make as good a father as a penguin?"

She swallowed, bit her lip, thought about that. Then she nodded. Very slowly, he kissed his fingers, pressed them against her lips, and smiled. "Thank you, again."

"You're welcome, again," she whispered, fighting the urge to grab him by the shoulders and pull his mouth to hers. Geez. What did a girl have to do to get a kiss?

"This doesn't mean I agree with what you said in that interview," he continued, as though he wasn't thinking about kissing her at all. "I don't believe men are as prone to infidelity as you think."

Marietta stopped thinking about kissing him. Instead, she thought of her former boyfriends, of Ryan Caminetti, of her father. "Yes," she said firmly, "they are."

Darlene Gardner

He kept his eyes steady on hers. "I haven't slept with anyone else since I've met you."

Something joyous leapt in Marietta, but she squashed it. She needed to think logically; bio-logically, to be specific.

"You're talking about short-term fidelity. What I think is impossible is long-term fidelity."

The night before he'd left for his business trip, he asked who'd hurt her, and she refused to answer. Now, he didn't say anything, and that very fact pierced her armor. She took a deep breath. Then she took a chance.

"All through high school, I had this great boyfriend named Bobby Lancer. He used to write me love poems and leave little surprises in my locker. On the night of the senior prom, I thought we were the perfect couple. Bobby wore a white tuxedo, and I had on this bubblegum-pink dress with my hair swept into this sophisticated updo. Before the night was over, I found him, without the tuxedo, in the back seat of my car with Betty Jo Kowalski."

She took a breath, stared down at her hands. Now that she'd started, he might as well hear the rest. "I was careful not to get serious about anybody for a long time. Then, in my junior year of college, I let another biology major talk me into moving in with him. I actually thought a love of biology was a positive trait until I caught him indulging it with a hot little number in our bed."

She glanced up at him for a reaction and saw empathy on his face. "They were boys, Marietta," he said. "Not men."

The bitterness she always tried so hard to bank spilled into her voice. "My father wasn't a boy, and for ten years he met Elvira Thorton at the Ramada Inn every Wednesday afternoon. On Mondays, he met Liz Applegate. I ran into him with different women so many times I can't even re-member all of them."

Jax reached out and took her hand, but she was so lost in the past that she barely noticed. "He used to call my mother his best girl and tell her how much he loved her.

She always believed his flimsy excuses when he wasn't home on time or when he'd miss some important family event. She might have kept on lying to herself about how he was spending his time if he hadn't had a heart attack and died when he was in bed with another woman."

He didn't say anything, but squeezed her hand, prompting her to go on. "When she was free of him, I thought she'd finally be able to live a little, to enjoy herself. But she died six months later of a brain aneurysm."

She brushed rough fingers over the tears on her cheeks, angered that her father's philandering still hurt years after she'd determined the biological reasoning behind his acts.

"What happened to your parents is terrible," Jax said softly. "But just because your father was unfaithful doesn't mean all men are unfaithful."

"Oh, come on." Marietta jerked her hand back from his. "Then let's talk about *your* father. Was *he* faithful to your mother?"

Jax dropped his head and didn't raise it for long moments. His brown eyes were flat, his expression as serious as she'd ever seen it. "I never knew my father. I don't even know his name."

His pain came through louder than the mating call of a bellowing alligator. Ignoring it was impossible. She reached out, stroked his cheek, took *his* hand. "I'm . . . I'm sorry."

"Yeah, me, too. I used to cry myself to sleep when I was a little kid. I couldn't understand why I didn't have a father like everybody else. Later, when I got older, I played sports. I'd look into the stands at every game, watching the other fathers cheer for their sons. Every time, I'd think that maybe my dad would show up to cheer for me. He never did. Even if he had, I wouldn't have recognized him. To this day, I don't know what he looks like."

"But I thought you had younger brothers," Marietta said, no longer afraid to show that she was interested.

"They're my half-brothers. We have the same mother, but different fathers. Not that theirs was much better than mine. He only stayed around long enough to get my mother pregnant twice in a little more than a year." Jax paused. "Billy's nineteen, and Drew's eighteen. That bastard who abandoned them missed out on seeing two great kids grow up."

Marietta could barely speak over the lump in her throat, because now she knew why he was so insistent on being part of their baby's life. He didn't understand that having a father in the home didn't ensure a happy childhood, because he didn't know his father. Not only had he been abandoned himself, but he'd watched two brothers grow up without a father. Two brothers he obviously adored.

"Tracy told me you went to Drew's high school graduation."

He smiled, turned over her palm, traced circles on it with his index finger. "I did. The day before the party, Drew got a letter of acceptance from MIT. He was so thrilled, he couldn't sit still. Every once in a while, he'd just let out a whoop."

Marietta smiled, picturing the boy. "He must be pretty bright to get accepted into MIT as a freshman."

"He is," Jax said, pride evident in his voice, "although sometimes I think he's too smart for his own good. Billy's smart, too. If you show him a plant, any plant, he can identify it. He's at Michigan State."

"Aaah. A scientist in the making."

"Yeah. He's one after your own heart. At this point in his life, I'm pretty sure he embraces that whole sex-without-love thing."

She didn't laugh, but her lips twitched.

"I don't envy your mother, having two boys in college at the same time," Marietta said, thinking of the spiraling tuition costs at Kennedy College. "What does she do?"

The Misconception

"Cooks, bakes, cleans, sews, gardens, cans, and worries about us. I'm always telling her to take it easy, but she's worked so hard all her life that I don't think she can."

Jax told Marietta more with what he hadn't said than with what he had. His mother was obviously no longer working outside the home. Neither of the men who fathered her children had stuck around to help her out, so that meant Jax had. If he'd helped out his mother, that probably meant he was helping his brothers, too.

"You're the reason your mother doesn't have to work, aren't you? I'll bet you're putting your brothers through college, too." Jax didn't answer right away, giving Marietta time to form another insight. "That's why you work so hard."

Jax shrugged his impressive shoulders. "Anybody in my position would do the same thing."

He was wrong, of course. Marietta didn't know many men who would take on the financial responsibility of their brothers as well as their mother. Jax truly didn't know how remarkable that made him.

"Why didn't you tell me about your brothers and your mother before?" Marietta asked after a moment. "Why did you tell Tracy that you were going to Drew's graduation and not me?"

He brought her palm to his lips and kissed it, sending delicious little shudders over her skin. "I didn't think you'd be interested."

"Not interested in my baby's grandmother and her uncles? The baby will be genetically related to your family, so it seems to me information about them will only benefit me."

One corner of his mouth lifted. "You won't let up, will you?"

She looked at him under her lashes. "I don't know what you mean."

"You won't admit that you're interested in my family, because you're interested in me."

"Of course I'm interested in you," she said, completely ignoring what she knew he meant. "You're the direct genetic link to our baby." She paused. "What are you grinning about?"

He squeezed her hand. "That's the first time you've said *our* baby."

"It is?"

"It is. Does this mean you're going to give us a chance?"

"It means," Marietta said slowly, "that I'm going to let you take me out to dinner tomorrow night."

His mouth fell in what looked like genuine disappointment. "I'd love to, but I can't. I'm flying out of town tomorrow afternoon."

"But you just got back!"

"My job's demanding, Marietta. I have to be on the road a lot."

"What kind of job—"

Before she guessed what he intended, he closed the distance between them and kissed her. She'd been thinking about this mouth-to-mouth contact far too often since the last time he'd kissed her to stop him. Even though his lips weren't operating on all symmetrical cylinders, the reality was even better than the fantasy. His mouth, even the slightly plump part, was soft and insistent against hers.

The heating pad slipped when she leaned forward to get closer to him, but she ignored it, opening her mouth and inviting his tongue to slip inside. He took the invitation as one of his hands tangled in her hair, and the other moved restlessly over her diaphanous nightgown until it cupped her breast.

Her nipples tautened, a hot ball of desire formed deep within her and her breath mingled with his. His mouth left hers to trail kisses over her cheek, along her jawline, into her neck. She reveled in the scratchy feel of his emerging beard against her smooth skin, of his hands on her body.

Then, maddeningly, he stopped. He lowered his hands until they rested on her waist, and lifted his head so his forehead leaned weakly against hers. She cried out in protest and tried to pull his mouth back to hers, but he put his fingers to her lips and traced the dark smudges under her eyes.

"There's nothing I'd like more than to make love to you all night and have breakfast, lunch, and dinner with you tomorrow, but I'm not so much of a cad that I'd take advantage of a tired, pregnant woman with a backache."

"My back doesn't hurt that much anymore."

He laughed, pressing a quick kiss to her lips. "As much as I'd like to believe that, I don't."

She was about to protest when her back began to throb again, surprising her. For long moments, the only ache she'd felt had nothing to do with her back.

"Tell you what," he said. "I'll take you to breakfast tomorrow morning and drive you to work. Then, on Monday when I get back, I'll take a raincheck. On everything." He caressed the side of her cheek and looked deeply into her eyes so she couldn't mistake his meaning. "Deal?"

She didn't hesitate in answering, because, in the last half-hour, she'd realized something amazing. She didn't just desire him. She liked him, too.

"Deal," she said, and they both smiled.

Chapter Nineteen

The Put Up With Us Players performed in a strip shopping center in Arlington in a space Marietta remembered as having once contained a shop for wild-bird lovers. The owner, who'd flown the coop after barely a year in business, must have concluded the feathered trade was truly for the birds.

As Marietta sat stiffly in a seat at a one-hundred-twenty-degree angle to the stage, she thought whoever designed the seating had done it with the flying critters in mind. Anybody else was in danger of getting a nosebleed.

Marietta supposed the towering perches made sense, considering that was the only way to jam seating for a hundred into the cramped space. Twenty minutes before showtime, however, the theater was barely half full.

Tracy had warned her the performances of the Put Up With Us Players didn't appeal to a mainstream audience, but she'd hoped the oddballs in the area would turn out.

Heaven knew there were enough of them. Why, just today, Vicky Valenzuela, president of the FOCs, had stopped by her office to ask her to autograph pictures of female elephants. Vicky had adopted the animal as a mascot for her organization after hearing Marietta talk about their independence from their male counterparts.

Marietta hoped Vicky didn't hire a live one for their next rally. She could picture it now. The pixie-sized feminist and the mammoth mammal.

If she'd known the theater would be so empty, she would have asked Vicky if she and the FOCs enjoyed improvisational theater. Chances are the title of the play would have frightened them away, though. How many people wanted to spend their time on a play that proclaimed itself *Insignificant*?

Another theater-goer entered the building, which Marietta viewed as a good thing until she saw it was Ryan Caminetti, looking darkly handsome in a long-sleeved khaki-colored shirt and worn jeans. Scanning the selection of available seats, his dark eyes fell on hers and locked.

Once upon a time, before he'd wronged Tracy, they'd enjoyed many evenings engaged in lively debate. Marietta didn't agree with Ryan about much, but always found his opinions informative and interesting. She'd even considered him to be a friend.

She hoped he would heed her stony stare and find a seat elsewhere, but knew he wouldn't. Ryan had never backed down from an argument. He wouldn't dodge a confrontation. He climbed the steps toward her, his lips curved in greeting.

"Hey, Marietta. Mind if I join you?" he asked, settling into the vacant seat beside her before she could answer that yes, she did mind. She shifted away from him and gave a brief nod.

"Ryan."

His Adam's apple bobbed as he swallowed, his jaw tightened, and she knew she was making him uncomfortable. She was perversely glad. She certainly wasn't going to try to make things easier on him.

"I haven't congratulated you yet on your pregnancy," he said after a moment. "I think it's terrific news."

She gave him a sharp look. "How do you know I'm pregnant?"

His dark eyebrows rose, calling attention to his equally dark eyes. His features missed being symmetrical by a few centimeters here and there, but he was still a very good-looking man. No wonder Tracy was still hung up on him. "Tracy told me. Is that a problem?"

It was, but there was nothing she could do about it now. "It's not common knowledge."

"I won't tell anyone, if that's what you're worried about."

"I'm not worried. I know you're not a gossip." She paused, because it had pained her to admit anything favorable about his character. "I just don't want people to know I'm pregnant yet."

"I bet that's hard on Jax. He probably feels like handing out cigars already. I know I would."

She blew out a breath. "You know about Jax, too."

"Why shouldn't I know about Jax? You and he are involved, aren't you?"

She didn't immediately respond, unsure of how to answer that. Yes, Jax was the man who'd gotten her pregnant. Yes, he lived next door. And, yes, she was considering sleeping with him again. Looking at it that way, she supposed there was only one answer she could give.

"Yes," she said. "I guess we are involved."

Ryan nodded, as though he'd known it all along. "Where is he? I would have thought he'd be here."

"He wanted to be here," Marietta said slowly as her brain worked. Since Ryan knew so much about Jax, did that mean Tracy was spending more time with her soon-to-be ex-husband than she'd let on? "He's out of town on business until Monday."

"He's a great guy, your Jax. Really funny, too. I bet he keeps you laughing."

230

Marietta's brows furrowed. "Are you sure we're talking about the same man? He tells the worst jokes. I don't think he knows a funny one."

"He must not have told you about the worn-out tires ending up on skid row. Or the refrigerator humming because it doesn't know the words." Mysteriously, Ryan chuckled.

"Actually, he has," Marietta said, then pinned him with a direct look. "What are you doing, Ryan?"

He returned her stare. "I'm waiting for the play to begin."

"That's not what I meant, and you know it. What are you doing back in Tracy's life? She was getting along just fine without you. Having you hanging around is just confusing her."

His jaw clenched, his nostrils flared, and she remembered how stubborn he could be. "Maybe I think she needs to be confused."

"What kind of statement is that? Your divorce will be final in a month. Tracy doesn't need you around jeopardizing that."

"I'm not the one who wanted the divorce," he said tightly. "I still don't want it."

"I knew it." Marietta shook her head in disgust. "I knew you were trying to get her back, but Tracy thinks you just want to be friends. How'd you manage that?"

"I do want to be her friend." He paused, and she could tell by the strain on his face that he wanted so much more. "If she can't bring herself to trust me, I'll have to accept that friends are all we can be."

"Trust you? How can she trust you after what we saw in that hotel lobby?"

Marietta expected shame to come into his eyes. To her surprise, she saw anger instead.

"Did you ever consider," he asked in a low, furious voice, "that you were wrong about what you saw in that lobby? Did it ever occur to you that maybe that woman invited me to have lunch at the hotel because she wanted to get me into bed?"

She hadn't considered it then. She wouldn't be gullible enough to consider it now. "So now you're going to tell me it didn't work?"

"Yes," Ryan said, and there was force behind the word. "That's exactly what I'm telling you. I'm guilty of being naive, but that's all I'm guilty of. You saw her kissing me. If you'd stuck around, you would have seen me stop her."

The image of Jax thrusting away the buxom, beautiful drunk the other night at Paddy's Pub sprang to Marietta's mind. If she had walked away a moment sooner, she would have believed the worst of him, just as she and Tracy had believed the worst of Ryan. For the first time, a sliver of doubt chipped away at Marietta's consciousness. Logic warred with it.

Man's propensity to stray was a scientific fact. She still couldn't quite believe that Jax hadn't known she was behind him when he'd rebuffed the woman just as she couldn't believe that Ryan was telling the truth. Especially since he'd rendezvoused with the woman at a hotel instead of a restaurant.

"So you make a habit of meeting amorous women for lunch at hotels?"

"She was a client who said she wanted to discuss the house I was building for her. She said she was staying at the hotel, because she was having problems with her husband. How was I supposed to know what she had in mind?"

"Oh, please." The doubt was mushrooming, but Marietta ignored it and made her voice heavy with sarcasm. "I'm a biologist, remember? A man doesn't turn away an attractive woman offering sex. Especially when he's the one who registered for the room."

He leaned closer, narrowing the gap between their faces. "I didn't do that, either. She used my name on the registration form, hoping I'd foot the bill for her room. When it comes to sex, she thinks the man should pay."

Marietta didn't reply, because, even though it sounded logical, what Ryan was saying couldn't possibly be true. Men were predisposed to stray. Hadn't she seen enough examples of that in her life? Hadn't her own father proved that?

"I don't know why I wasted my breath telling you that," Ryan said, shaking his head and sounding resigned as he leaned back in his seat. "Just do one thing for me, Marietta. Don't tell Tracy what we talked about."

"Don't tell her?" Marietta repeated. "I would have thought that *explanation* is something you'd want her to hear."

"What I want," Ryan said, "is for Tracy to ask me what happened that day and to reach her own conclusions."

Marietta started to ask what he meant by that, but the question fled her mind when she caught sight of a very large man walking up the creaky steps toward them. A very large, very symmetrical man who was thrown off balance by the white sling encasing his left arm.

"Jax," she mouthed, as new questions flooded her brain.

Across the distance, Jax grinned. The circumstances weren't ideal and the theater was nothing more than a stage and some rickety chairs, but he was headed exactly where he wanted to be. With Marietta.

Her brown-blond hair was back in its customary bun, and she was wearing a god-awful shade of green that did unflattering things to her skin. His libido hummed to attention. Cripes, she was sexy.

"Ryan, my man," he said when he reached their row, slapping the other man on the shoulder. "Could you let me through, pal? No offense, but she's prettier than you are."

Ryan, who was sitting in the seat closest to the aisle, returned his greeting and did as he asked. Marietta scooted over one seat, making room for him.

Darlene Gardner

"Did you break your arm?" Marietta asked before he could sit down, her multicolored eyes wide. Jax appreciated the concern, but dreaded the curiosity. He took his time settling into his seat, hoping he could get through the next few minutes.

"Hello, Marietta," he said, leaning over and kissing her. Her mouth went soft and welcoming. Her brain, unfortunately, stayed sharp. As soon as he broke off the kiss, she repeated the question.

"Did you break your arm?"

"It's my shoulder, and it's not broken. Just dislocated."

Marietta gasped. "You dislocated your shoulder selling stocks and bonds?"

"Of course not." Jax had a story ready, but he didn't want to tell it. Instead, he wished he could confide that he'd instinctively stretched out his arm to break his fall when Raving Maniac had slammed him to the mat with too much gusto.

"Then how did you do it?" The question came from Ryan, who was supposed to be his friend. Jax rolled his eyes. He was dying here. Didn't Ryan realize he didn't need this kind of pressure?

"Jax? How did you do it?" Marietta pressed when he didn't answer. Her eyes were soft with concern as she laid her small hand on his uninjured shoulder. The truth bubbled on his lips, but then he thought of how she'd react if she discovered he was the Secret Stud. He sighed aloud. And lied.

"In the gym when I was working out. I tried to lift too much weight. It's nothing. I have to wear the sling for a while, but it'll be good as new in a couple of weeks."

"But—"

"Shh," he interrupted as the lights dimmed. "The play's about to start."

He settled back in his seat, hoping she wouldn't take up the conversation later. He slung his good arm around her

234

shoulder and gave it an affectionate squeeze. Instead of batting it away, she turned and smiled at him. Guilt rose up in him like floodwater.

Damn, but he hated lying to her. Every time she brought up his job, his conscience screamed at him to tell her the truth. But how could he when she'd made perfectly clear what she thought of pro wrestling? How could he confide in her after the things she'd said about the Secret Stud?

Maybe it wouldn't be so bad if he shed the stud act and took up another. She might be more approving of something casting him as a savior, such as the Say-No-to-Drugs Dude or the Taboo-on-Tobacco Man. He might even be able to dream up an act throwing infidelity in a bad light.

He frowned. He wasn't only dreaming, he was stuck. Due to the long-running success of the Secret Stud, he ought to have some clout with the UWA brass. Yesterday, when he'd sent Star Bright to negotiate a change of acts, he discovered that he didn't.

The UWA wasn't about to let go of a proven crowd-pleaser. In fact, Lance Strong, the president of the UWA, was determined to give the fans more of what they wanted. According to the unscientific exit polls the league regularly ran, what they wanted was to see the Secret Stud unmasked. What Lance Strong wanted was an unmasking during the pay-per-view anniversary extravaganza, which unfortunately was scheduled after Jax's shoulder would be healed.

Jax had adamantly refused. He wasn't naive enough to believe the UWA wouldn't milk all the publicity from the unmasking it could get. A person as savvy about current events as Marietta would hear about it, especially if the mainstream press ran a photo of him. Unmasked, he might as well kiss his chances of becoming Marietta's husband good-bye.

She snuggled closer to him, and he got a whiff of shampoo. Not anything that smelled of flowers, papaya, or any of a myriad of other scents the shampoo industry was always promoting, but something simple and clean. Her shampoo was as straightforward as she was, as straightforward as he didn't have the courage to be.

Down on the stage, the curtains opened. Tracy and another man, both dressed entirely in black and white, appeared. Jax's eyes went instantly to the white top hat on Tracy's head, probably because of the contrast between the hat and her hair, which seemed to have been dipped in an inkwell.

"Why did Tracy do that to her hair?" he whispered to Marietta.

"It's a mood thing," she whispered back, which made absolutely no sense to Jax. Then again, even though Tracy had always seemed sensible to him, she *was* related to Marietta.

Nobody talked on stage, amplifying the occasional cough and fidget from the audience. The man next to Tracy stood absolutely still. Then, very slowly, very deliberately, with slow, staccato movements, Tracy removed the hat. Just as slowly, and just as jerkily, she examined it.

"What's she doing?" Jax whispered into Marietta's ear as, bit by bit, Tracy moved the hat toward a utilitarian pine table.

"She's taking off her hat and laying it on the table."

"I know that, but why is she doing that?"

Marietta shook her head, as obviously confused as he was. "This is experimental theater. Who knows why they do what they do?"

Beside them, Ryan leaned forward and put a finger to his lips. "Shhhh."

Jax looked back on stage, thinking he must have been missing something to warrant a *shhhh*. Tracy was removing a wristwatch with the same frustrating slowness.

He glanced back at Ryan, whose expression was rapt, causing Jax to wonder whether he thought Tracy was performing some sort of slow-motion striptease. At this rate, it'd be Christmas before the guy saw any skin.

A long while later, with the watch finally deposited on the table, the male actor spent an agonizing amount of time loosening his tie.

"What's he doing now?" Jax asked Marietta a few minutes later, close enough to her ear that he breathed in her scent.

"He was taking off his tie five minutes ago when I closed my eyes."

Jax laughed, Marietta elbowed him, and Ryan shushed them again. Jax supposed that was because, on stage, Tracy was getting into the act again. The man, sans tie, was making a pointed show of handing it to Tracy, who Jax supposed would deposit it on the table with the other items.

He wondered what the rest of the audience members would do if he stood up and yelled, "Would you just put the blasted tie down?"

Eons later, when the crew members pulled out a large white screen and the shadow dancers got behind it, Jax was already resigned to a long evening.

He entertained himself by playing with the hair that had gotten loose from Marietta's bun, expecting to get a slap on the hand. Instead she nestled against him, and he wondered if the craziness on stage had transferred itself to Marietta.

The small smile she gave him heated his blood, and he was insanely glad he was sitting next to her at the worst play he'd ever attended. Even if it had taken a separated shoulder and a forced vacation from pro wrestling to get him here.

The Old Town Alexandria nightspot known as Chrome and Mirrors was as far removed from the community's quaint streets as a peacock from a skinned chicken. Whereas the rest of the Old Town strove to keep the past alive, the Chrome and Mirrors resembled Jax's idea of a future gone glimmer mad.

Everything inside the place glinted. The chrome accents on the long, sleek bar and the solid chrome legs of the tall stools reflected off the diamond-patterned floor. Wall-to-wall mirrors enhanced the effect, nearly blinding Jax with chrome.

He drummed his fingers on the shiny chrome of the table separating him and Ryan from Tracy and Marietta, worrying about the effects of secondhand smoke on pregnant women and their unborn babies. They were in a booth at the back of the bar, away from the handful of smokers, but still he worried.

Across the booth, Marietta caught and held his eyes. She was different tonight, somehow softer and infinitely more approachable. He wanted her away from the smoke, but mostly he just wanted her. So how had he ended up sitting next to Ryan instead of beside Marietta?

Tracy fiddled with the skinny straw in her gin and tonic, looking anywhere but at Ryan, providing Jax with the answer. Tracy had practically dragged Marietta into her side of the booth, because she hadn't wanted to sit next to Ryan. Jax didn't want to sit next to him, either. He liked Ryan a lot, but their side of the booth was so full, it'd be grounds for assault and battery if either of them moved an elbow.

"You were great, Trace." Ryan reiterated what had become a familiar refrain since *Insignificant?* had come to a merciful end. "I especially liked the way you picked up that penny during the shadow dance."

Tracy glanced up at Ryan and just as quickly looked away. Considering heat had risen off the two of them the last time Jax had seen them together, he wondered why she was keeping her distance. "You knew I was picking up a penny?"

"Of course I did," Ryan said. "It was obvious."

No, Jax thought, it wasn't. He'd thought she lost a contact lens. Either that or she was in the early stages of keeling over from boredom.

The Misconception

"Speaking of obvious," Jax said, fishing, "how about the meaning of the play?"

A smile shadowed Tracy's mouth. "Yeah, wasn't that something? I wasn't sure the audience would get it, but I'm glad you did, Jax."

"I did?"

Tracy nodded. "It's a simple concept, but difficult to grasp. That every item, no matter how small, has significance."

"Oh, right," Jax said, finally understanding. Sort of. Across from him, Marietta's laughing eyes met his, telling him she knew he hadn't a clue what the play was about before Tracy told him. He winked at her, and her eyes laughed harder.

"I thought it was very clever," Ryan said. Tracy reacted to his compliment by squirming in her seat, which Jax took as the perfect opening to lighten the atmosphere with a joke. Not that he ever needed much reason to tell one.

"Speaking of clever, here's one for you. What would you do if a five-hundred pound gorilla sat in front of you during a play?"

Ryan was already starting to grin, reminding Jax of one of the reasons he liked him so much. "What?" he asked, giving Jax a pleasant surprise. When he was telling a joke, most people didn't participate.

"Miss most of the play."

Ryan laughed so hard he slapped his thigh, then he slapped Jax's, which, after all, was only an inch or so from his. Jax joined in, wondering how Tracy had ever let a great guy like Ryan go. Neither of them stopped laughing until a short, burly man appeared at their table, glaring at Marietta.

"You're that sex professor, aren't you? Dalrumple something or other," he said in an overly loud voice. His shirt sleeves were rolled up to reveal more dark hair than was atop his head. His jaw was beefy, his mouth slack with drink. While he waited for her answer, he swayed.

239

"It's Dr. Dalrymple," Marietta corrected, her chin high. "And I'm a biologist specializing in matters related to sex and evolution."

"You have the damn stupidest ideas I've ever heard," he spit out. "What do they call you? A bio-dummy?"

"Hey, watch your mouth." Jax's temper spiraled like a tornado. He usually left his aggression in the ring, but damn if he didn't want to pound the other man's face. "You owe the lady an apology."

"The bitch owes me an apology," the man shouted. "Where do you get off telling pregnant women they don't need a man around? Huh? What right do you have talking fucking nonsense like that?"

"It's not nonsense—" Marietta began, but Jax cut her off by rising to his feet and standing chin to chest with the smaller man. He nearly growled as the man's eyes traveled upward and filled with fear.

"Didn't you hear me?" he asked in a low, menacing tone. "You owe the lady an apology."

Nobody, and he meant nobody, was going to call the woman he loved a bitch. The thought stopped him cold, and his knees nearly buckled. The woman he loved. He loved Marietta.

He supposed he should have recognized the signs, starting with that lightning bolt that had struck him through the heart the first time he'd seen her. But, as infuriating as Marietta was, the bolt had been easy to dismiss.

Still, he should have realized he was in the market for more than a baby when he'd moved next door to her, when he'd lain awake remembering the exhilaration of making love to her, when he'd found himself admiring a brain that thoroughly confounded him. When he hadn't been interested in any of those come-hither women he used to find so desirable.

"Come on, man." The pleading voice seemed to come from a great distance, and it took Jax a moment to realize it was coming from the smaller man. "You can't agree with that shit—" Jax recovered his bearings and glared. "I mean that *stuff* she says. She's telling women we have no more control than animals."

At the moment, Jax's control was stretched so tight he wished he were an animal. Then he'd have an excuse to tear into the man.

"Dr. Dalrymple is not only brilliant, but she's spent years researching her ideas and forming her opinions. She deserves respect, and you're going to give it to her. Right now."

The man looked as though he was about to say something else, then apparently thought better of it. He stammered an apology and disappeared into the crowd. Jax's insides shook with the discovery he'd just made. He looked down at Marietta, wondering if she could see it on his face. "You okay?"

She didn't say anything, which answered his question. Her face was white, and she looked as shaken as he felt, making him think the last place a pregnant woman needed to be was a semismoky bar with professor-bashing patrons. He reached for her hand, and she let him take it.

"Sorry to cut the evening short, but I'm taking Marietta out of here," Jax told Ryan and Tracy as he helped Marietta out of the booth. A roomful of pro wrestlers intent on committing carnage couldn't have stopped him from leaving with the woman he loved.

"Go," Ryan said, barely refraining from helping Jax along with a push. All evening, he'd been plotting to get Tracy alone. The perfect opportunity had presented itself, and he was going to seize it. "Go, and don't worry about us."

After uttering a couple of quick goodnights, they were gone. Ryan's eagerness at getting Tracy alone wasn't reflected in her drawn, unhappy face. She looked at the salt-and-pepper shakers, at her nearly empty glass, at the vacant space in the booth across from him. Anywhere but at him.

Disappointment descended upon him like the curtain at the end of a play.

"I really should be leaving." Tracy started to scoot across the booth, and Ryan's disappointment turned to panic. She couldn't leave. Not when they were so close to putting things right again. Not when his happiness would leave with her. His hand shot out, trapping hers beneath it. She immediately stilled.

"Please don't go, Trace." His voice was pleading and so soft he barely recognized it. "At least, not until you tell me what's wrong."

"Nothing's wrong," she said automatically.

"I was married to you for fourteen months. Even if you hadn't dyed your hair black, I know you well enough to tell when something's wrong."

He looked down at the small, long-fingered hand under his, remembering how she'd once used it to transport him to the dizzying heights of passion. Now, she drew her hand out from under his and clenched it in her lap, breaking their connection.

"This isn't working, Ryan."

Her eyes finally rose, and they looked sad. He made himself ask the next question. "What's not working?"

"This . . . friendship." She indicated the two of them with the sweep of her hand. "I tried, but I can't do it anymore. I can't be your friend."

A fist clenched his heart and squeezed. "Is it something I did? I tried not to push you. I tried to give you space."

"No. It's nothing you did." Tracy shook her head, misery evident in her eyes. "It's just that . . . Well, it's too hard. We've been lovers, Ryan. I can't be around you without remembering how good it was to be with you that way."

Hope leaped in Ryan, brighter than a flaming torch. He'd taken more cold showers in the past month than in the rest of his life combined, but it was paying off. By not touching

Tracy, he'd shown her how difficult it was to live without his touch.

"Then be with me," he said simply.

"What?" Her head snapped up.

"We can be lovers again, Tracy, if that's what you want. It's what I want."

He saw her swallow, saw her consider the possibility, saw her reject it. "I can't."

"Why? Why can't you?" He pounded the table, caught himself, uncurled his fingers. "We're not divorced yet. You said yourself you still want me."

"I do," she cried, and tears shimmered in her eyes. "I do still want you, but that doesn't mean wanting you is smart. It doesn't mean wanting you is right."

"This is because you think I'll hurt you, isn't it?"

"You've already hurt me."

"Did I? Or did you hurt me?" Ryan wanted Tracy to believe in him enough, to trust him enough, to take it on faith that he wouldn't cheat on her. But maybe he was expecting too much. After all, he'd jumped to the wrong conclusion when she walked into Paddy's Pub with Jax. If Tracy asked what happened that day, maybe he should pull out all the stops to ensure she believe him. He took a chance by giving her a chance. "You never asked, Tracy, not once, about that day at the hotel."

"That's because I don't want to know." Tracy closed her eyes. He imagined her shutting her ears, too. "Seeing you with that woman hurt so much that I don't want to know the details."

"The details might change things."

Her eyes snapped open. "What, Ryan? What would they change? Nothing can change what I saw. I don't want to hear some explanation you've had almost a year to dream up. I don't want to hear anything about it at all."

Ryan stared down at the table. "That's your final word on the subject?"

He sensed her nod. "Yes. It's my final word."

"Then you're right. We shouldn't see each other anymore." He withdrew a few bills from his wallet and threw them on the table. "I'll sign the divorce papers and have my attorney mail them to you. You won't need to have any more contact with me."

He strode out of the bar, barely able to see because of the tears clouding his eyes. His heart felt as though it had been torn from his chest. He'd tried to be patient, tried to let Tracy see what kind of man he was, but she still didn't trust him.

This time, their marriage really was over.

Chapter Twenty

"There." Jax carried the tall glass into his leather-intensive family room and handed it to her. "One hot toddy, as promised."

Marietta stared down at the steaming white liquid, brought the cup to her nose and sniffed. Then she took a sip. "I thought a hot toddy had liquor in it."

Jax shrugged his good shoulder. "This one's a *virgin* hot toddy, made in honor of pregnant women who have been rudely accosted at tacky bars."

Because the shock of the confrontation had faded, she smiled at him and wrinkled her nose. "Pregnant women aren't virginal. Unless I'm mistaken, hot toddies are made with boiling water, not milk. I bet you didn't even put the sugar in."

He put up the hand that wasn't in a sling. "Guilty as charged. I thought a virgin hot toddy sounded more appetizing than a glass of warm milk."

She forced down a swallow of milk. He was being so sweet she was loath to tell him that she had begun to despise the white stuff. Her refrigerator was stocked with calcium-fortified orange juice, and she made a point of eating calcium-rich foods so she wouldn't have to drink more milk.

But tonight, after the way Jax had stuck up for her, she'd do just about anything for him. Including choking down a glass of milk. She might even moo if he asked.

She walked over to the mantel above his fireplace and picked up a photograph of two outrageously good-looking young men with the same flyaway blond hair. Jax's brothers. Billy and Drew. If you discounted their lofty cheekbones, they didn't much resemble Jax. Aside from the stunning symmetry of the halves of their faces, that is. Symmetry, it seemed, ran in the family.

"They're handsome, your brothers," she said, taking another sip of milk and barely refraining from gagging.

He nodded. "They're good kids, too. You'll like them."

He said it as though he didn't doubt she'd meet his brothers, as though her life had stopped running parallel to his and had converged with it. Exactly the way their lives had converged at the Chrome and Mirror when the drunk had insulted *her,* and *he* had taken it personally.

As though he cared about her. As though he had a stake in whatever happened to her. Deep in thought, she put the picture down.

"You do want to meet them, right?" He raised his perfect eyebrows, reminding her there was so much about their imperfect relationship they hadn't yet decided.

"Of course I do."

He reached out his unrestricted hand and laid two fingers on her lips. "Stop right there. Don't say you only want to meet them because they're related to our baby."

She gently removed his fingers and squeezed them. "I wasn't going to say that."

"You weren't?"

"No." She paused, wondering how best to bring up what was on her mind. "But there is something I'd like to ask you."

The Misconception

"I was kidding when I told you about Aunt Martha, Uncle Wilbur, and the insane asylum. Honest I was. As far as I know, the Jackson genes are top rate."

A smile tugged at the corners of her mouth. "I know you were kidding. This isn't about your family. It's about what you said to that man at the bar tonight." She paused, swallowed. "Did you mean it?"

His eyebrows rose, and he emitted a short breath. "Of course I did. I wasn't going to let him get away with insulting you like that."

"No. I meant the part where you said I was brilliant and that my ideas and opinions deserved respect. Did you mean that part?"

He didn't even hesitate. "Yes."

"But you don't agree with any of my ideas." She paced away from him to the opposite side of the room. "I'd even venture to say they drive you a little crazy."

His brow knotted. "That doesn't mean I don't respect them. It doesn't mean I don't think your ideas have some truth. It's when you take one of your general ideas and apply it to me specifically that I have a problem."

Curious, she paced back toward him. "Oh? Such as?"

"Such as that stuff you're always spouting about men being driven to spread their seed as widely as possible. On the surface, that's probably true. But it doesn't take into account the way a man changes once he's met the right woman." He took a step closer to her, and the air seemed thick with a warmth that enveloped her body and wrapped around her heart. "It doesn't take into account the way I've changed since I met you."

"How . . ." Marietta's voice broke on the word, so she had to start over. "How have you changed?"

"I don't want anybody but you. I can't see anybody but you." He removed the half-empty glass of milk from her trembling fingers. He set it on the mantle, never taking his eyes off hers. "You're in my blood, Marietta."

247

He picked up one of her hands and placed it on his chest. His heart beat strongly, erratically against her fingertips. Her eyes ran over his square jaw, sensuous mouth, and strong nose before stopping at his serious chocolate-brown eyes.

"You're in my heart, too," he whispered.

She didn't believe the heart was anything more than an organ pumping the blood necessary for life, but she couldn't deny the thrill that shot through her at his words. Her gaze fastened on his mouth, and she thought, at that moment, that her own heart would stop if he didn't kiss her.

He swallowed, licked his lips, and just kept staring at her with those hot, brown eyes, obviously waiting for a reply. But Marietta didn't want to talk. She didn't want to think. She just wanted to feel.

Anchoring a hand on his good shoulder and raising on her tiptoes, she kissed him. She drank in his taste, so heady she was drunk with pleasure from the mere act of putting her lips to his. Not able to help herself, she traced the beautiful line of his lips with her tongue and was awarded with his groan.

His mouth molded to hers as though it had been designed to fit the curve of her lips, and desire swirled through her like a drug. She angled her head, allowing him freer access to her mouth, thrilling at the stroke of his tongue and warmth of his breath. She moaned while his lips were still on hers, a primal noise that disappeared into his mouth.

He drew back and kissed the line of her jaw, the curve of her neck. "I love the little sounds you make when I kiss you," he whispered against her ear, nipping lightly on the lobe and making her whimper all over again.

He thrust his hand into her hair, coaxing the silken strands to fall down around her shoulders. He pulled back and stared into her face with eyes that burned like the embers of a still-glowing fire.

The Misconception

"I love the way you look with your hair down, all sexy and rumpled." His mouth was back on hers, and she could feel him smiling. "Definitely un-professor-like."

His free hand ran through her hair, over her shoulder and slipped beneath her unstructured jacket so he could caress her breast through the material of her shirt. She strained against him as her nipple pebbled and passion boiled in a steamy pool deep inside her.

He came up for air, his breath hot and erratic on her face. He lowered his hand, cupped her bottom, and brought her flush against his hard length. She rubbed against him, moaning. "I love the way your body reacts when I touch you, as though you can't get close enough to me," he said.

She buried her face in his neck to shower kisses wherever her mouth landed. "Look at me, Marietta."

His words were rough, insistent, and she raised her head, met his passion-dark eyes. "I love you. I think I've loved you since the first time I saw you."

She couldn't respond, couldn't think clearly. She didn't believe in love, did she? She'd stated repeatedly in her lectures that attraction between the sexes had nothing to do with love and everything to do with sex.

So why did a part of her thrill at hearing him say the words? Why did she want to make love to Jax instead of any of the other men she'd come across in her life? Why was the liking and the respect she had for him all mixed up with the desire?

Why did she want to kiss him again instead of pointing out all the biological reasons why he was mistaken?

His hand came up to her cheek. He touched it tenderly, like a lover would. "Make love with me, Marietta."

Her lips parted, but her vocal cords wouldn't work. So she nodded. The smile he gave her wasn't so much triumphant as exhilarated. His hand slipped from her cheek, locked with hers, guided her along as he moved through his house to his bedroom.

She had an impression of heavy wood furniture, earthy hues and painted walls that reminded her of the colors of a meadow. Then Jax dropped her hand and struggled out of his sling.

His shoulder! Marietta had forgotten all about his shoulder. She laid a hand on his good arm, alarm leaping in her breast. "Wait. I don't want you to hurt yourself."

His laugh was full-throated as he took his arm the rest of the way out of the sling. "Honey, it'd hurt a whole lot more if we stop right now."

"But . . ." Marietta began, then paused. She'd been about to argue against something she wanted more than university tenure. She swallowed as he slipped the jacket off her shoulders and began to unbutton her blouse. "You're sure?"

"Tell you what," he said with eyes that contained a fascinating combination of laughter and passion. "You can be on top."

"Oh, I couldn't . . ." she began, but lost her train of thought when his hands busied themselves in removing her clothing. His clever lips came back to hers over and over to dip into the well of passion she hadn't known ran so deep. Within moments, she was naked.

He stepped back to gaze at her, and she remembered how she'd looked that morning in the mirror after her shower. Embarrassed, her hand immediately covered her pregnant stomach.

"I'm showing," she said, and it sounded like an apology. "It's not very sexy."

"Not sexy?"

She wet her lips and shook her head. "Studies have shown that men are most attracted to—"

"Don't you dare start talking about hip-waist ratios again." He moved toward her, and ran a big, warm hand over her stomach. "Do you know how sexy it is to know it's my baby in there? That a part of me is living in a part of you? You're the sexiest pregnant lady I've ever seen."

He followed up on his words by taking her in his arms and kissing her senseless while his hands did a magic dance over her body. She fumbled at his clothing, wanting to feel his bare skin against hers, and within moments he was as naked as she was.

Then he was flat on his back on the neatly made bed, his body as beautiful as Marietta remembered, all muscle and brawn and . . . bruises. A large bluish mark marred his injured shoulder, but there were smaller ones below his ribs and over his upper thighs. She started to comment on them, but then he pulled her down on top of him. Flesh slid against flesh, making her forget everything but the terrible, wonderful yearning.

Her naked stomach pressed against his. Along with the liquid heat of desire that gathered inside of it, she felt a fluttering of life from the baby they had made together.

She lost herself in the moment and in the man so that, for that one brief space of time while they loved each other's bodies, she could almost believe she loved him, too.

Jax gathered Marietta's warm, naked body to his side, figuring the ache in his injured shoulder was more than offset by the pleasure still radiating through the rest of him. He kissed her sweet-smelling hair. "Stay with me tonight."

"Tracy—"

"Tracy will figure it out. Tracy's on my side."

He felt her smile against shoulder. "I hadn't realized there were sides."

"There aren't. At least, not anymore. I think I just got you to defect."

"Cocky? Aren't we?"

He laughed. "It's hard not to be after the way you were screaming my name."

"I was not." She sounded indignant.

"Were too," he teased, kissing her hair again and running his hand up and down her shoulder. "Did I mention how much I liked that? The sound effects, I mean."

"Is that all you liked?"

He chuckled. "I didn't just like it. I loved it." He waited a beat, timing his next words. "The way I love you."

Her body went rigid, the way he'd thought it might but hoped it wouldn't. But, damn it. She hadn't responded when he told her he loved her, and he wanted to know what was going on in that puzzling brain of hers.

"Love," she said flatly, "is a four-letter word for sex."

He swore ripely, pulled his arm from around her shoulders and sat up in bed. For the first time since they'd started making love, the ache in his shoulder caused real pain. He scowled. "For a smart woman, you can be pretty dumb. I've had sex before. I know what it is and what it feels like. What you and I just shared, that wasn't sex. That was love."

Marietta pulled the covers over her breasts and sat up across from him. She shook her head. "You're confused. Good sex can do that. You're confusing the afterglow with something else."

"Then why do I want to spend the rest of my life with you? Why do I love that confounding brain of yours as much as I love your body? Why do I want to know more about the woman who lives underneath all that tweed? Why does the way you'd do anything for your sister tug at my soul? Why can't I think of anything besides getting you to marry me?"

She didn't answer, so he reached out, cupped her cheek, and forced her to look at him. "You're going to marry me, Marietta. You know that's true."

She didn't deny it, which he took as a positive sign. He leaned down and kissed her, encouraged by the way her lips clung to his. Even though she hadn't told him she loved him, her body was saying it.

"This isn't about the baby anymore, although God knows I want to have a baby with you. This is about me and you. I've loved you since I saw you standing there at the airport, all prim and proper, wearing that ridiculous dress and waving that silly sign."

"You can't be sure that was love," Marietta said, but she no longer sounded so certain.

"Yes, I can." He kissed her again. "I love you, and you're just going to have to get used to it."

Chapter Twenty-one

"Jiminy, do you realize it's not even noon?" Tracy's annoyed voice penetrated the sensual haze that enveloped Marietta, and she reluctantly drew back in Jax's arms, just far enough to disengage their lips. "Don't you two get enough of that when the lights go out? Do you have to make out in the middle of the day, too?"

Marietta's gaze ran over Jax, taking in the way his broad, well-defined chest tapered to a trim waist and a compact, muscular behind that could make a chair deliriously happy.

"Yes," she answered, smiling into Jax's eyes.

"For cripe's sake, show a little restraint," Tracy complained, running fingers through hair she'd had cut boyshort. Obviously not everybody loved a lover.

Just days before, Tracy had bleached her hair blond and shed her black clothes, confiding it was time she stopped mourning the death of her marriage and started living. Her black mood wasn't as easy to cast off, and Marietta spent a part of each day damning Ryan for stirring things up again. If he'd stayed gone, Tracy would have had an easier time forgetting him.

254

The Misconception

"Restraint? What fun is restraint?" Jax let go of Marietta, swung Tracy into his arms and whirled her around. His laugh filled the townhouse as thoroughly as Marietta's carefully chosen period-piece furniture.

"Put me down, Cash Jackson. Put me down right now," Tracy warned, kicking her low-heeled red ankle boots like a horse with a burr under the saddle. "Think of your shoulder. You don't want to hurt it."

"Good try, but my shoulder's nearly healed. Seems to me some exercise will do it good," Jax said, keeping up the whirling until Tracy was breathless and laughing. When he finally set her down, he kissed her lightly on the nose.

"To set the record straight, Marietta and I weren't making out. I'm going out to do some errands, so we were kissing good-bye."

"Kissing good-bye. Kissing hello. Kissing good morning. Kissing good night." Tracy tapped her booted toes. "Do you get the pattern here? For nearly two weeks, all you two have been doing is kissing."

"That's not all we've been doing," Jax said, wiggling his brows at Marietta in a way that had her laughing. It amazed her that he could make her quiver with need one moment and shake with laughter the next. Almost as much as it amazed her that she'd been carrying on a torrid affair with him since the opening night of Tracy's play. She'd even let him serenade her with the theme from *Oklahoma*.

"You two are going to lunch, right?" He crossed the room to Marietta, pulled her into his arms again and made her forget that Tracy was sick of seeing them kiss. He drew back just before the kiss got out of hand. "I'll catch up with you later then."

"Just don't show up at the restaurant," Tracy groused. "I don't think the rest of the world is up for all the kissing you do."

An hour later, seated on the outdoor patio of the Grill and Go, Marietta sipped an after-lunch glass of decaf cap-

255

puccino as she regarded her sister across the table. The summer breeze was just strong enough that the afternoon sun felt agreeable instead of uncomfortable, and Marietta thought the day would have been close to perfect had her sister just smiled.

Tracy never responded well to pressure, so they'd talked of inconsequential things during lunch, avoiding the subject of her foul mood entirely while Marietta waited for her to bring up the reason for it. She only had to wait long enough for the waiter to clear the last of their dishes.

"I want to apologize for before, for the things I said to you and Jax. I don't know what got into me." Tracy grimaced. "Actually, yes, I do, but that doesn't excuse it."

Marietta didn't reply but waited for Tracy to continue. After a short pause, she did.

"My attorney called this morning to say she got the signed divorce papers from Ryan. All I have to do is show up in her office Monday for the deposition, and I'll be divorced." She swallowed, held up her left hand and wiggled her ring finger. "If I can't even bring myself to take off my wedding ring, how am I going to manage to get through that?"

Marietta's heart constricted at the pain on her sister's face. She reached across the table and covered her hand. "I'm sorry, honey. I'll come with you if you want. You know I'd do anything to make it easier for you."

"I'm sorry, too." Tracy swiped at a tear. "But I wasn't telling you so you'd feel sorry for me. I want you to understand why it's been so difficult for me to be around two people in love."

"Love?" Marietta repeated, her eyes wide. The thought that she was in love with Jax was laugh-out-loud ludicrous. "You're forgetting that I don't believe in romantic love, little sister. What Jax and I are having is a mutually satisfying affair."

"That's what Jax thinks, too?"

The Misconception

"Well . . ." Marietta ran her tongue over the outside of her teeth while she thought how best to dismiss her sister's question. "I'm not a mind reader. I can't vouch for what he thinks."

"You're telling me he doesn't tell you how he feels? That he hasn't said he loves you?"

Marietta's eyes slid away from Tracy's, because that was something she didn't want to think about. She preferred imagining he'd never said the dreaded three words at all. Jax, thank the stars, hadn't repeated his faux pas. He hadn't mentioned love in weeks.

"He has, hasn't he?" Tracy pressed.

"Maybe he has. You know the things people say in the heat of passion," Marietta said, trying to disregard that Jax had talked about love before and after they had sex, but not during the act itself. "It's a good thing I understand the dynamics of what's going on between us."

"Which is?"

"A sexual attraction based on deep-seated evolutionary desires to perpetuate the species."

"Oh, really." Tracy swirled the liquid in her glass with her straw. "Have you told Jax this?"

"Of course I've told him."

"Aaaah. But have you told him *lately?*"

Marietta wrinkled her nose. Tracy, it seemed, wasn't going to let the subject drop. "No," she said crossly. "I haven't."

"Why's that?"

"He doesn't like to hear the truth."

"The truth?" Tracy laughed. "So you're saying the truth is this relationship you have with Jax is based purely on sex, right? That you don't have any affection, any liking, for him?"

"Well, no. Of course I like him. He's really quite likable. He's funny, too." Marietta paused a beat. "When he's not telling jokes, that is."

"How about respect? Do you respect him?"

Marietta squirmed in her chair, growing increasingly uncomfortable by the questions. "What's not to respect about a man who's supporting his mother and putting both of his brothers through college?"

"So, let me get this straight. You're having an incredibly satisfying sexual relationship with a man you like, respect, and who just happens to be the father of your unborn child. Does that about sum it up?"

Marietta thought it was probably a trick question, but she couldn't find the land mine. "I guess you could say that."

Tracy raised her still-dark brows. "That sounds like love to me, kiddo."

Marietta banged her hand on the table, surprising herself so much that she took a moment to very deliberately raise her fingers and fold them demurely into her lap. She tried to speak calmly. "No, it's not. How many times do I have to tell you I don't believe in romantic love?"

"Whatever." Tracy waved a hand with such obvious disbelief that Marietta's blood pressure rose. Didn't Tracy understand who she was talking to? Didn't she realize somebody as educated in the ways of evolutionary biology as she was knew enough to avoid the messy emotional pitfalls of the nebulous thing some people called love?

Marietta didn't get a chance to ask her questions, because Tracy abruptly changed the subject. "You never told me why Dean Pringle called this morning. That's unusual, isn't it? For him to call professors at home?"

"Oh, that," Marietta said. She hadn't told her, because Jax had walked through the door seconds after she'd hung up, making her forget the call. Which most definitely didn't mean she loved him. She frowned. All it meant was that, with Jax around, she hadn't wanted to think about the ramifications of the call. "The dean got a call from somebody at *Morning Glory, Live.* They want me on the show next week."

The Misconception

"You mean the talk show starring Glory Green?"

Marietta nodded, and Tracy reached across the table to grasp her hands. "But that's big, Mari. Really big. I can't believe you didn't say anything about it. Glory's almost as big as Oprah. Appearing on her show will give your ideas the kind of national exposure you've been dreaming about."

"I know," Marietta said.

"So what's the problem?" Tracy peered at her. "Oh, I get it. You're afraid they're going to want you to talk about motherhood without males, aren't you?"

Marietta nodded.

"And you're not sure how strong an advocate you can be for it when you're days away from marrying Jax."

"I am not days away from marrying Jax."

"Okay. Weeks, then."

"Not weeks, either. Just because I'm having an affair with him doesn't mean I'm going to marry him."

"And this is because you don't love him?"

"Yes," Marietta said, nodding.

"Whatever." Tracy gave another disbelieving flick of her hand, making Marietta frown. She was a woman who prided herself on telling the truth. Why didn't Tracy believe her?

"Imagining yourself in love is like committing emotional suicide," Marietta said. "The minute—no, the second—you give somebody that kind of power over you, your life is no longer your own. You open yourself to all kinds of pain."

"You're talking about Mom and Dad, aren't you? You're thinking about how she stuck by him despite all the lies and all the cheating. That's why you don't want to believe in love."

"I'm thinking about you and Ryan, too," Marietta said softly.

At the mention of Ryan, Tracy's heart clenched. She wondered if she'd ever be able to think of him without this stabbing pain. But, then again, the lows wouldn't be so low if the highs hadn't been so lofty. "Did it ever occur to you that maybe it was worth it?" she asked.

"If what was worth it?" Marietta was obviously puzzled.

"Being in love." Tracy smiled. "Remember when Ryan and I first got married? He'd just sunk all his money into starting the business, and we didn't have anything but our little house and each other. I made curtains out of old bedsheets, learned a dozen recipes featuring the hot dog, and kept the heat down so low in the winter I walked around the house dressed like a snowman.

"Do you know that was one of the happiest times in my life? Colors were brighter. Birds sang louder. Flowers smelled sweeter. And it was all because I was in love."

Marietta didn't reply, but she was shaking her head, as though she could choose to disregard Tracy's message. What was it going to take, Tracy wondered, for her sister to realize that love doesn't give you a choice? That, when it strikes, it chooses you?

The noisy foursome at the table adjacent to them got up and left, providing Tracy with a clear view of the door leading to the air-conditioned part of the restaurant. Tracy's breath caught in her throat as a tall, dark-haired man stepped into the daylight, holding the door open for his companion.

Ryan. For just an instant, Tracy thought she'd conjured him up. But then the sun glinted off the blue-black highlights of the head of hair she knew so well, and a corner of his mouth lifted in that sexy grin she couldn't resist.

Of course it was Ryan. Hadn't she chosen this particular restaurant because it was his favorite? Hadn't she waited until Saturday to ask Marietta to lunch because it was Ryan's favorite meal to eat out? Hadn't she rejoiced when they got one of the coveted outdoor tables, because she and Ryan had always rejoiced?

The breeze blew a lock of hair over his forehead. She waited for him to swipe it back with the careless gesture that was second nature to him, but delicate fingers did it for him. Tracy stared, disbelieving, as Anna Morosco laughed up at him and stroked his cheek.

"Tracy, what's wrong?" Marietta's voice was sharp. Anna linked her arm through Ryan's, plastering herself against his side the way Tracy knew the other woman had been wanting to for years. For a moment, Tracy couldn't speak. "What are you looking at?"

Marietta turned just as Anna puckered up her plump red lips and kissed Ryan on the side of the cheek. Considering the way Anna had always panted over him, Tracy was surprised the kiss hadn't landed on his lips. Marietta instantly turned away.

"Oh, honey, I'm sorry you had to see that."

Tracy continued staring at the man she'd always loved with the woman she'd long mistrusted, and it felt as though a film covering her eyes lifted so she could see clearly. "I'm not sorry."

"You're right," Marietta said, "maybe it's best that you saw him with someone else so you can get on with your life."

"No, Marietta," Tracy said firmly. Suddenly, the picture was so clear she didn't understand why she hadn't been able to see it before. "You don't understand. Ryan's not with Anna. Not the way you mean, anyway."

"What do you mean?" Marietta's head whipped around at the exact instant that Ryan firmly disengaged Anna from him and shook her hand. Without a backward glance, Ryan left the restaurant. Alone. Anna stared after him, a pout on her poufy lips, her hands on her cinched waist. Then she left, too, traveling in the opposite direction from Ryan.

"I mean that they were having lunch together, as friends. Ryan wouldn't cheat on me," Tracy said. She thought back to their last conversation when Ryan pointed out she'd never asked him what happened that day she'd seen the blonde with the big hair and hourglass figure kissing him at the elevator. She'd said she didn't want to know. Now, quite suddenly, she did know. Big Hair Barbie had been kissing Ryan. He hadn't been kissing B. H. Barbie.

"Oh, my God. What have I done?" Tracy covered her face with her hands. Tears dampened her fingertips. "I broke up our marriage, Marietta. I did, not Ryan. I did, because I didn't trust him. I knew he loved me. How could I not trust him?"

"How could you not trust him?" Marietta blurted out the words, incredulity written on her face. "Mom trusted Dad, and look what happened to her! She spent a lifetime pretending she believed his lies. And six months after she was free of him, she died. She died, Tracy. Died before she had a chance to live."

"But it was her choice, Mari," Tracy said as the tears flowed freely down her face. Instead of blinding her, they cleared her vision. "Mom wasn't a victim. She could have left him, but she chose to stay. That's what she wanted."

"That's not what I want for you." Marietta's fierce mask dissolved, and tears pooled in her eyes. She reached across the table and squeezed Tracy's hands. "I don't want Ryan to hurt you, honey. I don't want you to let yourself be hurt."

Marietta's teary eyes fastened on hers, and Tracy saw in them what she always did: Fierce, unwavering love. For as long as she remembered, Marietta had rushed to her defense. In grade school, she'd pushed Jimmy Lee in the mud after he'd ripped the strap on Tracy's backpack. In high school, she'd gone to the soccer coach to argue her sister's case when she hadn't made the team. And ten months ago, she'd advised her to leave Ryan before she opened herself up to a world of hurt.

"This isn't about what you want. It's about what I want," Tracy said, swallowing. "I can't keep letting you protect me. I have to make my own decisions. Even if they're wrong. I have to live my own life."

"You do live your own life."

The Misconception

"No, I don't. I'm living the life you think I should live. If I had followed my heart, I never would have taken those anthropology courses. And I never would have left Ryan."

"But you had to leave him, honey. Biological evidence supports the fact that a man can't be faithful to one woman. It's not in their nature."

"That's what you believe. It's not what I believe," Tracy said, shaking her head. The tears came again. "Oh, Mari, I've been so miserable. I love him so much I can't bear to face the rest of my life without him. To think that I had that happiness in my hands, and I threw it away."

Marietta's lips parted and trembled, and Tracy braced herself to hear biology-supported evidence about how females can survive, and even thrive, without males. She remembered Marietta telling her once that flatworms could reproduce asexually and that whole-body regeneration occurs in starfish.

"I don't think you did throw it away," Marietta said instead.

"What do you mean?"

Marietta pressed her lips together as though the next words were difficult for her to say. "I think if you went to him," she said softly, "you'd find that out for yourself."

Tracy stood on the doorstep of the adorable little house she'd once shared with Ryan, worrying that she'd made a mistake in coming here. What if Marietta were wrong about Ryan? What if he couldn't forgive her for believing the worst of him? What if her distrust had killed whatever love he'd once had for her?

She lifted her hand and paused in the act of knocking, running her fingers instead over the heart-shaped wooden door knocker that Ryan had installed when she'd said she didn't like the sound of doorbells.

Other men wore their heart on a sleeve, he'd joked. He put his on a door.

She banged the heart, figuring she'd done pretty much the same thing to Ryan's flesh-and-blood organ when she'd let Marietta's views become her own and hadn't trusted him all those months ago. How was he ever going to forgive her? Could she even forgive herself?

A full minute later, when he still hadn't come to the door, she blinked back tears. He wasn't home. She'd drummed up the courage to bare her soul, and he wasn't home. Life, Tracy thought, was a bitch.

She was turning from the door when it opened. Ryan filled the frame, his hair wet from the shower, the first snap of his jeans undone, his shirt hanging open and unbuttoned to reveal a damp, masculine chest sprinkled with the dark hair she so loved to run her fingers through. Her lips parted, and her heart fluttered. Then her eyes went to his, which were guarded and unfriendly.

"What are you doing here, Tracy? I sent the papers to your lawyer. Don't tell me she didn't get them."

Tracy cleared her throat at the coldness in his voice. She wet her lips. "No, she got them."

"Do you want more money? Is that why you're here?"

The frostiness in his eyes nearly froze her vocal cords, and she winced. How could he ask that when he knew money had never been a driving influence in her life? His love was worth far more than any amount of money. "No. The settlement's more than generous. It's enough for me to open my own shop, even."

"Then what's the problem?"

She closed her eyes briefly and bit her lip until it hurt. This was even harder than she'd imagined. "Could I come in?"

He sighed heavily, but made room for her to pass. "Look, if you want something from the house, just take it, okay? I don't care. You always liked that lamp of my mother's. It's yours."

The Misconception

Miserable, Tracy shifted her weight from one foot to the other. "That's not what I want."

"You want my dad's old rocking chair? That's yours, too. Just take it and leave. I've got things to do. You can let yourself out when you're done."

He turned away from her, and snippets of their past appeared before Tracy's eyes the way that life's most glorious moments flashed before the eyes of a dying person. Ryan asking her to marry him amid the furor of a rock concert. Ryan's beautiful dark eyes never wavering from hers when he promised to love and cherish her until death parted them. Her bare-chested husband beckoning her to bed with a smile that reached all the way to his soul.

"Ryan, wait." The words were as strangled as the invisible vise squeezing her chest. She couldn't let their marriage die. If she did, everything vital inside her would also die. He stopped, but didn't turn, and she had to say something to keep him from going. "I don't want anything from the house."

He turned then, but his eyes were still guarded, his lips pulled taut. "Then what do you want?"

She wanted him, so badly she could barely stop herself from reaching out and running her fingers over the bare, warm skin of his achingly beautiful chest. She twisted the wedding ring she still hadn't been able to bring herself to remove.

"Marietta and I had lunch at the Grill and Go today." She cleared her throat. "We saw you with Anna Morosco. At the exit. Right when you were leaving."

Understanding dawned in his eyes. "You saw her kiss me, right? So, naturally, you assumed I have something going with her."

"Marietta did, but I—"

He swore ripely. "You listened to her? Even though you know Anna's always been like a kid sister to me, I bet you let Marietta convince you we're sleeping together."

Darlene Gardner

"No, I—"

"Here's a news flash for you." He advanced toward her, his voice so gruff and defiant that he was almost shouting. "I'm not sleeping with her. I'm not sleeping with anybody."

"Ryan, I'm trying to—"

"I don't want to sleep with anyone but you. I never did." His words came faster, more furiously. "I know you won't believe this, but it's time you heard it. Despite what you thought you saw at that elevator ten months ago, I never cheated on you."

"I know," she said calmly.

"The woman you saw me with, Mia Sullivan, she wanted me to come up to her room. She said she contracted me to build her a house *because* she wanted me. But just because she was willing didn't mean I was." He stopped, ran his fingers through his damp hair. The fight seemed to seep out of him like the air from a deflated balloon. "I don't know why I expect you to believe me now when you—"

"Ryan," Tracy interrupted, laying her hand on his bare chest, right over his madly beating heart. "I said I know you're not having an affair with her. That you never were."

Ryan had been waiting for those words for so long that he barely believed his ears. Something hot and sweet loosened in his chest until he remembered that he'd just done what he vowed never to do. Then the pain came back.

"Oh, I get it," he said, wishing he didn't. "You only believe me because I convinced you that nothing happened. The next time we're faced with something like this, I'd have to convince you all over again."

Tracy shook her head. "That's not true. I knew, Ryan. I knew the instant I saw Anna kiss you at the restaurant today that you've never cheated on me."

Hope leapt inside him, but he stopped himself from reaching for her the way he'd wanted to since she walked in the door. They needed to get this straight. For the sake of their marriage. For the sake of their love. "What are you saying?"

"You're not going to make this easy on me, are you?" The bleached strands of her hair were so short they barely moved when she shook her head. On another woman, hair like that would have looked outrageous. On Tracy, it was outrageously sexy. "I'm saying I was a fool. When I saw you in the hotel lobby, I wasn't thinking with my heart. I should have trusted you. I should have known you'd never cheat on me."

Underneath her heavy makeup, her eyes were sincere. But he needed to be sure he understood what he was hearing. "Are you saying all this because of what I told Marietta at the play?"

She looked confused. "Marietta? What does Marietta have to do with this?"

Ryan shook his head, unwilling to delve into how her sister's far-out theories affected her life. One day they would discuss it, but not today. Today, he was going to revel in the fact that she was finally offering what he'd wanted for so long. "You're saying you trust me."

Tracy nodded, and tears spilled down her cheeks, splitting his heart in two.

"I know it could be a case of too little, too late." Her voice broke. "And, if that's the way it is, I'll accept it and know I was the one who wrecked our marriage. And I'd understand, I would, if you still want a . . ." She stopped, sniffed, blinked, "divorce. Because if—"

"Tracy." By speaking her name, he stopped her torrent of words. She raised her watery eyes, and his own eyes teared up. He gently wiped the falling tears from her cheeks with the backs of his fingers and forced himself to ask the question. "Is a divorce what you want?"

Mutely, she shook her head. Both her chin and lips quivered as she tried to talk. "But if you don't love me anymore—"

Ryan took her face in his hands, looked deep into her eyes. "Not love you anymore? Whatever gave you that idea?"

"The red dress," she choked out. "When I wore it, you didn't touch me. I thought—"

"That I didn't love you?" He rubbed his cheek over her short hair. "Tracy, seeing you in that red dress and not touching you just about killed me."

"Then why didn't you?"

"Because I knew if I touched you, we'd end up in bed. I don't want you for just a night. I want you forever." He pulled back, looked deeply into her green eyes. "I love you, Trace. I want you in my bed. I want you in my life. But, most of all, I want you to trust me."

Fresh tears welled in her eyes. "Oh, Ryan. I do trust you. Can you ever forgive me?"

He kissed the tears away, the salty taste lingering on his lips. "I already have," he whispered the instant before he claimed her lips and reclaimed their marriage.

Chapter Twenty-two

Marietta stared down at her hands, noticing that the bright lights of the studio illuminated every vein. At least the veins weren't shaking as much as her insides. Maybe, if she remained perfectly still, Glory Green and her live studio audience wouldn't guess that a bad case of anxiety had her in a stranglehold.

Not that it wasn't her own fault.

She'd handled the entire episode poorly from the onset. She should have dealt with Glory Green's people herself instead of allowing Dean Gerard Pringle to act as a go-between. At the very least, she should have questioned him as to why the show needed an expert on evolutionary biology.

She would have, too, if she hadn't been so wrapped up in Jax that she spent her working days counting the minutes until she could be with him again.

She, Marietta Dalrymple, who was educated enough to know better, had let herself become blinded by a man's sex appeal.

Now, sitting on Glory Green's artfully designed stage, with the lemon-colored walls and vases full of morning glo-

269

ries, she was paying the price. A single mother was positioned on either side of her with Glory to the far left; none of them knew that Marietta's loosely constructed dress hid a pregnancy already five months gone. All were waiting for the audience furor to die down so Marietta could answer Glory's question.

Could you explain, Dr. Dalrymple, your controversial theory about the superfluousness of men after conception?

"Go ahead, doctor," Glory prompted, smiling her engaging talk-show host smile. "We've heard from single mothers, some of whom discussed the difficulties of raising a child on their own. We're all interested in what you have to say."

"First of all, I'd like to state that I'm presenting a *theory*," Marietta said, emphasizing the word. She took a deep breath. She could do this. She'd been reciting the words for so long that they should come automatically. "Because of the emergence of the economically independent female, mothers no longer need to rely on men to support and protect themselves and their offspring."

A contingent of women in the audience rose in unison and cheered, shouting encouragement and indulging in palm-punishing clapping. Marietta recognized their petite, olive-skinned leader and blanched. Oh, no. Vicky Valenzuela had brought the fan club to New York City.

In response to the support from the FOCs, another segment of the audience erupted into loud boos. Marietta pursed her lips, sure that Jax's response to her statement would be closer to a boo than a cheer. Although she'd been overwhelmed with guilt over her omission, she was suddenly fiercely glad she hadn't told him she was appearing on the show.

Glory, no doubt sensing that dissension made for good television, walked off the stage and up the aisle separating the two halves of the audience. A large black man with a shaved head and nose ring practically ripped the microphone from her when she called on him for his question.

"You don't know what you're talking about, lady. My kids need me way more than they need my ex-wife. She pays more attention to the bottle than she does them."

"I don't doubt—" Marietta began, but the noisy audience drowned her out. She bit her lip and thought how best to neutralize the situation.

Never, in all her years of academia, had she run into an audience like this one. *Morning Glory, Live* was a cut above the popular talk shows that sensationalized the bizarre, but the difference was that the other shows were taped. A live show, by its very nature, was unpredictable.

Expect the unexpected was the single bit of advice Glory's assistant had conveyed before sending her out to be slaughtered. So Marietta was only mildly horrified when Glory tripped lightly down the aisle stairs and stopped in front of a heavily pregnant woman who had trouble rising to her feet. She looked like she was about to either burst or keel over from exhaustion.

"Theory's all well and good, but reality's something altogether different." The pregnant woman spoke into the microphone in a voice that trembled. "I've got enough money, and I know I can support my child when it's born. I don't have a choice, seeing as my husband died a month ago."

"I'm sorry," Marietta said automatically, but the woman brushed her off.

"I didn't raise my hand for sympathy. I raised it, 'cause I got a question. If *you* were pregnant and the father of *your* baby wanted to be a part of *your* life, are you honestly telling us that you'd turn him away?"

The audience immediately quieted, waiting for the answer that was integral to the way Marietta would live the rest of her life. Without knowing it, the woman, in effect, was asking whether Marietta wanted Jax in her life. That wasn't something she wanted to answer on national television.

"I think some of you have misunderstood my position," she said. "Motherhood Without Males isn't for everyone. It's an alternative to the traditional method of child-rearing. Even in the animal kingdom, where it's prevalent, there are exceptions. Male emperor penguins and prairie voles, for example, are very attentive to their young. Their female mates might not need them, but they're happy to have them around."

"I'm not asking about penguins or prairie voles," the pregnant woman cut in. "I'm asking about you."

"I'm getting to that," Marietta said. "But first I want to talk about the coyote."

"The coyote?" Glory and the pregnant woman parroted in unison.

"They don't seem like the most noble of animals, considering they howl and bark and scavenge. Sheep farmers wouldn't agree with me, but I think coyotes are quite admirable."

"They are?" Glory asked.

"Coyotes mate for life. A singular male hooks up with a singular female months before either animal comes into heat, signifying that compatibility and not hormones is the basis for the pair bond. The commendable thing is that Father Coyote doesn't run off in search of greener pastures once Mother Coyote gives birth. He stays by her side, helping her care for the young. Those sheep he sometimes scavenges provide food for his family. Even after the young are grown, he sticks around."

The pregnant woman tried to take the microphone again, but Glory wouldn't let her. "I'm not sure how we got off on this coyote tangent, but we've lost sight of the question." Glory put her hands on her slim hips. "In light of your learned theories, Dr. Dalrymple, would *you* want the father of *your* child around if you were pregnant?"

"Wouldn't you rather hear about how the coyote's primary social unit is the pair rather than the pack?"

Glory shook her head emphatically. "No. I'd like to hear about you."

Marietta swallowed. A lifetime of telling the truth had brought her to this moment. Glory Green had asked, point blank, whether she was better off without the father of her child. Whether she was better off without Jax.

Mere months ago, her answer would have been heartfelt and immediate. Biology and its vital urges had compelled her to get pregnant, and she neither wanted nor needed a man. But that was before Jax had reappeared in her life, before her heart had started performing its unpredictable flip-flops.

Did she want Jax in her life? The time had come for her to face the truth.

"What all of you don't know is that I'm nearly five months pregnant." While she waited for the murmuring of the audience to die down, a funny thing happened. The anxiety pressing her into the seat lifted, and happiness replaced it. Because she knew, in that instant, that what she was about to say was unalterably right. "The benefits of parental involvement, of course, depend on the man. The father of my child happens to be a wonderful, caring man who will be an excellent parent. I'd no sooner cut him out of my life than I would my own hand."

Every segment of the audience, with the notable exception of Vicky Valenzuela's FOC contingent, clapped wildly. Glory Green's telegenic face, which had features nearly as symmetrical as Jax's, broke into a telegenic smile.

"What a beautiful sentiment, and a beautiful way to end our show." Glory wrapped things up. "Unfortunately that's all the time we have. Thanks for watching, and may all your mornings be as glorious as this one."

Bright, upbeat music filled the stage, signaling the end of the show. The other guests and most of the audience members rose, preparing to leave. Marietta felt as though her body had been secured to her seat with superglue. She'd just admitted, on national television no less, that Jax was as vital to her existence as a body part.

She stared out at the audience, and, for some unfathomable reason, her eyes went to the back row, near the exit. A larger-than-life man with the body of Adonis and a face of symmetrical perfection stood there, beaming at her. She blinked, but he was still there when she opened her eyes. *Jax.*

She would have kept on gaping at him if Tracy, waving wildly and wearing neon orange, hadn't stepped in front of him and fought her way through the crowd to the stage. She climbed the steps, took Marietta's hand, and pulled her to her feet.

"Please don't be angry with me for telling Jax you were going to be on the show," Tracy said, biting her lip. "It sort of slipped. Then, when he said he'd pay for us to come see you, I couldn't pass up the trip. I would have told you we were coming, but I didn't want you to be nervous. That's why we sat in the back row."

Marietta barely heard her sister, because she was looking over her shoulder, her eyes locked on Jax. His well-cut designer suit was deep blue, emphasizing the breadth of his shoulders and length of his legs. He was smiling his well-proportioned smile, looking so good he should have been arrested for inciting Marietta's hormones to riot. When Tracy let go of Marietta, Jax didn't hesitate. He just came straight at her and pulled her into his arms, heedless that half the audience was still watching them.

"Did you mean it?" he asked. He smoothed the hair back from her face, overwhelming her, as he always did, with the sex appeal that oozed out of his pores like an aphrodisiac. Mutely, she nodded, and his grin grew brighter than the overhead studio lights.

"You know what that means, don't you?" he asked.

She shook her head again, and he laughed aloud, a joyous, robust sound.

The Misconception

"It means you love me back." She opened her mouth, but he put his fingers to her lips, silencing her. "No, don't ruin it with any of that intellectual biological stuff. Just say you'll marry me."

She gave up. Her brain was so muddled, she wasn't sure what she'd been about to say anyway. All she could do was respond to the warmth in his eyes. An answering smile lit hers. "I'll marry you."

A raucous cheer went up at the same time that Jax pulled her to him for a promise-sealing kiss, and only then did Marietta realize that her microphone was on and the audience had heard every word she said.

But she was too far gone with happiness to care.

A man couldn't get any happier than this, Jax thought as Smashing Headhunter pulled him into a headlock and pounded his scalp with quick, staccato punches while screaming with blood-curdling glee. The punches were designed to be grazing blows meant to look like the real thing, but Headhunter's rhythm was off, and half of them connected with dull thuds.

Jax barely felt the pain. His life was brimming with such wonderful possibilities that the kind of physical pain Headhunter inflicted was superficial.

Jax, quite simply, had it all. A stimulating profession. Good health. A baby on the way. And a fascinating, sexy bride-to-be who he was crazy in love with. True, Marietta hadn't yet admitted she loved him, but she would. Once he proved that her theory about men and infidelity didn't apply to him, she wouldn't have a choice.

Smashing Headhunter released him, and Jax staggered around the ring the way they'd agreed on. In reality, he had enough energy to pick up the other wrestler and hurl him into the audience, but that wasn't in tonight's script.

Tonight, during the UWA's pay-per-view anniversary extravaganza, the Secret Stud was supposed to take a beating.

The rationale was that witnessing the beating of one of their heroes would fuel the fans' desire for revenge. Then the audience for the next pay-per-view event would be even larger.

Jax was more than happy to take a fall, especially because the UWA brass had dropped their pressure to have him unmasked. Star Bright hadn't mentioned anything about it in more than a week.

"Aaaaaiiiieeeeeeeeeeee." Smashing Headhunter let loose an otherworldly scream and hoisted Jax high into the air as he prepared for a predetermined finishing move called a back drop. Facing the other wrestler, Jax pushed off his shoulders with his feet and vaulted into the air. He extended his arms to create as much surface area as possible, being careful to let his feet and shoulders, and not his spine, absorb the impact of the fall.

The audience members moaned in unison. He heard copious weeping, letting Jax know he'd performed the trick to perfection. They really thought he'd suffered a grievous injury when, on the inside, he was congratulating himself on a job well done.

Because a hero was supposed to be tough in the face of adversity, he made it look as though he was struggling to a sitting position. Then he rose and pointed a shaking finger at the dancing, prancing Headhunter.

"You've won the battle, but not the war," Jax shouted with all the gusto of a seasoned performer. "I will avenge the deaths of my ancestors yet."

He turned with a flourish to exit the ring. At the last moment, a sixth sense alerted him that something was wrong. The Studettes had climbed into the ring, exactly where they were supposed to be, as they comforted him with hugs and kisses. The half-dozen women Star Bright had hired to pummel Smashing Headhunter when he exited the arena were positioned at the other end of the ring, exactly where they were supposed to be.

The Misconception

A large shadow, followed by hot breathing, told him Smashing Headhunter was behind him, which was not where he was supposed to be. Before Jax had a chance to turn, his archenemy's beefy hand reached around him, grabbed the bottom of his mask and tugged the material upward.

In the space of a heartbeat, Jax's face was naked.

All of the cameras, which seemed so skillfully concealed during the event, popped out at Jax. There was one overhead. One alongside the ropes. One at the foot of the ring. All of them were pointed at him.

"Aaaaaaaaiiiiieeeeeeeee."

Smashing Headhunter's scream rent the heavy air inside the arena, but it was Jax who wanted to yelp in panic. The identity of the Secret Stud was no longer secret. With a formidable effort, Jax stopped himself from rushing out of the arena. He called on his professionalism and played the part he'd been playing for the past few years.

"I'll get you for this, you fiend," he yelled at Smashing Headhunter, pointing in fury. "I'll have my revenge."

A few minutes later, while the crowd still buzzed with dazed excitement, Jax took his leave, the Studettes around him as he swaggered through the crowd as though he hadn't a care in the world.

The moment the fans could no longer see him, he rushed into the locker room, frantic to reach a phone. His heart beat faster than a hummingbird's, and he had to redial Marietta's number three times before he got it right.

All the while, he prayed she'd understand why the man she'd promised to marry masqueraded as the Secret Stud.

Marietta padded into her kitchen on stocking feet and pulled open the refrigerator door. The top shelf was two deep with cartons of calcium-fortified orange juice, which Jax had been buying her daily since she'd confessed her abhorrence of milk.

She smiled, thinking she missed him already even though he'd only been gone since that morning.

She closed her eyes briefly as the mind-boggling truth hit her. She, Marietta Dalrymple, naysayer of all things romantic, was engaged. Her refrigerator wasn't only stocked with healthy, calcium-rich food. Her dining room table was loaded with long-stemmed red roses and her ring finger festooned with precious gems.

She held her hand out in front of her face, delighting in the way the dozen tiny pearls circled the diamond centerpiece. A blush stole over her cheeks as she remembered the way Jax had presented the ring, on bent knee with his hand over his heart.

Her own heart had fluttered like the wings of a thousand butterflies, and her eyes had moistened with happy tears. Then she'd actually laughed aloud at one of his unfunny jokes. This one was about an optician who told the bride-to-be she'd have to wait to get fitted for glasses because he didn't believe in specs before marriage.

She didn't want to examine why she'd laughed or why she'd been acting so out of character, didn't want to think it was anything more than an extreme biological reaction to Jax's outstanding good looks and lovemaking techniques.

A bubbling sound escaped Marietta's lips, which she suspected might be her happiness overflowing. She took one of the orange-juice cartons out of the refrigerator, poured herself a glass and walked into the family room.

Her life had ceased to become routine, but there were some things a woman couldn't give up, and topping her list was the eleven o'clock news. She settled into her armchair, just then remembering she'd taken the phone off the hook after work because of pesky solicitors.

She started to get up, thinking Jax might try to call, but changed her mind. He'd left his phone number before flying off on one of the endless business trips she'd been too preoccupied to ask him about. She could call him after the news. If the sound of his voice didn't scramble her wits, she'd even ask him to explain again exactly what it was he did for a living.

Twenty minutes later, saturated with news of governmental scandals and faraway battles, Marietta let her eyes glaze over when the sportscast switched on. She might have dozed if something hadn't bumped into her stomach. She came instantly alert, reaching down to brush whatever it was away, but her hand encountered only air. She frowned.

The sensation hit her again, but this time it felt like bubbles bursting *inside* of her. She reached under the cool cotton of the maternity nightgown Jax had insisted on buying for her that weekend and laid her warm hand over her stomach. Her fingers jumped, helped along by what she'd just realized was a tiny hand or foot.

Her other hand flew to her open mouth as wonder filled her. The baby was kicking! Jax, she thought. If only Jax were here, the moment would be perfect.

A familiar blend of cheering and truly awful pop music wailed from the television, drawing her attention away from her miracle. The television newscast had switched to a clip of a packed sports arena. The camera panned in, focusing on two wrestlers locked in combat. The one wearing tattered trousers and combat boots was frighteningly large, but the slightly smaller masked wrestler in red snagged her attention. After a moment, she recognized him as the wrestler Jax had been watching on videotape a few weeks ago.

She squinted, trying to get a better look at him as the other wrestler lifted him into the air and dropped him. She winced as his back hit the mat, but kept watching. Something about the masked, spandex-wearing wrestler was familiar, more so than it should have been considering she'd only gotten a glimpse of him once before.

What had he billed himself as? The camera showed a shot of a trio of scantily clad, generously endowed women alongside the ring and she remembered. A studmuffin.

The women climbed into the ring and draped themselves over the masked wrestler, plastering kisses wherever their lips could reach in a disgusting display of sexism. The wrestler probably never saw his opponent grab what looked to be three shrunken heads dangling from a stick.

Marietta had just enough time to wonder what he was up to when he dangled the miniatures heads above the masked wrestler's head, let out a tremendous roar, and ruthlessly yanked off his mask.

The camera switched to a tight shot of a stunning dark-haired, chocolate-eyed man with perfectly symmetrical features. Marietta's eyes widened. Her mouth fell open. Her breath caught in her lungs.

Jax. The masked wrestler was Jax.

Before Marietta could fully process the information, the camera switched back to the sportscaster, whose blue eyes twinkled merrily. "There you have it. Tonight the Secret Stud's identity is secret no more after he was unmasked by his archenemy, Smashing Headhunter, at the Ultimate Wrestling Association's extravaganza. Back to you, Joy."

Joy, who was obviously the lead anchor, was also smiling. "With a face like that," she said, shaking her pretty head, "it makes you wonder why he was wearing a mask in the first place."

Marietta reached for the remote control, switched off the television and thought she heard booming in her chest. Jax didn't sell stocks and bonds, as he claimed. He wasn't a businessman. He was a professional wrestler.

He had lied to her, just like her father had lied to her mother, just like she swore she'd never be lied to. Was this searing pain the same as the pain that had sliced into her mother? Was this the price a woman paid for letting a man get too close?

Marietta had trouble taking in oxygen and realized it was because she was holding her breath. She made herself breathe, but the air felt ragged going down her throat, like she was swallowing a double-edged sword. One side was as smooth as Jax's lies, the other as jagged as his painful betrayal.

Much later, she realized her hand still covered her stomach, but the baby was no longer kicking.

Chapter Twenty-three

At nearly one in the morning, the taxi Jax hired after arriving at Washington D.C.'s national airport pulled up in front of twin townhouses. Jax's place was as dark as he'd left it before heading off for the UWA's extravaganza in Boston. Marietta's was glowing with lights.

That she was still awake meant he'd be able to tell her what he did for a living before somebody else did. He'd been trying to do exactly that since Smashing Headhunter had unmasked him earlier that evening, but Marietta's phone had been constantly busy. Finally, in desperation, he'd driven to the airport and booked a flight home.

Marietta wouldn't have subscribed to the pay-per-view event featuring his unmasking, but the news could get to her in other ways. Ryan was a wrestling fan, so Tracy could get wind of it and pass it on. Hell, the morning newspaper might even carry an item about it. The Secret Stud, after all, was an UWA icon.

Now that he was here, he found himself reluctant to move, which he wished he could attribute to the rain that beat on the roof of the taxicab like a bongo drummer. That, unfortunately, wasn't the reason. He'd come to a crossroads in his life, and turning toward one of the things he loved was going to take him away from the other.

"Hey, buddy. You gonna get out of my cab any time tonight?" Jax's gaze transferred from Marietta's townhouse glowing through the gray, steady rain to the taxi driver. "Understand, the meter's running so it's fine with me if you hang for a while."

The driver's jaw worked on a wad of gum. His expression was sour, as though he'd taken a bite of the world and didn't like the taste. Jax thought he looked as though he could use a good joke as much as Jax needed to tell one.

"Did you hear about the taxi driver whose cab was caught in a tornado and ended up dangling halfway over a cliff?"

The cabbie grunted, giving Jax all the encouragement he needed to continue. "When he called the dispatcher from his car phone to report he was caught in a storm, the dispatcher said, 'Don't worry. It'll blow over.' 'That's what I'm afraid of,' the man moaned."

The taxi driver fixed him with a stare so intent Jax felt like he was drilling twin holes through his forehead. "No," the cabbie said. "Wonder why I didn't read about that in the *Washington Post.*"

Jax's eyes narrowed worriedly. This guy had more problems than he'd originally thought. "If you don't know the answer to that, nothing I say is going to matter."

The cabbie stared at him a moment longer, then let out a long laugh and slapped the back of the seat. "You should see your face, pal. You really believed I thought that had really happened. Oh, that's a good one."

Dismayed at the other man's distorted sense of humor, Jax read the amount off the meter, mentally calculated a tip, and paid him. The driver's laughter followed him as he opened the car door and stepped out into the night. Rain slapped him in the face with wet drops, but he didn't hurry to Marietta's door. He was embarking on the death march of his career. Appropriately, that would take a little time.

Thunder crackled like the disappointment that was rumbling through him. He fully understood a professor as dignified as Marietta wouldn't want to be married to a pro wrestler. Still, he wished he could have stuck with the UWA for another year in order to pay off his brothers' college costs. Oh, he'd get the money some way, even if he had to take out a loan, but the loss of income wasn't why his chest ached at the thought of giving up the sport.

He'd come to love the pageantry, the gallantry, and the artistry of pro wrestling. He loved the cheers of the crowd, the challenge of staying in top shape, and the adrenaline rush of pulling off a particularly demanding stunt.

Despite that, choosing between his future wife and his future as a wrestler amounted to no choice at all. He loved Marietta far more than he'd ever loved anything, including wrestling.

In moments, his clothing felt heavy against his skin. He looked down at himself, recognizing the reason. He wasn't dressed in the fine suits and designer shirts he favored, but the gray sweatpants and shirt he'd pulled on after Smashing Headhunter had unmasked him. The workout clothes sopped up water like a kitchen sponge.

He raised his eyes to the dripping sky and let the wet breeze, which smelled of the nearby Potomac River, wash over him. That he had gotten on a plane looking like this meant he was further gone over Marietta than he'd thought.

He rang the doorbell and waited, wincing as lightning rent the sky. When Marietta pulled open the door, he smiled despite the turmoil inside and all around him. The green of her soft, flowing nightgown reflected in her eyes, making them look jewel-like and ethereal. Her hair was down around her shoulders, softening the angles of her face. Looking at her had always packed a sexual punch, but he hadn't realized, until that minute, how truly beautiful she was.

"Hi." He stepped forward, intending to come through the inner door and take her into his arms, but then realized her arms were crossed in front of her chest and her lips were unsmiling. He froze.

"Well, well, well." She drew out the words, speaking loudly enough to be heard above the battering rain. "If it isn't Jax Jackson, traveling salesman of stocks and bonds."

Jax narrowed his eyes, trying to read her expression through the rainwater that dampened his face. Did Marietta already know what he'd come to tell her? Her eyes were shuttered, concealing the answer. Jax hesitated, unsure of how to proceed. "I came back early, because there's something I need to talk to you about."

"One o'clock in the morning is a little late to talk."

"You're still awake."

"Only because you're standing here on my doorstep preventing me from getting to sleep."

Thunder boomed along with his heart. Her voice was colder than he'd ever heard it, filling him with a chilling certainty. He wasn't sure how she'd found out, but she knew he was the Secret Stud. Considering she'd clung to him less than twenty-four hours earlier before dropping him off at the airport, no other explanation made sense.

This wasn't the way he'd envisioned the evening, but he didn't believe the problem was insurmountable. He'd explain how he'd come to be the Secret Stud, then he'd tell her he was giving it all up. For her.

"Can I come in?" he asked. She didn't budge from her spot in the doorway. He cocked his head and tried a smile. "Please? I'm getting drenched here."

For a moment, she stood as frozen as an ice statue at a winter carnival, but then she moved away from the door, giving him a clear path to her sanctuary. He entered the townhouse, closed both doors behind him and stamped the water off the best he could.

She disappeared into the bowels of the house and returned holding a towel, which she tossed at him. He caught it, wiped the excess water off his face and clothes, and followed her into the living room. She didn't sit down, but stood in the center of the room, between the brocade sofa and barren fireplace, with her arms still crossed over her chest.

"You came here to talk," she said, her stare unfriendly, "so talk."

He looked down at the carpet, back up at her. "I have a feeling you already know what I'm going to say."

"What? That you dress in red spandex and strut into a wrestling ring to the cries of 'Studmuffin'?"

He winced, disliking her rendition of his act even as he admired her for not pretending to misunderstand his question.

"How did you find out?"

"You made the evening news." Her voice was tight. "It seems the wrestling community has been speculating for a long while on what you looked like under that mask."

He took a step toward her, stopped when the air around her seemed cold enough to form a wall of ice. "If it makes it any easier, I want you to know I never set out to be a pro wrestler. My mother had such a hard time of it that I wanted to make enough money to help her out. I thought I could do it through football, but I wasn't good enough to make the pros."

She continued to stare at him, offering no encouragement, but he kept talking, telling her what he should have told her months ago.

"I took a job as a phys. ed. teacher at an elementary school, but it paid next to nothing. Then one day, an old teammate of mine who'd been playing the Secret Stud got hurt and I had a chance to take over his act. It was an opportunity too good to pass up. I intended to get another act as time went by, but the Stud became so popular that I couldn't get out of it."

"So you're saying you didn't want to masquerade as a woman's sexual fantasy come to life?" She looked and sounded skeptical.

"Exactly," he answered.

"How about a pro wrestler who tells the woman he says he loves that he sells stocks and bonds? Who lies about where he got his bruises, dislocated shoulder, and *plump* lip? Are you going to tell me you did that against your will, too?"

"No, I did that deliberately," he said softly, feeling ashamed. "I didn't keep it just from you, Marietta. My mother and brothers don't know I'm a pro wrestler, either. I didn't tell you, or them, because I was afraid of what you'd think. I was afraid, most of all, of losing you." He took a deep breath, because he'd gotten to the crux of what he'd come here tonight to tell her. "That's why I'm going to give it up. For you."

Marietta shook her head in disgust, the way she'd done the first time they met, which wasn't the reaction he'd been aiming for. "That's what you think this is all about?" She cut the air with her hand. "You think this is about you being a pro wrestler?"

"Of course that's what it's about." He dragged a hand over the rough stubble on his chin, reminding him that he hadn't shaved prior to getting on the airplane, something else he never forgot to do before going out in public. He was more confused than ever. "Isn't it?"

"Do you really think I'd dump you just because you're a pro wrestler?

Jax screwed up his forehead. "Wouldn't you?" he asked. "Wouldn't you be afraid of what people would say?"

"Of course not. It doesn't bother me that most people don't agree with my views. Why should it bother me what people think of the man I'm with?"

The news was so staggering that Jax couldn't quite wrap his mind around it. Before joy could course through him that he'd be able to keep pro wrestling and Marietta, he noticed that she was still fuming. Her ears were in danger of turning into smokestacks.

"If my being a pro wrestler doesn't bother you, why are you so angry?"

"Because you lied to me." Her lips quivered but straightened into an unforgiving line so abruptly he thought he might have imagined the quivering. She paced from one end of the room and back again. "All these months, you let me believe you were a businessman. Oh, how you must have been laughing at me. So dazzled by your symmetry I couldn't see through your lies. I bet you were even sleeping with one of those Studettes on the side."

"You know I'd never laugh at you or cheat on you," he refuted. "And I'm sick and tired of hearing about how one side of my face is the same as the other. It's not my symmetry that's dazzling you, Marietta. It's me. You're in love with me."

"Oh, no," she said forcefully, running her hands through her hair. "Don't you dare say that to me."

"Why not?" he asked, advancing toward her. "It's true."

Marietta tried to glare at him, but she could feel her chin trembling. She would not cry, damn it. She would not cry because she'd been stupid enough to let this man into her life.

"It is not true. I don't love you."

"If you don't love me," he said, his eyes glittering with purpose, "then prove it."

Inch by inch, he came closer to her, but the moisture gathering in her eyes prevented her from seeing his features clearly. She could smell him, though, an intoxicating blend of soap, man, and rain that did uproarious things to her insides. Even though his clothing was wet, she could feel the heat of him as he drove his fingers through her hair and held her so she couldn't move.

"If you don't love me, tell me you don't want me to touch you," he whispered, his mouth a scant inch from hers. "Tell me you don't want me to kiss you."

The heat started somewhere near her heart, pooled between her thighs and spread all the way to her toes. She couldn't tell him anything, because it seared her voice box shut. With a groan, he captured her lips, kissing her with wild abandon. His tongue thrust hotly into her mouth. His hands left her hair and seemed to be everywhere at once, on her breasts, cupping her bottom, holding her to him.

She returned the kiss, straining to get nearer, mindless of his wet clothes. She rubbed the aching part of her against his erection, unable to deny, for even a moment, that she didn't want him.

Finally, he broke off the kiss. She moaned, trying to pull him back, but he wouldn't let her. He held her at arm's length, looking more determined than victorious. "That proves it. That proves you love me."

She stared back at him as his words blew away some of the sexual haze that enveloped her. "All it proves," she said, forcing herself to think of his lies, "is that you have all the characteristics that, through time, have attracted woman to man."

"Damn it, Marietta," he bit out, releasing her so abruptly she almost fell. "Are you really so stubborn you can't admit you're in love with me?"

"Love?" She laughed mirthlessly. "Love is for fools stupid enough to give somebody else the power to hurt them with their lies."

He peered at her so intently she had to look away. "This isn't about you and me, is it?"

"I don't know what you mean," she replied, still not looking at him.

"Sure you do. I don't know why I didn't see it before now. This is about your parents. This is about how your father hurt your mother with his lies."

She gritted her teeth as pain sliced through her at the old hurts. She tried sarcasm to deflect it. "So now am I supposed to believe that they give psychology degrees in pro wrestling school?"

"Don't be flip, Marietta. You think I'm going to hurt you the same way your father hurt your mother. That's why you accused me of sleeping with a Studette. Because your father cheated on your mother."

"What if it is?" There was no use denying it, so Marietta took the offensive. "In my experience, males have quite a bit of trouble with monogamy."

"What about coyotes?"

"Coyotes?"

"Yeah, the ones you talked about on *Morning Glory, Live*. They're monogamous. You said they bonded for life."

"You're not a coyote, Jax," she said tiredly. "You're a liar. How do I know you're not lying when you say you love me? When you say you'll be faithful to me?"

"If you looked inside your heart, you'd know," he said quietly. "I'm not your father, and you're not your mother. The only thing I ever lied to you about was being a pro wrestler, and I did that because I didn't want to hurt our chances of making a life together."

"We're not going to have a life together, Jax."

He shook his head. "You're pregnant with my child. You can't expect me to walk away from that. You can't expect me to walk away from you."

She blinked rapidly so the tears gathering in her eyes wouldn't fall. "I'll sign legal papers giving you visitation rights, but only on the condition that I don't have to have anything else to do with you."

"You can't mean that." His voice broke, but she didn't let it sway her from what she had to do to protect herself.

The Misconception

She angrily brushed away the tears that had seeped out of her eyes.

"Oh, but I do, Jax. This thing between us was all a big mistake. A misconception. It never should have started. Now I'm going to do what I should have a long time ago and end it."

Before he could reply, she turned and walked out of the room and up the stairs to her bedroom. A long while later, she thought she heard the front door open and close, but she couldn't be sure because her ears were filled with the stormy sounds of her own weeping.

Chapter Twenty-four

"The way I see it," Jax said as he leaned back in the soft leather office chair in a deliberate show of nonchalance, "you don't have any choice but to agree to my demands."

He surreptitiously gauged his effect on Lance Strong, the president of the Ultimate Wrestling Association. At well over six feet and two hundred pounds, Lance was nearly as large as the wrestlers he employed. The story went that he'd gotten the UWA where it was today because he bullied people into doing what he wanted. Bank presidents, television executives, and wrestling managers had all trembled in his presence. Jax was determined not to.

"Are you giving me an ultimatum, Mr. Jackson?" Lance regarded Jax with narrowed eyes as steely as his voice. Off to one side of him, Star Bright, who'd futilely argued against this meeting, desperately tried to get Jax's attention. His white hair seemed to be standing more on end than usual. Anger Lance Strong, he'd said, and your wrestling career is as good as over.

"Yes, Mr. Strong, I am." Jax crossed his ankles, consciously taking his time elaborating on his answer. "Having

The Misconception

Smashing Headhunter unmask me on national television without my previous knowledge or permission was a dirty trick."

"But great theater," Star Bright cut in. "Really great theater. The Secret Stud's archenemy, responsible for turning his ancestors into pinheads, striking again with villainous intent."

Lance Strong crossed his arms over his chest, ignoring Star and focusing on Jax, who continued to talk. "As you know, my contract runs out in another month. If you don't agree to my demands, I'll defect to the WCW or WWF."

"He doesn't mean that quite the way it sounds," Star said nervously. "Defect really wasn't the word he wanted. He meant something more along the lines of 'think really long and hard about leaving.' Did I emphasize 'long'?"

Again, Lance Strong ignored Star. The visible portion between his upper and lower eyelids got tinier. He tapped a big hand on the wide mahogany desk between them. "You haven't convinced me why I should agree."

The UWA president was so intense that Jax thought about telling a joke to lighten him up. He knew a good one about a boat carrying a shipment of yo-yos springing a leak and sinking forty times, but decided now wasn't a good time to tell it. Especially since Lance Strong's answer wasn't only integral to his career, but also his love life.

"I'm a crowd favorite and a proven asset to your organization," Jax said, concentrating on facts. "I've brought you fans and profit."

"The *Secret Stud* has brought me fans and profit. I have no doubt *The Stud* would continue to do the same. I don't have the same confidence about this new endeavor you're proposing." The UWA president sounded as full of bluster as the Wizard of Oz telling Dorothy to shoo, because he couldn't help her get back to Kansas. Jax reminded himself Dorothy's crew had persuaded the wizard, who wasn't nearly as frightening as he sounded, to their way of thinking.

"Then you'll have to take a chance, won't you?" Jax fixed his eyes on Lance Strong in an unblinking stare. "Because I'm not budging from what I want."

"When he says he's not budging, he doesn't mean he's not *budging*," Star said. "The last thing Jax intends to do is offend—"

"Shut up," Jax and Lance Strong spoke to the manager in unison, their eyes still locked. Jax thought he saw a glimmer of respect cross the other man's face.

"I mean what I say, Mr. Strong. Either give me the go-ahead to change my act or I'm cutting ties with the UWA at the end of the month," Jax said, shutting out Star's low, dismayed moan.

Jax watched the UWA president, admiring the way he kept his emotions from showing. He'd be a good poker player and probably, once you got him on your side, a better friend. He understood why others commonly backed down in the face of what Lance Strong wanted.

But Jax wasn't going to back down, because too much was at stake. Thanks to Marietta, he was through worrying about what others thought of him. As he'd explained to his mother and brothers when he broke the news that he was a pro wrestler, what he thought of himself was far more important.

His mother had been disappointed he hadn't confided in her, but she'd understood his reasons. Go-with-the-flow Billy pronounced it not a big deal. Drew made a couple of cracks about spandex and testosterone, but confessed his love of money outweighed his aversion to pro wrestling.

But love of money wasn't the reason Jax was a pro wrestler. When he was in the center of the ring with the crowd cheering, he got a rush second only to the one he experienced in Marietta's arms. If Jax got his way, he wouldn't have to give up either. It was past time he fought for what he wanted.

The Misconception

"Well," he asked Lance Strong, feigning nonchalance as though everything wasn't riding on the answer, "what's it going to be?"

Marietta placed the last of the dinner plates into the dishwasher and closed it with a soft bang. Tracy, a smile curving her lips, ran a damp sponge over the Formica counter as she hummed to herself. With her dyed blond hair, silver, midriff-baring shirt, and matching miniskirt, she looked like the perfect choice to star in a production of *Madonna Goes Alien.* Instead, she was acting like a contented housewife.

The little house her sister once again shared with Ryan was downright homespun, from the country kitchen with its walls covered in flowers-in-the-meadow paper to the plaid furniture in the family room. All that was missing were the two-point-five children who'd dash into the kitchen to ask for home-baked cookies, but Marietta didn't doubt they'd come in time. When they did, Dad would be just as likely to get the cookies out of the jar as Mom.

That wouldn't be a possibility in her home, because Jax, the father of her child, wouldn't be living with them. The thought gave Marietta a pang in the region of her heart. She ignored the pang the same way she'd ignored the pain at turning Jax out of her life. She'd done the right thing. Even if it hurt so damn much she could barely get through the days.

"Thanks again for having me over to dinner," Marietta said, trying not to think about Jax. "Everything was delicious."

"Ryan makes the best chicken lasagna," Tracy stated. "Did I mention the pesto sauce is from a recipe he came up with all by himself?"

"Three times," Marietta answered.

"Usually, he does the dinner dishes, but I told him we didn't mind cleaning up since he did all the cooking. Especially since he cleared the table. And made the pesto sauce. Did I mention he made the pesto sauce?"

"Tracy." Marietta laid a hand on her sister's arm. "You can stop trying to convince me that going back to Ryan was the right thing to do. I have eyes. I can see how happy the two of you are, and I'm happy for you."

"Really?" Tracy's expression lightened. "Do you mean that, Mari?"

"Of course I mean it," Marietta answered, no longer surprised that it was true. She'd harbored such resentment toward Ryan for so long that it had been hard to admit she was wrong about him. Once she had, the feeling was liberating. Her resentment had fled like a stir-crazy bird let loose from a cage. "I'm willing to concede you and Ryan are the rare couple who can buck overwhelming biological odds and not only stay together, but remain faithful to one another."

"Oh, Mari." Tracy leaned back against the counter, dismay evident beneath the sparkling silver shadow she'd slathered on her eyelids. "Do you still think so poorly of men? Even after Jax?"

"Jax lied to me about what he did for a living. It only follows that he'd lie to me about who he's sleeping with behind my back."

"Jax wouldn't cheat on you! He only lied about being a pro wrestler because he loves you and was afraid of losing you!"

Marietta cut off her sister's impassioned defense with a slashing gesture. "I don't want to talk about Jax, Tracy. And you, of all people, should know enough not to lecture me on fidelity. You saw what our father did to our mother."

"Yes, I saw," Tracy said, "but I didn't pay nearly as close attention as you did. If I had, I would have realized right away that Ryan isn't anything like Dad, instead of believing he was because that's what you believed. And you know what, Mari? Jax isn't like Dad, either."

"You don't know that," Marietta refuted. Tracy was indulging in wishful thinking, a practice she wouldn't permit herself. She'd admitted she was wrong about Ryan, but Ryan was a fluke that went against nature's grain. Wishing that Jax was another exception to the rule didn't make him so.

"Hey, it's nearly nine o'clock." Ryan came into the kitchen, looking casually rumpled in worn jeans and an old Washington Redskins T-shirt. "I was—"

He stopped speaking abruptly, and his dark gaze ping-ponged from one sister to the other. By the way he stiffened, Marietta could tell that he felt the tension in the room. His brow furrowed. "Am I interrupting something?"

"No," Marietta said firmly. "In fact, I was just about to leave."

"Leave?" Ryan's cry was plaintive. And puzzling "But you can't leave."

"Why not?"

"Uh, because it's early." He crossed the room to his wife and slung an arm over her shoulder. He appeared anxious, which was not a trait Marietta usually associated with him. "Isn't it early, Trace?"

"It is." She gave a nod so vehement the inside of Marietta's head hurt in sympathy. "It's early."

"You're forgetting that I'm pregnant and need my rest," Marietta said, heading toward the door.

Quicker than she could have imagined, Ryan let go of Tracy's shoulder and moved in a semicircular pattern until he was between Marietta and the door. He extended his arm, palm up, the way she'd seen the Supremes do on old variety-show clips when they sang, "Stop! In the Name of Love."

"Watching television is a good way to rest," he said.

"That may be so," Marietta said, "but I seldom watch television."

"Oh, but you should." Tracy was instantly at Ryan's side, forming a double-wide blockade. "You can rest your brain while watching television. It's a very undemanding activity."

"Yes, it is," Ryan said, "and we'd really like it if you rested your brain with us."

"Yes," Tracy said. "Yes, we would."

Marietta looked from her sister to her brother-in-law, who were nodding like those silly little dolls some people keep on their car dashboards. She didn't want to spend a minute more in their company. The two of them were so deliriously happy that it made losing Jax seem all the more tragic. A stubborn part of her subconscious still believed she and Jax could have been that happy, even though logically she knew that wasn't true.

"I really don't think—"

"Please," Tracy interrupted. "Please stay, Mari. I don't get to see as much of you as I did when we were living together."

Marietta breathed a sigh of defeat. Put that way, she couldn't refuse. "I suppose I could stay for a little while."

"Wonderful," Ryan said, and wasted no time in ushering them into the family room. Marietta's pregnancy wasn't so far advanced that she had difficulty maneuvering, but Ryan helped her into the armchair she knew was his favorite anyway. She snuggled into it, enjoying the pampering. Now that Jax was out of her life, she had precious little of that. She mentally slapped herself. She had to stop thinking about him.

"I have to admit, this is quite restful," Marietta said to take her mind off Jax.

"See, we told you." Tracy sounded nervous as she settled onto the sofa next to her husband, and Marietta wondered why. Ryan picked up the remote control, switched on a television station and the answer became immediately apparent. A black-jacketed emcee was bellowing into a

The Misconception

microphone about the ultimate in wrestling entertainment while a boisterous crowd shouted, "uwa, uwa, uwa."

Betrayal, swift and wrenching, cut into Marietta. The pair on the sofa regarded her warily, looking as though they were afraid she was going to rap their knuckles with a ruler and send them to the principal's office. If she'd had a ruler, she might have.

"How could you do this to me?" Marietta cried. "Did Jax put you up to this? Did he tell you to invite me to dinner so you could trick me into watching this?"

"That's not why we invited you to dinner," Tracy denied quickly. "We invited you, because we wanted to have you." She glanced at Ryan, as though seeking his support. "As for Jax, what did you expect him to do when you won't take his calls?"

"I expect him to stop calling, that's what." Marietta scooted to the edge of her seat, preparing to rise. "I certainly don't intend to watch him on television."

"Wait a minute, Marietta," Ryan said. "I admit it. We're guilty as charged. Jax is going to debut his new act tonight, and he asked us to make sure you saw it. What would it hurt to watch him?"

"Yeah, Marietta," Tracy chimed in. "What would it hurt?"

Ryan had the volume on the television set turned up loud. On screen, the crowd's cheers had died down and the absurdly dressed emcee straightened the tails of his tuxedo and yelled into the microphone.

"As you all know, in a daring show of bravado, the villainous Smashing Headhunter unmasked our own Secret Stud last week, gaining the upper hand in their ongoing battle of antagonism." The crowd greeted the statement with a chorus of boos. Marietta told herself to get out of the chair and walk away from the set, but couldn't seem to move. "But, as the Smashing Headhunter is about to find out, every action has a reaction."

Darlene Gardner

A sharp series of bestial barks closely followed by a prolonged howl caused the emcee to drop the microphone, which resounded with a vibrating bang. The camera panned to a large, bare-chested man wearing light-gray trunks and elaborate headwear. He sprinted the length of the walkway to the ring.

"That's Jax," Ryan said unnecessarily.

"Yeah, but what's he wearing?" Tracy sat forward on the sofa, her attention on the tube. "Oh, no. Don't tell me those trunks are made of fur!"

With animal-like grace, Jax grabbed a piece of rope and pulled himself to the edge of the ring. He howled another time before vaulting the ropes and picking up the microphone. The camera closed in on him, giving them their first good look at his headgear.

His face was exposed, but his thick, chocolate-colored hair was covered with the ugliest hat Marietta had ever seen. An animal's head, punctuated by a pointed nose and a feral, tooth-baring grin, stared out at the audience.

"Omigod, what's that on top of his head?" Tracy asked in obvious horror. "What on earth is he supposed to be?"

Jax let out another series of sharp barks, and, quite suddenly, Marietta knew. Her breath snagged in her throat as she tried to get her brain to believe what he was so obviously trying to tell her. Her heart thumped against the wall of her chest, threatening to break it down.

"Last week, you saw the end of an icon when Smashing Headhunter brutally ripped off the mask of the Secret Stud." Jax spoke into the microphone with dramatic flair as commanding as that of any actor who ever starred in an action flick. "Unmasked, the Stud has not only lost his mystique but his passion for wrestling."

The crowd lustily voiced its displeasure, from resounding boos to disbelieving screams to loud sobbing. A teenage girl, crying inconsolably, appeared on screen. Painted across her forehead were the words, "I love you." "Secret" was written on her right cheek, "Stud" on her left.

"But I assure you that the unmasking of the Secret Stud will not go unavenged. Today, you bear witness to that. For out of the ashes rises a newer, better, more determined wrestler. Out of the ashes . . ." He paused to give four rapid barks in succession, barks that arrowed straight to Marietta's heart and stuck. ". . . rises Coyote Man."

"Coyote Man?" Tracy's voice rose an octave. "Please tell me he didn't just say Coyote Man?"

Marietta tried to confirm Jax's new wrestling identity, but her throat was so strangled with emotion that she couldn't speak. Ryan nodded. "That's what he said, all right. I guess that explains why he's wearing the fur trunks and that coyote face."

"But that's the dumbest thing I've ever heard," Tracy exclaimed.

"As Coyote Man," Jax continued, "I propose to lead a new order of the Ultimate Wrestling Association which I will call the Coyote Pack. I implore my fellow wrestlers to leave an organization that allows barbarians such as the Smashing Headhunter to impose their own rules and to join me in the pack." He paused. "Together, we can strike fear in their hearts, because you know what they say about coyotes." He stroked the gray fur of his trunks. "Stay as *fur* away from them as possible."

Ryan chuckled. "Gosh, the man can tell a joke. I don't understand why he decided to be Coyote Man instead of The Comedian, like I suggested."

Marietta could no longer handle the emotions churning through her, and tears seeped out of her eyes, falling down her cheeks.

"Mari? Are you crying?" Tracy got up from the sofa and came to Marietta's side, smoothing the hair back from her face. Her eyes were wide with shock. "I don't think I've seen you cry like that since the fourth grade when Billy Bob Jones knocked you down on the playground and kissed you smack on the lips."

Her sister's sympathetic stroking only made Mari cry harder.

"Don't cry, honey. Jax's joke wasn't that bad." Tracy screwed up her forehead. "Okay, I admit it. It *was* that bad. But that's no reason to cry."

"I'm not crying about the joke," Marietta managed to choke out.

"It's the act then, isn't it? It's really dumb, I know, but maybe they go for things like that in the Ultimate Wrestling Association. Don't they have a wrestler named Mexican Jumping Ben who hops around the ring? That's even worse than the coyote nonsense, and it hasn't ruined his career."

Marietta sniffed and wiped at her eyes. "I'm not crying because I think Jax has ruined his career."

Tracy took a handkerchief Ryan produced and gently wiped the still-falling tears from Marietta's cheeks. "Then why are you crying?"

"Because he loves me," Marietta sobbed.

Tracy looked confused, delightedly so. "I know he loves you, and Ryan knows he loves you. But how come, all of a sudden, you know?"

"Because he's Coyote Man," Marietta said, but the pair still looked at her blankly. "Don't you get it? Coyotes mate for life."

On the television, Jax barked as he circled a hulking wrestler who was pointing at his chest and yelling, "You want a piece of me?" Jax ran full speed toward the ropes, turning at the last second so he could use them to propel himself into the other man's body. He slammed into his opponent, and they went down in a tangle of brawn and muscle.

"Coyote Man." Tracy sighed as she watched the wrestlers battle it out. "Isn't that just the most romantic thing?"

Marietta made a valiant effort to stop crying, because she had things to do. Her next step was as clear as the whites of the coyote eyes on the ugly hat that had fallen off Jax's head and stared sightlessly at the arena ceiling. "Ryan, do you know where the UWA wrestles next?"

"Miami. Tomorrow night."

"If I make the plane reservation, could you get me a ticket to the show? The best one left in the house? No expense spared."

The mammoth wrestler on the television set squeezed Jax, the man Marietta had just realized she didn't want to live without, into a bear hug and lifted him off his feet.

"As soon as Gargantuan Garth puts Jax down, I'll get right on it." Ryan's eyes never left the screen as he mused. "Wonder if Smashing Headhunter's going to fight tonight or if he's staying fur away."

"Just one more thing, Ryan," Marietta said, wincing as Jax hit the mat with a loud bang, "I want it to be a surprise, so don't tell him I'm coming."

"That's so romantic," Tracy said as Gargantuan Garth leaped and hovered airbound over a prone Jax before falling on him, "that I think I'm going to cry."

Chapter Twenty-five

The roving strobe lights in Miami Arena illuminated the fans with streaks of red, orange, and yellow as they broke into the series of yaps, barks, and whines that had quickly become the Coyote Man's trademark.

"Yip, yip, yap." The chant built to a crescendo as more and more voices chimed in. "Woof, woof, woof."

Jax stood in the ring, one foot resting on the chest of Smashing Headhunter, his vanquished archenemy, and tried to will away the headache that had been brewing since he'd talked to Ryan the night before.

Yes, Ryan had managed to get Marietta in front of a television set. Yes, she saw the debut of Coyote Man. No, he didn't know why she'd turned off her answering machine and wasn't answering her phone.

The entire scenario was enough to make a man go stark raving mad. He knew, with soul-deep certainty, that Marietta loved him. Just as he knew she'd spurned him, not because of his lie, but because she was afraid he couldn't form a pair bond.

By becoming Coyote Man, he'd hoped to prove that, like the animal he portrayed, he mated for life. Maybe his message hadn't gotten through. Either that, or she hadn't wanted to listen to it.

The entire sorry mess was robbing the joy from his life. Even inside the ring, one of the places he'd always loved best, she was all he could think about.

Because it was expected of him, as Leader of the Pack, Jax raised his arms high into the air and emitted the long, drawn-out howl that he and Star Bright had decided would signify victory.

He removed his foot from Smashing Headhunter, who struggled to his feet, holding his head as he went into a theatrical stagger around the ring.

"On this night, I vow revenge," Smashing Headhunter shouted. "Coyote Man has howled his last time at my expense."

The script called for Jax to turn three-hundred-sixty degrees, extolling the crowd to continue their joyous barking before he let out an in-your-face howl.

Jax got two-hundred-seventy degrees through his rotation when he stopped. A pregnant woman dressed in unattractive tweed who looked uncannily like Marietta was walking down the aisle through the cheering masses. Lights were shining in his eyes so he squinted, trying to get a better look.

"Jax, what are you doing?" Smashing Headhunter whispered through his snarl. "Why aren't you howling?"

Jax barely heard him as the woman approached, and the impossible became reality. Marietta. The pregnant woman in the god-awful tweed *was* Marietta. She stopped just beyond the ring, and their eyes met. He could barely believe what he saw in hers. Respect, affection, and *love*.

"Howl, Jax." Smashing Headhunter was right next to him, whispering furiously in his ear. "Howl now."

The other wrestler's words penetrated the haze that had enveloped Jax. He grinned, wide and long, before he threw back his head and howled with more gusto than any coyote has ever howled.

When the last of his plaintive cry died down, he gazed back at Marietta, who was smiling at him. Ignoring his archenemy, who was pretending to be enraged, he vaulted the ropes, dropping beside Marietta with a soft and graceful plop. He didn't touch her, but let his eyes rove over her face and then the stomach that was finally showing her pregnancy.

"What are you doing here, Marietta?"

"I wanted to see you," she explained, and bit her bottom lip nervously. It wasn't his symmetry that had her tongue-tied. It wasn't even his nearly naked state, although that was plenty distracting. It was the person inside all that gorgeous brawn, the one behind his perfect features. "I tried to get here sooner, but my plane was delayed, and I missed the beginning—"

"No, that's not what I meant," he interrupted. "I meant *why* are you here?"

"Because," she said, no longer afraid of what she was about to tell him, "last night I realized I was in love with a coyote."

The well-proportioned sides of his mouth lifted in unison, producing a dazzling smile. "Do you mean that?"

"Yes, I mean it. It seems like I'm going to have to dig harder for answers in my profession. Biology is an awfully good tool when it comes to the interplay between the sexes," she said, her gaze roving over the enthralling symmetry that she'd only recently realized was just a tiny part of his appeal, "but it can't explain everything."

Marietta took a step forward, intending to go into his arms, when she realized the entire arena had gone quiet. She turned her head left, then right, gradually realizing that all eyes in the place focused on them. A dramatic strobe light played over the crowd before bathing them in yellow.

"Everybody's staring at us," she whispered.

He gathered her into his arms. "Then now's a good time for you to tell me you'll marry me. Then I'll have witnesses."

The Misconception

His eyes twinkled. "I'm not going to let you get out of this one. Like the coyote, I pair for life."

"Of course I'll marry you," she said near his lips, "but only if you promise not to howl at home."

He laughed and kissed her. And every one of the fifteen thousand wrestling fans inside Miami Arena threw back their heads and howled.

Baby, Oh Baby!

ROBIN WELLS

The hunk who appears on Annie's doorstep is a looker. The tall attorney's aura is clouded, and she can see that he's been suffering for some time. But all that is going to change, because a new—no, two new people are going to come into his life.

Jake Chastaine knows how things are supposed to be, and that doesn't include fertility clinic mixups or having fathered a child with a woman he'd never met. And looking at the vivid redhead who's the mother, Jake realizes he's missed out on something spectacular. Everyone knows how things are supposed to be—first comes love, then comes marriage, then the baby in the baby carriage. Maybe this time, things are going to happen a little differently.

EUGENIA RILEY
The Great Baby Caper

Courtney Kelly knows her boss is crazy. But never does she dream that the dotty chairman will send her on a wacky scavenger hunt and expect her to marry Mark Billingham, or lose her coveted promotion. But one night of reckless passion in Mark's arms leaves Courtney with the daunting discovery that the real prize will be delivered in about nine months!

A charming and sexy British entrepreneur, Mark is determined to convince his independent-minded new wife that he didn't marry her just to placate his outrageous grandfather. Amid the chaos of clashing careers and pending parenthood, Mark and Courtney will have to conduct their courtship after the fact and hunt down the most elusive quarry of all—love.

TRISH JENSEN
Stuck
with
You

Paige Hart and Ross Bennett can't stand each other. There has been nothing but bad blood between these two lawyers . . . until a courthouse bombing throws them together. Exposed to the same rare and little-understood Tibetan Concupiscence Virus, the two archenemies are quarantined for seven days in one hospital room. As if that isn't bad enough, the virus's main side effect is to wreak havoc on human hormones. Paige and Ross find themselves irresistibly drawn to one another. Succumbing to their wildest desires, they swear it must be a temporary and bug-induced attraction, but even after they part ways, they can't seem to forget each other. Which begs the question: Did the lustful litigators contract the disease after all? Or have they been acting under the influence of another fever altogether—the love bug?

___52442-8 $5.99 US/$6.99 CAN

Marry Me, Maddie
Rita Herron

Maddie Summers is tired of waiting. To force her fiancé into making a decision, she takes him on a talk show and gives him a choice: Marry me, or move on. The line he gives makes her realize it is time to star in her own life. But stealing the show will require a script change worthy of a Tony. Her supporting cast is composed of two loving but overprotective brothers, her blue-blood ex-boyfriend, and her brothers' best friend: sexy bad-boy Chase Holloway—the only one who seems to recognize that a certain knock-kneed kid sister has grown up to be a knockout lady. And Chase doesn't seem to know how to bow out, even when the competition for her hand heats up. Instead, he promises to perform a song and dance, even ad-lib if necessary to demonstrate he is her true leading man.

___52433-3 $5.50 US/$6.50 CAN

Everyone loves a little ~~meddling~~ *help* from Mom . . .

A Mother's ~~Day~~ Way
Romance Anthology

Lisa Cach, Susan Grant,
Julie Kenner, Lynsay Sands

Is it the king who commands Lord Jonathon to wed, or is it the dia-
bolical scheme of his marriage-minded mama? After escaping her
restrictive schooling, Miss Evelina Johnson wants to sow her wild
oats. Mrs. Johnson plants different ideas. Andie never expects the
man of her dreams to fall from the sky—but when he does, her
mother will make sure the earth moves! Jennifer Martin has always
wanted to marry the man she loves, but her mom knows the only
ones worth having are superheroes. Whether you're a medieval
lord or a marketing liaison, whether you're from Bath or
Betelgeuse, it never hurts to have some help with your love life.
Come see why a little meddling can be a wonderful thing—and
why every day should be Mother's way.

___52471-6 $5.99 US/$7.99 CAN

Those Baby Blues

SHERIDON SMYTHE

Hadleigh Charmaine feels as though she has been cast in a made-for-TV movie. The infant she took home from the hospital is not her biological child, and the man who has been raising her real daughter is Treet Miller, a film star. But when his sizzling baby blues settle on her, the single mother refuses to be hoodwinked—even if he makes her shiver with desire.

Treet knows he's found the role of a lifetime: father to two beautiful daughters and husband to one gorgeous wife. Now he just has to convince Hadleigh that in each other's arms they have the best shot at happiness. He plans to woo her with old-fashioned charm and a lot of pillow talk, until she understands that their story can have a Hollywood ending.

Dorchester Publishing Co., Inc.
P.O. Box 6640
Wayne, PA 19087-8640

_52483-X
$5.99 US/$7.99 CAN

Please add $2.50 for shipping and handling for the first book and $.75 for each additional book. NY and PA residents, add appropriate sales tax. No cash, stamps, or CODs. Canadian orders require $5.00 for shipping and handling and must be paid in U.S. dollars. Prices and availability subject to change. **Payment must accompany all orders.**

Name: _____

Address: _____

City: _____ State: _____ Zip: _____

E-mail: _____

I have enclosed $_____ in payment for the checked book(s).

For more information on these books, check out our website at www.dorchesterpub.com.
_____ *Please send me a free catalog.*